CHANGEOVER MODE

"Lost lock on two of the guide points! That makes no sense. It's just a geometric relationship." She swallowed, forcing the acidic bile that was trying to rise from her stomach back where it belonged. "No . . . no problem. We're close now, I can tie the display to the radar and focus on where we're going." A glide path calculated to the nominal surface appeared, guiding her like a pathway. It was a lot better than nothing, telling her the right ratio and where she needed to think about changing modes to land.

Suddenly the ship bobbled, jolted; there was a rattle from the forward viewport. *Storm . . . entering the fringes.* Radar showed it shouldn't be too bad, though it was larger than she'd thought; it would be raining for a while.

In visible light, it was dark gray outside, and at this altitude mostly fog and rain; hints of terrain, maybe trees or something, began to appear as they descended. If she'd been relying on eyesight she would have panicked. But *LS-5* wasn't limited to visible light; in infrared and radar, the clouds and rain were practically gone. Wind might still push on the craft, try to distract her, but it couldn't blind her, and that was the important thing.

LS-5 bucked slightly, but she was getting a real feel for the controls, and she saw that she was staying pretty close to the middle of the glide path. Radar showed they were approaching the target area, clearing the higher ground in their path, dropping—

Just about there. She could see the lagoon up ahead. Final mode change time, to VTOL. Changeover initiated . . .

Suddenly a gust of wind struck *LS-5*, sent the shuttle swaying sideways through the air, just as the mode conversion began. The jolt made her pull a little harder than she intended, but the shuttle's dynamics had already changed. Desperately, Sakura shoved the stick back and sideways, trying to compensate, even as she heard the sergeant bellowing *not fast, not fast, don't overcompensate!*

But it was too late now, too late by far.

CASTAWAY PLANET

ERIC FLINT
RYK E. SPOOR

BAEN

CASTAWAY PLANET

This is a work of fiction. All the characters and events portrayed in this book are fictional, and any resemblance to real people or incidents is purely coincidental.

A Baen Books Original

Baen Publishing Enterprises
P.O. Box 1403
Riverdale, NY 10471
www.baen.com

ISBN: 978-1-4767-8134-1

Cover art by Bob Eggleton

First Baen Mass Market printing, February 2016

Library of Congress Control Number: 2014043636

Distributed by Simon & Schuster
1230 Avenue of the Americas
New York, NY 10020

Pages by Joy Freeman (www.pagesbyjoy.com)
Printed in the United States of America

This book is dedicated to three authors
who created and shaped the
genre of castaway fiction:

Daniel Defoe,
creator of *Robinson Crusoe*

Johann David Wyss,
who gave us *Swiss Family Robinson*

And Jules Verne,
author of *The Mysterious Island*
and many other novels

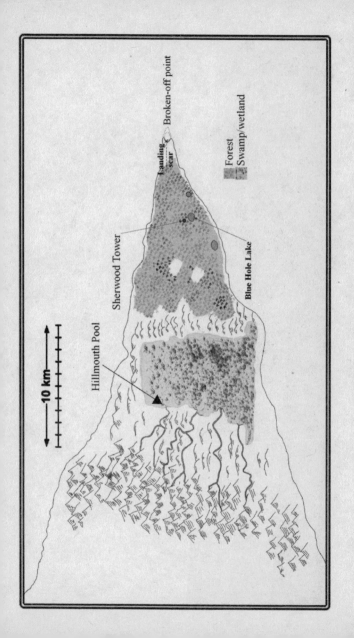

Broken-off point

Landing scar

Forest

Swamp/wetland

Sherwood Tower

Blue Hole Lake

Hillmouth Pool

10 km

CASTAWAY PLANET

Chapter 1

Sakura Kimei lay as still as possible on the set of pipes, listening for the creature's approach. It could be very near. She gripped the weapon in her right hand and steadied herself with her left, trying to breathe as quietly as possible.

Not for the first time, she was grateful that she was still "skinny as a rail," as her mother Laura often put it. There was minimal clearance between the pipes and the ceiling. No one with even a tiny bit more weight could have fit.

And that would have meant she had *nowhere* to hide.

The corridor wasn't terribly narrow and was pretty high—for Sakura, at least, since it was meant for adults to use, not just fourteen-year-old girls who hadn't quite hit their last growth spurt—but though only dimly lit, it was straight and without feature or doorway for a fair distance.

She tried to calm her beating heart. If it beat faster, she'd be breathing faster, and that could give her away.

The pipes under her felt both warm and cool, and she was doubly grateful for the advanced aerogel insulation that was able to keep them from being either

scorching or freezing without huge, thick coatings—
which would have made this hiding place impossible.

It had already been several minutes. Maybe she'd
lost him completely.

But then a faint sound reached her ears, and she
froze, holding herself as still as the walls around her.

Scrape.

That was not the sound of a human being walking.
It sounded vaguely like a leather bag being dragged
over the deck, but it was not a constant sound. It was
the sound of something moving rhythmically, slowly,
and as stealthily as it could. Straining her ears, holding her own breath, Sakura could just make out the
faint whistling of the thing's breath.

Shadows moved, coming from behind her, but
Sakura dared not move, not even to get a good look.
The creature's senses were very, very good and might
pick up on any movement, especially if it was still
behind her and might look *up* for an instant.

Focused as she was on being perfectly still, naturally
every tiny complaint or discomfort was magnified. That
tiny itch in her calf was suddenly almost unbearable,
demanding she move, reach down, scratch; the vague
irritation in her nose was now trying to burgeon into
a full-fledged sneeze. She clamped down with iron
will. *No! Can't screw up now! It's probably my only
chance!*

Slowly, below her, something came into view; waving
tendrils, curling and grasping at the air like corpses'
fingers, sharp black hooks showing themselves as the
digits worked back and forth. The tendrils moved
forward, showing there were actually three groups of
them, attached to three powerful forelimbs which bent

in the center to provide a sort of elbow. The creature was dragging itself along with two of these. One group of tendrils grasped a tubular affair something like a crutch; the thing's equivalent of a gun.

The body was generally triangular in cross-section, with the arms she saw at the front. She knew that between those arms and not visible from her vantage point, was a tripartite beaklike mouth equipped with a ripping, tearing tongue. At the rear, three stubby appendages similar to the arms splayed out, gripped, and pushed. Overall, the thing was several meters long and probably weighed five times what she did.

The thing could also go much faster than it was going now, even taking into account the fact that it obviously wasn't built for this kind of terrain. But it was moving quietly, trying to find her without alerting her to its presence. The front tendrils and rear "legs" were trying to keep as much of the creature as possible off the ground entirely. She was actually a little astounded. She knew the thing was strong, but this was way beyond what she'd expected.

Still . . . right now she was hidden. There was no sign he'd seen her.

She focused on timing now. The creature was almost past her position. She'd have to strike it right behind the eye socket and drive her blade down and back to hit the brain.

The ship's "gravity" came from spin; she had to guess just how much that would make her curve during the drop, because curve she would. Not much, but when centimeters counted you couldn't afford any slop.

Now came the most dangerous part. His eyes were passing below her; he'd have to turn now to see her.

But she had to ease herself sideways so she could drop off the pipes and onto the alien's back.

And that meant moving, and moving meant noise.

She exhaled silently as much as she could, lowering her height by a centimeter or less, but just enough to make sure nothing touched her back. Slowly she eased to her right. Over one pipe. Over two. Once she'd gotten past three pipes she could—

The creature suddenly halted. Maybe it had heard her, maybe it just realized it had come an awfully long way without seeing its quarry, but either way, it was now suspicious.

GO!

Sakura shoved off, dropping down, even as the thing tried to pivot around in a corridor much narrower than it was long. The girl twisted her body, stretching out, weapon held tight in her fist, reaching, even as one of the cruel taloned arms lashed around towards her—

And her hand drove perfectly into the gap between the right-hand eye and the thick, armored hide.

Instantly the arm froze, then collapsed to the ground.

"Oh, *stagnation*," the creature vibrated. "I almost got you!"

She laughed and jumped off, putting the play dagger away. "You caught me the last three times, it was about my turn to get you!" She hugged as much of him as she could reach. He was warm and leathery, something like she imagined an elephant might be, but smoother. The latter wasn't surprising. The Bemmies had been entirely aquatic when humanity first met them on Europa, and using genetic engineering to give them full amphibious capabilities hadn't given them any hair. "That was a good chase, though, wasn't it, Whips?"

Whips (more formally named "Harratrer") burbled agreement with a chuckle. "Half an hour, and you still caught me. I should remember you're thin as a bladefish."

"Want to do another round?"

"We don't *have* another half-hour," the big alien pointed out. "You've got pilot apprentice training and I've got my engineering apprenticeship work in fifteen minutes."

"Oh, blah. You're right, that's not long enough. Maybe we—"

A screaming klaxon ripped the quiet air to shreds, repeating in three sharp tones. *"Mandatory Emergency Drill,"* a calm electronic voice said. *"Mandatory Drill. All personnel, respond as to an actual emergency according to Section 115.2. Mandatory Emergency Drill..."*

"Dehydrate that!" Whips said grouchily. "Our lifeboat unit's all the way over on the other side of *Outward Initiative.*"

The young Bemmie's peeved tone hid nervousness— and not very well. Sakura knew the source of that, and gripped her friend's arm supportively. "Everyone else will be busy going to their lifeboats."

"But they'll still be able to...accidentally...impede me in one way or another." The voice was no longer grouchy; it was sad and hurt. Whips' flickering colors were muted and brownish.

She couldn't argue with him; it was true. Her family had grown up around the genetically enhanced creatures, but they were rare even in the home system; in fact, from what her father had said, Whips' family might be the first one allowed outsystem. There were concerns about physical and mental stability, long-term viability, and other things, some of which just boiled down to plain old-fashioned prejudice ... on both sides, unfortunately.

The engineered *Bemmius novus sapiens* looked, to human eyes, pretty much like their non-engineered Europan relatives, which was to say fairly nightmarish to a lot of people, and definitely not comforting to run into in a narrow corridor. To the normal Europan Bemmies, the effect might be worse, a malformed mutant with a flattened bottom and everything squished up much more in one direction. Normal Bemmies did have a sort of up-and-down orientation, but this was much more emphatic—and strange—looking.

Add to that the fact that such extensive redesign on an intelligent creature had never been attempted before. In fact, the techniques had only been perfected a few years before the project started. The end result was a perfect recipe for nervous mistrust, prejudice, or sometimes an almost more annoying coddling attitude that treated every twitch as a matter of concern.

Sakura looked down at Whips, but the continued whooping of the alarm klaxon told her she couldn't stay—or follow him. Then suddenly a thought struck her. "Didn't you hear that? Respond as to an *actual* emergency."

Whips turned two of his three eyes towards her. "Well, yeah, but so what?"

"So in a real emergency you're supposed to go to the nearest lifeboat, right?" She grinned. "And that happens to be *ours*."

Whips' tendrils curled in with uncertainty. "I don't know. What if ... ?"

"Come *on*. It'll be a little less boring if you're there!"

Whips snorted, but immediately started a hopping drag in the direction of the Kimei family boat, his colors rippling swiftly back to brighter, more cheerful patterns. "And I can't ever complain about it being boring with *you* around!"

Chapter 2

Laura smiled as she dropped through the entry hatch to see that her husband, Akira, had just finished strapping Hitomi into her crash seat. The six-year-old was behaving very well, clutching her winged-wolf plush and pretending it was flying back and forth in front of her, but otherwise sitting still. "You made good time," she said, giving Hitomi's inexplicably blonde hair a ruffle and kissing Akira on the cheek as she passed.

"Hitomi and I were taking a break in the exercise room," Akira replied, making sure his own long, black hair was firmly tied back, "so we were not far away." He glanced back to their second-youngest. "Melody, tighten your restraints."

"*Daaaad,*" Melody protested in the tone of put-upon children everywhere, "it's a drill, not an emergency, and the straps squeeze too much." She looked appealingly at Akira, her face and hair looking like a miniature mirror of her father's Japanese features.

"Don't argue with your father," Laura said firmly. "The point of a drill is to do everything right *all* the time, so that if a real emergency ever does happen, you don't have to think about whether you've done it right when it counts; you just *do*."

She finished locking down her carryon. "We're still two short. *Outward Initiative*, this is Laura Kimei. Where are Caroline and Sakura?"

The omnipresent AI that ran the starship *Outward Initiative* responded immediately. "Caroline is very nearly at your assigned shuttle. Sakura was in cross-corridor E-3 and will arrive in a few minutes."

Laura nodded, and tried to ignore Melody's predictable grumbles. Sure enough, *Outward Initiative* had barely finished speaking when Caroline dropped precisely through the center of the entranceway, landed, and walked to her location, locking down her own carryons with perfect, practiced motions. "All ready, Mom," she said, sitting down and locking in.

At least one *of my children is organized. Though sometimes a bit much for her own good.*

Laura sat down and strapped herself in, bringing up the telltales for the shuttle on her own iris displays. She couldn't pilot such a ship—few people could, and of her family the only one who had any idea how such a ship flew was Sakura—but she knew the check routines.

Landing Shuttle *LS-5* was one of over one hundred similar shuttles, spaced evenly around the spinning habitat ring of the giant colony ship *Outward Initiative*. The "Trapdoor Drive," which was how the ancient Bemmie word for the faster-than-light device translated, may have reorganized a lot of views of physics, but it hadn't given them the ability to generate gravity on demand, so habitat rings still spun, and probably always would. For a lifeboat, this was convenient;

to launch away from the main ship simply required detaching the links, and centrifugal force would hurl *LS-5* away from *Outward Initiative*.

LS-5 was already loaded with most of the cargo the Kimei family was bringing with them to the colony on Tantalus (formal designation EC-G5-4-100-11)—medical equipment and supplies, biological research and analysis systems, and the most current 3D manufacturing systems, which would produce just about anything given the right materials as input. They were just lucky they got one all to themselves, given that there were over a thousand colonists on this mission.

No, she corrected herself. *Not luck, just supply and demand. The only luck is that they needed both doctors and biologists, so we got double priority for me and Akira.*

Sakura suddenly plummeted through the hatch and instantly ran toward the pilot's console, dragging her carryall bag with her. The console wouldn't actually be active except in a real emergency, but Sakura had argued that if there was a real emergency, it only made sense to have the only person with any flight training already sitting there. "Hi, Mom, Dad, drill number one thousand six hundred twenty-seven can now complete! And look who's with me!"

"It's only drill number thirty-seven," Caroline corrected Sakura. "We do one drill a week on average and we're almost halfway to Tantalus. And what are *you* doing here, Whips?"

Laura saw Whips' arm-tendrils curl inward nervously. "Well, Sakura *said* the regulations claimed I should go to the nearest designated boat, and..."

"And she was perfectly right, Harratrer," Laura

assured him, using his official human name; the tendrils relaxed. "Just get your tie-downs on. *Outward Initiative*, let Harratrer's pod know that he's with us during this drill."

"They have been informed," *Outward Initiative* replied. "Proceed to Phase II of drill."

Melody sighed from her seat. Some drills ended once Phase I—getting to the lifeboat—was completed, but with Phase II—actual preparation for launch—being tested, there was no getting around the need to finish strapping in properly. "What a *pain* . . ." she muttered.

The display in front of Laura was a "reality overlay" that included status telltales as well as enhancing key images in reality. She could see everyone's medical condition and current location status, but there was still procedure to follow. "Everyone settle down, we're doing count-off. Laura Kimei, here and secured. Nothing to report."

"Akira Kimei, here and secured," her husband said immediately. "Nothing to report."

"Caroline, here and secured. Nothing to report," the seventeen-year-old said quickly.

"Sakura, here and secured! Nothing to report!" said the irrepressible black-haired girl from her pilot's seat.

"Melody, here and secured," came the bored voice of the ten-year-old in the seat behind her. "The straps dig into me. Otherwise nothing to report."

"Hitomi and Skyfang!" announced Hitomi proudly. "Ready to fly!"

"Harratrer of Tallenal Pod, here and secured," said Whips in his usual calm, slightly buzzing tones. "Nothing to report."

"All present and secured. Pilot's station, report status."

She could see Sakura straighten with pride. "Pilot Station reporting! Launch systems...green, on standby. Autopilot and AI Support, green, on standby. Maneuver rockets, green, all self-checks complete. Life support, all green, fully supplied. Cargo integrity, all green. Nebula Drive, green, seals intact, updates complete. Emergency Trapdoor Drive, green, seals intact, updates complete. Nuclear reactor, all green, on minimal operating level. Atmospheric jets, all green, secured and sealed. Variable configuration actuators, all green. Sensor systems, all green. *LS-5* ready for launch, Mom."

Laura smiled at the last word. Not *quite* the formal tone preferred, but she'd checked off all the vital systems. Laura could, of course, see all of that on her displays, and in fact the operation of *LS-5* would be done entirely by the onboard AI if a real emergency occurred. All AIs except the main shipboard AI were kept shut down at most times, of course, because the colonists would be on a world with minimal automation aside from whatever they brought with them.

"Good," she said, then went on with the procedure— it was her turn. "Medical station—all crew and passengers show green." Not surprising, of course; not only did she track her family's health, and that of over half the colonists on board, regularly, but modern medical treatment combined with the standardization of medical nanotech implants had virtually eliminated poor health for those who didn't simply abuse their bodies to the limit. *It won't be long before doctors become completely obsolete*, she admitted to herself. *And honestly? I think I'd be okay with that.*

The simple check procedure done and everything on *LS-5* showing green, Laura relaxed back into the secured chair. There was nothing to do now but wait while everyone else finished checking off and the usual wait to cycle through the launch sequence as though they were actually doing an evacuation. This week, unfortunately, the sequence was starting from the last shuttle and counting down, which meant they'd be waiting a while.

She activated the nose cameras, giving her a view of *Outward Initiative.* As the whole ship spun, not just the hab wheel, there was no relative motion, so the great ship's forward section, silver with multiple patterns of other colors from the logos and flags of its builders and supporters, glittered unmoving and stark in the exterior floodlights against the utter, unrelieved blackness of the . . . not-exactly-space that was generated around them by the Trapdoor Drive. Three kilometers long and well over a kilometer wide, *Outward Initiative* was one of the larger human vessels operating today—though not quite the largest.

She could never look at that sight, of the impossible-black space and the brilliant starship, without thinking on what it *meant* that she could be here, with her family, traveling at eighty times the speed of light to another star. *A hundred and fifty years ago, we were still stuck in our own solar system, all alone in the universe . . . and then it all changed.*

Changed, when Dr. Helen Sutter discovered an alien skeleton in earthly strata sixty-five million years old. Changed, when NASA and the Ares Corporation discovered an ancient alien base hidden within the Martian moon Phobos, and another on Mars itself.

And changed forever when Dr. Sutter, trapped beneath the ice of Europa, discovered that the aliens had left behind one last, incredible, wonderful legacy: a new, intelligent species that turned out to be as curious and eager to learn as any human being ever was.

Laura smiled and glanced back, seeing everyone—*even Hitomi, for a miracle!*—sitting quietly. Melody's slightly glazed look showed she'd brought up one of her immersive games to pass the time, or maybe one of the interactive books she liked. Whips was relaxed, his three-sided form rounded slightly from the pressure of the artificial gravity, and the rippling patches of light and color on his sides showed he was in a good frame of mind.

Her husband caught her eye and smiled and winked. *He's still as gorgeous as when I met him,* she thought. Akira Kimei was dancer-slender, delicate-featured, with black hair so long he had to pay constant attention to controlling it whenever he might be entering a low-gravity area—a *bishonen* even at the age of forty-three.

She winked back. *Of course, being forty-three now is a lot different than it used to be; I'm forty-five but I haven't aged that much since I was in my early twenties.* With average lifespans over a hundred and seventy-five, "old" had been redefined quite a bit.

Sakura's wireless link was active, and Laura smiled. Sakura never stopped talking even when she had to be quiet. Sometimes she was a bit sorry for Whips, but the Bemmie adolescent and Sakura had been best friends for years, even before they applied for the colony trip. She supposed he'd gotten very good at listening along the way.

She gave a satisfied sigh and settled back.

Alarm klaxons suddenly screamed, and as her stunned

mind tried to grasp what that meant, the pressure door to the hatch slammed shut and locked.

"Oh, my God..." Sakura said, and Laura heard fear in the usually fearless voice.

Stars bloomed into existence around them; *Outward Initiative* was—incredibly—no longer in the Trapdoor Drive mode.

No, her horrified mind said numbly, *It's worse than that.*

For one splintered fraction of an instant, she saw something in the displays that was utterly impossible; a ghostly shimmer of structures below them, as though part of *Outward Initiative* was here, with them, and the rest... not.

Even as she saw that, even as Sakura's shocked gasp was dying away, there was a *thud* and a virulent flare of green-white light, and *LS-5* was suddenly spinning away, uncontrolled, free-falling, lights momentarily flickering and threatening to send them into darkness. With only fragments of metal and composite following it, *LS-5* hurtled away into the emptiness of interstellar space.

Chapter 3

Sakura clamped her jaw shut to keep from screaming as *LS-5* whirled into the void. She gripped the arms of the pilot's chair convulsively. She heard herself muttering, "Oh my God, oh my God..." and her mother and father both whispering something that sounded very similar.

The whirling, dizzy, uncontrolled spin lasted only a few moments; automatic stabilizer jets fired momentarily and then cut off. She felt the odd floating feeling of microgravity; over the private channel she heard Whips' own half-formed prayers to Those Beyond the Sky.

For a few moments, no one moved; finally her father spoke. "My God, Laura, what happened?" Dad's voice was filled with the same disbelieving horror welling up through Sakura, filling her with cold shock. Whips' electronic link had gone blank, the loss so great that he wasn't even forming thoughts she could understand.

Her mother was silent. Hitomi was sobbing, the cry of a child who doesn't really understand, but knows something terrible is happening.

Then she felt a stirring in her best friend's link. *Are you okay, Whips?*

I ... must be. Panic is useless. His determined statement of that fact gave her a lifeline to hold to, and she sent him a smile that firmed his resolve. *I am a descendant of Blushspark herself, child of the Seven Vents, the people who dared the chance to become part of both worlds. I must get a* grip, *as you would say.*

Whips spoke aloud, answering Dad's question. "The light ... looked like a malfunction in the Trapdoor Drive," he said. "When a ship does the drop into the Trapdoor space, you'll often see a flash of about that color."

"So ... what, parts of the ship were dropping and others weren't?" Laura asked, her voice frighteningly casual. Her mother was scared. The thought almost made Sakura panic again. Her mother simply did *not* get scared by anything.

"I guess so." Whips squeezed his three hands together nervously. "A field instability—the field's usually kept larger than the ship by a fair distance, but if something went wrong ... I guess it could cause the field to dip down below the outer edge of the habitat ring."

"Are we going to die, Mommy?" Hitomi asked tearfully.

"We are not going to die!" Laura snapped, and Sakura winced at the underlying near-panic in her tone.

I'm in the pilot's chair. I should do ... what a pilot does. She bent over the displays, searching. "I don't see any other shuttles. *LS-5*, are you getting other beacons?"

There was no answer. "*LS-5*, respond!"

When the AI remained silent, she turned her attention to the displays on the board. *Oh ... no.* "Mom ... the AI's offline. And there's medical alerts—"

"What?" Her mother had the expression of a doctor discovering a patient had unexpected terminal cancer.

"What is it, Laura?" Akira demanded.

"Radiation. Huge spike, I've never seen anything like it. The diagnostics say it was a mixture of the common types plus some particle bursts that I don't even *know*."

"Does *that* mean we're going to die?" Hitomi's voice was almost a whisper.

Sakura saw her mother pause before answering. *She's checking. This is what Mommy does.*

Then Mommy smiled and shook her head. "No, Hitomi. It was bad—very bad—but LS-5 shielded us from the worst. We didn't get a lethal dose, and I'm already directing our medical nanorepair. We all might get a little sick in the next few days, but we'll be okay."

Hitomi relaxed visibly, and so did Sakura. She knew her mother wouldn't sugar-coat anything like this, so saying it was all right meant that it was, indeed, all right. But...

"Mom? What about Whips?"

She smiled. "His pod knows you spend lots of time with us, so his doctor gave me the data and access codes to his medical nanos too. He'll be fine."

"Thank you, Dr. Kimei," Whips said. "I think the radiation explains the problem with LS-5, although I'm not sure why our other systems are working."

"Trapdoor radiation surge," Melody said.

Sakura sensed the Bemmie equivalent of a headslap *of course!* from Whips, but no one else seemed to understand. "What do you mean, Mel?" asked her father.

"The Trapdoor Drive creates a surge of subatomic particles when it's used," Melody answered, in the tense, focused tone that she always had when she was thinking to keep herself from being nervous. "That's why the ship always stops talking whenever you're preparing for drive activation or deactivation; the particle flux isn't dangerous to *us* but disrupts the quantum channels the AIs use."

"She's right," Whips confirmed. "I should have thought of it myself. And the malfunction must have caused the dangerous radiation surge; we were sitting *on* the Trapdoor interface. But I'm surprised you'd know that, Mel."

I'm not, Sakura thought. *She's the family genius— heard Mom once say to Dad that Melody might be smarter than both of them put together.*

Melody looked pleased, even though still worried. "I studied up on it when I knew we were leaving."

"Whips, can you get the AI back up and running?" Laura asked.

Sakura saw the rippling pattern of hard thinking on her friend's skin. "I . . . don't think so," he said, finally. "I'm not nearly finished in my training, and anyway the only way I think might work we can't use right now. We'd have to shut down all associated systems and extract the cores, then do a clean memory restore. We *have* a memory backup onboard in the central repository, I think, but the other part means shutting down most of *LS-5*."

"Can we handle things without the AI?" Akira asked after a moment. "Shutting down *LS-5* and living in our suits may be necessary."

"There's still a lot of basic redundant automation in the systems," Sakura answered, looking at her readouts again. "Exterior comms aren't working—I think some of the antennas got fried or something—but all the interior systems seem to be okay, and most of the sensing systems are still running." She halted, staring at the readouts, and felt as though an ice cube were sliding down her spine. "Oh, crap."

"What is it, Sakura?" her mother asked tensely.

"The piloting and navigation. The automation there is based on the same kind of quantum-channel circuitry as the main AIs, and it was up and running for the drill."

"My God," said Akira in a soft voice. "Does that mean we're dead in space?"

Sakura flipped the controls from *Auto* to *Manual Control. Please, if there's anything listening . . .* She gripped the joystick and pulled.

LS-5 immediately spun smoothly about its axis, and Sakura felt a relieved smile spreading over her face. She did a quick, sharp test-fire of one of the rockets, and then ran through manual checks of the other systems. "No, Dad. We're not dead in space. The manual controls are all operating, and systems all check out."

"Can you run it all?"

She swallowed, then sat up. "I . . . I guess I have to, don't I? I've got the basics down—the sergeant said I was doing really well. And . . . well, I think I can pilot *LS-5* with Whips to help and Caroline to work with us to figure out destinations and courses."

Laura looked to Whips. "What is your honest guess as to how long it would take to get the AI back up and running, if we try that? That would bring back our automation, right?"

Whips' arms curled backward in a momentary defensive posture. "Um, Dr. Kimei, I . . . I'm not *sure* we can get it back up at all. I'm just learning, still, you know! If I tried . . . well, several days, at least. If it worked. And it's possible I'd mess something else up while I was doing it."

"Mom, Dad," Caroline said after a moment, "I think we'd better stick with what already works. If Whips tries and breaks something by accident we could be royally sc . . . er, in a lot of trouble."

Laura looked uncertainly at Sakura, and there was suddenly a private channel. *Sakura? Honey, this will put a lot on you. Are you really okay with this? Do you* really *think you can do it?*

Mom was being serious, and that meant she had to be serious too. The controls and readouts suddenly looked bigger, more intimidating, and it sank in that what Mom was really saying was *we'll all be depending on you to do it* right.

Sakura took a breath and made herself really think about it. *Look first, jet later,* Whips reminded her. *Not the time for your usual charge-forward, Sakura.*

I know, Whips. Don't nag. Still, she knew he was just reminding her of her own worst failing, and she couldn't argue with him. She considered all the controls, everything she'd have to do—if they could survive at all, something she didn't want to contemplate. It was terrifying.

But at the same time, part of her was *excited*. At most she'd expected to get a solo shuttle flight many months from now, with the automatics handling most of it and the sergeant, or another pilot, hanging over her shoulder. This was scarier . . . but it was *real*. She, Sakura Kimei, would be the honest-to-God pilot of a real spaceship.

Whips? she sent. *Can you keep everything else running?*

Everything that's not damaged now? Yes. I can.

She looked over at Caroline, who met her gaze, frowned . . . and then smiled and nodded.

Relief burst in on her. *Yes, Mom. Me and Whips can run this little ship, I promise.*

"All right, then," Laura said decisively. "It's not the way I'd have wanted Sakura to get her real flight experience, but I guess it's our best choice."

"Yay!" Hitomi said happily. "Does that mean you're the Captain, Sakura?"

That caused a faint chuckle around *LS-5's* interior. "No, Hitomi, Mom's the Captain. Dad's the First Officer. I'm just Navigation. Whips is Engineering, and I guess Caroline's sciences or something." She looked over to her mother, who was smiling fondly at Hitomi. "So what next, Captain Mom?"

"'Mom' or 'Captain' please, the two together are just silly." Laura looked out the viewport. "Can we get any comm beacons?"

"No, sorry, Mom. Remember I said most of the comm system's down. Just internals."

"Can't you use the other scanning systems?"

"Maybe." Sakura thought a moment, then after poking around in the controls was able to check out the infrared and radar scans. "Radar's still working—don't know why, that's an RF-based system too. Umm . . ."

After a few minutes, she shook her head. "I'm not getting any radar patterns that look like other shuttles, no IR glows, either, at least nothing nearby."

"There might not *be* anyone else," Whips said bluntly. "I . . . wasn't looking carefully, but can't we play back the recording of those last seconds?"

Laura looked at him. "I'm sure we can . . . but why?"

"Because I don't think I saw any other of those Trapdoor flares. If I'm right that means that we'd be the only ones who fell off, so to speak."

"Or," Sakura said slowly, "that if there are any others they'd be somewhere else along *Outward Initiative*'s path, dumped whenever the instability reached their area of the hab ring."

Hitomi brightened. "So once they realize what happened, *Outward Initiative* can just come back and pick us up, right?"

Sakura winced, and she saw her mother close her eyes before turning to face Hitomi. "I'm . . . afraid not, honey. If it's just us, well, they still probably lost a big chunk of the hab ring. There's going to be a lot of damage to the ship and they won't dare stop. They'll have to get to the nearest colony and get repairs, even if they think we might have survived."

"And with our comm systems out . . ." Sakura swallowed, but made herself go on, "well, with them out, even if they did come back there's so much space for them to look through that they'll probably never see us."

"And if our comms are out, the same is almost certainly true for anyone else who escaped, so if there are others, we may never see them, and they may never see us," her father pointed out. "The important thing is to determine what we do next. Are we equipped for a system survey?"

Sakura checked, but got the answer she expected. "Sorry, Dad. No, there's no survey software installed. No reason to have any. *LS-5* is really meant as just a shuttle between orbit and ground and vice versa, and maybe a small ship for moving around a known system. Even in a lifeboat context, it's assumed we're in some inhabited system. Surveys are done by big ships, usually."

She sensed her Bemmie friend suddenly close off, as though he'd had a terrible thought. His next words brought that thought out for everyone to look at.

"Sakura...most of space is...well, very empty. If we're not in a solar system..."

She saw her mother's eyes widen, and Caroline's too; they both understood the implications. "It's not *that* bad...I think. The Shuttle's got its own Trapdoor Drive, so we can go FTL...in hops, because we have to charge the loops to run it—takes more power than the reactor can generate by itself. So...in effect it's about a third the speed of a regular Trapdoor."

"So that's about...what, twenty-five times the speed of light or so?"

"A little more, but yeah."

Her mother frowned and looked towards the back, and Sakura suddenly understood what she was worrying about. Whips. His people were amphibious, and he had to immerse in water fairly often for his skin and other biological functions. She knew that wasn't necessary every day, but...

"Honey, let's say we get to a good solar system. How long will it take to go from, well, wherever we get in the system to landing?"

"Depends on where we come out of Trapdoor," her sister Caroline said. As a planetographer, Caroline had a good grasp of distances and times in solar systems. "Could be only a few days—long enough to get a good look and choose a landing site, or get noticed by anyone already in-system—or could be several weeks, maybe over a month."

"A month." Mom shook her head. "And each light-year will be a couple of weeks, roughly, at the speed we can reach in *LS-5*. Then . . . we really have to hope there is a solar system within one or two light-years. Normally two weeks is pushing it for a Bemmie. I've got some ideas on how to stretch that—there are recommendations in the literature—but I don't know if I can stretch it more than two months."

Sakura tried to hide her dismay. The chances weren't great that a star was that close. They weren't *terrible*—maybe one in two or three—but still, not certain. And even if there were stars nearby, they might not have good planets. *And even if it weren't for Whips . . . there's not all that much food on board, especially since Whips'll eat more than one of us. We've got a nuclear reactor with power for years, but our supplies won't last that long.* She glanced at Hitomi—staring back with wide, terrified eyes—and Melody, gripping her seat's arms so tightly the knuckles were white—and then at her mother and took a breath.

"First thing to do is find out where the nearest star is, I guess," she said. "I mean, if we *are* in a solar system, no problem. Everyone keep an eye out."

Her hands tried to shake, and she paused and took a breath before she reached out to the controls again. *Simple. Just a full look around. Methodical, careful, controlled, just like in training.*

The gyros and stabilizers could be used to spin the ship without having to use any of the limited reaction mass, so she used that, carefully rotating *LS-5* around its axes so that all portions of the sky slowly drifted across the forward field of view.

Stars swam by, and everyone in the ship watched

tensely. The beautiful river of light that was the Milky Way pinwheeled around them. Bright stars, dim stars, stars with a hint of red or yellow or blue or pure white shone unflickering against the absolute black of space.

"Anyone?"

The others shook their heads. "I saw some pretty bright stars," Whips said, "but nothing that looked like it had a disc. At a light-year away, I think the Sun would only look like a bright star—"

"Magnitude about minus three," Caroline said. "So yes, even if we're close to a good star, if it's even a large fraction of a light-year away, we won't see it as a disc. And without knowing what kind of star I'm looking at, I can't make a guess as to how far away it is."

Sakura knew what she meant. Given how much stars varied in their actual light output, a really bright star could be a tiny red dwarf just a fraction of a light-year away, or a supergiant star hundreds of light-years off.

"But . . ." Caroline continued, smiling, "we don't need to worry about that. Sakura, just charge up the Trapdoor Drive and give us a few hours hop in any direction."

Sakura laughed, feeling some slight relief. *At least we can find out how bad we're screwed.* "Parallax, right?"

"Right. Move only a little ways and we should be able to see movement of a nearby star against the background of the others. You recorded the whole globe of stars around us, right?"

"Yeah. And really, only the *very* bright ones matter, I think—over first mag, probably."

"I'd guess you're right. That's only twenty or so back home, probably not much more than that here. We can track that pretty easily."

"Okay, then—can I do that, Mom?"

Her mother smiled. "Of course you can. 'Make it so,' navigator."

Sakura heard the first chuckle since the disaster go around the cabin. "Aye, Captain!" She turned back to the controls. "Unsealing Trapdoor Drive controls. Drive shows green. Coils charged."

Despite the desperate circumstances, she felt a thrill go through her. Her first solo flight . . . and she was doing a hop in interstellar space!

"Since we have no idea which direction we want to go, I'm just jumping the way we're pointing. Set for four hops, total distance a few light-days. We'll check the big stars after each hop, while the superconductor storage coils are charging. Okay?"

"Sounds good to me, Sakura."

She found herself holding her breath as she reached out and touched the activation button.

Without a bump or jolt, the universe outside disappeared, and the Trapdoor Drive sent *LS-5* hurtling on its unknown course. "Trapdoor Drive activated! We'll be under drive for . . . about one hour and ten minutes."

This is going to be the longest hour ever.

Chapter 4

The stars shone out again, and she bent forward. "Coils recharging. Doing a full survey of the sky again . . ." She tumbled *LS-5* once more around its axes. "Generating full sky view . . . okay, everyone, start looking. I'm blinking our virtual displays between the first panorama we got and this one. I'm sending different areas of the sky to—"

"*Got one!*" sang out Caroline. "Brightest star in our sky just jumped a beautiful, beautiful big fraction of a degree! Measure that arc, Sakura!"

"It's . . . about an eighth of a degree," she said after a moment, feeling a smile spreading over her face. "That's less than a light-year off, right?"

"About zero point two seven light-years, I think, which given the brightness means we're probably looking at a G-type star!"

G-type star. She heard the words with a tremendous lightening of her heart. That was the best possible candidate for a world they could live on.

She heard both her parents let out their breaths in a sigh of relief. "That's wonderful, Caroline, Sakura," her mother said. "But let's not jump the gun. See if any other stars move."

28

No one else spotted any that they were sure of, and by the time they were done, the second jump had begun. After another tense-yet-boring wait, Sakura repeated the maneuver and started the comparison running again. This time, Hitomi spotted two more that she thought moved. A close comparison showed that she was right, but the movement was small compared to the now very noticeable movement of the first star. One appeared to be a red dwarf about three light-years out, and the other a brighter star five light-years away. No very bright stars were directly ahead of or behind them, so they weren't heading straight towards or straight away from any possible candidates.

That was enough for her mother. "All right, then. Sakura, cancel those other jumps and get us headed towards that star, okay?"

"Yes, Mom—I mean, Captain." She felt much steadier this time as she set the course. "Given that we're this close and moving as fast as we will be, I don't need to do a fancy navigation calculation. Just point the nose at our target and drop out to adjust our course maybe once a day. We'll be about there in a little less than four days."

"That's just fine, honey. Hold off on the jump for a little bit. Everyone, unstrap for a moment so we can all talk together," said her mother.

The others unsnapped quickly. It took Whips a little longer to release all his hold-downs.

"First . . . all of you, come here," Laura said. She reached out and hugged little Hitomi to her, and gestured the others close.

Then her mother looked up as the family gathered, straight at Whips. "You too, Harratrer."

She could sense a momentary protest that he was too old to need special treatment. "Come *here*, Whips," she said, and heard her voice waver. "You're our family too."

The patterns that rippled chaotically over Whips' skin showed that he, too, was close to the equivalent of tears. He drifted over to the others and wrapped all three arms around the Kimei family; Sakura and the others gripped his arms and hands, and even though he was so very different . . . it was still exactly like a hug from their own family.

For a few moments they all hung there, not moving, just accepting that for now, they were together, and a family, and safe.

Mom smiled finally and spoke up. "That's right. We're all here, we're all alive, we're together, and no one's hurt. Right?"

Hitomi nodded, brightening. Melody, eyes still huge and frightened, also nodded. *She's smart enough to know we're not anywhere near safe yet.*

"Right!" said Sakura; her attempt to sound confident and ready didn't fool Whips, she was pretty sure, and probably not her parents.

"Of course, Mom," Caroline agreed.

"Exactly right," Dad finished. "I won't pretend we're not in trouble—not even to you, Hitomi. But we could be in much worse trouble."

"We're already trying to figure out where we are, and where we have to go," Mom said decisively, letting go, and allowing the others to slowly drift back to their seats. "I've never heard of a Trapdoor Drive failure before, but then I suppose if it happened it would be hard to get news of the failure. Is it possible we're somehow near our destination?"

"I wouldn't expect so," Whips said slowly. "I mean, I'm just an apprentice right now, but I've been studying real hard to understand all the key engineering stuff. We were only halfway there. I don't know how it'd be possible for us to jump the rest of the way so fast. If 'fast' is a reasonable term, I'm still finding the swimming *really* hard with understanding relativity and such. Still, it looked like the field just...deformed and dropped us off. We're still probably about halfway to our destination."

"But space is pretty much empty," Melody said, her voice trembling a little but her tone going to the lecturing one that she liked to use whenever showing off what she knew. "And our destination was EC-G5-4-100-11 Tantalus, which doesn't have any stars I know of right along our route."

"Can we tell if this is the right star?" Akira asked.

Sakura thought, then shrugged. "How? If we get close enough or we find a planet we might be able to tell. *LS-5* doesn't have any spectroscopic software on board."

"My omni does," Melody said.

A ripple of stroboscopic surprise washed down Whips' body. "Why in all the oceans would you have spectroscopic software?"

"I was playing with chemical analysis packages," Melody answered defensively.

"It's all right, Melody; he wasn't saying there was anything wrong with it, he was just surprised. As am I," Caroline said, "but if you'll let me access your omni we might be able to use it."

Melody gestured vaguely in the air, and her omni-personal communicator, database, toolkit, entertainment center, and more in one—generated a green light. "Go ahead."

"From the designation," Caroline said, "we know that Tantalus' primary is a G-5 star and Tantalus itself is the 4th planet out from the primary. So the first thing to do is to find out what type of star that is." She looked at Sakura. "Which camera input should I use?"

"Umm...Hold on a minute." *Where are the specs on all these things? Oh, there's the info tags... Okay!*

"The forward nose camera is continuous spectrum sensitivity from deep infrared through far UV—that's between about twenty-four microns down to two hundred nanometers," she said finally with relief. For a moment she had wondered if in fact there were any full-spectrum, unfiltered cameras available. She refined the alignment of *LS-5* and made sure the target star was centered. "There you go, Caroline."

"What's the camera designation?"

"Sorry. It's simply designated as camera Alpha in the main systems."

"Okay, I have the input stream. Melody, direct your spectroscopic app output to my omni, okay?"

"Okay."

A few minutes passed, then Caroline sat back with a smile. "Based on the spectrum and apparent temperature, I'm reasonably confident—though not certain, because these aren't ideal conditions—that we're looking at a G-3 main sequence star. So it's not Tantalus' system, but it is, at least, the type of system we'd like to be in."

"The Sun's a G-2, right?" Whips asked.

"That's right," Sakura answered, glad she knew some of this. "A G-3 will be just a little tiny bit cooler and smaller than the Sun, I think, but we won't notice the difference." *If there's a planet to land on, anyway.*

"Well, in that case," Akira said, "I think it's time to get things started and for me to get out some food. It's past lunchtime, after all. Hit the jump, Sakura."

He looked apologetically at her friend. "I'm afraid... we don't have very many rations for Bemmies, Whips."

"I didn't expect you would," Whips said calmly. Sakura bit her lip. The Europan Bemmies weren't obligate carnivores, but they did need a lot more protein—of the generally animal sort—than anything else. The more "balanced" human rations wouldn't be terribly good for Whips, and he'd have to eat a lot more of them, even in proportion to his size. How long would their supplies hold out?

"We'll have to make do," her mother said. "I know they're not ideal for you, Harratrer, but we have I think three months' supplies. Even with you onboard, we should be able to keep going for two months, and that should be more than enough now." Unspoken was the fact that immersion issues might become acute long before then.

"Thank you, Dr. Kimei." Sakura could tell that Whips' formal-sounding voice hid much more relief and gratitude.

They'd found a good star. The drive was working. Maybe they'd get out of this after all.

Chapter 5

The unnamed star glowed before them, a visible disk, as *LS-5* came out of the Trapdoor Drive. *Now the next cycle of worry begins*, Whips messaged to Sakura, who gave a tense, wry grin. *Finding a good star was excellent luck...but we cannot live on a star.*

Yeah. But let's take one problem at a time. He saw her shove the worries out of her mind and concentrate on trying to figure out their location. *We're already moving some with respect to the star, so if I can get any parallax at all that will give me a good idea of distance. I can sorta guess based on the likely diameter of the star, probably about one and a quarter million kilometers, but it could be significantly more or less than that.*

Finally she shook her head and sat back. "I've got a rough guess as to our distance, but it'll take a while to refine that and get a velocity vector. At a guess, we're maybe two AUs from the star."

"I *thought* the star looked a lot more than Europa-sized," Whips said. "I mean, the size the Sun looks from Europa."

"Yeah, that was really all I had to go on, given

the uncertainty in the Trapdoor transit distance. If it's a yellow supergiant I'd be totally wrong...but I don't see all the gas and stuff it should be shedding if it was a supergiant, and if that's what it was we'd be pretty much out of luck anyway, so it *has* to be a regular G-class."

Caroline nodded. "Besides, if it was a yellow supergiant it would have been *incredibly* bright at a quarter light-year distance. Trust me, it's a regular G-3."

"Why do we have to wait to get parallax?" Laura asked reasonably. "Just do a quick jump with the Trapdoor Drive."

"We *could* do that," Whips said, since he saw Sakura looking uncertain. "But the Drive doesn't come up and go down fast; what happened to separate us from *Outward Initiative* is almost certainly partly due to something trying to do a fast adjustment on the field. You're deforming spacetime itself, after all, and that's something you need to do very, very carefully. So... in practice you don't want to do jumps shorter than, oh, thirty seconds or so, which since that's going to be a full continuous jump instead of one that's interspersed with recharging moments, that's a minimum jump of...well over seven hundred million kilometers."

"Oh." Laura's brow wrinkled as she accessed the data. "Ah. That means that even the shortest practical jump covers a distance almost as far as Jupiter from the Sun."

"Roughly, yes," Whips agreed. "There are special drive designs that can do shorter, faster jumps, or ways to tune these for that, but..." he gave the rippling gesture of arms and color that was his equivalent of the human's shrugs, "I'm an apprentice. I know the theory, but no way am I going to try doing that in practice."

"We wouldn't want you to!" Sakura agreed emphatically. "So that means we need to just let our own speed give us the parallax, and then we can deploy the Nebula Drive to get us to our target."

Whips actually looked forward to that. The "Nebula Drive," or more technically the "dusty-plasma sail" had been originally invented by *Bemmius secordii sapiens*—not his direct ancestors, but the ones who'd seeded his ancestors on Europa. Human scientists such as Dr. Robert Sheldon had theorized it was possible, but it wasn't until an ancient *Bemmius* relic had been uncovered and repaired that the Nebula Drive was simultaneously reborn and renamed, a method for using ionized plasma to inflate a magnetic field to immense sizes, confining dust and gas within the field and providing the most ethereally beautiful, and low-cost, way to move around a solar system.

"*Can* we get closer to the star?" her dad asked. "I don't want to worry anyone, but I know the only other long-distance capability we have comes from the Nebula Drive, and that's sort of like a solar sail, right? So I can see how it can push us *away* from the star, but..."

"Remember that we're not just sitting still with respect to the star," Whips said. "So the real key is which direction you are orbiting the star, and at what distance."

"Right," said Sakura, picking up the conversation, "To oversimplify, you just point your sail so you go against your orbiting direction, and that'll make you go closer. You can tack with a dusty-plasma sail just like a regular sail. If we can find a good-sized gas giant somewhere, we can also use the gravity assist to send us in the right direction."

Hitomi spoke up. "And we need to find a planet to land on. So we should be looking for planets now!"

Whips was impressed with his friend's self-control, as Sakura managed to keep a smile on her face at Hitomi's innocent assertion. Whips didn't need to read the datastream from Sakura to know what thoughts were going through her head. *There might not be a planet to land on. Probably won't be. Only one of ten stars like this have good planets in the habitable zone—which is a whole ocean of a lot more than they used to think there would be...*

Aloud, Laura Kimei said, "Hitomi's completely right. Caroline?"

Caroline looked uncomfortable. Whips knew that she hated doing things halfway, or out of order, or, well, just not the right way—and there was nothing "right" about this situation at all.

But she sat up straighter and nodded. "The most puzzling thing to me is that this star is just not on the charts. I checked with what I had from Earth, and if we did just drop off where I think we did, there *aren't* any stars where this one sits. Nothing. If there was, the big wide-baseline telescopes in our home system would have mapped any planets in detail, especially habitable ones, even if no one actually went there. But there's nothing. This star shouldn't be here...but it is here, and I guess we should just be grateful it is.

"But that does mean we've got to do all the survey work ourselves, without a single clue as to exactly what we're looking for or where it is." Caroline sighed, pursed her lips, then nodded again. "We'll need to get all our omnis linked in to the different cameras and do running background comparisons. Stars don't seem to move appreciably at orbital speeds, so what we're looking for are dots that move with respect to the background of the stars." She sighed. "If *LS-5* were meant for this kind of work, it could run the whole comparison by itself while we slept even without the AI, but it was just meant to follow beacons to orbits and landings and take sights only when it knew pretty well what it was looking for. And when we were looking for a nearby star, well, we were looking at the few very bright stars in the sky. Planets might be pretty dim stars, especially depending on what angle we're viewing them at."

"Can you program the omnis to do the comparison?" Whips asked.

Caroline hesitated, then nodded. "I have a comparison program from my studies, actually. It can be transferred. But..."

"But...?" Laura Kimei prompted.

"But... well, without any benchmarks it's going to be really hard to know what we're looking at. Oh, you can tell the characteristic banding on a gas giant pretty easy, but how do you know if you're seeing one that's closer in or farther away? We don't even know which direction we are going yet."

"Never mind that," Laura said firmly. "First let's find planets. By the time we find some, I'm sure Sakura will have gotten enough data to tell us how fast we're moving with respect to our star and we can really start nailing things down then, right?"

"Yes, Mom," Caroline said after another hesitation.

They all acquired the running comparator program a few moments later. "I've picked out some bright stars as landmarks," Sakura said. "*LS-5* will use those to keep our orientation the same, so each of us has our own camera to focus on and the view won't shift."

Maybe a silly question, Whips sent to Sakura, *but what if you've picked a planet as one of your landmarks?*

Oh, come on, *Whips, don't you think I* thought *of that?* The transmitted voice came with a grin-symbol, so he knew she wasn't really annoyed. *I put full magnification on each one to make sure it didn't change size and got a partial spectrum off each using Melody's program; they're emitters, not reflecting the local sun, so yeah, they're all stars.*

Good. He hesitated, then, *You know the odds are... not good?*

Yeah, she sent back after a few moments. *One out of ten chance there's a decent candidate, and then there's the question of the biosphere.* She looked at her father, who had subtle frown lines on his normally cheerful face.

He knows—better than anyone else—what those odds are.

They're great *odds... if you're not worried that your life's being bet on them*, Sakura sent back.

That much was true, he had to concede. Out of all of the extrasolar planets found to harbor significant life, one-half had a biosphere that was, astonishingly, compatible with Earthly (and Europan) lifeforms. *Why* this was true was a source of spirited, not to say flamingly acrimonious, debate between biologists and allied professions. Some held that it was simply a matter of chemistry. There were only so many easily assembled building blocks of self-replicating chemistry, and the ones that Earth and Europa were based on were some of the most easily synthesized, and so it was just likely that similar lifeforms would evolve. Others had championed the old idea of Arrhenius' "panspermia," that life had evolved somewhere else a long time ago and been spread through the universe by light pressure or similar phenomena. But so far no one had found an unambiguous example of such spaceborne spores.

No matter the actual source, it was true that half the lifebearing planets found had compatible biospheres— although "compatible" did not in any way guarantee it was safe, or even easily digestible. The other half . . . were not compatible and generally lethal. *And vice versa, of course—an animal of those biospheres eating me would likely die in agony.*

So . . . one chance in twenty, then. We beat odds like that all the time in those card games.

Sure, agreed Sakura, darkly. *But if we lose this game we won't be starting another.*

Little Hitomi grew bored of the comparator fairly quickly and drifted through the air to start climbing on Whips, playing with her stuffed flying wolf along the way. Whips sighed, but tolerated it. He was bigger than everyone else, so she'd bother him less than the others. Besides, there was more of him for her to climb on. He quickly found he could keep her amused by wiggling his rear anchors gently so she had to hold on—and sometimes came off to drift away, so Hitomi had to bounce her way back, giggling.

It was still somewhat distracting, but he was able to focus on the comparator data. The running comparator would flick back and forth between images in the field of view of interest, and kept the original images as the start point while constantly updating the second image with new data. Any planets, then, would show an increasing oscillation as the images flicked between original and new images.

"One here!" crowed Akira suddenly. "Definitely moving back and forth!"

"Wonderful, Dad!" Caroline said. "Show me!" She studied it for a moment. "All right, Sakura, I'll need our full magnification on that location for a minute."

"Hold on . . . I'll rotate us. Okay, there, we're steady."

The built-in telescopic optics in the forward imaging system gave Caroline a high-quality image to look at. "Ohh, how *pretty!*" she said a moment later, and projected the picture onto the forward screen for everyone to see.

Whips had to admit it was quite pretty, even to his perceptions, which weren't quite the same as those of his human friends. It was a good thing they had displays which actually emitted the intended wavelengths, instead of that old human red-green-blue system; or he'd only be able to make out shapes in those displays.

In the projected image floated a slightly flattened sphere, banded with rippled stripes of startlingly bright colors. Based on what he knew of human perceptions, they ranged from bright red through purple and even some definite green, though he'd use different names for the colors back home. "That seems even more spectacular than Jupiter. What is it with all those colors?"

Caroline shook her head absently. "So many possibilities. Though I looked at the spectrum of the star, and this planet, and I'm pretty sure this system's got more heavy elements in it than ours. So it might be a higher concentration of complex compounds in the atmosphere."

"Well, that's one gas giant," Laura said. "We need to find others, presumably closer to the star. Sakura, have we gotten enough parallax to estimate distance?"

"I think so." Whip's friend stared vacantly into air for a moment, seeing her own display. "Um, yeah. Looks like we're just a hair over one point two AUs from the primary, which refines all my other estimates!"

"Where's the Goldilocks Zone?" asked Hitomi, startling them.

"I'll tell you in a second," Caroline said, but Melody, who'd been mostly silent, interjected, "Centered at one hundred thirty-seven million kilometers."

Caroline looked at Melody. "How—"

"Well, I'd brought up the data on calculating it earlier, so I just caught Sakura's data and threw it in."

"So *what's* the Goldilocks Zone?" asked Hitomi.

"You remember the story of Goldilocks and the Three Bears?" Sakura asked. When Hitomi nodded, Sakura went on, "Well, then, the Goldilocks Zone is the region around the star that's 'just right'—not too close and hot, not too far and cold—for planets like Earth."

"Oh! That makes sense!"

"Sakura, my measurements agree with yours," said Caroline. "If that's the case, then Whips and Mom have the best views of that region, at least where we currently are. But some of the Zone is going to be out of sight or hard to differentiate behind the primary."

"Let's allow the system to accumulate more movement," Akira suggested, "and take a break. The bathroom's fortunately able to accommodate a Bemmie, as they made all the shuttles from the same design, so why don't you take a turn if you need it, Whips?"

He *had* been feeling that need, so he flickered gratitude at the black-haired Akira Kimei. "I will, thank you!"

The others took their turns once he came out, and in the meantime he took a long drink of water and added some salts. He didn't say anything, but he caught Mr. Kimei looking at him with grave concern. Since Laura had the girls helping her to put a dinner together, he drifted over to Akira. "Don't worry, sir."

"It's not terribly dry in here, is it?"

"Not too bad, Mr. Kimei."

Akira Kimei shook his head. "Laura is working out a treatment."

Whips had no doubt that Laura Kimei was trying— and probably would succeed. But..."Sir...Mr. Kimei... if we're out here very long, we're probably not going to live anyway. The fact that I'm drying out...well, I'll stop needing rations—"

"Stop that right now, Harratrer!" The use of his real name made him stiffen, just as he might if his mother were there. "We are *all* getting out of this, or none of us."

"Sometimes one must leave the Pod for it to survive," he said, quoting one of the oldest rules.

"In this case, if we can't find a world to live on, none of us will. So don't worry about it."

He had to admit that Mr. Kimei had a good point, so he rippled his arms in a "you win" gesture, and went over to see about dinner. He might as well stay as well as he could until they knew if there was hope...or none.

Chapter 6

Akira's arms hugged Laura tightly for a moment. "Are you all right?"

"I think so," she answered on the same channel. One good thing about having private comm channels was that you could have a private conversation even in the middle of a not-too-large cabin. "But my God, Akira." Even after four days it was still hard to grasp what had happened, and only now that they had successfully reached that target solar system had she started to allow herself to think beyond the question of whether something would happen to the little shuttle's Trapdoor Drive.

"I know. We weren't prepared for this."

She rotated around to face him and then retightened her sleeping tether. "No one even knew this could *happen*. I wonder if this is the first time, or whether it's happened to other ships, too."

He shrugged. "No way to know, Laura. And doesn't matter now."

"Now that we've found a good star . . . what are our odds?"

She felt him draw a deep breath. "One in twenty

that there's a planet we can live on—in theory. If Sakura can land us."

That was one of the things that worried—no, to be honest, terrified her. She didn't doubt Sakura normally, but without the AI running, everything would depend on one fourteen-year-old girl piloting a ship from orbit to landing.

"Stop worrying about that," Akira said firmly. "First, it's useless; we can't change what we have to work with. Second, the main automatics may be gone, but there are still some basic stabilizers and other safety devices to help her. Third, she's been studying and doing calculations with Caroline every spare moment. Caroline, Whips, and Melody have been working on display apps for Sakura's omni to help guide her down. Sakura will do fine."

"You're sure?"

He kissed her quickly. "*Sure?* Nothing about this is sure, Laura. But what I am sure of is that Sakura will do her best, and that's all we can ask her to do. If we die trying, well, we'll die anyway if we don't."

She smiled and nodded. "I suppose you're right. It's not like we have much choice."

"No. Sakura's the only one of us with any idea how to operate this ship. And so far she's doing just fine. I can tell how proud you are of her, too."

"I'm proud of all of them. No panic, yet. All listening, all pulling together. I'm most worried about poor Harratrer."

Akira was silent for a moment. "Well, we're only a few weeks from the Goldilocks Zone, if Sakura's current estimates of speed and what the Nebula Drive can do are right. I checked our stores and what you gave me on his biology. We can keep everyone well-fed, even Whips, for longer than that. The ship was pretty well-supplied. And if there is a livable world, it will have an ocean that he can probably handle; remember that we made sure they had the adaptations to deal with wide variations in water salinity and mineral content."

That much was true, and just hearing Akira repeat the facts calmly helped to relax her. When the Europan Bemmies and human beings had established long-term contact, the relatively primitive aliens had turned out to be surprisingly open to understanding. They had shown little of the signs of culture shock that had plagued various human societies—although that was probably at least partially because the Interplanetary Research Institute and its sponsoring U.N. had managed to strictly control interactions with the aliens at first.

The Bemmies, AKA *Bemmius pelagica sapiens* Sutter, were not identical to the similarly named aliens who had, sixty-five million years before, set up bases in humanity's solar system and then nearly killed themselves off in a war, but were instead evolved descendants of lifeforms with which *Bemmius secordii sapiens* had seeded Europa prior to leaving the system. But evolution had taken them down a similar path, and to human eyes the two species looked very similar. The Europan natives had been fascinated by the idea of a real world beyond the sky—given that the most prevalent religion on Europa had been about gods that lay "Beyond the Sky," which meant above the crust of ice that covered Europa, this was not surprising.

It was impractical, to say the least, to have starships filled with water (for many reasons, ranging from sheer mass to electronics issues), so for a while it seemed that only a rare ambassador, scientist, or student from Europa might travel from their homeworld. But then one of the aging survivors of the first Europan venture, A.J. Baker, had suggested that—just possibly—the Europan Bemmies could be adapted to live in air and water, as had their long-vanished distant cousins. "We've seen what we can do with genetics in the last few decades—life extension, engineering healthy organs, engineering new versions of lifeforms for our own use—and it's not like it's a new idea. Heck, it's the exact idea Bemmies used when they seeded Europa to begin with!"

There was much reluctance at first, but to many people's considerable surprise, once word of the idea got to the Europans, some of them practically *insisted* that this be tried, none of them more vehemently than Blushspark, the Europan Bemmie who had made First Contact. And with careful, painstaking work... the design had succeeded.

Laura sighed. "I've figured out a way to wet him down without choking us on mist. It won't work forever but... a few weeks, yes, though I don't think he'll be in top shape. Now... if there is a decent planet?"

"I can't give odds on unknowns. What I know of biology tells me that we will probably be able to find something to sustain us there." He glanced at her with momentary concern. "That is, if you can keep our medical nanos going to filter out incidental toxins, and maybe convert some materials to any vital nutrients we're missing like the vitamins."

She thought about that for a moment. "I think so. *LS-5* has a good nano updating installation onboard, and I have my medical kit. I'm not sure we'll be able to update them like we do at home, though, and over some time the concentration may drop. Medical nanos are strictly limited in self-replication."

"If you can get *LS-5* to do so, I'd have it replicate some nanos now for a reserve. No telling what demands we'll put on it later. We've got a few weeks at least."

That was an excellent suggestion, and she checked *LS-5*'s systems. "Yes, I think I can do that, and it shouldn't interfere with other operations. Good thinking, love. What about other survival issues?"

"*LS-5* is nuclear powered, and there's a lot of equipment and material we can use in her. We were, after all, going to a colony world that's just opening up. She'll serve as excellent shelter for a long time, and we can move around as we need. Don't worry, Laura, if we find such a planet, we'll be okay."

She looked over at Whips, who was floating at his own station, clearly awake, probably observing the comparator. His people, Laura remembered, didn't generally sleep in the same cycles as human beings. They went into a sort of not-entirely-unconscious torpor for a few hours, then woke for several hours before going back into the recuperative torpor. Only when they were severely exhausted or injured did they seem to sleep deeply the way humans did—although they did, in torpor, have something like human dreams. "It's a good thing he is so close to Sakura."

Akira glanced in that direction, some of his black hair trying to escape its netting. "Yes. He has a connection to us and that should help against the loss of his pod."

Suddenly, Whips stiffened, and then shouted in his deep, vibrating voice, *"Found one!"*

The others jolted awake, Sakura blinking blearily at

her friend, Hitomi giving a little *yip!* of startlement, and Melody glaring at the big alien. But Caroline seemed instantly alert. "A planet? Where?"

"Here—I'll send you the coordinates in my viewing field."

Sakura unsnapped and drifted herself over to the controls. "Everyone secure? I'm going to turn us towards the coordinates so Caroline can use the telescope."

Laura checked on everyone, especially Hitomi, who had a habit of unsnapping herself at the most inopportune times. "Everyone's secure, Sakura."

The ship pivoted and turned and the stars swirled by, then steadied. "Okay, Caroline, that should do it."

Caroline studied the view, her hands twitching slightly with control gestures. Suddenly she stiffened. "Oh. My. God."

"What *is* it?"

For answer, Caroline sent the image to the main channel. Laura heard herself give a gasp.

Floating in the star-speckled blackness was a world, illuminated in a crescent by the nearby sun, a crescent that showed swirls of white and brown but mostly a beautiful, rich green.

"Caroline?" Akira said tensely. "Where is that? Is it—"

"Measuring now, Dad. Sakura, can you check me?"

"Now that you've bullseyed it, I can track back through the data for the parallax, yes."

Another few moments passed, then Caroline leaned back, and her voice was shaky. "I put it at one hundred nineteen million kilometers from the primary, a little inside the middle of the habitable zone."

"Yes, yes, I check you, Caroline! It's there, it's a planet in the Goldilocks zone."

"It's the right size, too," Caroline said, her voice showing almost as much excitement as Sakura's. "I make it about thirteen thousand kilometers across."

"Caroline," Akira said calmly, "give me the feed, please. And Melody, your spectroscopic app?"

"Yes, Dad," they both said. Laura understood what he was looking for, and said a silent prayer to whoever, or whatever, might be out there.

Hitomi was staring at the image of the planet. "It's so *pretty!* What's its name?"

She smiled. "It doesn't have a name yet, little girl. We get to name it."

Hitomi stared up at her with huge eyes. "We *do*?"

"We do."

The six-year-old looked back at the screen and then gave a nod so emphatic that it would have caused her to spin if she hadn't been strapped in. "Then I wanna call it Lincoln!"

"Lincoln?" repeated Melody in a puzzled tone. "Why would you ever call it after President Lincoln?"

"Presi—who?" Hitomi looked confused. "No, because that's its color—like the clothes those men wore in that story!"

"Those men—Oh!" Melody suddenly laughed. "You mean Robin Hood's Merry Men, and they wore Lincoln green!"

Laura smiled. "Well, I think that's a perfectly good name. What do the rest of you say?"

As Laura had expected, while obviously Sakura and Melody had hoped to name the planet (and, she admitted to herself, so had she), none of them wanted to disappoint the excited Hitomi. "Then Lincoln it is."

"Why are the oceans green?" asked Sakura. "I'd think they'd be blue, like Earth's."

"It could be due to any number of reasons," Caroline said. "A different mineral/particulate suspension in the water than we have on Earth. Or—"

"An abundance of chlorophyll-bearing creatures," their father interjected. He was smiling broadly, and pointed to the virtual display they could now all see, a pattern of dark bands on bright. "We're down to those odds I couldn't guess. Chlorophyll. A beautiful, unmistakable variation on chlorophyll, and a perfect indicator of life like our own. The other ecologies use other pigments."

As the meaning of the words sank in, the others cheered. Hitomi didn't exactly understand, but she knew good news when she heard it, and cheered as well.

"It's possible it may even be a seasonal thing," Akira continued. "Something like huge algal blooms that periodically make the sea brilliant green across most of the globe, then fade away. Even on Earth you can sometimes get very green water that's visible from orbit."

Laura felt immense relief go through her. "Sakura?"

"Yes, Mom?"

"This is your Captain speaking, Navigator."

Sakura snapped her an exaggerated salute, grinning from ear to ear. "Yes, Ma'am! What are your orders, Captain?"

"Set a course for Lincoln and give us an ETA."

"On it, Captain Mommy!"

Sakura immediately went into conference with Caroline and Melody. Laura had to admit after a few moments that she honestly didn't really understand the discussion. Unlike her offspring, physics calculations and orbits and vectors just didn't interest her much. But she could tell the three girls were arguing over the best approach to use the Nebula Drive and heard terms including "constant acceleration," "orbital transfer," and "least-time course." Whips drifted over and joined the debate. She noticed that the Bemmie's normally smooth, flexible skin already had a fine network of lines over it, like dry human skin.

After a few more minutes, Sakura nodded and the other three seemed to have reached agreement. The fourteen-year-old strapped herself back into the pilot's chair and carefully manipulated several controls before turning back to them. "Deploying Nebula Drive dusty-plasma sail. According to calculations, ETA is three weeks."

Laura finally felt herself relax. That was well within Akira's estimate of their food supply and, she thought, her ability to keep Whips in functional shape. It wasn't going to be easy, no. But they had a livable destination, they could get there fast enough, and they had the tools and equipment they needed.

The worst was over.

Chapter 7

"Nebula Drive fully retracted. All smart dust now stowed away. Recovery of materials at 95%," Sakura reported, partially to herself. The routine, reporting each detail of her tasks, helped calm her, slow the heart that threatened to accelerate out of control.

It's all on me.

The thought was terrifying, more so because she knew she couldn't show it. Melody and especially Hitomi could panic if they realized just how scared their older sister was.

But she *was* scared. Lincoln now loomed up before them, as beautiful as it had been at first with drifting streamers and coils of white cloud across the green ocean and brown-green of islands and continents. It was the salvation they needed, a real, livable planet with an oxygen-nitrogen atmosphere and water and animals and plants...

...if fourteen-year-old Sakura Kimei could manage to land *LS-5.*

"Stop worrying," Whips said. "I can tell you're ready to jet yourself into blackness with this, and it's not doing you any good. We've chosen a landing spot, the apps we've got for your display will help guide you, and all you have to do is keep calm."

A hand touched her shoulder. "Whips is right, sweetheart," Laura said to her quietly. "You told me yourself, didn't you?"

"I know, Mom," she said, and tried to keep her voice from trembling. "But still, I'm going to—"

"You're going to do just fine," her father said from the other side. "Just take some breaths and relax. Even choosing the points isn't happening right now. You want to select them once you're sure where we're setting her down."

"Yes, Dad."

She turned back to the console, bringing up the physical controls. "In a real emergency situation," her instructor Sergeant Campbell had said, "you do *not* rely on the projected interfaces. Understand this, boys and girls, projections can fail. Our wireless toys can go haywire, even today. Your local net can shut down. But the real console controls, the ones built into the shuttles, those won't fail you unless the ship itself is bad, bad damaged. So you can practice all you want on your virtual toys, but in this class you will do everything on real, solid controls, do you understand?"

I understand, Sergeant. She remembered him, a craggy-faced man towering over her, seeming almost two meters high and as intimidating as a thunderhead— but really one of the kindest and most patient teachers she'd ever had. *I hope I won't screw this up after all your lessons. I . . . just wish I'd had about a hundred more lessons.*

The controls of *LS-5* responded exactly like the simulator's. She gave very brief test actuations of all systems to make sure they responded as expected. "All controls active. Test burns all green. On course for deorbit and landing on Lincoln."

Lincoln was starting to take on more the aspect of a wall than a planet. She checked all the sensors that still worked, which wasn't many. "Huh."

"What is it?" asked Caroline.

"There's some . . . strange, really long-wave stuff that the radar's just able to pick up."

Her mother's head snapped up. "You're not saying it's . . . *inhabited*, are you?"

"I . . . don't think so. It's kinda like some signals you can get from gas giants like Jupiter, random noise at funny wavelengths, and there's no sign on our tele-scopic images of lights or anything like cities." It was disappointing, of course. Discovering a new intelligent alien species would have been awesome.

"Should we wait? See if we can figure out what it is?"

Caroline shook her head. "Mom, that's an unbounded problem. Looking at the waves, Sakura's right. It's got the patterns of some type of natural phenomenon, and they're hardly intense enough to be dangerous, or even interfere with our systems. We could spend months surveying this planet. But we don't *have* months."

Her mother frowned, then nodded. She knew the truth as well as any of them; Whips was starting to show signs of real skin dehydration, even with every-thing her mother could do to try and slow it. They couldn't afford to wait long.

"Besides," Whips pointed out, "we *have* done a basic survey on approach, as Lincoln rotated. We know there are several small continents and many smaller islands. We've got a basic map of their locations. As

Sakura says, we've seen nothing to indicate that it's inhabited—though I guess it could be, especially if the inhabitants are like my people, in the water and not making lights or fires. We also know that there don't appear to be any huge mountain ranges—largest altitudes we can guess are maybe three hundred meters or so. We've got good candidates for landing locations. We know that the atmosphere's close to Earth's ratios of nitrogen, oxygen, and carbon dioxide, which means we all should be able to breathe there just fine."

"Right," Caroline agreed. "We also know that there's the type of salts we expect in the ocean and my guess at the concentration puts it at an acceptable level. With our limited sensors, Mom, we can't expect to get much more." She said the last uncomfortably, her preference being for complete and detailed answers.

"All right," Laura said. "Then I'll shut up and let the pilot . . . pilot." She smiled at Sakura, and Sakura felt a warm glow and a boost of confidence.

Lincoln's white-and-green filled the viewport. *Close enough.* She looked at the projections on the screen. *We're in orbit . . . if we get ready to deorbit, another orbit and a half . . . that brings us* here. She studied the general area they would have to land in and saw one of the sites they'd already discussed, one of her favorites. *There, the end of that small continent. I can use the very tip of that, and these points on the nearby islands.* The tip of the small continent ended with an almost circular lagoon, with long, gently inclined slopes preceding the lagoon; sheltered access to the sea, easy terrain for exploration, and part of a nice large landmass—fit all the criteria they were looking for. She designated the guidance points to her display app as they swept over the target area. *I'll refine it with radar scans just before we do the deorbit.*

"We've got almost two hours before reentry," she said, trying to sound calm. "Everyone use the bathroom or whatever before then."

Nervous as she was, she used the bathroom three times. How could time seem to be dragging by, yet going so fast?

As she sat down for the third time, she saw her timer alert go to yellow. Sakura took a deep breath and raised her voice. "Everyone please make sure you're strapped down right, it's going to be a rough ride even if there's no trouble. Mom—I mean, Captain, can you check for me?"

"Hitomi is secured. Melody, tighten your straps just a bit, honey."

Melody's muttered, "What a *pain* . . ." brought a quick smile to Sakura's lips.

"Caroline?" asked her mother.

"Secured, Mom."

"Harratrer?"

Whips' voice was very matter-of-fact, showing how tense he really was. "All hold-downs fastened, all secure."

"And I've already made sure I'm locked down," said her father.

"All secure, Sakura. Don't worry about us now."

"Yes . . . Captain."

Focus. Eyes on the instruments and controls. Find those points!

The target location came into view again, the last time before—hopefully—they landed. *Get the angle . . . clouds starting to cover the one, but no problem, I can see through the clouds with radar anyway... radar painting them... designation...*

The guide app considered, blinked green. It now understood the geometry. "Caroline? I've got the estimates. Can you make sure everything's right?"

"Of course." A pause. "I make our first deorbit burn as being in eight minutes, fifty-two seconds from... *mark.*"

"Checked," Melody said.

This is it. Sakura knew that reentry and landings were the hardest part of spaceflight. "Eight minutes, twenty seconds to burn on my mark... *mark,*" she said. "It'll be about one *g* for eighteen seconds. We'll have lowered our orbit and my, Caroline, Whips, and Melody's apps will track our reactions to the first fringes of atmosphere, verifying their models of the planet's atmosphere and the performance of *LS-5*, before we do the final deorbit burn, which will last for a few more seconds and drop us low enough, to about eighty to ninety kilometers altitude, for the atmosphere to do the rest of the work. That's when it's going to really get rough, but we might feel a little something before then."

"Okay, Sakura," said her father.

She watched the countdown tensely. This much, at least, she could automate, putting a simple timer in line with the engine controls. Still, she poised her hands over the actual controls in case it didn't work. A few minutes later, the main engines roared to life, pressing them into their seats with a full gravity of pressure. Sakura watched, ready to cut the burn off if it didn't stop of its own accord, but it shut off exactly on time.

Maybe it was her imagination, but in the minutes that followed, she thought she felt phantom quivers, twitches in the big shuttle, as the very outermost fringes of the atmosphere began to touch on this intruder from a distant solar system.

This was one of the sticky parts. The problem with a deorbit and reentry was that there was a very narrow band of reentry angles—slightly more than one degree, in this case—between the extremes of striking the atmosphere too sharply and burning up like a meteor, or literally bouncing off the atmosphere back into space. They had to hit this exactly right, because there were also limits to the g-loading they could take, and what the thermal protection system (TPS) on *LS-5* could handle.

"Reconfigure for reentry, Sakura. We want as blunt a profile as we can get," Caroline reminded her.

Fortunately, *LS-5* could shift between multiple design configurations; landing, it looked not terribly different from the original Space Shuttle, a boxy airframe with stubby wings, but it could transition from that to a sleeker hypersonic configuration, a lower-speed, wider-winged subsonic craft, and even reconfigure for vectored thrust as a VTOL aircraft. She made sure the shuttle was in the first configuration. "Locked into reentry mode. TPS shows all green."

After a lot of checking and rechecking, Caroline and Melody finally agreed with Sakura on the landing calculations, and put the guidance data into her guide app. "This is it, everyone. We're landing!"

Hitomi cheered, Melody said something like *"Finally!"* and Whips sent her an image of thumbs-up, a gesture he was incapable of really making himself.

"This won't be fun at the beginning," she said, looking over the stats. "We've tried to figure the easiest reentry we can manage with our configuration, but we'll have some moments above 4.5 g."

Whips twitched. She couldn't blame him; for Bemmies, 5 g was just about the limit because they were originally water creatures, and they were so much larger than the average human. "How long?"

"Only a few seconds. Mom?"

She saw her mother check the restraints and Whips' medical readings. "I think it should be all right, honey. Aside from his hydration issues, Whips is in good shape. Just try not to tense up against it too much, Whips; your internal shift-plates need to flex with the pressure, not try to fight it."

"Okay, Dr. Kimei."

Everyone else settled back into their seats. Sakura swallowed hard, then took the controls firmly in hand. She couldn't let go now until they landed, really. The guide visualization counted down the seconds and projected a simulated view for her, with a generated guide path. It couldn't control anything for her, but it could help her know when she was going wrong—and she would, inevitably. But with these apps, she'd probably know in time to fix the mistake.

"Full deorbit burn in three, two, one . . . now!"

The second burn finished, and then there was no doubt that atmosphere was touching *LS-5*. A faint vibration and a rumble, and Sakura sealed all ports, making sure the TPS was in place and showing green. "Reentry beginning. We'll temporarily lose most sensors in the next few minutes, lasting until we've slowed down to a few Mach numbers."

Breathe. Calm. Hold the controls firmly but not tightly, guide the ship. Don't react quickly! Fast maneuvers will kill us.

The manual controls transmitted more strain, more buffeting vibration as the rumble from outside rose to a frightening crescendo and the hull sensors showed that *LS-5* was careening through the atmosphere like a meteor, blazingly hot, but the vibration was less than she'd expected. Deceleration crushed her down, but she forced her hands to stay rock-steady, even though her heart was racheting itself into ever-faster beats. Yellow along the guide path and she restrained her panic, forced her hand to move the tiniest, most controlled bits. Green again, and they were holding to the original calculated glide pattern as though running down a set of tracks.

Hitomi gave a series of yelps as the deceleration peaked, forcing them into their harnesses with more than four times their own weight. Whips burbled something in the Bemmie native language and she wanted to reassure him, but she didn't dare take her eyes from the guide display or hands from the controls.

At least if it screws up here it'll be fast...

But now the pressure began to ease, and she felt a smile starting as the temperature sensors showed they were past the peak.

As the temperature continued to fall, Sakura finally caused the forward shields to be retracted. They were at around Mach 5 and dropping, heading towards their destination. The three points should be coming into view soon.

As the speed fell to that of normal atmospheric craft, Sakura triggered the mode shift from a reentry configuration (minimal surface area, all-refractory surfaces with ablative covering) to that of a high-speed aircraft, larger wings, multiple control surfaces, more capable and responsive. "Activating atmospheric engines," she said. Jet intakes opened and Sakura felt the vibrations as the nuclear reactor heated the incoming air and hurled it out the back through jet turbines. Great! All engines were operating just like they were supposed to.

LS-5 now tore through the sky at Mach speeds, fast but far, far slower than it had been. "Atmospheric reentry complete—guys, we're a plane now!"

A rippling, pained sigh from Whips. "Thank the Sky Above. That *hurt*."

She shot a glance at her mother. "Is he—"

"Just some strains, Sakura. No injuries. Just focus on flying."

Below her, green and brown with occasional splotches of brighter color streamed by. "We're over the target continent. Expect to see our landing site any minute. Transitioning to subsonic flight."

The third configuration deployed larger wings, gave her more control. She tested this new setup. It responded just like in the sims. Maybe she could do this after all.

A bank of clouds was moving in over the target region, but that shouldn't be a major concern, Sakura thought. She had infrared and radar to penetrate the clouds, and it didn't look like a big storm. The long-range radar located the tip of the continent, built up an outline picture of a gently sloping section of land coming down from the small mountains she was approaching, a section of land narrowing to a narrow tip with a nearly circular lagoon—like a gigantic arrowhead with a huge hole punched through the tip. Beyond the lagoon was a narrow, triangular section of the continent and then the sea. To either side were two smaller islands.

Her guide program recognized the three points she'd designated—the triangular tip and the other two islands—but, oddly, showed yellow for the correspondence. Sakura didn't understand that. She could see clearly it was the same group she'd chosen. She redesignated, the display went back to green, and the guide path solidified.

There were no flat landing fields here. She'd have to go to VTOL configuration at the end, which made her a little nervous. That was the hardest mode to control and she maybe hadn't practiced that one as much as she should. Still, she only needed to hold it together for a few seconds, enough to get them down.

She was grateful—so very grateful—that everyone else was staying calm and quiet. They didn't need to see her worry. And she couldn't do this with Hitomi screaming or worrying in her ear.

Gingerly she tested the controls as she began the final approach. They were exceedingly responsive—almost too much so. She nearly spun *LS-5* out before getting a feel for the ship's performance. Fortunately, Hitomi took it as a fun stunt rather than thinking something was wrong.

Then the two island key points went yellow again. "What the—?"

"What is it, Sakura?" asked Caroline.

"Lost lock on two of the guide points! That makes no sense. It's just a geometric relationship." She swallowed, forcing the acidic bile that was trying to rise from her stomach back where it belonged. "No . . . no problem. We're close now, I can tie the display to the radar and focus on where we're going." A glide path calculated to the nominal surface appeared, guiding her like a pathway. It was a lot better than nothing, telling her the right ratio and where she needed to think about changing modes to land.

Suddenly the ship bobbled, jolted; there was a rattle from the forward viewport. *Storm . . . entering the fringes. That was sleet or something.* Radar showed it shouldn't be too bad, though it was larger than she'd thought; it would be raining for a while.

In visible light, it was dark gray outside, and at this altitude mostly fog and rain; hints of terrain, maybe trees or something, began to appear as they descended. If she'd been relying on eyesight she would have panicked. But *LS-5* wasn't limited to visible light; in infrared and radar, the clouds and rain were practically gone. Wind might still push on the craft, try to distract her, but it couldn't blind her, and that was the important thing.

LS-5 bucked slightly, but she was getting a real feel for the controls, and she saw that she was staying pretty close to the middle of the glide path. Radar showed they were approaching the target area, clearing the higher ground in their path, dropping—

Just about there. She could see the lagoon up ahead. Final mode change time, to VTOL. Change-over initiated . . .

Suddenly a gust of wind struck *LS-5*, sent the shuttle swaying sideways through the air, just as the mode conversion began. The jolt made her pull a little harder than she intended, but the shuttle's dynamics had already changed. Desperately, Sakura shoved the stick back and sideways, trying to compensate, even as she heard the sergeant bellowing *not fast, not fast, don't overcompensate!*

But it was too late now, too late by far. Still moving at well over two hundred kilometers per hour, *LS-5* heeled over, slammed diagonally on its tail into the alien soil of Lincoln, performed a spectacular somersault (had anyone been outside to see it), smashed back down and skidded uncontrollably, the cabin inside now filled with horrified screams and curses and cries of pain. Careening onward through the storm, *LS-5* carved a trail of destruction straight down to the shore of a storm-lashed lagoon, where it dropped over a sharp incline into the water, flipped, and came to rest, tail-first, with a thunderous *crash*.

Movement ceased, and the storm roared its triumph.

Chapter 8

Despite the sledgehammer impacts, the cabin of *LS-5* remained cheerfully, invariably lit as the world spun, and now, as the ship quivered to stillness, they stayed on, as though nothing had happened.

Laura could see that Sakura, at least, was unharmed; her seat had locked properly and the girl's one arm was visible, white-knuckled with tension. Hitomi's sobs of terror, though heartrending to hear, were paradoxically comforting; those were cries of a frightened little girl, not one badly injured.

The local net was readjusting, and Laura could access the biosignals. "Is everyone all right?"

"I seem uninjured, love," answered Akira.

"I'm fine, Mom." That was Caroline, the shakiness in her voice belying the casual words.

"I'm sorry, I'm sorry, I screwed it up, I—"

"Sakura!" Her daughter's name came out much more sharply than she intended, and Laura took a deep breath, let it out. She had to stay calm. "Sakura, honey, don't apologize. Are you all right?"

"I . . . I think so."

"Good." She turned her seat to face the others.

That felt very odd, because with the way *LS-5* was sitting, she was now looking *down*, held in her seat by the restraints.

"You were right, Mom," Melody said. "I *did* need those straps that tight." The ten-year-old's face was white as a sheet, and tears were starting from her eyes, even though she was rigidly controlling her expression.

Laura chuckled a little at that, and Melody gave a tearful but sheepish smile. "There's a reason for what we tell you. I'm glad you listened." She looked over to the next seat. "Hitomi, come on, little girl, just tell Mommy if you're all right."

The sobs slowed, and Hitomi lowered Skyfang from her face; the hazel eyes were wide and frightened, but her head nodded, and a mumbled "Okay," managed to make it through the winged wolf's fur.

"I'm . . . a little battered, Dr. Kimei," Whips volunteered, "But I think everything's okay."

"Good. Now everyone just stay still for a few minutes; I'll check your vitals to make sure that we really are all okay."

It was almost quiet inside the crashed shuttle except for the howling fury of the wind outside, which managed to penetrate faintly even through the soundproofing. *LS-5* occasionally quivered under what Laura guessed were either waves or extremely strong gusts of wind. She carefully examined all of the readings and, finally, relaxed.

"All right, everyone. We've landed, and we're all fine. Sakura—"

"I'm sorry!"

"Young lady," Akira said mildly, "your mother told you not to apologize. I think what she—what we both—wanted to say is 'well done,' actually." Her husband turned so the others could see him. "You already knew there were no automatics. But when we were on final approach, we went into a small storm... and even so, Sakura kept us up and flying until the very end, all by herself. I think there are plenty of professional pilots who might have had trouble when the wind hit *during* the conversion."

Melody grinned—a very shaky grin, but with much of her spirit and returning, and Laura felt herself relax again. "That old saying you told me, right, Sakura?"

Sakura sniffed, obviously trying not to cry, but there was a tiny chuckle there too. "Any landing you walk away from... is a good landing."

"Exactly!" Whips said. "By the Beyond, Sakura, you kept us flying right to the end, and I think if that wind gust hadn't hit at just the wrong time, you'd have brought us down perfect."

Hitomi sat straighter and clapped. "Hurray for Saki!"

Laura laughed and suddenly they were all clapping. Sakura turned her chair around and they could see she was blushing, but smiling, tears finally drying. "Okay, I did *awesome* then. And we're really all okay, Mom?"

"Really. Sitting like this is going to be a little uncomfortable, but that storm won't last forever, and once it's over I hope we can get out. What's the condition of *LS-5*?"

"Checking."

"I have to pee," Hitomi said suddenly.

Laura shook her head. "All right, hold on." A thought struck her. "Um... will the toilet work in this position?"

"I think so, Dr. Kimei," Whips said after a moment. "It works in microgravity and when we were attached to *Outward Initiative*, and in the position we're sitting . . . yes, if we keep it in the microgravity mode I think it will."

"Good. Then since you're farthest back *and* the biggest can you help—"

"Of course."

As the big Bemmie assisted Hitomi to get out of her harness and move to the rear of the cabin, Sakura spoke up. "Well, the bad news is that we're not flying *LS-5* again, not any time soon anyway. We skidded along on most of her exterior and ruined most of the thrust nozzles, ripped off her wings, crushed her tail. Took off most of our exterior sensors, too, so right now I can't get much from outside.

"But that's most of the bad news. All that stuff getting ripped off and crunched . . . well, it took a lot of the crash energy, let our harnesses do their work, which is why we're all in good shape. Internal systems all seem pretty good, and the starboard lock shows all green so we shouldn't have any trouble getting out. Cargo looks like it all stayed secure." She looked troubled. "Getting the cargo out, though . . . we'll have to move *LS-5* until we can open the rear loading doors. Right now we're *sitting* on them. And this thing weighs tons. Lots of tons, actually."

"Worry about that later. Are we close enough to land to be able to get *out*?" Laura was particularly concerned about Hitomi, who still needed help swimming.

"I'm pretty sure we're in that little lagoon that's a few hundred meters short of the end of the continent; that was my target, I wanted to set us down near the edge. If we'd come down farther along we'd have been in trouble, but we're not bobbing up and down, just twitching a little, so we're sitting on something solid. And the recordings of our path tell me that we were running on solid ground right up to the end when we fell."

"We can't get *any* information from outside?"

Sakura shook her head. "The cameras all got wrecked in our cartwheeling across the ground. Radar's out, too. There's one working external microphone, but that's just hearing a lot of wind and rain, and a little thunder once in a while."

"Well, that's all right," Akira said. "I'm sure we will be able to get *LS-5* out of the lagoon with a little work and some of the smaller equipment on board, and once we get into the cargo we should be much better off. I believe we have everything, really, that we could want for this emergency on board, right?"

As was often true, Melody answered. "We have a Dust-Storm Tech Nanofacturer VII 3D manufacturing system in the cargo, Dad; that was meant for the whole colony. With raw materials and power that'll make anything we can spec out well enough. Whips can probably run it, and *LS-5*'s reactor has enough power according to the datasheet."

A full manufacturing system! Laura found herself grinning. "We'll be able to make our own little colony easily, then."

"Especially since we've got you and Dad's stuff, too," Sakura said, excitedly. "You've got the full medical equipment list, and Dad's bio research stuff is *perfect* for this—I mean, really, he was supposed to be doing research on Tantalus, but we'll have to do the same kind of research here, right?"

Akira laughed. "You're exactly right, Sakura. Same

kind of research—what's safe, what isn't, how all the species interact, that kind of thing."

Laura noticed that Melody, oddly, seemed somewhat let down. "What is it, Mel?"

The black-haired little girl flushed. "Oh . . . Just being stupid. Never mind."

She caught a flash of data from Melody's omni and realized that the girl had been reviewing old books like *Robinson Crusoe* and some of the outdoor survival shows that had been popular a century or so back, and couldn't *quite* keep from smiling. The laziest of her children was still hoping for a big adventure. Thank goodness she wouldn't get it.

"So . . . we're really going to be okay?" Hitomi said, as Whips lifted her back to her seat.

"Really," Laura assured her. "Oh, it'll be a rough few days or even weeks getting everything ready," she saw Melody make a face, "but we'll be just fine." She smiled around at the others. "So let's sit back, relax, and let this storm blow itself out."

Chapter 9

"Okay, Sakura, now cycle the lock again, exhausting to the outside."

Whips wasn't taking any chances. Before letting *anyone* step out of the shuttle, he wanted Dr. Kimei and her husband to check the air readings. So they'd put Laura Kimei's omni, which had a lot of built-in sensors for medical purposes, into the starboard airlock, let it open to the outer air, and left it there for an hour to gather data. The omni hadn't been able to communicate well through the lock, so they had to bring it back in to check the results. Everyone was accordingly in environment suits.

It had better be okay, Whips thought. Because they couldn't stay in environment suits the whole time.

Laura reached into the lock as it opened and brought out her omni—a Scanwise Gold Five that looked like an Egyptian bracelet. "Well, it looks all right." She tapped into the local net and checked the data.

A few minutes later he saw her pull off her helmet and knew the answer. "All clear, everyone. Oh, there's some pollen and other such things in the air, but nothing immediately toxic."

"Did it see anything through the open lock?"

"Not terribly much. Mostly a lovely blue sky and a few distant flying somethings."

Dr. Kimei tied back her hair tightly. "All right, I'm going to take a look."

No one argued. Whips knew that Laura Kimei was not only the tallest and strongest of the humans, but much more agile than he was out of the water. If he remembered right, she was also the daughter of a policeman and trained in some hand-to-hand weapons, overall making her the best choice for first person outside. In her hand she held the only ranged weapon that had been available outside the cargo storage: a SurvivalShot 12mm, designed for use on worlds with no ammunition manufacturing in place.

Not that she was going far. They saw her go to the lock, look out cautiously, then lean out farther, looking down, around, and up, then back down and out for several minutes.

She turned back to them, smiling broadly and holstering the pistol. "Well, Sakura, we can see exactly where we came down; there's a big trench cut through the landscape pointing right back to the heart of this continent.

"Better news is that I can see a shallow ridge below us. I think the water there is no more than a meter deep, so we can wade to shore, though someone has to carry Hitomi."

"Very good!" Akira said. "What's our plan, then?"

"First we need to scout out some temporary headquarters. It has to be near to the water, for Whips' comfort, but high enough that we're not going to get caught by waves and tides. It also needs to be sheltered, so that wind and such won't get in too much. Everyone take some of the rations with you. We'll probably be camping outside the *LS-5* until we get her out of this lagoon and lying flat instead of mostly on her tail."

Akira nodded. "Whips, since you're the strongest, if you don't mind I'd like you to carry the winch?"

"And the carbon-composite cable and block-and-tackle, yes, sir." The compact high-powered winch was a standard piece of equipment in the shuttles, available to install on the nose or the rear loading ramp or into the standardized sockets on the colony work vehicles. And, with enough mechanical advantage—like the block and tackle—it might just be strong enough to pull *LS-5* out of its current inconvenient position and up onto the land. The carbon-composite cable, of course, was more than strong enough for the job. From his engineering work he knew that he could probably suspend three or four shuttles from that single cable.

"Good." He smiled down at Whips. "I'm very glad you're with us, Harratrer."

"So am I," he said quietly. Inside, he wondered if any of the rest of his family, his pod, had escaped. The thought that all of his family—little brother Pageturner with his eyes always in a book, so much like Melody that at times he'd wondered if they could somehow be related despite all the obvious biological impossibilities; his father Kryndomerr, called Numbers by everyone for his mathematical genius; Windharvest, his mother, whose real name was Rillitrill but who was proud of the nickname that told of her success in making more efficient and easily manufactured wind turbines; and his big brother Dragline, hunter and athlete—the thought that they all might be gone was enough to dim his light even inside, make an ache spread from within to the very tips of his hands.

Am I unstable? Is that my stress limit?

He forced himself not to think of it. That would just make it worse. And perhaps they weren't gone. The rest of *Outward Initiative* might have survived. And here he also had a pod, with the twin sister of his heart Sakura (who he liked to think of as "Jumps-first" in the way of his people), and her family who had welcomed him without hesitation. He forced the light back into his skin, mind, and heart. Yes, it would get worse later. He could feel it. But he knew they would be very, very happy to know he was alive and with the Kimei family.

He waited for the others to go out; make sure everyone else was clear before trying to get down himself. Crawling to the lock, he stuck his forearms out and grabbed the climbing rungs, pulling himself forward enough to get a good look out.

For a moment he just stopped there, admiring the view.

Below, shadowed slightly by the sharply inclined *LS-5*, the waters of the lagoon sparkled and shimmered in blue-green, a lighter line of pale green showing the shallower ridge that began right at the hull of the shuttle and ran to the shore. From this height he could see that the seafloor dropped sharply to either side of the ridge, down to at least five meters depth; there were hints of movement in those depths which told him there would be prey aplenty—if he could eat it.

The shore, which the Kimeis had just reached, was a three-meter-high cliff which had a big bite taken

out of it, right where *LS-5* had finished its crash.
Along that line he could see the trench the armored
shuttle had dug from its impact almost a kilometer
distant. The brilliant blue sky contrasted with the fluffy
white of clouds, and with the deep, pure green of the
forested hills or even low mountains in the distance;
he guessed that some of those rolling ridges reached
several hundred meters in height. Trees—or something
very like them—grew at no great distance from the
shore, broad and feathery-looking crowns casting deep
shadows beneath.

He looked down again. This might be a little tricky.
The climbing rungs were of course there for climbing down the shuttle when it was set down properly,
which was to say sitting on its belly, rather than
standing almost vertically on its tail. The rungs now
provided only a stabilizing handhold, with the winged
shuttle's side dropping away below. The humans had
gone down a rope, but that was something he really
didn't want to try.

On the positive side, though, the tremendous damage on the outside of *LS-5* had taken great scrapes,
dings, and divots out of the hardened exterior. He
was pretty sure he could use those—especially since,
unlike the humans, he had three arms with a very
wide reach. If he stretched them out, he could reach
almost four meters from tip to tip, and that meant he
could hook fingers into a couple dozen places at once.

Stretching that far stung, as well as ached. Despite
everything Dr. Kimei had been able to do, his skin
was drier by far than it should be, little sore cracks
opening as he pulled on normally flexible hide. But
they were down, and near an ocean. He could take

this, and the aches from the deorbit and crash. They were down and they were safe.

Feeling more confident with that thought, Whips carefully slid his lower first arm out as far as he could, locking fingers and extending his graspclaws to catch anything they could. His lower second arm followed. His top arm anchored itself to the doorframe and twined around the rope. Not without some trepidation, he slowly spun his body and let it slide over the edge.

"Whips," Laura called to him, "Make sure you close the inner hatch, okay? I don't expect any problems, but no reason to let the local wildlife have easy access."

"Right, Dr. Kimei." He stretched out part of one arm and touched the control, closing and sealing the inner door. Since he was using the doorframe as an armhold, he couldn't close the outer door, but that shouldn't be an issue anyway.

As he let the whole weight of his body finish the slide to the vertical, a couple of fingers lost their grip, but more than enough stayed firm. With exquisite caution he carefully released the grip of his top arm and moved it lower, gripping at other scars on the shuttle and the rope. Then, one by one, the fingers of his first arm let go, dropped, and found others.

He could, of course, have just dropped into the deeper water . . . but a quick splashdown like that would surround him with bubbles and be momentarily disorienting. That was a perfectly good entrance to use—if you were confident nothing was waiting to eat you. It wasn't likely there was something waiting in those depths to ambush him, but it wasn't at all impossible, and why take chances?

A few minutes later and he was down on the shallow

ridge. He inhaled the water. So fresh! He'd forgotten what real, honest seawater of any world tasted and smelled like. Lincoln's seas smelled exciting, a tingle of salts just slightly more concentrated than Europa's, not quite as concentrated as Earth's seas, but different, with other smells and vibrations and tastes that promised something dangerous yet thrilling. Sharp pain sparked momentarily at the places where his hide had started to crack, but the overall sensation on his skin was wonderful. He paused for a moment, just letting his skin *soak* in the water of a natural ocean.

There was definitely movement in the water not far away. He wanted to see what it was, but restrained his curiosity; he did, however, take advantage of the fact that a meter of water was more than enough for him to jet his way to the shore in one quick spurt of motion, running right up onto white-green sparkling sands next to Sakura.

The whole family clapped. "That was great, Whips!" Laura said appreciatively. "You're quite an acrobat for someone who's normally slow on land."

"I'd be a lot slower climbing *up*, Dr. Kimei," he said modestly, though he was very proud of how well he'd managed the descent.

"Most people are."

They gazed up into the interior, shouldering their packs—even little Hitomi making sure the backpack her mother had given her was settled properly. "You know, Laura," Akira said after a moment, "I think our best bet might be to just go up this trail to near its beginning. Everything's been cleared out of this region, so there isn't much chance for surprises, and even larger things were probably scared off by that crash, and it makes a perfect path to the ocean. We'll haul *LS-5* up the trench as soon as we get a few things settled, or at least see if we can get started."

"Makes sense to me. Let's take a look."

So, my crash gives us a good shelter! Clever of me to arrange that! Sakura sent.

But if you hadn't *crashed, we could still be using* LS-5 *as our main shelter,* Whips pointed out.

She sent an image of her sticking her tongue out at him. He smiled (though the smile was mostly a matter of particular light and color patterns rather than the human equivalent, which wasn't something he could actually do) and was pleased by the fact that Sakura was cheering up and able to take a joke or two.

Glassy-winged *somethings* zipped quickly by the newcomers, but dodged aside before approaching too closely. They probably smelled very strange to anything native. That'd keep most things away, at least for a while.

He crawled along higher on the edge of the trench than the humans, to give himself the same vantage point. Once he thought he heard something larger approaching from the high side, and extended his top hand. *Let's try my favorite trick.*

Bemmie articulation was very different than human. The linkages of the arms, in particular, could both stiffen selectively in various ways, or be relaxed to the point that the appendage was as flexible as a hose ... or, in this case, as a whip. There was, of course, always some risk in this trick; even though the arms and fingers were quite tough, it was possible to dislocate, break, or—in rare instances—rip off the tips of fingers with the particular trick he was going to try.

But it was what he was famous for. With practiced, focused ease, he bobbed and pulled the arm, causing a ripple to travel all along the extended arm and finger tendrils. At the far end, this hastened as he yanked the arm back, and the fingers at the very tip suddenly snapped around, multiple whipcracks of sound echoing loudly across the trench. His fingertips tingled, but didn't hurt. *Ha! Got away with it again!*

Whatever it was, the thing didn't like that sound at all; he heard a sudden and speedy movement away.

"What was *that?*" The Kimeis had all spun to face him, and Laura had the pistol out.

"I don't know, Dr. Kimei, but it sounded bigger than most of us, so I scared it off."

"Darn near scared *me* off," she said, with a half-smile. "I still can't imagine how you do that without breaking your fingers."

"I know other Bemmies who can do it. Not as good as me, though," he admitted, proudly. "After all, that's where I got my name."

"Seems to already be coming in useful. The more we can chase things off and the less we have to confront them, the better we'll be." Laura looked up. "Oh, that's promising."

LS-5 had struck hard on first impact, gouging out a considerable trench with one of the tailfins in the underlying corallike rock, a trench that actually had considerable overhang on one side. Caroline, not only the closest they had to a geologist but one who had previously gone caving, mountaineering, and freeclimbing, moved cautiously under the overhang and started checking it. After a few minutes, she nodded. "At least this section along here looks stable—no deep cracks or flaws I can see. We could use this as a windbreak and partial weather shield and let the shelter set itself up right here."

"Looks good," Laura said, and Whips, after examining it himself, agreed. "All right, everyone, dump the first load here. Whips, that means the winch and such too, even though I'm pretty sure we'll be bringing it down near the water's edge again."

He complied gratefully; the little winch was still pretty heavy, and all the cable—neatly tied or not—was clumsy. He noticed small shapes scuttling away from their feet and gear, lashed out and caught one.

The thing had a shell shaped like the shields of knights that Sakura had showed him in one of her books, and pulled its limbs and head under the shell when he grabbed it. What he could see indicated eight limbs and the head showed glints of sharp-edged mandibles or something like it. Some of the ventswimmers were similar. "I think we need to make sure our stuff is protected soon. These things might be able to dig through the packaging."

"Spread out the shelter," Melody suggested, plopping down with exaggerated exhaustion on the ground. "We have to do that anyway to let it set itself up properly. We can put all our other stuff on top of it until we trigger the setup."

"An excellent idea, Melody," said Akira. "Hitomi, can you and Melody start doing that?"

"Why *me?*" asked Melody plaintively.

"Because the rest of us have other work to do, like running all the way back to the shuttle for more supplies, and figuring out how we're going to move it," her father said.

Whips felt a grin ripple across his back as he watched Melody glance down the long stretch of somewhat broken terrain back to the shuttle and then up the several-meter-high climb to the airlock. "Okay," she sighed. "Come on, Hitomi."

"Akira, hon, I want you and Caroline to stay with them. Sakura, Whips, and I will go get the rest of the stuff. I don't want Hitomi left with just Mel, and with Caroline the two of you will be able to get some of the preparation work done."

"All right."

The three of them started back. "Sakura, have you any idea what happened to your guidance app?"

His friend shook her head. "Not really, Mom. What I got after we landed and I queried the data made no sense. It claimed that the points I designated weren't the same points, that they had different geometry than the original points, and the same thing happened when I told it to reacquire. It tried to follow them but couldn't hold a lock. Something had to be wrong in its calibration or something."

"Whips? Any thoughts?"

He dug through his knowledge of the assisting app they'd devised for the landing. "I don't know, Dr. Kimei. We designed that app to be close to foolproof, but I suppose it's possible we missed something about how perspective affected the apparent distances. I *thought* we had that all nailed down, but..."

Laura nodded. "Well, I don't suppose it matters right now." She stopped by the water's edge and looked up, studying the shuttle as it stood, tipped to one side, in the water; it looked somehow slightly more tipped than it had been, but he couldn't be sure. "Whips, I think we need to know what's holding her up—and especially if there's anything under her that might catch on her when we try to pull her off."

That did make a lot of sense. He could see her looking at him uncertainly, and understood. "No problem, Dr. Kimei."

"Oh, please, Whips, I know I'm your best friend's mother, but please stop calling me 'Dr. Kimei.' Call me Laura. We're going to be stuck here for a long time no matter what, we don't need that much formality."

"Okay, Laura." It sounded a little strange, but he could understand getting tired of formality. "It's okay, Laura. None of you could do that a tenth as well as I can, and if there *is* anything dangerous down there, well, I'm still the one you want." He flickered a smile. "Besides, I really want to go in and swim. I haven't done that for like a *year*."

"All right, then. Get in, do a quick check around the base of the shuttle, then come back and report."

"Yes, ma'am!"

He slid easily into the water, retracting his arms for minimum friction. The exciting, tingling smell refreshed him and the cool water buoyed him up. All his senses were now on full alert, especially the skinsight that was by far the most powerful sense his people had in the water. Oh, you could get a lot from acoustics—soundsight—and from eyesight, from smell, and so on, but the electromagnetic skinsight—analagous to the lateral-line and ampullae of Lorenzini found on Earthly sea life—was the most useful of all underwater. In the air it was barely active, with a range usually of only a meter for minor things, but in water . . .

Now he could sense movement, living things moving

throughout the lagoon. There seemed to be nothing very large, at least not moving, and no strong signals of something bigger than he was. But there was a dead zone—near the ship, not surprisingly.

Whips jetted slowly off the ridge and down to the deeper areas. As he got lower, he could see what appeared to be a *very* steep dropoff below the mangled jets; it seemed to be a trench, broadest just under the shuttle and narrowing to either side. He hesitated, eyeing the shuttle. There was the faintest grinding resonance, as though the shuttle were shifting against the rock, but it seemed stable enough.

In and out quick, then. If it started to fall, he was plenty fast enough to get out from under it as long as he paid attention. Just duck into that gap and get a look, then get out.

He pulled in plenty of water, then jetted forward and down, flipping his body so he streaked vertically into the crevice beneath the shuttle.

For a moment, he was simply too stunned, too disoriented, to make sense of everything. There were no returns from his quick soundpings, no safe aligning of walls and surface with depth once he passed a scant few meters, barely more than a few body lengths. Sounds and skinsense and sight scanned down and down and sideways and sideways and on and on and on, and found nothing except above...

And then there *was* something below, something rising, rising *fast*, and the soundpings returned slowly, yet faster, and he could not grasp, not even with all arms, what it was he was feeling because it made no *sense*...

Then it *did* make sense and horror struck him,

overwhelmed him with utter, unreasoning panic. He spun about, jetting frantically, streaking upward, past the tail of *LS-5*, up, up, so fast that he flew across the dry sands, almost bowling over Laura and Sakura.

As he left the water, he shouted, trying to tell them, and scrambling with tail-anchors and arms to push himself farther up, farther. "No *bottom*, a void, so huge, nothing, something *coming!*"

Sakura stared, confused, but Laura seemed to understand his panic, if nothing else, and snatched up her daughter, ran, up the slope, passing him even as he grasped in desperation and pulled himself another meter forward.

The ground quivered.

At the same time, three *somethings* erupted from the water, gray-blue-green, stretching up, pointing to the heavens like curved daggers as they rose, trailing foaming water into the air with them, towering up, far, far above *LS-5*. Even as they reached their apex, casting sharp-edged terrifying shadows across the three refugees, *LS-5* tilted sideways, falling...

And the far side of the lagoon, too, slid sideways.

Whips froze alongside his friends, unable for a moment to grasp what he was seeing. The towering... claws? Tentacles? Fingers?... were subsiding into the water, but *LS-5* was bobbing in the disturbed water, its airlock now flooding (*but the inner door's closed, that should be fine...*), but what held their gaze in disbelief was the far side of the lagoon, the shore that had been just a hundred meters or so distant, rising now into the air, higher, revealing a craggy, dark, weed and growth-encrusted underside, rising higher as the farther end, the very tip of the land on which they stood *sank*, and as it dropped the portion near them continued to rise, fifty, sixty, a hundred, three hundred, almost five hundred meters towering into the sky, pouring a cascade of dirty water and squirming, chittering, shocked creatures down into the sea below. Then a part of it broke, and began to fall with exaggerated apparent slowness.

"*RUN!*" Laura screamed, and Whips was galvanized back into desperate motion, climbing up, up, have to get *higher*—

A two-hundred-meter mass of stone, shedding greenery as it plummeted, landed squarely on *LS-5*, piledriving it into the impossible depths below, sending a huge wave thundering outward and up, inundating the shore. Whips gripped a rock with his tail anchors and reached out, catching hold of Laura and Sakura with one arm even as the other two realized there was nowhere to run, then latched onto everything around him with the other two arms and held on.

The water rumbled up and over him, clawing at him madly, but somehow he kept his grip against that titanic force—barely—and then it began to recede, slowly running back. Blinking his eyes clear, he saw to his relief that the wave had not managed to reach the rest of the family, nearly a kilometer distant.

But the *LS-5* was gone, gone as though she had never existed at all . . . and everything she had held was gone with her.

Chapter 10

Laura stared in uncomprehending shock. Bobbing ever so slightly, the vast wall of dark, wet stone still loomed up less than a kilometer distant. The piece that had fallen from it—a solid mass the size of a skyscraper—should have been towering over them even nearer. There was no *possible* way that the lagoon before them could have been two hundred meters deep, no, not even a *tenth* of that!

Yet that monstrous fragment had plunged down effortlessly, irresistably, neither slowing nor pausing, and taken their hopes with it into the impossible deep.

Even as she thought that, the seething water bubbled more, darkened, and that same fragment surged from the depths, shedding water and stripping itself of soil, a massive bulwark of varicolored stony outcroppings and dripping mud. It bobbed slowly, rising and falling in diminishing cycles. She hoped against hope that she might see something else, smaller but oh so very much more valuable, also bob to the surface . . . but there was nothing more coming from the mysterious depths.

Sakura was clinging to her with a deathgrip, and Whips' tendrilled arms were only just beginning to relax. Slowly Laura forced herself to stand. "Are you all right, Sakura? Whips?"

Sakura managed a tiny nod of her head, eyes so wide that white showed all the way around them. She was otherwise silent, and did not release her grip.

Whips buzz-clicked something in his native language before catching himself. "I . . . I am all right, Dr. Kimei . . . Laura," he said slowly, uncertainly.

Her omni buzzed. "Laura!" came Akira's shaking voice. "Are you all okay?"

"We're . . . fine, Akira. But . . ."

"We saw," he said. "*LS-5* is gone?"

"It . . . looks like it. I don't know if there's anything to salvage. Whips is the only one who might be able to even try."

The big Bemmie—only an adolescent, but still out-massing her by at least two to three times—shuddered, a rippling motion accompanied by jangling, discordant patterns of light and color in his skin. "I'm . . . not sure I can."

Laura knelt next to Whips. "Harratrer, honey, I know that must have scared the wits out of you. But I really need to know exactly what you saw, what it means, and that might mean you have to go down and really *look*."

His back quivered under her touch, and she wondered for a moment . . . but the clenched tendrils relaxed slightly. Then he heaved a long, wet—sounding breath and shook himself something like a long, flat dog. "You're right. No one else can do it, you don't have the senses or the equipment to do it right. And I . . ." a quick flash of bright patterns that were like a chuckle, though a very nervous one, ". . . I really *didn't* understand what I saw, and I have to see it again to really know."

"If you're afraid of that . . . *thing* we saw—"

"A little, but really, something that big isn't going to bother coming after something like me unless I make myself an obvious nuisance. I think."

Laura bit her lip. Maybe this was a stupid idea. "On second thought . . ."

"No, I'm doing this." Whips turned and moved back towards the former lagoon. "You'd do it, if you were me."

Laura couldn't argue. "But you're . . ."

". . . *Bemmius novus sapiens*," he said bitterly, and she understood now what drove him.

"No," she she said, and put her hand on the base of one of his arms; Whips twitched, but didn't move away. "I was going to say, you're not an adult yet, you're like one of my own children, and I wouldn't force them to go."

His discordant colors quieted, went to a calm blue-green. "Sorry . . . Sorry. I just . . . this is what we have to do, isn't it? Do what we can? If I don't . . . if I can't . . . then maybe they're right about me, about *us*." He contracted, then raised himself up. "I can't be afraid to go in the water. I'm still fast, I'm still smart, I can't let this keep me out. And if I don't go in now, it's because I *am* afraid. And I am. I really, really am." He shuddered again. "But I'm not going to let that stop me."

With a swift, decisive movement, Whips sent himself sliding over the edge and into the water.

Sakura finally let go. "M-Mom? What happened? That didn't make any *sense*, the whole end of the . . . the land, it tipped *up*, and it's over *there*," her voice was rising higher and shaking, speaking faster, "like, floating, and the *LS-5*, it was hit and then it's gone and we're—"

"*Sakura*." She spoke her daughter's name firmly but quietly, taking her by the shoulders, looking her in the eye. "Sakura. Stop."

The girl's brilliant blue eyes locked on hers. With an obvious effort Sakura forced her mouth closed and stood there, shaking, then closed her eyes. Slowly they opened again, but they were less wide, more focused, more *there*, and Laura let herself relax a tiny bit. "Sorry, Mom."

"It's okay, honey. We're all near that panic. We just can't let it catch us. And I have no idea what happened."

There was a splash, and they saw Whips emerging from the water. "I'm back, Laura."

The dull colors on his back echoed his tone of voice. "I still can't believe what I've seen."

There were sounds of running behind them, and she turned to see Akira, with Caroline, Melody and Hitomi close behind. They came here as fast as Hitomi could run, she guessed.

She took a moment to hug her other daughters and take a rib-straining one from her husband. Then she turned back to Whips, whose colors were now brighter but slowly rippling. "All right, Harratrer, what did you see?"

"A lot. But . . . I don't know exactly what it all means." He took an audible breath. "Once I get out past where you can see the shallow water, it just . . . drops away. Farther than I can ping. Even when I shout as loud as I can, there isn't a return from the bottom."

"But..." Melody started, then stopped.

"Go on, Melody," Laura said.

"But... I thought your people could ping to the bottom of the Europan ocean."

"Some of us can. I couldn't manage that, but... there are other noises. I think the bottom's a long, *long* way down below even that level."

"We're sitting on a cliff *tens of kilometers* high?" Caroline said in disbelief. "That's impossible. Even underwater that should—"

"Not a cliff," Whips said, cutting her off. "I don't know what we're standing on, but... once I get down maybe thirty meters or so, there's nothing but water in *all* directions. Well, that's not true, I detect *some* stuff in the direction that's, well, inland, but there's always water in that direction eventually."

Laura and Caroline exchanged disbelieving glances. "Whips, are you saying that, well, there's nothing supporting the land we're standing on?"

"Nothing as far as I can tell."

For a moment they all stared at each other, trying to come to terms with that ridiculous, impossible statement. Laura turned and looked back at the immense stretch of land behind them, vanishing into hills on the horizon, then over to the black wet towers of what had been the land across from them. "You looked at that piece that... well, is floating there?"

"Yes. It *is* floating. Nothing under it anywhere."

"Coral," Caroline said slowly. "The rock... I noticed it looked rather like coral. But I never thought..."

"Coral?" repeated Melody incredulously. "But shouldn't that *sink*?"

Caroline bent over, searching, and found a chunk of

rock that had been broken off by *LS-5* in the crash. Laura watched as her oldest daughter flung the rock far out into the water.

The white-pink rock plunged into the sea. And a moment later, bobbed to the surface.

"There were cases of floating coral on Earth," Caroline said, her voice starting to become more animated, excited, "and some pieces could drift for hundreds of kilometers, last for many months. Mom, Dad, this is amazing. If Whips is right, we're floating on an ocean so deep that no landmass *could* rise out of it, not for more than an eyeblink on a geologic scale, because you can't *get* that many kilometers of rock to stick up above the rest. There are plenty of water worlds out there, some of them with oceans over fifteen *hundred* kilometers deep, so deep that geological forces probably can't even make themselves felt on the surface. Since this one has life like ours, though, trace elements, some kind of active geology just *has* to be working here to get all of that into solution. But with the gravity here, by the time you get a hundred kilometers down it'll be all solid, ice-six, maybe ice-seven, but then there's heat from below..."

She broke off. "Sorry, got carried away. Anyway, something must have evolved here to keep itself up on the surface, where it got the advantage of all the light energy from above, or maybe harvesting things like diatoms or whatever that did use the light energy... maybe also keeping it away from a lower-down eco-system like the one on Europa, where everything revolves around the vents. And that turned into colonies, and then other things started taking advantage of the colonies to support them..." She looked back inland, eyes shining. "We'll have to get samples, get a look at the actual geological history... only it's not really geological, it's... coral-ological? Alcyoneological?"

"*That's* why the guide app got confused," Sakura said suddenly. "It was *right*. The geometry shifted. We assume that land doesn't shift detectably over any reasonable timescale—a few centimeters per year, right, Caroline?" Caroline nodded. Sakura went on, sounding finally like her regular self. "But these things aren't land, they're *floating*. Floating islands—floating *continents*—and they're moving with wind and currents, so they must've been drifting at centimeters per *second*, maybe even more, and so the guide app lost certainty on the targets because it was like trying to get a fix on... I dunno, a set of waves or something. The app and the sensors could see small changes that I couldn't with my eyes."

Laura was still trying to grasp it. *Floating islands... floating things hundreds, thousands of kilometers in extent?* Her mind balked momentarily at the idea. The material in question would have to remain buoyant for a timescale of... how long? To build something that huge, get *forests* growing on it? How strong would it have to be, how flexible, to keep from shattering into pieces at the first storm and waves flexing it?

"That *is* fascinating, Caroline, Sakura," Akira said after a moment. "And we will of course be studying this as time goes on. But I think the first order of business is survival, and I don't think it matters, for that, whether we're on regular land, an island of floating coral, or the back of a giant turtle."

Laura couldn't keep from smiling at the last, and the others burst out laughing; even Melody ended up grinning. "No, love, you're right. We've lost *LS-5*, but we haven't lost any of *us*, and that's the important thing. This isn't going to be easy," she said, looking at her family steadily, reassuringly, "but we *will* survive."

Akira took her hand, and the others—even Whips— gathered around for another hug. "Now, everyone—let's go back to our camp and figure out what we need to do next."

Inside, Laura was still shaking, still worried. But she could see her family—including, now, one juvenile Bemmie—straightening up, wiping away tears, taking that new breath and focusing on the moment, ready to face whatever Lincoln held for them, and that was all that mattered. *If Akira and I stay strong, they'll be strong. And that's what we need right now.*

Chapter 11

"The seven wilderness survival principles," Melody said, obviously looking at her omni's display, "are positive mental attitude, first aid, shelter, fire, signaling, water, and food."

"Not a bad list," Sakura said, dusting off a nearby chunk of coral-rock to sit on, "but some of that won't work. Signaling isn't going to be something we do any time soon, if we can do it at all." She didn't like thinking about that, but it was true, and avoiding it wouldn't get them anywhere.

"Still, let's go through that list and talk about it," said her father. "Positive mental attitude—that's an excellent point for us as castaways. If we focus on what we've lost and on what terrible things could happen, we'll be undermining ourselves every minute. We talked a little about that on our way here, but that little list reminds us about how important keeping that attitude is, even when things set us back—like now."

Mom nodded. "It's not always going to be easy, I know that, and I want any of you who start feeling it's too much to come to me right away about it. Depression will rob any of us of our strength and our courage, and..." she looked back at the stretch of empty water where *LS-5* had once been, "...it would be perfectly understandable for any of us to get depressed after this."

"Okay, Mom. I think we all get that, right?" Caroline looked around to the others, who all nodded. Even Whips gave a bob up-and-down that he used for a nod.

"Okay, so next is first aid. All of us are okay right now, so we finished that part of the list." She smiled and patted the broad circular silvery pad she and several of the others sat on. "We've got the emergency shelter right here and it responds right to signals, so we can get it set up in a little bit. So that's covered, right?"

"For now," her mother agreed. "We'll have to find something more permanent eventually, but those shelters were meant for use while people built themselves real houses at the colony, so it's actually exactly the purpose for which it was designed.

"For the other points on that list...I think we need to look at what we already have."

"We've all got omnis, Mommy!" Hitomi said brightly. *I don't think she's quite understood that this isn't like an extended camping trip,* Sakura thought. "That's good, right?" Her expression shifted to a slight pout. "But mine's not connecting to the Jewelbug app."

"That's because there's no server in range, Hitomi," Melody said; Sakura noticed that Melody did try to minimize her "sarcastic know-it-all" tone, which was good.

"But her point's very good," Whips said. "We *do* all have omnis, which means at least some computation and data storage and, for some of them like Dr....I mean, Laura's and Akira's, sensor capability."

"Something even better," Sakura said, finding that as they talked it out she was feeling more and more her old self. "Communications. Okay, there's no satellites or relays here, but still, our omnis will have some comm range, right?"

"I would think so," Akira said, "but I admit I'm not sure. Melody, is that a piece of trivia you know?"

Sakura grinned as she saw Melody straighten up even as Melody tried to hide how proud she was that her father was asking her for that kind of information. "Um, yes, Dad. Most omnis have about a kilometer or two range, depending on what gets in the way. Yours and Mom's are probably pushing the two-kilometer range—mine too because you got me the top model just before we left, I think I might get three kilometers—while Hitomi's is probably below a kilometer. If there were satellites we could link to them even from much farther away, but there aren't any."

"Very good. What else do we have?"

Sakura dug into her pocket and pulled out what looked like a handle attached to a small cube of metal with clear crystals on either side. "I have my Shapetool!"

"I was hoping you did," her mother smiled at her. "I have mine, too."

Melody looked crestfallen. "Oh, darn. I left mine in our cabin on *Outward Initiative*."

"I still have mine, too," said her father. "Anyone else?"

No one else had one of the transformable multitools, but Sakura thought that having three of them was pretty good as a starter. Akira went on, "I've got my pocket laboratory, too. Laura—"

"I did not forget my little black bag," her mother answered immediately, and Sakura relaxed a little bit more. It sure wasn't as good as having a real medical facility, but it was a heck of a lot better than nothing.

"We've got some food," Sakura said, looking at the small pile of material in the center of the flattened shelter. "Those are compressed reconstitutable . . . how much is that, anyway?"

"More than a week," Hitomi said brightly. "I counted when we were piling them up. Three for each of us a day, except Whips who gets *twelve* a day. That's thirty per day, and there were three hundred and fourteen in the load we'd brought with us, so that's about ten and a half days, right?"

Sakura's renewed optimism took a sudden dive towards depression and worry. A week and a half of food, on a planet they'd only just landed on?

She could see that both her mother and father had similar thoughts, but their expressions barely flickered. "That's all right for now," her mother said, pushing back a lock of her chestnut hair, "but it definitely makes finding food and water a priority."

"Water shouldn't be a terrible problem," Caroline said. "We're in a latitude where I'd expect fairly frequent rain showers. We just landed in one, obviously. Given that we see forests of some sort and there are storms like the one we landed in, I'd think there are probably streams and ponds and such a little farther inland, as well. I think we saw a fair number of those when we did our orbital survey. All we need are containers; I'm sure we can figure something out. I've seen things that look sort of like seashells, so if there's any big shells for snail or crab type things we'll be set for that, anyway."

"And we're forgetting one other *big* resource," Sakura said. "Whips."

"I'm not sure if I should be pleased or insulted to be noted as a 'resource' along with multiform tools and food packages," her friend responded, with a shimmering pattern that showed his amusement.

"Be pleased," Akira said. "Sakura's very right. We've already heard something large approach us—and be scared off by you—and you are undoubtedly much bigger and stronger than any of us humans. And of course you can work underwater, which we cannot for any length of time. On a world like *this*," he gestured to the surrounding ocean, "I think that makes you terribly valuable."

Over the local link Sakura could sense Whips' embarrassment. "Well . . . thank you, Mr. Kimei. I will do whatever I can to help, you know that."

"We need to be organized about this," Caroline said briskly. "Let's lay out what we need to do and start figuring out how to do it. I've already made a list while we were talking and I think it's in order of priorities."

That was Caroline, always a list and a set of orders. But Sakura guessed she was right about doing this in an organized way.

"First, fresh water. That's probably covered. We already have some, and I don't think we'll have trouble getting more as long as our floating continent doesn't go too far out of these latitudes." She frowned. "That's so hard to imagine. Continental drift happens over millions and millions of years, not in human time. But drift and shifting of continents—and weather patterns—will happen in real-time here."

"Let's focus on the immediate term, Caroline," her mother said.

"Right, Mother. Next pretty much *has* to be a defensible shelter. Like Dad said, we know there's some pretty big *somethings* on land already, not to mention," she gave a visible shudder, ". . . whatever that thing was that we saw in the ocean."

"We're not defending ourselves against anything like that, though," Sakura pointed out.

"Of course not," Caroline said, slightly nettled. "The point is that while our portable shelter is reasonably tough, and we can protect it some by erecting it in this overhang here, but it probably can't take any serious attack by something hostile, unless the lifeforms here are a lot weaker than I think they are."

"All right," said Whips. "So we have to figure out a way to build, or locate, a shelter that we can defend from something pretty big wanting in."

"Right. And one pretty close to the water so that you can stay with us." Caroline's eyes defocused momentarily, looking at her invisible list. "Okay, so next is food. We really need to figure out how to get new food fast; a week and a half isn't very long."

Hitomi looked suddenly worried, but her father hugged her reassuring her. "I think the best course there is fishing, Whips. If anything here is edible, I expect it will be more likely to be animals, or at least that a larger proportion of the animals will be edible. Whips and I together should be able to get a sample of things living under and upon the shoreline. This coral island does seem to have many characteristics of regular islands, so I would expect a shoreline ecology of some robustness."

"I hope you're right, Dad. Anyway, the next thing is tools and weapons. Right now we have no weapons."

"Not quite," her mother said, indicating the SurvivalShot 12mm. "And Whips is something of a weapon by himself."

Caroline cracked a smile at that, and Sakura grinned at Whips. "You're right, Mom," Caroline said. "The SurvivalShot uses evolved hydrogen to propel anything you can fit down the barrel, so it's a great weapon. But we only have the one, and at most you can fit a dozen objects into the magazine. If there are hostile creatures, we'll want more weapons than that. And we'll need all sorts of tools—knives, levers, hammers, saws, all that kind of thing—which means stuff to build them from, and to make *other* things from."

Sakura suddenly smacked herself in the head. "Duh! Caroline, we've got tons of stuff to make tools from."

Melody's bored expression vanished. "Oh, yeah! The *LS-5!*"

"Um . . ." their mother looked puzzled.

"I know the main shuttle sank, Mother," Melody said quickly. "But what me and Saki mean is that when we crashed there were huge pieces of *LS-5* ripped off. We go back along this trench in the ground and I bet we'll find metal, composite, ceramics—all sorts of stuff we can use."

Both her mother and father looked simultaneously chagrined that they hadn't thought of it, and relieved. So was she. Even if they weren't ideal materials, there'd be a bunch of stuff that would be better than sharp sticks.

"The next item," Caroline said, moving on, "might be a problem in a while. Clothes."

Sakura paused in mid-thought. She hadn't thought about that.

"That is a challenge," admitted Laura. "But probably not for a while. These outfits we're all wearing are pretty tough. But you're right, we will have to find some source of clothing—a way to make cloth and similar materials. Anything else on your list?"

"Just one," Caroline said. "Signaling for rescue."

Melody snorted. "With what, a fire? Spelling out our name on the beach?"

"Don't be sarcastic, Melody," their mother said sternly, and Melody immediately fell silent; when Mom used *that* tone she was not joking around.

"Melody may have a point," Whips said after a moment. "I mean, even if we had a radio and it was powerful enough—and it would have to be very powerful to make sure anyone noticed—it would take years for it to get to the nearest colony. If we are somehow halfway to our destination, I think the nearest colony is well over ten light-years away."

"But *Outward Initiative* may not have been destroyed," Caroline pointed out. "And if they *do* come back looking, we need to be ready to show them where to look."

Sakura frowned. How could they even try to signal them? If they put all their omnis together they'd barely be noticeable even for someone not too far away looking for it. A comm satellite could link to them, but that was a specialized system no one was going to be putting up unless they were planning on using it.

"I agree that we should keep it in mind," her father said. "But that will definitely be a long-term project; we'll have to figure out how it might be possible to do this, with anything else we might find."

"But we do have some clear priorities," her mother said, smiling. "And it's time to get on them."

Sakura bounced to her feet. "Yes, Ma'am, Captain Mommy!"

Chapter 12

"No, Akira, you keep it," Laura said, pressing the pistol into her husband's hand.

Whips could see he was still reluctant. "But you're the one going—"

"I'm the only one here who actually knows how to fight. Police background, remember? And Whips is coming with me and Sakura on the scouting expedition, so that means that you'll need something to protect yourselves with while you get things set up here and start scavenging the crash scar nearby. Tomorrow you and Whips will do your fishing expedition, and then I'll take the gun."

Akira nodded, and looked over to Whips. "Keep an eye on them for me, all right?"

"Of course, Mr. . . . Akira."

"Come on, Mom!" Sakura was already at the top of the ridge of earth carved out by *LS-5.*

"If you keep trying to get ahead of us, Sakura, you will stay behind with your father," Laura said bluntly. Sakura immediately froze. "Honey, I'm glad you're enthusiastic—God knows we need all the positive attitude we can get—but you can't go running ahead much. We have no idea what we're getting into out there, and staying together is vital. You understand?"

Sakura nodded—but with a bit of a stubborn tension, Whips thought. *We are a lone pod now, Sakura,* he said over their private link. *Don't be angry that your mother wants us all safe.*

The young girl's shoulders relaxed slightly, as both Whips and Laura came up next to her. She turned to her mother. "Sorry, Mom."

"It's all right." She lifted her head and looked up and out. "Now that's quite a view."

For the first time, the three beheld the floating continent they stood on clearly. Sparse shrubs or something like it were scattered here and there nearby, with serrated, split leaves of the same brilliant Lincoln green that Hitomi had noticed and named the world after. There was also short-cropped ground cover of multiple sorts, most of it the same shade of green but occasional spots of blue, red, and purple. Shimmering and brightly colored somethings moved through the air, glittering with the iridescence of dragonfly wings. None of these things came near them yet.

Perhaps half a kilometer off, larger, treelike growths began, drooping what seemed spiral leaves nearly to the ground and standing closer together in what swiftly became a forest of deep emerald and aqua, with splotches of brighter color. Something much larger than the little things near them darted up and in and out from the trees, soaring and diving like ventsprites on Europa.

Farther out the terrain spread out and rose higher, stretching towards the sky. Now that he realized that the entire thing was a floating mass and not a continent, he was astounded by the size. Hundreds of meters above meant at least that much below. "These things are bigger than anything like them on Earth, aren't they?"

Caroline answered over the omni's link. "Masswise? This one probably outmasses every coral reef on Earth put together. I'm betting that when I go through the actual structure it'll turn out to have a lot of carbon in it, used as natural reinforcement fibers or something."

"All right, we're off," Laura said briskly. A brief wave of static drowned out her next words, so she paused and then repeated, "As I said, we're off. Akira, I don't intend to go very far outside of that two-kilometer maximum range, but with interference we might well be out of communication for a while."

"I promise not to panic," Akira said. "Just be careful, all of you."

"We will."

The three began walking—well, in Whips' case sort of dragging—inland, keeping along the edge of the scar left by *LS-5*.

At first, Whips tried to keep as much of himself off the ground as he could, and he noticed that the others were stepping as carefully and gingerly as they could. Finally, though, he sighed. "I *can't* keep this up all the way while we're exploring. I guess I have to assume that the ground's not much more dangerous than it is on Earth or our planned colony, right?"

Laura laughed, as did Sakura. "You're right. If it's really that much worse, we're in real trouble. Just keep an eye out for, oh, the equivalent of snakes or something."

He rippled assent, and focused his two lower eyes

on the ground. The upper eye, though, could keep
watch ahead, and he noticed something that seemed
to stick out. He stretched out his topside arm and
pointed ahead of them and slightly to the side. "What's
that, do you think?"

Lying on the ground a hundred meters or so away
was what appeared to be a very large broken column,
slightly tapered, wound about with vines.

"What is that?" murmured Sakura. "A *building*?"

"What?" Akira's voice and the others echoed the
startlement.

"Calm down, everyone," Laura said, not without a
smile. "Sakura, it does look interesting, but I would
bet that it's natural."

It took a little longer to reach it than Whips had
expected, because it was much bigger than he'd thought.
The wider portions were over four and a half meters
across, and the whole thing was well over thirty meters
long. It was clearly recently broken, with sharp edges
around the visible white-pink exterior. The twining vinelike stuff seemed oddly . . . *plated*, Whips thought, but it
didn't react to prodding or, after a moment's hesitation,
cutting, when Sakura tried a Shapetool blade on it.

"It's broken off here at the base," Laura said musingly.
"Except I don't see the actual base it broke off from."

Sakura pointed off to their right. "In the trench,
Mom!"

Sure enough, there was a squat circular something
in the trench which seemed the right size and showed
the same bright white-pink material. "Oh," said Whips,
understanding, "we must have hit it during landing and
made it fall." From this angle he could look back and
see down the center of some of the pieces; the column

was hollow. "It seems to be a floatcoral structure of some sort, not engineered. Sorry, Sakura."

"Darn. Still, it is pretty impressive." From her greater height the young Kimei squinted ahead. "You know, Mom, I think that some of those trees in the forest are actually some of these columns."

Whips raised himself on his two lower arms and focused all three eyes in that direction. "I think you're right. There seem to be some scattered trees that actually don't have those top fronds."

"Well, let's go take a look at the forest. We haven't seen anything that I'd want to test as edible yet—experience shows that it's the plants that tend to be more toxic, and I'm not quite ready to try catching the equivalent of ants for dinner," Laura said. "How're you doing, Whips?"

"Not bad, Laura," he answered. He realized he meant it. Despite the panic and confusion earlier today, he felt better now than he had in a couple of weeks. It was amazing what a couple dips in a real ocean had done for him. "Really. I know I look clumsy on land, but I can keep up with you guys for quite a while. Don't worry about that."

"It does look harder than walking, but I guess you should know. Just make sure you tell us if you're getting tired enough to turn back; remember that we'll have to walk all the way back, too."

"I know. I will."

As they approached the forest, the undergrowth became higher; Whips found himself plowing through it, and then paused in startlement. *What was that?*

"What is it, Whips?" Attuned to his movements and moods, Sakura had noticed his reaction first.

"Wait." He concentrated and relaxed, reaching out with that sense which was usually so useless above water...

And there it was. A faint chime, a tiny vibration in the world. He pushed experimentally at one of the thicker "plants" he'd been shoving through, and the chiming increased slightly, shifted in tone. "Wow. Sakura, Laura, some of these probably are plants, but some aren't. These things," he nudged the shiny-stemmed, multibranched object with what seemed greenish threads trailing along the branches, "they're alive more like we are. They react fast, they're like some of the animals in the ocean. They look like plants, but they're not."

"You mean like hydroids or barnacles or something of that nature?" came Akira's voice faintly over the comm. "That's a surprise. There are definite limitations to such creatures out of water, and I would think that would prevent colonization. Or at least that the land-dwelling forms would lose the harder shells which must be very energy-intensive to form."

"I don't know, sir, but I know what I sense. Skin-sense is pretty good about that, and if I can feel it at all here out of water, it's actually an active sender, not just passive."

Laura bent over, studying it. "Here's some images, hon. You can look them over while we keep going."

"Thanks so much, Laura. Oh, my, this is fascinating. Melody, take a look at this..."

The three explorers moved on; Whips felt a little sorry about mashing things under his admittedly broad belly pad, but there weren't any paths. None of the squashing seemed, so far, to be dumping anything irritating onto him, but he still was nervous about running over unknown creatures.

A *tap...taptaptap...* sound ahead under the trees caused all three of them to halt. "Sounded like something walking," Laura whispered. Whips bobbed his agreement as Sakura nodded. The three of them waited to see if the unknown creature would approach or flee. After a moment, Whips made a single heaving step forward; there was an explosion of tapping steps that dwindled into the distance, and Whips relaxed slightly.

"If it runs," he said, "it's less likely to try to attack us."

"On the downside," Sakura pointed out, "if it knows enough to run, it means there are things it expects to run from. *Wow!*"

He turned his gaze up just in time to see something disappear into the foliage far above, the spiraling leaves rippling for a moment. "What was it?"

"I...don't know." She played her omni's recording back, showing them something zipping from one tree to another. It seemed to have a long, pointed head, two pairs of wings or something like them, and two or maybe even four tails. Unfortunately, the images were blurred. The omnis were in lower-power mode, and so high-speed image capture was disabled by default. Even with high-efficiency solar cells the omnis would take a bit to charge and no one wanted them to run out while they were separated. "Looks like it was about a meter long. Probably won't bother anything as big as us, but we'd better keep an eye on the trees, too."

It was really becoming clear to Whips that he had to treat this like an expedition into an unknown vent region on Europa. Even now, a hundred years after contact, most Bemmies still explored their world with spears and courage and not much else, and you never knew what was hiding in the next crevice. And up here, he had no skinsense, and the soundsense was pretty limited too. He could do a sort of acoustic ranging at ten meters or so, but nothing like the sonar his people were accustomed to. On the other hand, he *could* still use a loud enough soundpulse that it could hurt at close range, and he was much better at tracking sounds and getting direction out of them than his human friends.

"Well, now, this looks more promising." On a tall bush, or low tree, were growing several teardrop-shaped blue-purple things. "Whips, is this a plant or an animal?"

He reached out and touched it gingerly. Nothing. "I'm pretty sure that's a plant. Do you think those are berries?"

"They might be. Worth a sample, anyway." Laura reached out with gloved hands (her medikit had several reusable pairs, Whips knew) and plucked one cautiously. There was no reaction, so she dropped it into a sample bag which had been one of the ration packages.

As they turned to move on, something lunged part-way from a hole in front of them and *hissed*.

Whips didn't think about it. He just saw jaws with black-blue teeth extending towards Laura and reacted. One arm shoved both Laura and Sakura back, and the other two lashed out, griptalons extending, whipping around and *pulling*.

The thing was braced in its burrow, but Whips' talons struck deep. His over two hundred twenty kilograms of mass far outweighed the target. It flew from its hole, trailing soil, and Whips spun, smashing it into the scale-shining bole of a nearby tree. It shrieked and fell limp, twitching slightly. Above, the foliage rustled as other creatures fled in startlement.

Laura was just recovering, eyes wide; Sakura was helping her to her feet. "Are you all right?" Whips asked.

"Fine," she answered, a bit shakily. "I . . . you know, I don't think it was actually attacking."

"Probably not," Whips admitted, feeling a little embarrassed now. "It was a threat display, as Akira would say. I just . . ."

". . . reacted to protect us. Thank you, Whips." Laura looked down at the creature he'd just killed. "And honestly, I don't think I would have wanted you to wait."

The thing was over two meters long and thicker around than Laura's thigh, with multiple legs spaced in four rows down its sides. It had four eyes, one pair top and bottom, and a mouth like a spiky four-section door. In general nastiness it reminded Whips of a smaller version of the huge miremaws, ambush predators native to Europa.

But the thought of miremaws, which were as delicious as they were savage, did bring to mind the other question. "I wonder if it's edible?"

Laura smiled. "Worth a sample or three." With the Shapetools providing maximal blades, it didn't take very long to cut sections from the creature in several locations. The blood, Whips noted, was red-purple in color. As they cut it apart, Laura reached out and carefully pulled out one of the dark fangs. "Hmm . . . yes, Whips, take a look at that."

The very tip of the fang had a small hole in it. "Venomous."

"Yes. And a quick analysis indicates a nasty neurotoxin. A good thing you killed it before it could fight back. That means we need to be very careful. These creatures could easily kill any of us—including you."

"Can't you make an antivenom?" Sakura asked.

"I might, and certainly our medical nanos will do their best to prevent untoward effects, but everything has its limits." He could read the concern on Laura's face. "Remember, honey, all I've got is my kit. I did— at your father's advice—have a lot of extra nanodust made up, and I have some of it here, but we have to remember there aren't any hospitals, no medbays, nothing but what I carry with me."

Sakura looked more sober as they moved on, and Whips felt a quivery tension in his guts. *It's funny, a century or two ago I wouldn't have even known what a "nano" was; now I'm afraid of not being able to rely on them.*

"Here it is!" Sakura sang out suddenly. "Wow, it's big."

In front of them, looming over everything else in sight, was the undamaged twin of the column they'd seen. Whips was impressed. Standing, the thing was huge, farther across than Whips could stretch his bottom arms and extending beyond sight through the canopy above. Scaly vinelike things twined around it, and other plants, or plantlike things, grew on its sides, mostly the same shades of green but with occasional splashes of color; most evident were round green cylindrical bulges about the size of Laura's fist with a puff of brilliant scarlet feathery fronds extending something like fifteen centimeters out in all directions. There were other objects affixed to the trunk that were less spectacular; ovoid, dark-colored, ranging in size from smaller than his last finger's claw to as big as Laura's head.

"Mom? I'm going to go up, see what I can see from a higher vantage point."

Laura hesitated, then nodded reluctantly. "I know how good you are at climbing. Just be careful; if you don't see a good handhold, you stop right away. And try not to touch anything other than these vines, which we've already looked over, okay?"

"Okay. Well, there's those leaves up there, but I'll check them before I try going through." She tested the stability of the vine, seemed satisfied, and began climbing.

Whips admitted he envied Sakura her climbing skill. He was very strong for his size and he could, in fact, climb using his three arms to get him up into things that even human climbers had a hard time with, but he was generally pretty slow. Sakura was like a monkey, making her way up now with an assured speed that ignored the possibility that she even could fall, let alone ever actually would.

Sakura reached the point at which the column penetrated the canopy, then took out her Shapetool and turned it into a long, slender rod. She smacked all the leaves nearby and poked through the area she intended to climb. Small creatures fled at her actions. A few moments later she disappeared from sight through the foliage.

"Wow. Mom, I can see a *long* way now," came Sakura's voice from above. "Those hills keep going quite a distance—I can't see the end. We've got a couple more lagoons off to, um, I guess it's south? They've got lighter water color, too, so I think they're shallow

water we might be able to fish in or something." A
pause. "Holy *wow*, you should *see* the scar *LS-5* left.
It goes on and *on*, even farther than I thought. I can't
believe we survived that! It's totally awesome, though."

"Anything else?"

"There's . . . like paths or something through the
trees—I can see places where they're not as tall or
they're separated by a little bit. And there's some kind
of big clearing off to the west, almost straight west
from where we are, before the hills. Might be the edge
of the forest, actually. Maybe if I got a little higher,
but I'm almost out of handholds I trust. Oh, *neat*."

"What?" Whips demanded. It was really quite
annoying to hear someone else talking about things
you couldn't see.

"There's a hole in the side of this thing, and it's
hollow, just like the fallen one. I can feel a cool breeze
coming out of it, too."

"Don't go in!"

"*Mom*, I'm not *stupid*, that other one was hollow,
it'd be like a what, twenty-meter fall?" A pause.
"Okay, I got the best imagery my omni could get,
I'm coming down."

Sakura descended almost as quickly as she had gone
up. The path was slightly different as handholds that
were easy to reach from below might be harder than
other hand- and footholds for the way down. As she
passed close to one of the scarlet puffs, the fronds
suddenly flicked out and Sakura gave a combined
scream and curse, nearly falling, catching herself.
"*OW!* Ow ow *OW!*"

"Hold on, honey! Just keep coming down as fast as
you can!" The worry in Laura's voice was the same

as in Whips' heart; if one of the native creatures was dangerous, what about these?

"Coming, Mom . . . oh, that *hurts* . . ." Sakura nearly missed a grab. "Oh, crap. Mom, I feel . . . funny. Shaky. And things look a little blurry."

Whips slid up to the base of the column, then opened his arms high and wide, keeping the griptalons sheathed—except for a few on his lowest arm-branches, which were gripping the base of the column. "Drop down."

She gave a quick glance down and, blurry vision or not, understood what he was doing, and let go.

Sakura plummeted the final eight meters like a dead weight.

Chapter 13

Laura restrained the urge to leap forward. Panic would not help her.

Even as she scanned the data from Sakura's internal medical nanos, she categorized the symptoms of the shaky girl. *Skin reddening...pupils dilating... heart rate increasing.* Sakura was also looking dizzy, disoriented.

The data from the nanos confirmed her guess. "It's a hyoscyamine derivative, something like atropine. And a few other chemicals, too." Thankfully, she knew how to counteract that kind of thing. It was in the basic medikit data.

She first directed the medical nanos to counteract some of the symptoms—bring the heart rate under control. "It's okay, honey, I can handle this. Are you with me?"

"Funny...hard to think. Hurts." Sakura was clearly working hard to focus on her mentally as well as visually.

Heavy dose. But the nanos can slow the reaction, and the kit's able to do a physostigmine variant. Timed and controlled release to the proper sites, then

*the nanos can finish adapting to the toxin and start
cleaning it out.*

Laura made the injection, feeling her own heart
starting to slow down finally as she took action. The
bright red color faded and slowly, slowly Sakura's pupils
began to contract. "Feeling better?"

"Yes, Mom," Sakura answered, and shakily sat up,
then leaned back into Whips' supporting arms. "It
still hurts bad, though."

The stung area was a twining pattern of reddened
welts with dark and light banding. "Looks very much
like a jellyfish sting." Laura looked up. "A land
anemonelike thing, then." She studied the details
from the internal nanos in that area. "Yes, there's
cnidoblasts or something like it. Mostly inactive now.
The pain's mostly from an associated toxin, probably
meant as a warning to accompany the main poison.
Even if the sting doesn't kill you, you'll remember
it. I've got the nanos doing some anesthetic damping.
Better?"

"Lots." She watched her little girl—*not so little
anymore, but she'll always be little to* me, *anyway*—
close her eyes and relax.

"That scared the light right out of me," Whips said
quietly. Laura could see that even now Whips' colors
were subdued.

"An important lesson for us, though. We had started
to relax after getting through all that underbrush
without trouble. Now we know that even things that
look like red flowers could be dangerous."

Sakura smiled weakly. "Don't think I want to be a
demonstration again."

Laura reached out and hugged Sakura tightly,

letting the tears flow finally. "Neither do I. Thank God you're all right."

After a few moments she let go and wiped her eyes. "How do you feel? Can you stand up?"

Sakura was a little wobbly, but in a few more minutes she seemed steadier on her feet. "I'm getting better."

"End of an expedition?" Whips asked.

"Yes. We don't want to push things any farther, and I want Sakura back to camp and lying down until tomorrow. We don't know for sure if there are any other effects of those toxins, and without a full medical system I can't simulate it well enough. I'm also not getting any contact with the base camp, so we need to get closer before we can even update them."

Laura took the lead, with Sakura in the middle being partly supported and watched over by Whips. It took longer to get out of the forest, but by the time they reached the open area in front of the forest Sakura was moving almost as well as she normally did, though she was still holding her arm well away from anything that could touch it.

Suddenly her omni pinged. "Laura? Are you there?"

"We're on our way back, sweetheart. Something stung Sakura—"

"*Stung* her? Is she all right? I'm coming—"

"Akira, don't panic," she said in her most confident tones. "She's walking fine right now. It was dangerous for a few minutes, and we've learned a lot, but I think everything's okay. You stay right where you are. We came out of the woods a little farther west than we went in, but it shouldn't take more than, oh, forty minutes to get back to you."

"All right. Sorry," he answered, his voice a tiny bit sheepish.

"It's all right, I'd react the same way."

"So," he said in a more normal voice, as they continued moving back toward the camp, "you said *stung*. How?"

She described the events, from the time they'd left the fallen column to the time Sakura had recovered from her sting. "So I think we're looking at something like a land-dwelling anemone."

"Or hydroid, which is probably also what those plantlike things that Whips noticed are like. Yes. Very interesting. I'll have to get some samples of all these things later. I'm also very interested in your samples of potential food—and that ground-dwelling attacker. Did you keep its head?"

"No, honey, sorry. I didn't want to burden us and thought we'd go farther and get more samples."

"Don't worry about it. Unless it was one of a kind, which I very highly doubt, I'm sure we'll run into more. Hopefully without being bitten."

"That does worry me, though," Caroline put in. "We don't have multiple outfits, and none of us have good hiking boots."

"We'll have to start thinking about how to address that," agreed Laura. "but for now let's take one problem at a time." They came to the edge of the crash scar, and Sakura gave a delighted laugh. Laura smiled as well. "It seems that you've helped solve one of the problems, anyway."

Tucked slightly under an overhang from the crash, the inflatable temporary shelter looked large and solid, a rounded, almost igloolike shape with a tall entrance hall and two rounded lobes extending out to each side. Transparent windows were visible, allowing natural light in when desired, and the faint, dark sheen on the outer side of the shelter showed that it was coated with active, high-efficiency, rugged photovoltaics.

She could see Melody, sitting on a flat-topped stone a short distance from the shelter, and her husband was visible now, just coming around the other side, but... "Where are Caroline and Hitomi?"

"We're on our way back. We went up the scar some distance and we've been picking up metal and composite junk that might be usable."

"I found bowls!" Hitomi announced proudly.

"Bowls?" echoed Whips. "What do you mean?"

"She found empty shells or carapaces that are close enough in size that we can actually carry them pretty easily, and look like they could work as bowls or small pots," Caroline answered. "They're quite tough, too, so I think we can use them freely, if there isn't something poisonous in the material."

"Can we determine that?" Akira asked cautiously.

"Definitely," Laura said, picking her way down the slope. "My medkit will certainly be able to do that much. Melody, why are you sitting down reading when everyone else is working?"

Melody flushed slightly. "I helped put up the shelter."

"I know, honey, but you can't just stop because you finish one task. Why don't you go inside and see if you can figure out the best setup for our living and sleeping space? You like solving space puzzles."

Somewhat to her credit, Melody managed to restrain a roll of her eyes, and stood up. "Yes, Mom."

Laura shook her head as Melody disappeared inside

the shelter. "Where does she *get* that from? Neither of us were like that."

Akira laughed and came over to hug Sakura. "My love, you didn't know me when I was young. Melody reminds me rather forcefully of me, which is why I try not to encourage her." He looked down at Sakura. "Now *you* go lie down and rest."

"But I'm—"

"Don't argue with your father. Or your doctor, who happens to be your mother," Laura said with a smile. "I wouldn't have had you walk at all if we'd had any choice on the matter. After what you've gone through, you should get a lot of rest. Melody," she said to her omni, and saw the ten-year-old acknowledge the signal, "pull out Sakura's bed now."

"You okay, Saki?" Melody's laziness was no longer evident when asking about her sister.

"I think so, but Mom and Dad don't want to take chances."

Laura noted that Sakura's gait wasn't nearly as bouncy as its usual habitual rhythm as she went inside. Whips obviously saw it too. "She's more tired than she lets on," the big Bemmie said.

"I'd be astounded if she wasn't." She pulled out the sample bags. "Let's check out what we found."

"While you do that, I'll go make myself a land-nest," Whips said. Before she could say anything, Whips continued, "Dr. . . . Laura, I'm a lot bigger than the rest of you and I'm also a lot tougher. I don't mind being outside; if it rains, that's just fine with me. If you don't have to squeeze me into the shelter, you'll be a lot more comfortable. If I bury myself in dirt and sand, it'll be hard for anything to just come bother me, anyway."

"He's right," Akira said. "It makes sense. Plus if he has to go to the sea for any reason, it will be much easier from here in the open than trying to go out through the entranceway. He's also got better senses than ours in some areas, so he might help protect us that way. I've set up Caroline's omni as a security monitor, but it can't hurt to have someone outside who can be a second line of defense."

She couldn't argue the logic, even though a part of her still felt that it was like marginalizing the young Bemmie to a less-desirable neighborhood. Quashing that irrational feeling, she nodded. "All right, go ahead."

The two adults bent over their analysis devices and studied readouts. After fifteen minutes, Akira shook his head. "Those are indeed berries, but they've got alkaloids or some close analogues which are quite toxic in them. On the other hand, their very *existence* gives me hope that we will find other fruits which are, in fact, edible."

Analysis of the meat went somewhat faster, partly because they were both getting used to this much more primitive setup, and Laura found herself grinning foolishly at Akira as they finished. "Completely edible . . . and nutritious," he said, and the two of them hugged. "Food, honey. There *is* food we can eat here!"

"That's worth celebrating," agreed Caroline's voice behind them. The oldest and youngest of her children came around the side of the shelter in the now-setting sunlight. Caroline had a large bundle of assorted junk on her back, strapped together with what appeared to be salvaged cable. Hitomi was doggedly half-carrying, half-dragging a string of moderate-sized objects. "Of course, let's hope it doesn't *taste* terrible."

"Look, Mommy—bowls!" Hitomi held the string of objects up.

The shells were of a peculiar shape—effectively flat-bottomed, with perhaps a tiny curve, generally cylindrical, and the top flared out in small ripples around the edge. Something about the shape and green color tugged at her memory; then she realized the truth and laughed again.

"What is it, Mom?"

"I think what Hitomi's picked up are a bunch of shells of the same kind of creature that stung Sakura," she said.

Akira glanced at them and then looked over the footage that Laura had brought back. "I do believe you're right."

"I'm going to go show her!" Hitomi said, but Laura caught at her sleeve.

"Wait a while, honey," Laura said. In her monitor, she saw Sakura, and her vital signs. A faint snore came from the girl.

"Wait a while," she repeated and smiled over at Akira. "She's sleeping like a rock."

Chapter 14

Whips wallowed his body back and forth, feeling the coral-based sand squish reassuringly under him. "Hm. That will be good."

It had been quite a while since he built a land-nest—years ago, when he and his father had gone on a camping trip with the Kimeis, and that was long enough that he'd had to think about just *how* you did this right. His first attempt, about three meters away, hadn't quite worked and ended as a loose sort of sand crater. It was supposed to be soft in the middle but still packed at the edges in certain ways.

This one felt right. He thought he would be able to crawl out of it and get back in without it collapsing, which was the way a land-nest was supposed to work.

Night had fallen on Lincoln—well, their part of Lincoln, anyway—while he'd been busy digging. Built-in solid-state lights illuminated the area near the shelter, and Laura was bent over her medikit while Akira cooked on the portable stove that had come with the shelter. Carefully, Whips pulled himself forward and up, and slid from the nest, keeping his anchors carefully pulled in. He glanced back once he was far enough away. It was still intact!

Feeling better at that minor triumph, he began moving towards the stove to see what Akira was cooking; as he slid along, though, he noticed Caroline almost directly in his way, apparently staring upward. "What are you looking at?"

"The answer to one mystery, I think," Caroline answered absently.

"What do you mean?"

"I mean I think I understand why this system could be here, halfway to Tantalus, without it being anywhere in the databases. Because any G-type star would definitely be in the databases."

"Okay, well, don't keep me waiting. Why?"

"Look up, about there."

Used to following human pointing fingers, Whips reared up and gazed in the indicated direction. There were stars of all colors and sizes scattered across the night. "Where, exactly? I see a lot of night sky."

"Your omni active? Okay, here."

A set of dim crosshairs materialized in his field of view, and he turned his attention there. "Just night sky and stars there. Well, there isn't a star exactly there, but—"

"That's the key. See, *exactly* there is where the Sun should be. At about magnitude 5.8, but with my omni's enhancement and your naturally sensitive eyes, that should be easy to see."

"Oh, my," came Laura's voice. The tall woman joined them, looking up. "So something is between Lincoln's sun and ours."

"And has been for probably a few centuries, at least, so it wasn't ever mapped out. Lincoln's star would be pretty dim from Earth-magnitude six, I think, what with being a little dimmer than the sun overall—so naked-eye astronomers might not have caught it regularly. And if our relative motion to Earth's solar system isn't big, a pretty small nebula could cover it up for quite a while—a Bok globule, maybe. I don't know how the *nebula* couldn't have been seen, though. It should have been one of the most interesting objects in the sky, and any exploration of it should have found Lincoln's sun." She shook her head, puzzled.

"But wouldn't the other colonies have noticed the new star?" Whips asked. "I mean, they're going to be looking from another direction, so the same cloud of stuff isn't going to be in their way."

"Maybe. But like I said, it's going to be pretty dim from any reasonable distance, and most colonies aren't going to be looking for new, close-to-home stars that we missed." Caroline continued staring up. "Maybe, if *Outward Initiative* didn't get totally destroyed, they'll check images of that region of space and figure it out, though."

She glanced down suddenly. "Do you . . . what do you think the chances are that *Outward Initiative* . . . well, didn't get totally wrecked?"

Whips bunched inward slightly, tense. He knew why they'd asked him. He was as close as they had to an engineer or physicist; he knew more than anyone here about how the ships worked. But . . .

He thought about it seriously. He'd studied those brief, terrifying sequences of images, the fading of most of *Outward Initiative* with only a few ghostly pieces of the hab ring remaining before the disaster, and in the weeks it had taken to get here to Lincoln he had, in fact, spent a lot of time mulling over what had happened, what *could* have happened.

"I can't give you a...well, a good probability estimate," he said finally. "But I think there's a chance it survived. The hab ring's built with a lot of redundancy in the structure, and the ship itself has a lot of safety cutoffs that should cause it to reduce rotation or otherwise adjust if it suddenly lost chunks of the hab ring. If the Trapdoor field wasn't just oscillating out of control, then it was some kind of glitch that probably only lasted a few seconds on the outer perimeter of the field. There's some minor instability in the field all the time, it's just that the wavering of the field is usually kept many meters away from any actual components of the ship. If you got a really huge peak in that instability...I think they'd damp it down in ten seconds or so, and after that they'd be okay."

"Will they come and rescue us?" Akira asked from the stove.

Whips waved his arms in a shrug. "If they survived? They'd have to somehow guess that someone could have survived falling off the interface; I never heard of anything like that, and I think I would have in my studies. Maybe their records will have ghost images of that happening, like we have ghost images of part of the hab ring, but without that...maybe."

"No point in worrying about it," Akira said firmly. "Our job is to survive, to build this into our home, and if rescue comes, wonderful. If not, we leave for the people who will, eventually, come after us a record showing that we didn't despair, but we did everything we could to survive and prosper."

He rapped on the table set a ways from the entrance. "Now come on over and let's find out if the native food's going to be a trial or a treat."

"Oh, wow! That's what you were doing, Dr. . . . I mean, Akira?"

"Since you'd brought enough to cook up, yes. It's not much, and we'll certainly all have to have some rations, but it seems to me that we might as well have a taste right away."

"Not leaving *me* out of this!" came a sleepy voice from the tent doorway. Despite her heavy-lidded eyes, Sakura was moving a little better than she had when she went into the shelter; Whips felt relieved.

"Me! I want to try some!" Hitomi said excitedly. Melody emerged from the tent as well, but hung back. "I want to see what happens with the rest of you first."

"Suit yourself, Melody. Though either way we'll have to eat it sooner or later; our rations won't last forever, and in fact I'm going to require we stop eating them as soon as we find enough sources of food that we have an assured supply," Laura said. "I want as many rations left as possible for emergencies, travel supplies, and so on. They'll last more than ten years, so having them as a backup will be something very comforting."

Whips looked at the dark fried pieces of meat on his plate, reached out and gingerly picked one up between two fingers. "Warm. All right, here we go!"

The texture was reassuringly meaty—tougher than many vent-dwellers, softer than some patrolling creatures like orekath. Overall it was something like mire-maw or, for Earth creatures, beef. The taste was . . . good, actually, now that he tried another bite. *Really* good! It wasn't exactly like anything else, but . . . "I'd forgotten what fresh meat tasted like after being in *Outward Initiative* so long!" he said finally.

"It's like...alligator, I think," Akira said slowly, a relieved smile spreading across his face.

The others' faces wore the same expression, as they realized that not only was there something to eat, but it would be something worth eating. "A stronger taste than that...but you're right, Dad," Caroline said after a moment. "It's got that cross between land and sea taste going."

Hitomi had already cleared her plate and was looking hungrily at the chunks on Melody's plate. Whips couldn't help but laugh when Hitomi's face face utterly plummeted as Melody snatched up one of the pieces and stuffed it into her mouth. As Sakura and Caroline echoed the laugh, Hitomi looked at first betrayed... and then suddenly started laughing joyously herself.

Then he noticed Laura. "Laura? Are you crying? What's wrong?"

Everyone else immediately stopped, staring, worried. "Laura, honey, what is it?" Akira asked softly, going to his wife and putting his hand on her shoulder.

The tall human woman blinked fiercely, but the tracks of shining tears were obvious, and her voice was a little thick when she answered. "I'm sorry. Oh, God, I feel so silly. It's..." She shook her head, wiped her eyes, and smiled brilliantly. "I was just so worried about everything. About Sakura, about having to live on our own, about how many things might be out there waiting to cause another disaster for us, and... well, just suddenly seeing everyone sitting here, eating food we found on our own planet, eating *good* food we found here, seeing us all smiling, laughing..."

She shrugged helplessly and laughed, still with tears in her voice. "I just felt everything let go in me, and I was so relieved, so happy that we did survive, that we're all here and alive and living..."

Whips felt the strange tight tingle of the same painful, joyous whirl of emotions, knew his skin was shimmering in a clash of colors, and then saw that all around the table, the other Kimeis were also crying in exactly the same way, even little Hitomi.

Akira hugged Laura tight, and suddenly, without any word or gesture, the others all gathered around and hugged, as they had after they knew they had survived and found a destination. Whips enfolded his whole adopted family and squeezed tightly, as he would have twined arms with his mother. *Now we know we* can *survive, that this world is a place* worth *surviving on. And so now, we* will *survive, no matter what Lincoln has to throw at us.*

Our family will survive.

Chapter 15

"Can't I *please* come with—"

"No." Her mother's answer was firm. "You seem recovered, mostly, but you were in very bad shape for a while yesterday. I don't expect to see any more trouble, but for today you're staying near camp. You'll have plenty more chances to explore, I promise."

"Sorry, Saki," her father said, and gave her a consoling hug. That didn't exactly make up for it, but it was a hug, anyway.

Akira straightened and beckoned to Melody. "Come on, Mel. You were hoping for an adventure a while back, now's your chance."

Sakura saw the momentary excited jump up, and turned away to hide a smile. Melody was normally lazy, and she cultivated the bored appearance at times—why, Sakura didn't know, it wasn't like she was old enough to be acting like that—but that was right now clearly fighting a battle with Melody's curiosity and desire to be one of the people who found something *new* on this planet.

Of course, she suspected that Mel had another reason for volunteering to be the third member of the expedition.

Whips waved to all of them, and the three disappeared over the edge of the landing scar, heading for the shoreline, which they planned on following for a considerable distance to observe what the local sea and shore life was like.

"All right, Caroline," Laura said briskly. "It's up to you and me. Sakura, you're in charge of continuing camp setup and keeping an eye on Hitomi."

"Yes, Mom."

"And you call me if you feel *anything* wrong, you understand?"

"I will, don't worry." She meant that. She wasn't going to forget the terror she'd felt as the poison worked its way through her, not any time soon. If there was a slower-acting component to the thing's venom, she had to admit there was no better place to be than in shouting range of her mother.

And it did, at least, give her an excuse to not be digging the deep disposal pit, which was where they'd put the, well, crap that would eventually have to be emptied from the shelter's toilet facility.

"C'mon, Hitomi. We've got chores to do before we get to play."

Hitomi made a face, but stopped her run towards the edge of the landing scar and came back.

Sakura first had Hitomi help scrub out the shells she'd brought back with sand, multiple times. Her mother's tests had shown that the tough little shells were a mix of carbon-based material and silicate, but didn't have any toxic components of note. The same couldn't be said for the remnants of stinging land-anemone or whatever that was inside, so they had to get every little trace of the animals out.

This was, fortunately, exactly the kind of thing Hitomi was good at. Get her focused on one task that she could keep doing and that needed a lot of attention to detail, and she could keep doing it for a long time. Sakura didn't find this task quite as engrossing, but it was nice to see the things cleaning up so well, becoming smooth, shiny white-green bowls. They'd have to rinse them out with water too, but if they got all the hard part done with the sand it'd go a lot easier.

After that was done, she and Hitomi carefully swept out the shelter, using a bundle of frayed wiry fibers from the crash tied to a broken support rod. She glanced at the sun, noting how far it had risen, and checked her omni. "Hey, Mom, it's been a while—I think it's lunchtime."

"Really?" There was a pause, then, "You're right, Saki. I was thrown off by the sun. Makes it look more like, oh, ten-thirty in the morning."

"Thirty-two hour rotation instead of twenty-four," Caroline confirmed. "That's going to be a little confusing."

"Yes, we'll be out of synch with the light cycle," Akira's voice came over the omnis. "Our natural cycle will still stay around twenty-four hours, so our "morning" will migrate from actual morning to afternoon to late night and back to morning again over three of Lincoln's day-cycles."

"You're still in range, hon? It's been several hours, I'd have thought—"

"—I'd have gotten farther, eh? Well, love, first of all we *are* quite a ways away. But we have Melody's omni, which does have better range, and I moved Caroline's up to the highest point near the camp so it could be a relay. Also, we're following the coast.

We're probably about a kilometer and a half from you as the four-winged whoosiwhatsis flies."

Sakura and Hitomi were getting out some of the rations as her mother and Caroline came trudging up the slope. "So how is the expedition going, Akira?" her mother asked.

"Oh, very well. Unlike the broken area near the ex-lagoon, which got rather well cleaned out by the fall of that mass of rock, most of the shoreline does, in fact, have an extensive mass stretching out underwater—a beach and shore or surf zone. Whips has done some quick survey work and says in places he can scan it can go out two kilometers or more."

"That should be a good thing for us, yes?"

"Very good, yes. Shallow-water ecosystems like that will be easy for us to harvest from, and will tend to keep the worst predators from getting too close in to shore."

"How's Melody doing?"

"Occasional minor complaints, but she's been taking pictures with her omni and making muttered notes to herself. Whips didn't encounter anything too large in his quick dips, but he thinks he's found underwater burrows of creatures similar to the one he caught before. We'll try to catch a couple and bring them back for dinner when we're returning."

"And what have you been up to?"

"Sampling everything I find, of course. There are a couple of tentative observations I have, but I'm going to need a bit more data before I draw conclusions from it." He paused. "Melody's calling me; I had better go see what she's found. Talk later, Laura; love you!"

"Love you too." Her mother smiled as she put

the omni back on her belt. "Oh, thank you, Sakura, Hitomi. That was lovely of you."

"We'll need to find water pretty soon, Mom," Sakura said hesitantly.

"I know, hon. I'm sure your father has an eye out for that, and we'll keep looking until we find it."

After lunch, Hitomi and Sakura cleaned everything up. Sakura stopped her little sister before she crammed the plastic wrappings into the disposal at the side of the shelter. "Wait on that, Hitomi."

"Why? It's trash. Mommy says to always put the trash in the trash as soon as you're done."

"Because stuff that's trash back home might not be something we want to throw away here," Sakura said slowly. "Mom?"

She heard her mother give a pained grunt, obviously lifting something heavy. "Yes?"

"Should I be keeping the wrappings from the rations? I mean, I don't know if there's a use for them—"

"Oh. Keep them for now. We'll talk that over when everyone else is together. Now, honey, don't interrupt me again unless you absolutely have to, Caroline and I are working hard on this together."

"Yes, Mom."

"Saki? Can we go up there?" Hitomi pointed up to the land above the landing scar. "I haven't seen where we are yet."

I should be doing something useful . . . Sakura's gaze lit on the pile of salvaged material that Caroline had brought back yesterday. *There's an idea.* "Okay, we can, Hitomi. Just let me get a couple of things."

The route the family was using to climb up to the higher ground was already starting to look like a path.

That made it easier to climb, too, Sakura thought as she led Hitomi up, carrying a bundle of stuff with her.

"Wow, it's so pretty!" Hitomi exclaimed, and started to run.

Sakura dropped everything she was carrying and snagged her sister. "Slow down, Hitomi! You listen to me. Are you listening?"

Hitomi looked slightly hurt, and shocked by the sudden yank. "What?"

Sakura knelt down and looked seriously into her little sister's eyes. "Hitomi, we've just gotten here. We don't know everything that's safe, and everything that's dangerous. You have to stay near me. You can't go running off by yourself somewhere. Be careful. Watch what you're touching. We know that most of this stuff doesn't seem to cause any problem just by walking on it or sitting on it, but," she held up her arm, where the sting marks still showed, mottled red-brown, "we've already seen something else that will kill us if it can."

Hitomi's eyes were wide, and Sakura could tell she now had her sister's full attention. "I'm not saying to be terrified of everything, either. Just be careful, and if anything nips you, stings you, pricks you, you let me know right away. And stay near me."

"Yes, Saki."

"Okay."

Hitomi watched as Sakura took the jumble of wreck materials over to a nearby flat-topped boulder and spread them out. Sakura sat down, and picked through the pieces. She'd chosen a bunch of reinforcement fibers which had been ripped free, a chunk of metal about the size of her fist whose origin was uncertain, and some smaller shards of metal, along with a rod of composite about a meter long and some composite pieces.

Okay, let's see. We already talked about needing weapons, and if we're going to protect ourselves and hunt, it's time to start on that.

The smaller shards of metal were of generally triangular shape—ideal, Sakura thought, for spearheads. But she'd need to get them to a pretty symmetric shape and get them sharp on the point and edges, plus have something—a haft? she wasn't sure of the right name—which she could use to connect it to a shaft, like the rod she had brought up.

Her Shapetool could of course configure to exactly what she wanted, but if it was strapped onto a spear shaft she couldn't use it for anything else—and if it got used and the spearhead came off, they'd have lost one of their most versatile tools. *Mom'd kill me. And that would be taking the really easy way out, anyway.*

The three pieces she had to choose from were roughly the same size, but one of them actually had a bit sticking out which might be good for the . . . Sakura paused and checked her omni's database. *Tang, that's the word!* That should be good for the tang.

The rest of it came to a nearly symmetrical point. One side had a thick edge, the other a ragged but much thinner edge. If she could hammer the one flatter and smooth out the other, it might make a good spearhead.

The hand-sized chunk of steel would make a good hammer. It fit nicely into the palm of her hand. She took a good grip, steadied the putative spearhead on the flat rock, and brought the hammer-chunk down.

There was a sharp, buzzing *whack*, and she could see the impact had left a significant ding in the other metal. *Ha! It's softer than the hammer!* Encouraged, she hit the thick side several times. *It* does *seem to be flattening!*

"What are you doing?" Hitomi asked.

Sakura explained her idea. Hitomi immediately wanted to try, but it was pretty obvious that she didn't have the strength to hit hard enough; it wasn't easy for Sakura, truth be told. "So what can *I* do?" she asked.

She's in a helping mood. That's good, if I can figure out something... An idea struck her. "You know what? I think there *is* something you could do that would help everyone, especially Mommy and Daddy." Sakura fiddled with her Shapetool and handed it to Hitomi, now configured into a two-sided tool that was a pair of gripping tongs on one side and a cutting shear on the other. "Go over the local plants and things and get a sample of each one. Pile them in order on that other rock, there. That way Daddy and Mommy can go over them and see what kinds of things we have. The shear will let you cut pieces out and the tongs let you pick them up safely, just in case."

"I can do that!" Hitomi said proudly. She took the Shapetool carefully and walked to the waving grass-like stuff nearby. Studying the stalks intently, the little blonde-haired girl very methodically selected one, clipped off a stalk, picked it up with the tongs, and carried it to the other rock; without being told, she took another loose rock and put it down on top of her sample, to keep it from blowing away in the light breeze. Hitomi went back, studied the grass, and cut another stalk.

"Isn't that the same stuff? We want samples of different—"

"This isn't the same!" Hitomi said defensively. She brought the newly cut stalk over, gripped in the tongs. "See these bumps? They're not the same on the other one."

Sakura put down her hammer-chunk and went over to the first sample with Hitomi. Sure enough, the "bumps"—which looked to Sakura sort of like the joints seen on things like horsetails—had a different pattern that really did argue for them being different species.

"Sorry, Hitomi. I should know better than to argue with you." Hitomi's attention to detail, when you got her attention at all, was legendary. "You keep doing that and Mommy and Daddy will be very excited."

Hitomi smiled brightly and skipped back to the surrounding greenery.

Sakura turned her attention back to the piece of metal. *I've seen stuff kinda like this on some of the immersives I've played, but never really did any of it. Still, how hard can it be? Just pound the metal into the right shape, then sharpen it by grinding it down. I'll bet I could use this coral-rock as a good grindstone kinda thing.*

She started pounding methodically, working her way up and down the thick edge so that she hopefully wouldn't flatten one area much more than another. It took a while to figure out the right angle and force to use to not jolt the heck out of her arm and hand and still get the metal to move a bit on every impact. Sakura paused and checked on Hitomi; her little sister had moved somewhat around the perimeter but was now carrying, very carefully, what looked like a dark green puffball in the tongs and placing it on what was already a fairly impressive array of pieces of plants and, probably, plantlike things. *She's focused now; she'll do that for hours, probably, unless something distracts her.*

Reassured, Sakura went back to her work. *Now that I've figured this out...*

But as time went on, Sakura found, to her chagrin, that what looked really easy in an immersive sim... wasn't nearly so easy. The side she was pounding on was thinning, yes, but it was also mushrooming out, and parts of the metal were splitting slowly. There was no sign of a nice, clean edge appearing. She thought her Shapetool might be able to trim off some of the edge, but she had to, grudgingly, admit that her cavalier assessment of how easy this should be had been badly wrong. *They make it look easy in the games—smith heats metal, pounds it, grinds it, got a blade. Sometimes just pounds on the metal.*

She studied the mass of junk again. Making a blade wasn't easy. Whips would probably be laughing at her for trying it that way. But maybe there was something else.

The long reinforcement fibers were like braided cord—and very strong. But they wouldn't do as a whip; she'd intended them just for tying things together. The meter-long rod wouldn't make a very good club; it was too light on its own. The hammer-chunk of steel wasn't shaped in a way that would make it easy to attach it to something. She thought about various types of weapons. *Well, tough cord could be used for a, whatchacallit, garrotte, but that's not a hunting weapon. I've seen something people throw to tangle up prey . . . a bola?* Her omni had a little information on those, including how to determine the right weights and lengths of cord.

But learning to use them would take a lot of time, and they'd be pretty useless as a defensive weapon up close. Sakura wanted something they could use for hunting or for protection.

She looked at the rod, then a thought occurred to her. She took it and tried to bend it. The rod bent, then sprang back to its original shape as soon as she let go.

Bow and arrow?

The problem then would be arrows. They'd need something pretty straight, the right thickness, and a way to put heads on them—and making the heads would go right back to the problem she was having with making spearheads. Or maybe you could just take the stuff you used for the shafts and sharpen it? *Fire-hardening, that's what I'm thinking of. There's some kind of trick to that.*

"Well, Saki, what are you up to here?"

She jolted to her feet, startled. *"Dad?* I thought you were out exploring!"

"We were, but it's been a long day." Akira Kimei showed traces of sunburn and a lot of sweat, and his hair was disarranged and filled with sand and salt, but he was grinning widely. Behind him, Melody was trudging up, carrying a bag of samples, and the scraping sound and movement behind her showed Whips was also approaching. "But a very good day overall."

She saw a potential disaster in the making as Whips emerged from the surrounding vegetation. "Watch it, everyone—Hitomi's samples are on that rock. Don't walk over it."

"Hitomi's samples?" Akira smiled. "Well, that should be interested. Where *is* Hitomi?"

With a shock, Sakura realized that she'd lost track of time—and she didn't remember, now, seeing that movement out of the corner of her eye that told her Hitomi had brought in a new sample. "I . . . I don't know!"

"Don't panic," her father said quickly. "Hitomi! *Hitomi!*" he called.

There was no answer.

"*HITOMI!*" she called as loud as she could.

There was still no answer. "Dad . . ."

"If she was making this collection, she can't have gone too far. Let's all look around." Her father's tone did not quite conceal his worry, and Sakura's gut tightened. How could she have been so stupid?

She hesitated, took a deep breath. *Got to think. Part of me must have heard her, must have seen her, last time she went by. Which direction?*

She turned slowly, until a part of her said *yes*. She couldn't put her finger on exactly what told her that was the right direction, whether she'd heard some faint noise, seen some shadow, or what, but she was pretty sure this was the direction Hitomi had gone.

Please be okay, please be okay . . .

"Hitomi! Come on, answer me, *Hitomi!*"

Her omni pinged. "What's wrong, Sakura?"

"Mom . . ." she heard her voice quiver. "Mom, I . . . I lost Hitomi."

There was a sharp intake of breath. "How could you—" her mother began to snap, then stopped. "You're looking for her now?"

"Me, Dad, Mel, and Whips. They just got back. Oh, God, Mom, I'm so—"

"Don't, Saki. Find her."

She filled her lungs again and shouted, *"HITOMI!!"*

She heard the others calling too, in different directions, pushed on. There were so many things they didn't know; so many things that could have hurt her. She had a grisly vision of one of those hole-dwelling things striking, dragging her little sister down . . . She shuddered, felt nausea rising. *Or something could have stung her . . . poisoned her . . . God, I'm so stupid, stupid, I should've watched her . . .*

"HITOMI!"

Nothing.

She drew another breath, then stopped. *What . . . ?*

Ahead, and a little to the right, she heard a rapping sound.

She waited.

There it was again. It sounded like rocks banging together.

If she gets absorbed in a project . . .

She ran towards the sound. Sparkling, darting things flew in panic from the plants. Something else scuttled away, making a faint wheezing noise as fled.

Sakura burst through a group of jointed-stalked plants into a tiny clearing.

Hitomi was sitting there, a rock in her hand, carefully banging on another rock that was covered with plants. In that momentary glance, Sakura had the impression the unpounded ones looked something like very skinny celery.

Sakura felt her knees wobble, realized that the combination of yesterday's poisoning and this new panic was catching up with her. "Everyone, I've found her!"

Hitomi didn't even seem to notice immediately. She

took another handful of plants, placed them carefully on the rock, and started pounding on these new additions. Sakura walked shakily closer, then laid a hand on Hitomi's shoulder.

Her little sister jumped, then looked up with a suddenly guilty expression. "I'm sorry!"

Sakura dropped down on her knees and hugged Hitomi fiercely. "It's okay, I just . . . just should have kept a better eye on you." She looked at the green-spattered rock. "What in the world were you doing?"

"Oh! I was cutting a plant, and one of them . . . *squished* funny. And I saw it had these, like, strings? In it. And the way it squished was funny, and I wanted to see what happened if I squished more, but there were only a couple, so I kept looking until I found a lot of them in a big clump . . ."

Sakura shook her head. It was *so* very Hitomi. She got an idea in her head and it literally took over. "Well, look, Dad's back. Let's get back to camp."

Hitomi looked back at the rock reluctantly. "But I want to bring it with me."

"A bunch of squished plants? Hitomi, how could we carry it? It's stuck to the rock! Even if it wasn't, it'd just be a big squashy mess!" To prove her point she grabbed a mass of the fibers at the edge and pulled.

Most of the mass of pounded plants peeled off the rock in a single sheet, translucently green in the sun.

Chapter 16

"Barkcloth," Laura repeated wonderingly, looking at the green sheet which was slowly coming apart under repeated handling.

"A beginning to it, I think, yes," Caroline said. "The Polynesians made something like this, called *tapa*. We'll have to do some experiments, but ... I think Hitomi might have found us something really important."

Hitomi looked very proud.

Laura bent down. "But you also could have gotten yourself hurt."

The youngest Kimei looked down. *And she looks so tragic it makes me want to hug her and tell her it's all right. But I can't. Not here.*

"Your sister told you to stay near her, she explained why, and you still didn't listen."

"I'm sorry!"

"*Sorry* is good, honey, but it's not good enough. We can't trust you to listen yet, I guess. You're still young. But that means you have to stay with someone all the time from now on. That could slow down everything we're trying to do, because whoever that is won't be

145

able to concentrate on something else. They'll have to be watching you."

Hitomi looked up, tears running down her face. "I'm *sorry*, Mommy!"

"So are we, Hitomi. We're very glad you're safe, and this cloth-stuff you've accidentally invented might really be important, but you could have been killed. If you behave *very* well the next week or three, maybe we'll change the rules."

Hitomi sniffled, but nodded. "Okay."

Now I can give her that hug. With Hitomi still clinging to her neck, she glanced at Sakura. "You aren't—"

"—I know, Mom, don't you think I know it was my fault? You left her with me and I lost her."

The tears and shakiness in her second-oldest child's voice told her the lesson had been taken to heart. "All right. Don't forget this. You know what could have happened."

"Yes." The reply was almost a whisper. "I didn't think of anything else all the time I was looking for her."

"Then I'll let it go." She turned to Akira, putting down Hitomi. "Now what is that thing you've brought with you?"

"Not thing, *things*," her husband corrected. "What we carried with us is a sort of crustacean—a general observation, not a biological classification, let me note—and two of those hole dwelling ambush predators. 'Minimaws,' Whips wants to call them."

Now Laura could see that what she'd taken for a creature with two long tentacles around a huge blocky body was a blocky, cuboid creature bracketed by two things like the one Whips had killed. "Why minimaw?"

"They look and act something like miremaws," Whips answered, "but they're so much smaller."

"Good enough. Minimaw it is, then."

"I'm going to have to come up with proper Lincolnian taxonomy and nomenclature," Akira said.

"I suppose we're going to try that crustacean thing?"

"Tests show it should be edible—well, the main meat. I think the internal organs are questionable. Whips and I dragged it down to the water's edge and gutted it first. I should note that was *not* easy; the shell is extremely tough."

"Awfully large to drag. I'm surprised you got it all the way here, Whips."

She could tell by the way the colors rippled and his arms curled that he was a bit embarrassed by the praise. "Well, we didn't want to waste it, and it had sort of forced us to shoot it."

"Came after Melody when she was between a couple of rocks and couldn't get away easily," explained Akira. "Took three or four shots—I'm not sure if it was dead when I fired the fourth time or not, but I wasn't taking chances, and I was very grateful you had convinced me to take the gun with me anyway. That armor is *tough*."

Laura looked at the shell; like many creatures, it shaded to light beneath, but the top of the shell, both on the body and on the legs, was a beautiful mottled green. "That could be useful. Plates, big bowls, and such. Did you test the shell itself?"

"You wouldn't want to cook with it. It's got enough metallic content that would probably leach out if you put the wrong kinds of things in it and applied heat. But we could use it for just putting things on, and certainly for wearing, carrying, making things out of, it should be fine." Akira poked at two ridges on the upper portion of the shell; things that looked like jointed spines projected from the ridges. "I think this does share some lineage, somewhere, with the minimaws and other creatures. You'll notice these spinelike things are actually degenerate legs—I think for defense, possibly venomous—which means that it had that effectively fourfold symmetry of the minimaw and those flying things we've seen."

He looked up and grinned apologetically. "Sorry, getting into my professional habits. How were your days, barring the last-minute panic?"

"Tiring," Caroline said honestly, "but we got the disposal pit dug. It goes down a couple of meters and about that long. Until we figure out a better method we can just dump stuff in, bury it, and extend the pit a little each week or so."

Sakura held up a somewhat mangled piece of metal. "I thought I could make a spearhead at first..."

Whips gave a whooping snort accompanied by diamondlike color patterns they all recognized as laughter. "You thought you could just...what, pound it into being a blade?" He laughed again.

"Oh, shut up, Whips!" Sakura's face went red with embarrassment. "Yes, I know, it was stupid. I guess we'll have to figure out some way to make them, though."

Whips settled down. "Grinding works on just about anything. With the right metal, forging can work well, but we'd need to be able to maintain high heat for quite a while." The adolescent Bemmie's engineering training was showing clearly. "Right now we're able to keep the superconductor loop batteries charged with the sun, but if we try rigging up a forge I'll bet we'll be using it way faster than we can recharge."

"Still might be worth a try if we can figure out how to make the furnace—a few hours forging, a couple days off, try again?"

"Mmmmph. Maybe. I'll have to do some calculations. It'd be better if we could actually build a fire, but I'm not sure anything here is going to be burnable—or safe to burn, even if it will."

Laura stood up. "Let's start getting dinner together, everyone. There's going to be plenty to talk about, but we can't leave these things sitting here."

Dressing the miremaws wasn't terribly difficult. The way they were built it was something like gutting and cleaning a long, skinny fish, though you'd get narrower steaks or fillets out of it because of the four-sided design. The blockcrab—as Melody named the large, squarish creature—was more of a challenge. Laura eventually figured out a workable method to get the legs open and get at the meat: score it deeply along the sides with her Shapetool, then lay it across a rock and let Whips pound on it with another rock until it split along the carved seams.

"What do you mean about it being safe to burn, Whips?" asked Caroline.

"Well," Melody answered almost instantly, making Whips twitch slightly, "We know that the plantlike things are—"

"*Melody*," Laura said sternly.

Melody blinked. "What . . . oh."

"'Oh' indeed. The question was asked of Whips. I know you like to show off what you know, but let the people asked answer. Don't be rude."

Melody bit her lip. "Yes, Mom."

"See that you remember it."

Whips himself had an apologetic pattern rippling on his skin. "Dr. Kimei—"

"Whips—Harratrer—I know what you're going to say, but it's necessary. We may be the only people around for ten light-years, but we still need to be reasonably polite to each other."

"Sorry, Whips," Melody said. There was in fact a note of genuine regret, even if part of her posture still said *But I knew the answer!*

"It's okay, Mel," Whips said. "To answer the question, Caroline, it's because we don't know what this stuff is made of. In Europa, of course, we didn't have fires—we used vents for cooking—but even there, some vents were safe to cook with, some weren't. Here, well, we don't know yet if there's anything like wood. Wood's just cellulose, mostly, and burns pretty well, but if I remember right there were still some plants you didn't want to burn even on Earth."

"Quite a few, actually," Laura said. "I remember a neighbor of ours who got exposed to oleander smoke and got pretty sick. There's quite a few others in different parts of the world."

"So," Whips went on," we don't even know if any of the stuff that looks like trees and plants will burn—well, I mean, will burn well enough to make fires with—and if it will, we haven't got any idea if any of it will be safe."

"We'd better see if we can find out," Akira said slowly, even as he started up the stove. "If anything happens to our stove, we'll need *some* way to cook our food—maybe even to heat wherever we end up living, if our continent drifts into a less comfortable region. And fire has, historically, been one of the best defenses against any dangerous animal."

"Might be less effective on things which have never encountered fire—if things don't naturally burn here," Sakura pointed out.

"Ha! A definite point, Sakura. They'd have to learn what it feels like to get burned, rather than just avoid fire in general."

"I was wondering about fire anyway," Sakura said. "After my complete failure at making a spearhead, I thought we might be able to make a bow with that flexible support rod, but needing arrows with points put me back to the problem of spearheads, but then I remembered reading something about—"

"—fire-hardened arrows!" Melody burst out, then immediately looked contrite.

"'Sokay, Mel," Sakura said with a grin. "I was going to say I don't know much about it, so if you do . . . ?"

"I was reading . . . well, some survival stories and things, so I looked up a lot of stuff on that," Melody said, "and it's still in my omni. Basically you put the tip into a bed of coals and rotate it, pull it out and rub it with a coarse stone to get char off, and repeat until you've got the point you want. According to my references, doing the repeated rubbing with a good stone often helps by embedding bits of stone in the wood, but the real effect is caused by driving out the moisture in the wood and polymerizing other parts of the plant into a harder form." She got a thoughtful expression. "But we don't know if there's real wood here, so that technique might not work."

"Couldn't we cut out arrowheads from the blockcrab's shell?" Hitomi asked. Akira put some fried minimaw in front of her. "Yum!"

Conversation was temporarily interrupted as the food

was served. Laura thought the blockcrab meat was very tasty, though a bit chewy, but both Hitomi and Sakura spat it out. "Ugh!" Sakura said, with Hitomi concurring. "Bitter, *nasty* bitter."

"That's strange," Caroline said. "I taste hardly any bitterness. It tastes sort of . . . like lemony duck with a lobster texture."

"Well, *I* taste bitter. It's almost like wine—that alcohol taste."

"Ah," Akira said with a nod. "Specific sensitivities to tastes, like cilantro. Many people think cilantro tastes like soap, while most other people don't taste a hint of that flavor. Well, then, everyone else can have some more blockcrab, and I'll serve you and Hitomi more miremaw. Hopefully we can find some vegetables or fruits that are edible, and perhaps there are ways of eliminating the taste you don't like." He continued, muttering about different ways of marinating or preparing meat.

Whips wasn't saying anything; based on the way he was shoveling the blockcrab into his mouth, Laura figured he liked it far too much to waste time talking.

After dinner, Hitomi wanted to go back up and look for more of the possible barkcloth plants with someone, but Laura shook her head. "Hitomi, it's time for bed."

"But Mommy, the sun is still up!"

"I know, honey, but that's because the day's much longer on this planet. Little girls still need their sleep on time."

Hitomi kept protesting as she was dragged inside, but by the time Laura had made sure her littlest girl was all clean and given her bedtime story, Hitomi's eyes were sagging shut all on her own, inside the cool dimness of the shelter. That wasn't surprising, Laura thought.

By her omni, it was actually the equivalent of nine in the evening—well past Hitomi's usual bedtime. Sakura was already getting herself ready for bed, with Melody having just gotten out of the minimum-water bath.

They'd have to find more water soon. Put the main shell of the blockcrab out to catch water in case it rains? That might work.

She went out to join Akira; he gave a gesture, closing a file he must be viewing in his omni, as she approached. "Sun's finally starting to go down."

"Yes; I'm afraid it'll be full nighttime by the time we hit our next day cycle."

She shook her head and smiled. "It'll take some getting used to." Laura looked back at the shelter, and then over to Whips digging in for his vigil and torpor. "Whips can extract water from the ocean, right?"

"Yes, he's not in any danger of dehydration now." He slipped his arm around her shoulders and pulled her close. "You're worried about our supply."

"Well, of course."

"I think we'll be all right. It looked to me like there might be a stream a couple of kilometers up from where we stopped our exploration. We'll check that out soon enough."

"And if there isn't?"

Caroline answered from behind them. "Then we can probably dig a well."

"A well?" Laura was puzzled. "Caroline, we're surrounded by the sea here, and most of the rock looks... awfully porous. Won't we just end up with salt water?"

Caroline looked up—at only 165 centimeters she hadn't much choice when talking to her mother, who topped her by nearly twenty centimeters—and shook her head. "I don't think so. You see, salt water is denser than fresh, and in many island settings that means that if you get a reasonable frequency of rainfall, a 'lens' of freshwater forms on top of the salt water trapped underground. Since the pores in the ground don't let the water move fast, waves and such aren't going to mix it up. So you get a pretty thick layer of fresh water if you're fairly far inland."

"Planetography studies are coming in handy," Akira said.

"Well, the geology parts," Caroline said modestly.

"And your knowledge of suns and planets," he reminded her.

"We are very lucky," Laura said bluntly. "Just seven of us and we have an expert biologist, a doctor, someone who's *almost* a planetographer, and people who know something about other fields." She looked across the water. "Imagine getting wrecked here without any of that."

The three were silent for a few moments. "Well, we aren't without that," Caroline finally said, "and we'll be all right, I hope." She glanced back at the shelter and up at her omni, perched above as high as Akira had been able to mount it. "I'm exhausted, Mom. I'm going to bed now."

"Go ahead, hon. We'll go to bed after you," Laura said. Honestly, she *was* tired—and she could see Akira was, too—and it was just about time to turn in, no matter what the confusing sun said. But while waiting, she could just lean against her husband, and he against her, and relax, looking at their new home, which—just maybe—wasn't going to succeed in killing them.

Chapter 17

Whips jolted awake as a loud, strident *beep! beep! beep!* sounded from somewhere above him. That was the camp alarm! Something was coming through the perimeter!

The night of Lincoln was, by Earthly standards, pitch-black; even if one of Lincoln's two moons had been up, they were too small to shed very much light.

But Whips' ancestors were from the utterly light-less sea of Europa, orbiting Jupiter in the farther reaches of the solar system, living beneath kilometers of solid ice cold enough to freeze air. There, the only light came from other creatures or strange natural processes, and any creature that could see at all had eyes that could wring every possible bit of data from every photon they could catch. To Whips, the blazing stars above made the black night nearly as bright as day.

Plowing its way up the gouged scar of *LS-5*'s crash was something huge—ten, maybe fifteen meters long. Its hide glistened wetly in the starlight and air hissed from it as it breathed, a round, wormlike thing with rings of serrated white at intervals along the body, crowned with a writhing mass of tentacles surrounding a mouth like a grinder.

It was also headed straight for the shelter, and Whips knew it would be a matter of seconds only before someone came out to see what the alarm was—emerging right into that tentacled mass.

Whips heaved himself up out of his land-nest and simultaneously bellowed loudly, even as he sought around desperately for something to throw or swing with.

The movement and bellow did, at least, accomplish what Whips hoped. The monster slewed around, facing directly towards him, and started flowing in his direction. Whips humped backwards as fast as he could, grabbing with tail grippers, curling his body back and shoving back with the elbow pads on his lower two arms. The tentacles lashed towards him but he wasn't—quite—in reach yet.

Laura shoved her way out of the tent flap and said something shocked and probably rude, but at that moment the thing gave vent to a howling roar which drowned her out. Despite the insulated walls of the shelter, Whips could hear responding startled screams from inside.

The thing gathered itself and lunged. One thick, velvet-looking tendril brushed Whips and he heard himself let out a steam-whistle shriek of pain. That stung!

With horror he realized he'd slipped in the sand; the thing was about to catch him!

Two sharp reports rang out as Laura fired the SurvivalShot twice. The creature gave a low-pitched bubbling growl and swung about towards her.

"Look out, Laura! It's like the anemones!" Whips felt a faint numbness radiating from the sting, but his internal nanos and his own self-awareness told him the damage was actually minimal. A human getting stung, however, might be really bad.

Laura dove to the side, the deadly tendrils smacking the shelter and causing it to shudder, but missing their target.

But Whips realized that if it followed Laura, something that size could probably rip the shelter apart, or crush it if the rigidity currents keeping it up failed. He took a breath and then charged forward as fast as he could, synchronizing rear anchor-feet and arms, and threw himself on the monster, arms spread wide.

He felt dozens of his attack barbs sink deep. The creature's pained, writhing attempt to escape caused the barbs to rip gashes in its hide. But the force of the thing's twisting motion yanked Whips around, dragging him across the sand, slamming him down like a ball on a string. Two of the tentacles wrapped around him, and it felt like two belts of fire strapped to his body. Grimly, he hung on, dug in, tried to pull himself closer. If he could just bite the thing...

The SurvivalShot popped again, twice, and the other Kimeis were shouting, screaming, out of the shelter, but were they safe? Whips didn't dare let go, he couldn't bear the thought that he might let this thing go too soon and get his friends—his adoptive family—killed. At this range he let the agony focus his cry, let go with a stunshout that rippled the creature's skin as though it were struck. Then he heard half a dozen small impacts. Rocks? Were they throwing *rocks*?

Another tentacle caught at him, but he pulled as

hard as he could, clamped down with his beak and let his tongue start ripping into the leathery, bitter-tasting flesh. The venom was starting to work its way through him, his resistance being overcome by volume, but he refused to let go, even though he found his vision becoming distant, his arms trying to become shaky...

Suddenly the monster wrenched itself around, trying to flee. The Kimei family were still pelting it with rocks and debris from the crash, with more shots from the hydrogen-powered pistol slamming into it. The thing rammed into the ridge of the crash scar, and Whips, finding he could hold on no longer, was scraped from the thing's side.

But it didn't take the opportunity to turn on him. It just continued swiftly slithering away, back into the water from whence it had come.

The sounds now were distorted, strange, like they were if your sound membrane was half-in, half-out of the water, and everything was painful and drifting and distant at the same time. "Whips? Oh, God, look, he's been stung all over!"

"Settle down, Sakura. I've got his nanotelemetry." That was Laura's voice, but somehow Whips couldn't tell which of the figures over him, shining bright lights, was which.

"Will he—?"

"*Quiet,* all of you!" Akira's usually quiet voice was raised, worried, but filled with iron authority. The others went silent. *Wow,* Whips thought disjointedly, *he bellows like an Old One...*

"Neurotoxin," a voice muttered, wavering in and out. "But there's natural resistance...similar to other poisons..."

Vaguely, Whips realized he was losing consciousness, finding himself unable to understand the noises around him. He couldn't feel more than the most distant jab of fear, though. The numbness had spread to his brain and even thought, fragmented already, was fading.

Light faded, dwindled, became gray fog.

But then the gray brightened, and sound began to come back, at first just incomprehensible murmurs, and then faint, almost random words: "...responding...hope that...killed..."

His eyes finally began to respond. He felt shaky, sick as he had ever been, but his mind was slowly clearing. He turned one eye, saw Laura kneeling next to him. Pain like fire burned across most of his skin, but it seemed to be fading now. "Everyone...okay?" he managed to ask.

"Okay?" Laura repeated, and then shook her head; a pair of tears suddenly rolled down her face. "Whips, *you* were the one hurt!"

"Knew...if it got any of you...probably kill you," he managed. It still hurt a lot.

"You were right," she said, voice and eyes back in control. "Your people have a higher resistance to some toxins, of which this was fortunately one. Even so, closing in on it and letting it sting you—"

"Didn't have much choice," he said. The sickness was rising inside, like something coming to a boil. *Oh-oh.* "Um, excuse me..."

His shaking body tried to betray him, but he somehow kept control until he reached the waste pit and voided everything he'd eaten into it. He lay there, gasping and shuddering, letting his tail hang over the edge in case another fit hit him. So much for dinner.

Sakura had suddenly reached him, and her fierce embrace made him feel a tiny bit better. "Whips, are you okay?"

"Feeling a little better, maybe."

"It'll take a while. I had to use what was on hand, which wasn't ideal," Laura said apologetically. "Your nanos and your natural resistance kept things under control long enough for me to fake up something like an antidote, but it's not perfect."

"As long as I'm going to recover, that's good."

"What *was* that?" Melody's question was somewhat rhetorical—it wasn't like anyone had any better answer than she did—but she was terrified, and Whips couldn't blame her. "Why did it attack us?"

"That's a good question, Melody," Akira said, his calm voice making even Whips' pained, sick mind feel a little steadier. "Why would it attack us? It crawled a long way out of the water to get here. How could it have sensed us?"

Something about the question nagged at Whips. "I don't think it did sense us. Not out there, anyway," he said slowly.

"Hm? But then why come here? Do you think this is just the way it normally hunts—comes up on land and looks for things that are sleeping?"

Whips concentrated, trying to force his brain to work. "No. Well, maybe . . . but it has to have some way of choosing where it comes up."

Melody suddenly froze. "Oh. Oh, I think I know, Dad." She pointed over to the now-tumbled tables and chairs. "The blockcrab—"

Now he heard Akira Kimei swear. After a moment, he shook his head. "*Baka*. We gutted it and then dragged it up to camp, leaving a perfect trail of blood straight here."

Whips waved his hands affirmatively. "That was just what I was trying to think of. Predators like that in Europa will follow scent-trail."

"Well," Laura said, "no real harm done. We've learned that lesson and won't do it again."

"But that's only a temporary fix, Mom," said Sakura. Now that she was sure that Whips wasn't dying, she was hugging a still scared and crying Hitomi and getting her to settle down.

"I know it," Laura said. She knelt down and hugged Whips. Even though touching the stung areas hurt, it was still comforting . . . and the pain was fading. "First . . . thank you, thank you so very much, Whips. If you hadn't distracted it, it would have grabbed me when I stepped out. And without you fighting it, I don't think we could have stopped it."

"I second that," Akira said gravely. "Our pistol—and throwing rocks—stung it and infuriated it, but I really don't think we did enough damage by ourselves to drive it off, or that we could have without someone getting killed. You risked—"

"Nothing, sir," Whips interrupted, feeling so embarrassed that the pain and sickness were secondary. "I'm not going to survive without you either. You're my *family* now, right? And we always fight for our family. Together."

The two Kimei parents were quiet for a moment, Akira in particular wearing an expression that looked oddly like vindication, and then they simply nodded. "You are our family, yes," Laura said unsteadily, and he could see the tears again. "And we will fight for you. Together."

"Always," agreed Akira and Sakura, and the others echoed it—even little Hitomi, who reached out and patted him gently.

Then Laura looked out into the dark, where the thing had fled. "But we don't want to do fighting we don't have to, and now we know we are in danger here. We have to find somewhere else to live—and do it soon."

"But that," Akira said, "will be something for later."

Whips nodded, and finally felt himself relaxing, the sickness starting to ebb...and exhaustion coming close behind. "Later," he repeated, and closed his eyes.

Chapter 18

Sakura cut, perhaps with unnecessary viciousness, at a bamboolike stalk that blocked her passage. The machete—cut and ground down under Whips' direction from one of the pieces of steel that had formed a major wing support—sliced cleanly through the stalk, which fell, spattering her with drops of blood and an explosion of crimson tendrils from the flowerlike ends; these were, fortunately, not venomous. "Oh, ick."

"Sakura, slow down," her father admonished. "You don't need to break all the trail yourself. And if you insist on chopping your way along like some old-fashioned axe murderer, you can't expect to stay nice and clean."

For some reason, the forest on the farther side of the floating continent—at least in their area—was thicker than on their side. This expedition, with her, Dad, and Caroline, was an attempt to cut straight across from the column where she'd been stung to the other side, which should come out somewhere near where Dad thought there might be a stream.

Water was dripping on her from above, too. There had been a heavy rainstorm last night, which had at least reduced the worry about water, but they still

163

didn't know anything about Lincoln's seasons. This might be the "rainy season" and the dry season could leave them without water for weeks.

At least the dripping water helped her wash the icky stuff off, but the combination of heat and water wasn't very pleasant.

Sakura slowed down, waiting for the other two to catch up. Whips would have come along but he wasn't quite recovered from his fight against what Melody had named a direworm, causing her father to lecture everyone on the differences between worms, cnidarians, echinoderms, and how none of that applied here—and then agree that direworm was a very good name for the thing.

"Hey, Dad," she said once they were caught up and had started pushing their way forward again, "you'd said you thought you'd figured out some things about our native life here?"

"Hmm?" Her father had been studying a small creature like a green box with bright lavender eyes, apparently spinning a web of some sort. "Oh, yes. Well, it's nothing staggeringly surprising, but it is very indicative. From what I've seen, most things here—with the possible exception of our four-winged quadbirds, as Laura's called them—have evolved to be able to survive both on land and underwater, at least for a time. This is rather what I expected to find, of course, but it's exciting to have it confirmed."

"And a little worrisome," Caroline said.

She looked at Caroline. "Why?"

"I think Caroline means because of what it implies," her father answered. Caroline nodded, and he continued, "If these islands stayed stable for, oh, millions upon millions of years, you'd expect obligate air-breathers to become fairly common. There's a biological cost for keeping both options open, so to speak, and something that can just focus on one should gain a considerable advantage. The ocean-dwelling ones certainly are nicely focused."

Sakura thought, then understanding dawned. "Oh. You mean that if they're all ready for either one, then these islands break up, roll over, whatever, fairly often on an evolutionary scale."

"So I would guess, yes." They rounded another of the great columns, this one slightly shorter than some others, and pushed on into another cluster of heavy jungle. Sakura watched every unfamiliar object narrowly; the last thing she wanted was to end up stung again.

The path ahead lightened, and suddenly she could see into a moderately sized clearing. "Oh, wow," she whispered.

In the clearing, apparently grazing on the blue-crystalline semi-grass that carpeted the little meadow, was a herd of creatures. They had blunt heads with big, rounded eyes, bodies supported by several squat legs, and a pair of ridges extending on either side of the body. But what was surprising was that they were covered with a lovely blue-green material that looked—at least from this distance—like fur. The animals measured about two meters long on average, but Sakura could see several much smaller, but generally similar creatures, trotting around and between the others, nuzzling their flanks, and generally being treated the way that young animals are everywhere: as a beloved but sometimes having-to-be-tolerated nuisance.

"My goodness," Akira said bemusedly. "Their top jaws seem to have fused, though the bottom still splits. Other than that odd tripartite jaw, they have an almost Earthly look about them. Like . . . like a capybara, in a way."

"They're *adorable*," Sakura said. "I wonder if they're dangerous."

"We have to assume so," Caroline said.

Two of the creatures nearest them straightened and looked at the humans at the edge of the clearing. The two gave warbling chirps, and the rest of the herd moved restlessly. Other cries were heard, and Sakura could see the youngsters moving closer in.

"Defensive reaction to the unknown. They're tightening into a better defended group," her father said, in a fascinated tone. "The scouts or guards have moved closer too, but they're staying on the outside and watching us, obviously ready to defend the others."

He frowned. "This isn't a new reaction. They obviously do this often."

"Which means there must be some pretty big and mobile predators around," Caroline said slowly.

"I'm afraid so. But this may be a very big find. Those animals might be tamable, if we can figure out how to make use of their herd instincts."

"You mean domesticate them? What for?"

"I'm not sure—yet. But anything from meat to draft animals. We have soil, we have water, there are undoubtedly plants we can eat here—agriculture seems like a good idea. But trying to plow a field by hand . . . let's say I'd rather find an alternative."

Caroline nodded. "The larger ones are about the size of . . . oh, what was that breed . . . Shetland ponies.

Not exactly massive draft animals, but still pretty big, and strong enough for a lot of things. If they can be domesticated. I have no idea if that's possible, though."

"It's worth thinking about."

Sakura grinned. "I could ride one!"

"If it didn't decide to bite you," Caroline pointed out.

Her father finished getting imagery of the creatures and gestured. "Let's move on. No need to keep these things on edge."

As the three of them moved around the edge of the clearing, the small herd of animals edged cautiously around, trying to keep the same position with respect to them, moving under some of the large treelike growths fringing the clearing in that direction.

Without warning, something lashed down from above, grasped one of the blue-green capybaralike creatures, and yanked it screaming out of sight into the forest canopy above. Sakura gave her own yelp of startled shock, and heard similar sounds of consternation from her father and Caroline.

For the herd it was not consternation; it was panic. The entire mass of creatures stampeded away, even as a second pair of tendrils streaked out and slashed at one of the rearguard, sending the animal tumbling. One of the littler animals gave a trilling shriek and ran towards the one that had been struck. The bigger animal let out an emphatic bellow and got up, running with a pronounced limp; the little one turned and fled just ahead of the limping one. A mother and its baby?

Something leapt from the trees just behind the fleeing herd and thudded to the ground. It scuttled on multiple jointed legs and held two tentacles coiled back, waiting to strike. It looked ungainly, like a cross between a lobster and a squid, but it moved shockingly fast. It was closing the distance between itself and the limping creature.

Sakura didn't know what caused it. Maybe it was the pitiful trill of the baby as it saw the thing coming, or the sight of the parent creature obviously trying to keep itself between the baby and the oncoming predator. But something drove a knife of empathy and rage straight into her heart and she was suddenly charging out, her father and sister screaming at her.

Part of her—most of her—realized how stupid this was—and how it was even more stupid than she'd originally thought. They might think she was another predator trying to attack!

But instead, the running herd merely split around her as she ran. The limping creature and its cub were streaking closer, but the tentacular predator was faster still. *Got to . . .*

Instinct and reflexes of a born pilot were the only thing that saved her. She saw a ripple on one side of the predator and dove forward, the striking tentacle passing just over her head. She rolled to her feet, feeling the ice-cold of adrenaline washing through her. The predator was now less than a meter away, but she swung hard—

The concussion of impact tore the machete from her hand and sent her tumbling away, bruised and dizzy. Sakura heaved herself back up, trying to focus as the predator shrieked in rage, but she knew she didn't have any more weapons.

Abruptly her father was there, plunging an alloy-tipped spear straight into the thing's shrieking mouth, rolling aside as the tendrils ripped through the air he'd occupied. Then Caroline, pale as paper, brought down her own machete with a two-handed blow that split the thing's carapace. It spasmed and went limp.

Sakura shook her head, clearing it, even as her father—with one more glance at the creature to make sure it wasn't moving again—ran to her. "*Sakura*! Sakura, are you all right?"

"I . . . I think so, Dad. Just a little shaken up . . ."

Her father's face suddenly transformed from concern to fury, more angry than she had ever seen him. "*Bakame!* What the hell were you doing? A little shaken up? I . . . you . . . I should give you a shaking you'll never forget!"

"And I'll be there to help!" Caroline stomped her foot as though that might be the only thing keeping her from slapping her sister. "Of all the utterly idiotic things . . ."

"I'm *sorry!*" she said, and she was. That was so *stupid*.

The shock and fear and guilt overcame her and she started crying. "I know, I was so stupid, I'm sorry, I'm sorry, Dad, I don't know why . . ."

Akira sagged to his knees, then touched her shoulder. "I know perfectly well *why*. But we can't do that, honey. We can't afford to lose anyone. And even if we could, your mother and I would be devastated if—"

"I know. I know . . ."

She looked up and then saw movement beyond her father.

The wounded animal and its baby were standing maybe fifteen or twenty meters away, looking at them. Farther behind, the herd waited, shifting restlessly.

Her father and Caroline turned slowly, and for a

moment all was still; the blue-green animals with deep green eyes staring at the humans, the humans looking back and wondering.

Then the parent-animal snorted quietly, and turned and walked, still limping slightly, away. The baby looked back and followed. There was no sign of hurry or concern in the herd now.

Her father took a shaky breath, let it out. "That . . . could be very promising." He looked down and the anger was back, though more muted. "But that does not excuse your behavior, Sakura. If you cannot control yourself, you're little better than Hitomi, and I may have to ground you—even though we really cannot afford that."

She looked down. *No way I can argue. He's right. I saw the little animal running and the mother—I assumed it was a mother—hurt, and I just acted, no thinking. No better than Hitomi. Maybe worse, because I know better than that.*

She forced herself to look up and meet her father's gaze—and with him looking so angry, that wasn't easy. Akira Kimei was almost never the angry one, that was her mother who brought down the wrath of God usually. "I know, Dad. I won't do anything like that ever again. I promise. I knew it was stupid as soon as I found myself out there, and I know I was luckier than I deserve."

He closed his eyes, then opened them and nodded. The anger had faded to a warning behind his gaze. "All right. Then let's keep going; if you're not hurt, we've still got work to do." He looked to the body, lying not far away. "And the first work is to take a look at this beast."

Sakura nodded and moved towards the body. She glanced towards the trees from which the thing had come. *And another way I was lucky; what if these predators had decided to protect each other? We'd all be dead.*

She gripped the handle of her machete and ripped it out of the body. *I won't endanger my family again. I won't!*

As she bent over the animal and listened to her father's discussion of the thing they'd killed, those words echoed deep inside her, not merely a decision, but an oath. *I won't endanger them. I won't.*

Never again.

Chapter 19

"Oh, my. It's *beautiful*."

"It is that."

Laura stared in admiration at the large pond, or small lake, that stretched out before her, a pure blue that deepened to blue-black in the center. "Sakura said it was the bluest blue she'd ever seen, but I have to admit I doubted her."

"Oh, she was right." Akira put his arm around her waist. "I'm pretty sure that what we're looking at is the Lincoln equivalent of a 'blue hole' on Earth. I saw a couple when I was doing my graduate work in bio. Tests show that the surface layer, at least, is fresh water, as is the little stream we followed up here."

"Tides don't reach up this high?" Laura asked.

Akira chuckled and shook his head. "Another area where our assumptions conflict with Lincoln. We're *floating*, Laura. There's a bit of a ripple and lag given the size of this drifting island, but not much; there aren't tides of any sort we're used to. So there's no real equivalent to the tidal zone as such, just the wave area; we do of course get waves and such, but you don't get the slow progression of water coming in and then going out."

"All right, you've made me feel stupid. I should have thought of that."

"I have no doubt we'll constantly be noticing things that we should have thought of, but didn't. Lincoln's a very subtle trap; things seem so close to things we know from Earth, or Whips knows from Europa, and then suddenly we come face to face with the difference of this place."

"So," she said, changing the subject, "Why did you bring me out here? Not that I mind having a few minutes alone with my husband," she noted, and gave him an unhurried kiss before she continued, "but we can't afford to not be doing things that are useful, either."

"Caroline's taken the responsibility to give us this time. She, Sakura, and Hitomi are making barkcloth, now that we've figured out how to make it really work, while Melody and Whips work on cutting the meat of the three minimaws we caught up for drying." He glanced at her. "That was a brilliant idea you had on making a solar grill."

She felt a touch of heat on her cheeks. "Oh, I'm sure that Whips or someone would have—"

"Maybe, but they didn't, and you did."

Truth be told, she was proud of that. "The shape of one of the side vent mounts that we found was what suggested it."

"Well, it's working. We can cook without using our limited supply of electricity, and that's so very important. There's no reason to assume our solar cells or batteries are going to run out any time soon—they were designed with at least fifteen-year lives, after all—but we needed some way of surviving without them. The heat box that Whips made out of some of the crab shells should allow us to dry out food for use later."

Akira led her around the edge of the blue pond. Laura could see, by traces of cut plants and plantimal-things along the way, that the prior expedition had come this way as well. "But to get back to your question, I wanted to show you Sakura's brainstorm, which almost made up for her nearly getting killed."

"It was that bad?"

He nodded gravely. "Laura, I was at the point that *I* could have killed her . . . for almost getting killed, if you know what I mean. All trying to save a couple of capys from one of their natural predators."

"Capy?"

"I mentioned they somehow reminded me of capy-baras, so the name stuck. That predator, though—it's an ambush and fast-dash type. We have to keep our eyes up as well as down; they disguise their tendrils as vines and such, and when something wanders underneath . . . *bam!*" He mimed a lightning snatching motion.

Laura glanced uneasily up into the forest canopy. There were a *lot* of loosely hanging vines . . .

"But as I told you, she seems to be taking the lesson to heart. You noticed there wasn't a single protest about being told she'd stay in the camp doing work for the next two weeks. Just asked if she could help make the barkcloth with Hitomi."

"Yes. That was uncharacteristic of her. Or," she amended, "maybe not. She wants to help, and she just learned how following her impulses can cause a lot more problems."

"Yes." Akira grinned and pushed his hair back out

of his eyes as he led her onwards. "They're all holding up well. But I'm worried about that."

She knew what he meant. They were getting past the time where pure shock and emergency were keeping people focused, and where novelty was starting to wear off. "Anyway, what was this brainstorm?"

"We're almost there... Ah! Look ahead. *That* is her brainstorm."

Laura saw, in a small clearing, an absolutely immense column—perhaps one and a half times the height of the others they'd seen in the forest before, and at least twice the diameter, a monstrous cylinder fifty meters high and eleven meters across at the base. Various growths, from vines to the bright red flowery creatures that had stung Sakura, adorned the column. "What about it?"

"We wanted a place to live. She pointed out that this would be perfect."

Laura stopped, staring. The thought was another of the obvious in-hindsight ideas that could stun you for a moment. The columns were hollow—they already knew that—and one this large... "Doesn't anything already live in them?"

"Probably—although most of it will have to be quite small. Lower down there are only relatively small openings, and anything that can reach the top can't be very big."

"Don't *you* go making assumptions, Akira dear. Your arboreal predator-things could probably climb up that column and drop into it very easily. Might make a good hiding or nesting place."

Akira winced. "Oh, well played, Laura. That'll teach me. Yes, I would say you're very right. We'll need to get a good look inside. But still, what do you think?"

"I think it's brilliant, as you said. We'll have to figure out a nice safe way to anchor floors and such, and figure out good ways to cut through safely without imperiling the structure's integrity, and so on . . . but I like it, I really do. An armored treehouse, almost." She studied the column. "But getting up and down . . ."

"Solved, by Whips, when I talked with him last night. Gearing and solar batteries—and a backup hand crank—combined with the winch. Remember the winch?"

She couldn't help but laugh. "The one we thought we'd be using to bring *LS-5* up onto the shore?"

"Yes. We didn't lose it, and the capacity of that thing is just incredibly beyond anything we'll need. Put our solar cells from the shelter up on the top of the column, where they'll always be getting maximum light in, and dedicate a battery or two to the winch, and we should have guaranteed elevators—keeping us from having to climb with stuff in our hands, yet letting us live well above the forest floor. Build a rampway, too, so we can get up and down that way as well."

She walked over to the great column and laid her hand on it. "That sounds like a good plan to me. We should test methods of cutting through the material before we try it here, though—maybe on the column that's fallen near our camp."

"I agree. We don't want to ruin this column by using it for practice."

Laura found herself smiling as she looked up at the huge column. "What will we build with?"

"The trees and treelike things have support elements that are nontoxic and usable, I think. And I've got another surprise for you, and everyone else." She looked down to see his smiling face above a ragged cube of pinkish...

"...wood? Is that *wood*?"

"Close enough, love. It's a very close analogue, I've tested it and it burns... and it's not toxic. Well, not any more than wood usually is, you wouldn't want to breathe in lots of smoke from a standard hickory or oak fire, either."

"Oh, that's... that's wonderful, Akira!" *Wood*. Something that could be burned, or—much more importantly—cut, carved, shaped, used for floors, barriers, cups, bowls, without dealing with the issues of metal or the frangibility of many shells... "That's *wonderful*."

He looked up at her with the same expression she remembered from their dating days—something that was so intensely focused on her that it gave her a thrill down her back, the same thrill she'd had then, too. "And that's why I waited to tell you first. I wanted to watch you smile like that again."

"Oh, Akira..."

There was no decision or thought, just another kiss. And like all the others, it was both familiar and new.

Finally they pulled apart, and she smiled again. "Alas, I don't think it's safe to do anything else here."

"Decidedly not. But I most surely appreciate the implied sentiment. *Domo arigato*." He looked back at the piece of wood. "Such a simple structure, really, sugar molecules interlocked in a layered polymer... and it could be one of the most valuable things on the planet."

She looked around the forest surrounding them and the huge column. "How common is wood here?"

"Oh, it's far from the main component, but there's a sizeable minority of wood-bearing plants. We'll want to be careful about our harvesting habits, but there's plenty for our purposes." He looked back at the column. "So, soon we'll have a home."

Suddenly, a quiver ran through the forest. Debris sifted down from above; the trees swayed. Her hand grabbed Akira's and they stood stock-still, waiting. The swaying and rumbling died away, and in a few moments all seemed back to normal.

"What was *that*?"

Akira frowned. "Caroline was afraid of something like that. The whole floating continent is lifted up and down, moves with the tides, and so on. It *must* have to shift with such motion, and that will sometimes not be a smooth process."

"So even here we'll have earthquakes."

"Yes. We have to assume that they won't become too bad—because we really have no chance to survive if this semi-landmass breaks up on us. We've seen what that looks like in miniature, and it would be utterly lethal. But," he said, turning back towards the pond, "it does mean we'll have to build our house to take a little shaking."

She nodded, and looked around her. A last long, yellow-green leaf was fluttering down from the forest canopy, a reminder that what was up...could fall down.

Chapter 20

"Well, that sort of works," Whips said grudgingly, looking at the centimeter-wide hole in the side of the downed column. "But if we have to do that for all the holes we want, that have to be something like twenty or thirty centimeters wide, this could take *years*."

"I know." Sakura felt irrational frustration welling up in her and managed, barely, to resist the urge to kick the massive stony thing. "That hedral is pretty acidic, but that's only by comparison with other things; it's more like a lemon or orange. Tastes kinda like one, too."

The "hedral" was one of the fruits that Akira and Laura had cleared for consumption, with a fresh, sour taste that came from citric acid, just as in Earth citrus fruits. That particular chemical was a common part of certain metabolic pathways which were nearly universal. Laura had dubbed the fruits "hedrals" because they came in faceted shapes somewhat like polyhedral dice.

"It proves we were right; concentrated acids will weaken the material. Probably carbonic acid in the atmosphere slowly dissolves them too. If we had a stronger acid . . ."

"But we don't. Not right now. Mel and Mom have been looking into making chemical stuff, and from what we've got right now, things like nitric acid and sulphuric are just not in the picture. You might get some hydrochloric out of animals' stomachs or something, and Mel said that one of her references says something about making it by heating salt in clay vessels, but that sounds like something really dangerous to me." Sakura heard her voice rising slightly unsteadily, sounding much angrier and more worried than made sense.

Whips either didn't notice or chose to ignore it, instead just waving his arms in agreement. "Hmm... yes, that could work. High-temperature steam and salt... that would produce hydrochloric acid and soda, which could be useful. But you're right about needing to be very careful. I'm not sure we've got anything quite like clay, anyway, but it would be a problem."

Sakura took a deep breath. She knew she'd been touchier than usual and not just because of her stupid moment that almost got her killed. She had to make sure she didn't start snapping at people. She glanced over at other parts of the fallen column. Attempts to just chop or gouge through the massive walls of the thing had mostly failed miserably; her father thought that if they had a good hard-steel pickaxe and someone strong enough to use it well they might get somewhere, but almost all the metal they had was much more lightweight and not at all suited for that kind of purpose—even if they could forge something that large and heavy, something that Whips wasn't sure of even with a large solar furnace for heat.

A black-edged hole was visible a little ways down

the column—demonstrating that fire could also weaken the material over a fairly wide area. "If we had a *blowtorch* we could get this done a lot faster."

"Yes," agreed Whips. "But we don't."

"You're a lot of help."

"Your sarcasm is no help at all."

"Makes me feel better." That was a lie, a part of her realized. It released the anger but not enough of it.

"Well, it makes *me* feel like you're just dismissing me, throwing silt in my face!" Whips' voice had an edge in it now, a sudden edge, and he turned and slapped down hard on the column, pulling back with a ripping sound as he tore a wide swath of vines from it.

The action was so abrupt and violent that it shocked Sakura out of her own brown study. "Oh. I'm sorry, Whips. I wasn't thinking."

The adolescent Bemmie was staring at the tangle of torn plants and plantlike things in his one set of arm-talons with a bemused expression. Slowly he retracted the sharp claws and the stuff dropped with a rattling hiss to the ground. "I guess I wasn't either. Just letting my currents carry me without thought. I didn't mean to snap at you." The sudden frightened undertone in his voice echoed his other concern: *I'm not unstable!*

Sakura looked down. "Well, I deserved it. I was being nasty for no reason."

"Not for no reason," Whips said after a moment. "It's just getting harder, isn't it?"

She couldn't pretend to misunderstand him, but that just meant she really had to face it, and that... that really hurt. "You mean...that this isn't going to change. The situation, I mean."

He hesitated a moment and visibly deflated. "That we're stuck here, with only a few remnants of technology to help us? Yes. Probably forever. Even if, somehow, *Outward Initiative* survived, and guesses we did too, it will be at least a year before someone could possibly get a rescue mission up. And how will we even know they're there, or be able to signal them? They'll be looking for the lifeboat transmitters, maybe even a beacon buoy, not searching every centimeter of the planet. If they recognize the new planet, maybe a scientific expedition will come out here...in ten years. But there's an awful lot of planets already being studied, there's nothing hugely important about just one new one."

"But Lincoln's unique. I've never heard of anything like these floating continents, have you?"

Whips snorted. "No, never. But noticing that will probably take years of study by one of the remote telescope arrays—if someone bothers, rather than just doing a quick survey that says 'here's the major landmasses, it's got typical livable biosphere,' if you know what I mean there."

"Yeah." Sakura forced the frustration down. This was getting them nowhere. "Where were we before we started getting all snippy with each other? Oh yeah. The lack of a blowtorch."

"It would be such a perfect solution," Whips said mournfully. "The columns are really hard to catch on fire, since they've got a lot of silicon-based structure, but since they've also got carbon-based structure you can break that down with fire easily and that really erodes the strength. Once you've done that, you can bash it apart with a rock or dig it away with a shell.

But no way to direct the fire. If we had something like thermite paste—something that would stick to the column while it burned—now that would be perfect."

"About the only way to make a paste that burns here, though, would be fat . . . and that's just going to melt and run down the side. Not what we want."

"If we could just lay it down like this one, it wouldn't be a problem."

The two of them sat quietly for a few minutes, thinking. Sakura finally went to the bucket they had nearby—once a small blockcrab shell—and used her drinking shell to dip up some water. "If we could lay it down and put it back up, I think we'd have to have technology that made it no longer important."

"Yes. I . . ." Whips trailed off, staring at her with all three eyes.

When he didn't move for a moment, she looked behind herself, then back. "What is it?"

"Cups," he said, slowly.

"What?"

"Cups!" Whips said, with more force, as if a sudden revelation had struck him.

"Cups?" She looked down at her own, and suddenly it was snatched from her hand. "Hey!"

And Whips was pressing it up against the side of the cylinder. "See?"

Now she *did* see. "Whips, that's perfect! We just have to drill little holes like those to support a sort of . . . firebox, I guess—that gets held up against the column and burns until it's weak enough to get through! Then . . ." She frowned. "We have to keep burning our way through—those things are *thick*."

"Sticks on fire, stuffing the hole?"

"Might work. Maybe we need to get some kind of burnable oil or alcohol or something. It's kind of porous—maybe we could soak it and set it on fire in steps?"

"There's an idea. If it can hold its own fuel, it can self-destruct according to a design." Whips gave the tightening of the arms that equated to a frown, combined with a dull rippling pattern. "Liquid burnable material is going to be the limit. The side cup approach doesn't need liquid, but packing a hole with burning solid material probably won't work very well."

Sakura sighed. "Then maybe it's not good enough. We have to get through a couple *meters* of this stuff. Even higher up it's going to be half a meter thick."

"Right."

She thought again about their limited supplies. The only powered machine of note that they had was the winch and its associated block-and-tackle and cable. All the winch could do would be to lift things...

"Wait a minute," she said, an idea slowly dawning.

"What is it?"

"This stuff isn't harder than the titanium alloy fragments we have, right?"

"Nnnoooo," Whips responded slowly. "It's tough, but sawing away at it with some of those pieces made cuts without apparently blunting the alloy much. But it's far too light to make a—"

"I know that—besides, how would you—or Dad— swing a pickaxe thirty meters up? But what about a *drill*?"

"Drill? We don't have a—"

"Put a sort of drillhead, faced with the titanium pieces, in the center of a wheel. Run the winch's line around the wheel. Maybe use some trick to gear it up—I'm not an expert in such designs—but get it spinning and then push it into the column!"

Whips sat stock still for a moment, even his colors drifting to neutral as he thought intensely. Then slowly colors began to ripple brighter and brighter. "That might work. And we could combine it with the fire approach. Weaken the exterior, start drilling through. Perhaps even gear it up to spin something like wood at speeds that heat it up and drive it in with the heat of fire? I don't know, but maybe, just maybe, we can figure something out."

"Let's go back and talk to everyone else. For once everyone's here today."

But as they got close to the main camp, Sakura heard a sound that sent a cold shock through her; Hitomi, crying as though her heart were broken. Sakura broke into a run, sprinting towards the camp. *Is she all right? Are Mom and Dad—?*

She practically tumbled over the edge of the crash scar before she could finally make out the repeated words blurred together in the sobs: "I want to go *home!* I want to go *home!*"

She could see her mother kneeling in front of her youngest sister, who pushed her away and kept crying. Melody was turned away from everyone else but from her vantage point Sakura could see that Mel's face was screwed up in an unsuccessful attempt to keep from crying herself.

The repeated phrase hurt, because she felt exactly the same way. She didn't know what had triggered it, but she, too, was tired of sleeping in the temporary shelter, tired of a menu that was only very slowly expanding and never nearly diverse enough, of days spent hammering fibers into cloth or smoking meat or trying to drill holes into stuff that didn't want holes in it. She hated the rough barkcloth and having to figure out how to stick softer things inside it to cushion the rubbing.

And she was tired of seeing the same faces *all* the time, no one else, no calls, no visits, no one to interrupt or vary the monotony.

"—and I want my *own* bed, I don't *wanna* do any more work, and I want new Jewelbug adventures, and I want to eat . . . want to eat . . . something that's not from *here!*" the little girl sobbed.

"Hitomi, honey, I'm sorry," her mother said, and the sympathy in her voice at least managed to get through; Sakura saw—through the slight warping of her own tears that were trying to get through—Hitomi let her mother pull her over for a hug.

"When's the ship coming *back*, Mommy?"

"Hitomi, we've told you before," her father said, kneeling next to Mom, "we're lost. It may never come back. Maybe it will, but we can't live based on that hope."

That set off another round of sobs, as Hitomi tried to argue against the reality the rest of them—even Melody—knew. Sakura wanted to help, but the whole subject felt like a dull knife in her gut. She felt exactly like Hitomi, and the excitement at the possible solutions she and Whips had found was now gone. Sakura sank into one of the nearby chairs and put her face in her hands, trying to pull some of her own courage back up from the depths.

Even Caroline was silent. Her methodical and

organized approach to life had been utterly shattered by their being marooned on Lincoln, and while she was older and more controlled, Sakura could tell without even looking that Caroline didn't have anything left to give either.

I just... can't. I'm so tired of this place. It's beautiful... and it's scary, and uncomfortable, and there's no one else here. We're all alone.

She glanced at Whips, who was draped above, not even bothering to finish coming down. His arms were almost completely limp and his colors were dull and sluggish. It had to be so much worse for him. At least Sakura had a family. He didn't even have another member of his species here.

That worry about her best friend was enough to grab onto. She forced herself to sit up, but looking around almost broke her again.

Even Mom and Dad look helpless.

We've beaten the crash and all these other things... but I think we're all beating ourselves now...

Chapter 21

Laura tried to comfort Hitomi, but the dull ache in her own heart, the exhaustion in her own mind, echoed that of her little girl entirely. She saw Sakura come down and collapse. Caroline, trying to organize their assembly of homemade tools and utensils, just stopped in the middle and dropped a handful on the ground, sinking to her knees. Melody had her back turned, but Laura could see the shaking of sobs from behind. Even Akira's hand on her shoulder felt perfunctory, a matter of form. There was no strength flowing from it, nothing telling her *this will be all right*, and that was terrifying. They'd been each other's support since they were married. If she couldn't support him, and he couldn't support her . . .

She'd known this was coming. They'd discussed it, she and Akira, what . . . only a week, no, two weeks ago, Earth measure? When they visited Blue Hole Lake and the Great Column. Now that it had happened, though, she had no idea what to do. She could see Whips, dangling so dull and limp that he was nothing but a faded shadow of himself.

Then she saw Sakura glance at her best friend, and

her jaw set, and she straightened. Her face was still devastated, frightened and lost and tired, but she still straightened up and looked, with those fear-stricken yet determined eyes, straight at Laura.

These are my children. I'm not going to let them down.

Slowly, Laura reached out and hugged Hitomi to her tighter. "I know it's hard, sweetheart." She raised her voice. "It's hard for all of us. Even us."

Hitomi looked up for just a moment, uncertainly.

"Yes, honey, even us. I know that sometimes Mommy and Daddy have you do things you don't want to do because they think it's a good thing, but that's not what we're doing here. If we could call the ship back, we would. You all know that. Hitomi, I'm sorry, but you have to accept it."

Hitomi sobbed harder.

"Hitomi," Akira said softly, and after he repeated it a few times, the little six-year-old looked up uncertainly. "Hitomi, do you want Daddy and Mommy to lie to you? Tell you things that aren't true?"

Hitomi blinked away tears, then looked at both of them for a long minute. Finally, she shook her head.

"Good. Because we don't want to tell you lies, either. But that means that when the truth isn't the one we want, we still have to hear it. We *all* would like to be back on the ship, or even at our colony, or back on Earth. And if there is any way to do that we will, Hitomi, I promise. But right now, there isn't. And that means we're stuck here, doing everything we can to live."

"I'm just so tired of it all!" Melody burst out, kicking the shelter in a sudden rage. "I don't have a room, and I can't access *anything* that I don't already have, and . . . and . . . and . . ." She started crying loudly, unable to hide it anymore, obviously not even able to say exactly what she felt but knowing it hurt.

Hitomi was blinking around with big, teary eyes, and the new heartwracking sobs from Melody threatened to break Laura's new resolve. She saw tears starting again from Sakura's face, and Caroline's head sag down.

But then Hitomi suddenly pulled away and ran over to Melody, and put her arms around her sister. "I'm sorry," she said.

Melody's sobs caught, and she blinked, looking down at Hitomi. "You . . . you don't have anything to be sorry for."

"I'm sorry you're sad. I didn't want to make you sad!"

For once Melody's usual sarcasm deserted her. She just reached down and hugged Hitomi fiercely. "Not . . . your fault." Melody mumbled.

"No, it's not your fault," Laura said emphatically. "We all feel the same way. We're alone, we've got so little that we *want* to do that we can do, and so much we have to do to stay alive. It's . . . very wearing. And we still are just learning about the world, so we're still worried just about taking walks, or sleeping out in the open. We know how hard it is."

She felt her resolve firming up again, and Akira's arm was strong around her as she stood. She looked at him and though there were a few tears on his face too, she saw him nod. *We are two rocks, and we will support our family.*

"That said, I think we've got to take some time to make things better for us all. We've found food. We've got water. We've got shelter. We've got clothes—even if they're scratchier than we'd like, we can pad them with driftseed fluff. We're working on a house that—if we can build it—will give us all our own rooms, a chance to at least have a real *home*.

"But we need something to help us feel like our old selves, and that means something fun that isn't just part of survival."

She saw with relief and pride that all of them were drying their tears and coming towards her and Akira; even Whips' color started to ripple more brightly, and he finished coming down into camp.

"But what can we do, Mom?" Melody asked.

"Well, first...we can set times for each of us—or the group of us—to spend doing things we want to do. We should sit down and make a schedule so we know when that is, and then keep that schedule. Caroline, once we work it out, I'm going to leave it to you to track."

"Yes, Mom."

Organization was her favorite thing. Giving her the chance to help with that as part of her organization should work. "Now...for entertainment, we still have our omnis. Together we can make our own little network, and do some cooperative games—and single ones." She looked at Hitomi, then over at Sakura. "Sakura, Whips, do you think that you and Melody could make some new Jewelbug add-ons for Hitomi's favorite app?"

"Why, I..." Whips was obviously caught off-guard by the question, but paused. "Hmm. Well, I see the package came with add-on specs...I can certainly code it, but—"

Melody stood up and nodded. "I'll script some of the best Jewelbug adventures *ever*. I promise!"

Hitomi looked up at Melody with surprise. "Really? You *will?*"

Her voice was still thick with tears, but Melody gave a grin that was much closer to her old self, and Laura felt the strange pain that accompanies pride that nearly makes you cry. "I will. You'll see. If Whips and Saki can help with figuring out how—"

"I'll do it!" Sakura said emphatically. "And ... you know, Dad, didn't you used to play a lot of games when you were younger? Could you help make something for all of us?"

"I did, yes," Akira said slowly. "And ... well, it won't be as immersive as we'd get with the shipboard nets, but there are certainly adventures I remember that none of you will have seen. I could write those up— with some technical help—easily enough. And there are other games that we can play with the same help, and that won't strain our resources. Everything from ancient board-games to more modern ones. Maybe your mother could read us all some stories some nights, too?"

"Yes!" all four of her children said quickly.

Laura blushed. "Really?"

"Mom, you're like the *best* reader," Caroline said emphatically. "You do all the voices, the accents, even mime the movements. It's almost like having the autoperformance on, but it's better because it's *you.*"

"She's right, you know," Akira murmured softly. "You read to all of them when they were young, but since we crashed you've hardly read to even Mel or Hitomi."

"All right," she said, with the knot in her chest slowly dissolving. "Story night sometimes, too. We'll do that tonight. I'll have to pick out something for all of us, but I'd be happy to do it. Other than that, we will work out this schedule today, and get the network set up. Caroline's omni can still be part of it, can't it?" She looked at the glittering device which they'd placed high up as a security monitor.

"No problem, Laura," Whips said, looking almost back to normal. "The security functions only take up about five percent of its operational capacity. Caroline's can serve as our central node and direct network operations."

"That's good." She looked over at Hitomi. "Are you all right now, Hitomi?"

The little girl nodded, then ran over and hugged Laura, almost making her cry again with relief. "Okay, Mommy," she said, mumbling into Laura's barkcloth dress. "I'm sorry."

"It's okay, honey." She bent down and picked up her smallest daughter and hugged her close; Hitomi's arms went around her neck and hugged back, one of the most wonderful and comforting sensations any parent ever gets. "Not your fault. And we'll be okay now."

She wasn't fooling herself into believing there wouldn't be other outbursts like this; they'd lost their entire world, after all. But having gotten past this, she was pretty sure she could handle them now... and the later ones, she hoped, wouldn't be as bad.

"Now, let's get things set up and have dinner. No more work today that we don't have to do."

"Um...Mom, can we talk about our work?"

She and Akira looked at each other and started laughing. She quickly damped it down when she realized that, with the unstable sea of emotions still washing through her, it could easily turn into a much more unsettling and uncontrolled laugh. "Of course you can, honey. I didn't say we were going to pretend we weren't here, after all."

"Oh, good. Because Whips and me—"

"Whips and *I*," corrected Caroline reflexively. "Remember, it should be said the same way you'd say it if you didn't include Whips."

"Oh, yeah. Whatever. Anyway, Whips and I came up with a couple ways of making holes that might work..."

They discussed the new ideas during dinner. Both of them would be harder to work out than it seemed, Laura was sure, especially getting the right kind and amount of fire, but there were possibilities there. It was certainly worth exploring.

"Um...Dr. Kimei?"

Whips' nervous, formal address came as she was scrubbing off some of the plates with sand in preparation for a rinse. She looked up, startled. "What is it, Whips?"

"Um," he said again, and hesitated. "Could I...I know I'm not one of your children, but—"

"Do *not* say that," she said emphatically. "You're part of the family, which means that as far as I'm concerned, you're one of my children—no matter how strange that may look."

He gave a rippling laugh, sparkling colors over his skin. "Okay, Mom."

She reached out and gripped the base of one of his arms in the best analogy she could manage to what a real Bemmie adult would do. "Now what is it?"

The colors and patterns were those of nervous embarrassment. "Well...I was wondering...could *I* request a particular story?"

"Of course you could—as long as it's something I can read to Hitomi, too."

"Oh, it is! Um . . . I'd like you to read the translation of *The Skyspark*."

She smiled suddenly. "The story of the first human-Bemmie contact as written by Blushspark herself?"

"Well, yes . . . It's like a piece of home."

"Then I will happily read it."

And so, a couple of hours later, she began: ". . . It started so long ago, when the Vents sang louder and the Sky was a perfect, impenetrable shield above the world . . .

Chapter 22

"Are we in position, Whips?"

He looked from his perch, clinging tightly to the side of the great column with his two side arms. Drifting from below he could detect the smell of the borefire that had been slowly eating its way into the column. The smell varied between simple wood-burning and a sharper chemical stench as the carbon-based components of the column—and trapped organics of the things that had built them—yielded to the primitive power of flame.

After multiple tests on the downed column near the crash site, they'd come up with a multiple-method approach that seemed to work: first, point heat and weak acids to allow them to put pins or spikes into the column. The pins held curved holders—made from some of the largest pieces of metal left from the crash—in which were built borefires that the holder kept pressed against the column.

Once the fires had eaten in and weakened the column enough, then a pointed log could be rammed against the weakened area to actually make a hole all the way through. It was painstaking, difficult work, and it was going to take a *lot* of work over the next month or so, but they'd knocked six successive holes in the test column, and the last three had been exactly the size and rough shape needed—good enough that hand tools hammering and chipping away could finish the job.

It was probably going to be made much easier by the fact that there were small holes spaced around the columns fairly regularly—Sakura had found one of those on her first climb—and while the spacing wasn't quite up to engineering precision, it was good enough that you could use a lot of them as starter holes. Akira suspected that the holes were for water circulation, to keep the things that built the columns alive.

He wished the idea of a drill head had worked out, but the problem was how to embed the hard pieces well enough to not just pop out. No one had a solution, at least not yet.

Now they were about to knock the first hole in the real column, the giant that Sakura had found near Blue Hole Lake. Whips focused all three eyes on the pointed log, directed his omni to follow the gaze and triangulate.

Not quite aligned. The log would have to strike dead-center, several times, to bash its way through, if their test experience was any guide; hitting the unburned area of the column would blunt even the fire-hardened point in a single blow. The pointed battering ram was held up by cable from the winch, with guidelines held by Sakura and Laura, and Akira, Caroline, Melody, and Hitomi holding it pulled back for a strike. "Saki, we need to raise it by about . . . thirty centimeters."

"On it." Sakura and Laura pulled slowly on the lines, and the whole rig rose up. "Tell me when."

"Now!"

"Okay, are we aligned?"

"Pull it a little to the left, Laura . . . sorry, no, your right. Little more . . . okay, that's good." He checked the alignment once more. "Right. I think we're ready. Bring it in slowly . . . slowly . . . Oh, perfect." He saw the black point of the ram hitting dead-center on the fire-scar on the column. "Pull it back to full ramming position!"

"Are you braced, Whips?"

"Holding on tight, Akira," he said, making sure his hooks were firm. "Let it go!"

With a slow, majestic curve, the fire-blackened log swung and slammed with a mighty impact into the column. A spray of black and gray shards and dust exploded from the impact location and a shudder went through the entire structure. As the log rebounded, Whips could see a deep, deep indentation exactly where the firebox had eaten into the column. "Bullseye! Pull it back and we'll go for another strike!"

"Great!"

"Do you think we'll get all the way through?"

He would have liked to say yes, but . . . "Probably not. I think we'll have to build another borefire inside. These things are thick—which is good!—but it'll take time."

Still, the progress was impressive, and with the prior work aligning the log ram, the people on the ground were able to get repositioned much faster. In came the log again, *WHAM!* and more debris fountained out.

Something screeched from overhead.

Whips' gaze snapped upward, to see something—no, *three* somethings—crouched on the top of the column, tentacular legs balancing them, two other tendrils coiled back, armored bodies and working, sharp-edged mouthparts. He instantly recognized them as canopy krakens—the same things that had nearly killed Sakura when she tried to defend a pair of capys.

Then the creatures were descending, screeching again. *Lair!* They were protecting their lair!

There was nowhere to run and he didn't dare try to just leap for a nearby tree. He wasn't, after all, built for that kind of thing, and he was too high up to afford a fall. So he gathered himself and waited as the things dropped towards him at terrifying speed.

At the last moment he struck with his upper arm, hooks extended, and *bellowed*, an attack pulse as intense as he had ever generated, one he'd never have dared use if the Kimeis were any closer to him.

Underwater, such a sonic pulse could severely injure. In air, it could not hurt directly so easily, but it was a shock tactic second to none. Combined with the slashing impact of his arm and gripping hooks, it startled and intimidated the canopy kraken that had come directly for him, unbalanced it, and let him rip it free. He cast the creature away from the column to plummet uncontrollably below.

But that left two more, which backed slightly but came down on either side of him, using the tactics of practiced hunters. He fended off two blows by the hunting tentacles, but was forced to drop down, lower....

Lower?

He had no breath to speak, but he still had his link to Sakura's omni. *Sakura! See!*

For a moment she didn't respond, but then: *Yes! Got it!*

He dropped again, sidling out of the way. One tentacle slammed his body, but his tail holdfasts kept that from knocking him off of the column. Almost there, almost . . .

"NOW!" came a shout from below.

As the second canopy kraken scuttled towards him, its body crossed a fire-blackened hole—and at that moment, a huge log suspended on cable *impaled* the hard-shelled creature, stabbing through it like a fork through a shrimp.

Now there was only one, and it and Whips were about the same size. The kraken had two striking tentacles, but Whips had an arm that flowered into multiple branches, covered with black griphooks. The kraken's edge-filled mouth, insectoid in appearance, was also no more dangerous looking than Whips' black and yellow beak with its ripping, tearing tongue.

Still, this was its home territory and not his. The kraken battered at him, successive powerful blows of the striking tentacles trying to dislodge or kill by sheer impact. The others were shouting from below, and he realized that the kraken was too close for Laura to dare shoot.

Another hammering impact came, but that finally crystallized a thought. *It can hit harder . . . but not so accurately.*

He let go with one arm and swung around sideways. Such a maneuver wasn't very surprising to the canopy kraken—it probably did similar ones all the time—but that did force it to reposition and gave Whips a vital fraction of a second to focus closely on the thing's head, its construction . . .

His central arm whipped out, the fingertips with claw-hooks fully extended—

—to rip straight across the thing's upper two eyes.

The canopy kraken's shriek was ear-piercing. It convulsively tore away, fleeing into the neighboring trees, disappearing finally in a diminishing wail of pain and rattle of branches.

"Whips! Are you okay?" Sakura shouted up, and her mother called at the same time, "Harratrer!"

"I . . . think so." His body ached all over.

"Get down here so I can check you over."

That wasn't a hard order to obey. He really wanted something solid under his belly pad right now.

Laura was waiting at the bottom, and immediately engaged full diagnostics. After a few moments, she nodded. "You'll be okay. Some very deep bruises, I think. A few strains, too, but nothing really serious."

"Why did the monsters attack Whips, Daddy?" Hitomi's voice was frightened.

"Don't call them 'monsters,'" her father admonished calmly. "They're simply predators, and we were bashing in their home, I think." His simple, matter-of-fact approach quieted Hitomi, and everyone else began to relax. Laura might be the more dynamic one, but he was often the rock the family leaned on.

"They probably like to use the top of the columns as a roost or lair," Whips agreed, still trying to get his body to slow down from panic mode. "I guess we'll need to put a cap over the top of the column when we're done, to keep things from getting in that way."

Akira nodded. "We'd want to, anyway. We don't need rainwater pouring into our house from above, at least without directing it into something that can hold it."

"We can't go through that again," Laura said, worried. "Whips got off without serious injury this time, but that was partly just luck."

"I don't think we need to worry about that now," Akira said. "Two of the three are dead, one is injured. The top of this column is, I would suspect, marked with scent or other markers showing there are or were krakens lairing in it, which will tend to discourage other things from moving in right away. We're going to be burning and pounding on this column fairly continuously for the next few weeks, I think, so I really doubt anything else is going to try to move in. At most we'll have some cleanup of dung or other detritus to do, depending."

"Actually, Dad," Caroline spoke up, "I don't think we'll even have to do that. Well, there's probably some stuff on the insides of the column, but this one probably doesn't *have* a bottom to collect stuff."

"What? Everything has to have a bottom, Caroline."

"Well, okay, but not one we can reach. Saki mentioned feeling the air coming out of the one, and Whips has mentioned the breeze he gets coming from the holes, or sometimes seeming to go in, right?" The others nodded. "Well, in a cave, that's called 'breathing,' but it only happens because there's a really big volume of air inside that's reacting to atmospheric pressure outside."

Sakura blinked. "So you're saying...what?"

"I think the bottom of the column—the bottom we can see, down here—isn't actually the bottom. I think it opens up into the inside of the continent. Into a big chamber, or network of chambers, like caves—probably there's a bunch of different ones across the whole floating continent system, and they provide buoyancy and adjustment to pressure regimes."

Whips found himself shimmering in agreement.

"That makes sense. Maybe when these things are underwater, they exchange water through the columns, build more of the island. Who knows?"

"So you think that there's a lot of empty space below our chosen home?" Akira frowned. "Something could crawl up, couldn't it?"

Caroline shrugged. "Maybe, but the canopy krakens were nesting up there. If I'm right, our column's a hole in a big, *big* roof, so anything that wanted to come up would have to crawl for a long time along a ceiling over a tens-of-meters drop to rock or maybe water. I wouldn't expect big things to be crawling up. We'll just want to put a really solid bottom floor in that things can't come through."

"I'd want to do that in any case," admitted Laura. "Suspended over even a twenty-meter drop, we need floors that can't break."

Whips shook himself. "Well, all this talk is good, and we'll need to finish that part of the design— which fits, by the way, with what we were already working on—but right now, we've still got a hole to finish punching."

Ignoring the pain in his body, he began to clamber back up the column. *Not going to let a little thing like being attacked by three predators stop me!*

Chapter 23

"Hi, Caroline!" Sakura said, finally spotting her older sister at the base of the landing scar. Caroline was chipping at something with one of her few metal chisels, hammering with a rounded piece of stone.

"Hey, Saki," Caroline answered absently. "Don't step in my samples."

The warning was just in time. Sakura stopped herself with one foot on the edge of a neatly arranged array of pieces of what looked like dirt, pebbles, and stone chips. "Brought you lunch." She waited impatiently for Caroline to look at her. The older girl tended to maintain focus on what she was doing for a long time.

But after a few moments her sister finally realized that Sakura was standing there for a reason, and turned. "All right, what is it... Oh. Oh, my, is that what I *think* it is?"

The reaction of complete stunned joy was everything Sakura had hoped for, and she almost jumped with the excitement. "Flatbread."

Caroline stared. "Bread... from *what*?"

"Driftseed," she said proudly. A seed of some plant they hadn't quite identified yet, the seed or kernel of a driftseed was held in the center of a sort of fluffy donut formed by two graceful curves of delicate white, green, and gold feathery fiber. Melody had given it the name, not because it floated—it more bounced and rolled, being a bit too heavy to do the same thing as dandelion seeds—but because it would accumulate in drifts along fallen logs or ridges.

"It was partly my idea and partly Mel's," she went on. "When we started trying to harvest them for padding, Mom checked to make sure the fibers were safe, and after she said the driftseed fluff wasn't toxic in any way, I asked her if the seed was edible, and she said yes; I chewed a few and they didn't taste too bad.

"So once Whips figured out that sort-of-carding machine using the bristlethorn stems so we could get a lot of the fluff, I started saving them, but I didn't know quite what to do with them. Mel pointed out that breads were made from ground seeds. So we made it a private project to see if it would work; we dried them out so they wouldn't squish, then got Whips to help us make a mill—though we wouldn't tell him why."

"Make a mill? How?"

"Basically a couple of stones, one on top of another—we had to check for different types of the coral stone until we found one that was strong enough—and you put some grooves in the bottom one to catch and shove the flour out as you turn the top one, that you've put some kind of handle on. We took turns on our days off. Then we sifted it to make sure we didn't get lots of stone chips or something in it, and it was flour! So then we made bread, and you're the third person to get some."

"You and Mel first, I presume?"

"Right." She bounced impatiently. "Well, are you going to try it?"

"You don't need to worry, I want to." Caroline brushed her hands off on a rough barkcloth rag nearby, then grabbed the wrapped sandwich. "I never thought that feeling something like bread would make me want to cry." She looked into the end of the sandwich. "Minimaw with green sweetweed? Works for me."

She opened her mouth and took a big bite, chewed. The look of surprise was gratifying. "Omrrgrd," she mumbled, then chewed and swallowed. "Oh my God," she said again, this time clearly, "It's almost like, what is it, rye. With a hint of some kind of spice, but that's *bread*, Saki, it's bread!"

"I know!" Sakura said, and felt that ridiculous pain in her heart and stinging in her eyes. *Really, I feel so stupid. Getting all emotional over bread.*

But Caroline obviously didn't find it silly. She ate the whole sandwich in its irregularly shaped wrapping and caught even the crumbs jealously. "Thank you, Sakura. Really. I feel as though I just had a vacation in five minutes. That's really good bread. I think I'd think that even if I hadn't been missing having bread for months. What's in it?"

"Driftweed seed ground up, water, salt—from the salt-drying racks Mom had us set up—and that's pretty much it. We got really hopeful when the dough started to squish instead of crumble and fall apart. And then we just heated one of the flat rocks you found last month in a fire and put the dough on it, flattened. It took a few tries to not burn it up, but now we know how much time to cook it."

"So I guess driftseed's going to have to be a major crop, then. It's good for stuffing, lining, and now eating."

"There seems to be a lot of it, but I'll bet in the end we'll need to start farming for that. That's why Dad and Whips are off observing the capy herd; Dad thinks we might be able to domesticate them, and then we'd have some small draft animals and maybe meat, too." Sakura looked at the array of samples. "So, learning anything?"

"Oh, I've learned a lot!" Caroline pointed. "These all come from different layers of what was exposed when we crashed. I came up to this end of the crash scar because I wanted to see what I found at the farthest inland point. You can see I've cleaned off this face of the scar, here."

The area Caroline pointed to was obviously cleaned up—all the crumbling debris cleared away, the three-meter-high vertical cliff almost straight up and down now, showing multiple layers. "That's more structure than I expected."

"It's incredibly exciting, and without the crash scar it would have been a lot harder to dig down and find all this. So, the first thing I can tell you is that this continent—or at least this part of it—has been around for something on the order of a million years."

"A *million* years?" Sakura knew that getting things to float wasn't easy. Something this size persisting for a million years seemed crazy.

"Well, I said 'on the order' of a million years."

"Meaning that you're sure it's over a hundred thousand and less than ten million, right?"

"Close enough, yes. So that means we don't have to worry *too* much about the whole thing breaking up on us. It's not impossible, but the chances are pretty low. But it means a lot more than that."

Learning more cool things about Lincoln was important, and Caroline looked happy and enthusiastic; Sakura sat down to let Caroline lecture. "Okay, tell me."

Caroline flipped back her arrow-straight hair and knelt down in front of her array of samples. "Well, first, we have an absolutely *classic* soil structure here, which is very good for potential farming. The 'O' layer of debris on top—leaves and such—followed by humus—rich soil in the 'A' layer that's obviously turned over fairly well by the worm-equivalents and other subsurface fauna. A layer of deeper earth here, the subsoil or 'B' layer, which I think actually shows evidence of being water-deposited. I think those streams we've seen meander pretty widely and so they're depositing stuff all over."

"That's pretty bright red."

"It's got a lot of iron oxide in it; a lot of the crustacean-type creatures have high mineral content in their exoskeletons, so I'm guessing that's where it comes from." She smiled and pointed to the next. "But here is where it gets really interesting. Feel that."

Sakura reached out and touched. "That's rock. So?"

"So it's not the substrate of this island. That's a sedimentary rock, forming under the deposits above it. Some of the stones we found before made me suspect this, but it's still amazing. This isn't a rocky continent, yet rocks are being formed on it—enough that in at least some places you have major portions of soil which are derived from rocks which are, themselves, derived from hundreds-of-thousands-of-year-old deposits that managed to solidify. Only *here*," she pointed to the base of the cliff, showing brilliant white and green striping, "do we actually hit the real bedrock, the material that's built up by the corallike creatures that make the foundation of these islands."

"So . . . there's active geology here?"

Caroline chuckled. "Well, sort of. We don't have ordinary tectonic forces, or volcanoes that can reach us—though I *have* found a layer of what looks like pumice mixed with water-deposited debris, so on at least some occasion an eruption must get close enough to the surface to produce it. Those must be massive vents to get that high, though. The mechanisms to get even near the surface couldn't possibly be stable, not with the depth we estimate for this ocean.

"But we do have erosion, redeposition, cementation, and from what I see here there's at least some indication that the main structure lives for at least some time after being above the water, and certainly is being maintained somehow underneath." She gazed down towards the distant water at the far end of the scar. "I'll bet that if we watch carefully underwater at the end where it broke off, that you'll see it extending itself slowly out underwater, rebuilding what was lost. There's probably a huge set of symbiotic species which specialize in keeping this floating structure afloat and dealing with damage to the structure. This whole ecology depends on being within a hundred meters or so of the surface."

"That's really amazing," Sakura said, and meant it. Every time they learned more about the way Lincoln worked, the more fascinating the world became. And with the occasional games and stories and breaks, she found she wasn't resenting its differences so often. "So if something damages the colony enough, would it have defenses?"

Caroline paused. "You know . . . I think it might. I think Dad, and maybe Mel, mentioned something like that before."

"Hey, Mel," Sakura said into her omni.

A moment later, Melody's voice answered. "What is it, Saki? Did Caroline like the—"

"I *loved* it!" Caroline said, loudly enough so the omni would pick her voice up. "That was one of the best surprises I've ever gotten."

"Great!" Melody's voice was genuinely happy. "Saki, you'd better get back here pretty quick, we need to make enough for everyone for tonight."

"Sorry, yes, I know. Then we'll be almost out of seed."

"Worth it for a meal, and we'll start getting more."

"Anyway, I called to ask—have you ever heard of symbiotic animals that defend the thing they're a symbiont with? We were wondering if these islands have anything—"

"Oh, yes," Mel interrupted. "Besides some trees that have ants to protect them, there are corals that have crabs and such living in them. The crabs can sense the approach of predators, like that giant spiky starfish . . . *Acanthaster planci*, that's it . . . and they go out and drive the starfish off. There's also things like that near some of the Europan vents. I'll bet that Dad could give you a hundred other examples from a dozen planets."

Sakura looked at Caroline. "Then we might want to be a little careful about how we work here."

Caroline nodded slowly. "But I wouldn't worry too much. What we're doing is so small, on the scale of this floating continent, that we're probably unnoticeable."

"Probably. Anyway," Sakura bounced to her feet, "Mel's right, I have to get going!"

"Thanks again for that wonderful lunch!"

"You're welcome!"

Sakura found herself skipping a bit on the way back, and then laughed. Little things sometimes made a big difference.

Chapter 24

Laura looked down from her perch on the Great Column—a seat of braided barkcloth suspended in front of one of the support holes finally bored and smoothed through the column's meter-plus thickness. She could see Hitomi, well out of the way of everyone else. The monitor of Laura's omni showed that her youngest girl was busy playing her latest Jewelbug adventure, which Mel and Whips had finished the other day. That would keep her occupied for hours.

There was no concern about lurking canopy krakens. Akira had been right. Nothing had attempted to set up housekeeping in the column with them constantly working on it for the last several weeks. They were sure of that because Whips periodically went up and checked. Caroline's theory about the depth of the hole had also been confirmed. The column had no actual bottom they could reach.

That did make the fact that the broken-off one in their landing trench had possessed a bottom somewhat puzzling, but both Caroline and Akira thought there were several possible reasons.

The others were all at their positions. Caroline,

Sakura, and Melody were holding the ropes to lift or lower things with; while the powerful little winch could easily do such things, it was such a power hog that it would be very difficult to do a full day's work depending on it. One or two crucial operations would certainly use it, but for these, individual control and endurance were more important.

Akira and Whips were up at the top. Whips, as their chief engineer and designer, was overseeing the work. He was also the one most likely to be able to act safely in case of emergency, with his three powerful, wide-spreading arms to both anchor and grab. He'd proved that when he had to fend off the krakens.

They had already lifted the cover which would go over the top, hung off the side and suspended by a length of the winch's carbonan-core composite cable. Just approaching the top of the column was the first of the supports which—if this worked—would provide the foundation for the first floor of their new home.

The support was a slightly arched, huge section of wood taken from one of the largest trees they had cut. If they didn't have wood, she wasn't sure they could even do this. But they did have wood, and wood growing in a forest never cut in its lifetime. There were thousands of forest giants waiting to be harvested, even allowing for the fact that only twenty percent or so of the forest included real wood, and of that Laura and Akira had agreed to not permit cutting nearly all in any given area.

Cutting and shaping such massive pieces of wood was itself a challenge, but Whips, Melody, and Sakura—with her help and that of Akira—had managed to find ways, combining fire, carefully-made stone and coral tools, judicious uses of the winch's power for moving and positioning, and a lot of patient effort, to make what they needed.

In theory, what they were doing was simple: the supports each had a long, slightly curved end that would go into one hole, and a shorter, straight end that would slide into the opposing hole. You just lowered the support until the long end slid into the first hole, pushed that long end all the way over so that the support was just a little shorter than the distance across the hole, then lowered it until the shorter pieces sticking out could be slid into the opposite hole. The long piece was more than long enough to make sure plenty stuck out the other side, while the second end was about as long as the thickness of the column, so you'd end with a bit sticking out of one side that you'd lock down with pins, and you'd pound anchors into the other side.

Easy . . . in theory.

The first support was nearly to the top now, a flanged and solid arch slightly over eleven meters from socket-point to socket-point. There were three more of them, and each was cut slightly differently so that in the end, they had extensions and were interlocked to provide multipoint support for the floor that would rest on them.

Whips had taken no chances he could avoid. After all the pieces had been produced, the whole family had assembled the entire structure beforehand on the flattest area they could manage, interlocking all of the supports and putting the floor pieces in place, then measuring how much the weight atop the supports caused them to bow outward. Only then had Whips bored the holes for the locking inserts.

"All right, that's got it. You're well above the top

of the column," Whips called out to the girls below. "Hold on. Akira?"

"I have it, Whips." Now Akira was pulling the support over the support with a guide rope, but the key here was just to get the support inside. Whips held another line loosely which would allow him to assist Akira in turning and positioning the support.

"It's coming. Girls, give me about half a meter slack."

"Half a meter slack, yes, Dad," answered Caroline. The three girls let a little rope slide between their fingers, giving the support the chance to move towards the column.

A few more maneuvers, and Whips called out, "There! That's it! Sakura, Caroline, watch your omni displays, and begin to pay out the line slowly. Stop when you see the red highlights."

To her credit, Melody didn't complain about not having her omni, which was currently being borrowed by Caroline because Caroline's was still on security duty at the main camp. *Against her will, I think my third little girl has been getting over her original laziness,* Laura thought, smiling to herself.

Looking at Caroline, streaked with dirt and hair askew, grinning as she held tight to the cable, she realized that Melody wasn't the only one changed. *My constant organizer who hated anything out of order has learned to adjust, too.*

Probably, she admitted to herself, *we all have changed. Had to, with Lincoln driving us.*

The support descended smoothly into the darkness of the column, scraping occasionally as either Akira or Whips lagged slightly in keeping the column tilted enough.

There! For the first time she caught a glimpse of the lower end of the support, entering the view from inside the great column. "I see it!"

"Great!" Whips answered. "Now comes the tricky part. Laura, make sure you're seated to the side, and extend your omni just far enough to look in."

She adjusted her seat carefully, and checked to make sure that the locking pins were also suspended safely but reachably out of the way. Caroline would normally do this climbing bit better than Laura would, but this needed someone pretty tall and stronger than she was. Since Whips pretty much had to be at the top, that left Laura. "I am in position. Are you getting the video feed?"

"Coming through perfectly. Activating the guidance application now."

With the omni's remote display still on her head, Laura could see the swinging support highlighted in yellow, with arrows showing directions. "All right," Whips said. "Everyone seeing the display?"

"I do," Akira answered, echoed by Caroline and Sakura. Below, Laura saw that even Hitomi had put away her game to watch this first—and crucial—assembly.

"All right. Arrows show we need to lower by about one hundred twenty more centimeters. Lower away."

The arrows shortened, shortened . . . and suddenly there was a short arrow pointing up. "Whoa! Too far. Pull it up slowly . . . slowly . . . *perfect!*"

Laura could now see one end of the support that looked to be almost exactly on her level. If things worked according to plan, the long, somewhat curved end of the support would be coming through this hole.

"All right, Akira, pull to the right . . . sorry, watch

the arrows, I mean your left! Slow ... slower ... good. Okay, let's try this ..."

In theory, now, all they had to do was let the one end drop while the other end rose, and that rising end would go straight through the hole in front of her.

There was a tremendous *THUD* that she felt through the column itself. "*Silt!* A few centimeters off. Pull back! Up ... Girls, I think we need a tiny bit more down. *Tiny* ... good." The display flickered with green and yellow tiny moving arrows. "Okay, I think that's right. Akira, let's try again ..."

Another *THUD*. This time Whips used a word in the Bemmie language that Laura knew shouldn't be translated. "Now we're hitting on the other side!"

"You've only allowed about two to three centimeters of extra space on each side, Whips. It's not going to be easy," Akira pointed out.

"I *know*," the young Bemmie replied, his tone that of someone trying to banish nervousness and not succeeding too well. "But I don't want the holes too loose, either. We can put in wedges afterward, yes, but the looser the holes, the bigger the potential disaster if a wedge comes out."

Another set of adjustments. *THUD*. This time it was Akira saying something that she didn't think needed translation. "Maybe we should have made those holes bigger anyway."

"I'd hate to give up," Whips said reluctantly. "Widening all the holes will be a hell of a task. How are you girls doing down there?" he asked.

"It's getting ... a little hard to hold it," Caroline confessed. "Even with the leverage advantage."

"I'm pretty sure we're on the right level," Whips

said after a moment. "Can you lock it down exactly where you are?"

"I think so. *Hitomi!*"

Laura was glad to see how quickly Hitomi came running over. "What?"

"See that lever? The one marked with red?"

"Uh-huh."

"Pull it hard towards me. That's right . . . perfect!" Caroline eased off, but the line stayed taut, held by the carved wooden lever clamp with its blunt teeth now dug into the line. "Locked down, Whips; your lock's holding great!"

"Good. Make sure it's fully locked, then sit down and rest for a bit, while we curse at this thing some more."

"I think it was a little off to my right . . . your left . . . that time."

"Try again. But this time if it hits, don't pull back. Let's get it resting right against the side of the column."

"Oh? Oh, I see. Yes, that's probably a much better idea."

The *thud* was a tiny bit muted, and seemed to come from the hole before her, too. On the omni's screen, she could see something almost entirely filling the hole.

"Aha!" said Whips. "Right level, we're off by about ten centimeters to . . . to my left, again."

"But it's resting against the column wall, right? So if we pull it to your right, slowly . . ."

"I think so. Laura, pull your omni out of the way."

She did. There were a few seconds of scraping, and then suddenly, even as she heard a triumphant shout from above, an immense red-brown shaft of wood slid into view, mere inches from her face. "It's in!"

"Can you get in the locking pin?"

The farther end was just out of reach. "Pull it up, just a little."

Wobbling slightly in the hole with a *crunch* noise, the support slid backwards half a meter. "Okay, okay, hold it!"

Laura reached down and took the first locking pin in hand. "Do *not* let it move now."

"Holding as steady as we can."

The locking pin for the support was an eight-centimeter-diameter dowel of the hardest wood they'd yet found, tapered slightly, as was the hole it went into. She reached out and slid the pin into the hole, then hit its end several times with a stone hammer to make it tight. "In the hole. I'm putting in the cotter pins now."

The "cotter pins" were actually just other pins that hammered into both ends of the locking pin itself, as they didn't have any spring steel to make real cotter pins out of. She hammered in the nearest one, climbed carefully on top of the slightly shifting support, hammered in the other. Only once she'd returned to her safe seat did she report, "Done!"

"All right, last part of this... let's hope I didn't screw anything up," Whips said, now even more tense.

The support end slid out farther now, to the limit of design; she could hear the thicker portion hit the column interior. "All right, let's see if we can drop it into place!"

There was a distant scraping; taking their cue from the successful insertion on her side, her husband and Whips were obviously sliding the other end down the inside of the column, hoping that when it reached the opposing hole it would catch and then slide in. On her side, the curved end rose slightly higher as the end remaining inside descended.

Abruptly she saw her end shudder, then slide forward over half a meter. "*You've got it!*"

A cheer echoed from below and above. "I think you're right...Yes, yes, we're *in!*" shouted Whips jubilantly. "Akira, let's give a pull, make sure it's seated all the way."

The support ground forward another decimeter or two. "There, that looks good. Laura, check the marks on your end?"

"You're within two centimeters of the black mark going back into the column."

"Perfect! All right, Akira, belay me. I'm going down and putting in the locking pin for the inside, then Laura can make her way around the other side and pound in the anchors for that end."

"On belay."

A few moments later she heard Whips on the other side, pounding his locking pin into place. "It's set! I'm going to put in the seating wedges on my side, too, make sure it stays level, then go to the other side and wedge that one."

More sound of pounding, a pause, and then more distant hammering, still transmitted somewhat by the massive support beam. "And...we're *done!*"

"It worked!" she heard Melody shout from below.

"It sure did!" Whips sounded euphoric. "It's not easy, but by the Sky it *worked*, and the rest will be easier, just knowing it will work!"

"When can..." Hitomi began.

"Be a little bit yet," Akira answered. "We've got

several days of work just to get the supports and floors in, locked, stabilized so that the only thing that can bring them down would be the column cracking or something. And we'll still have to do our hunting and other work in the meantime. But still...I think in two, three weeks, old-home time, we will be moving in!"

Laura joined in the cheer, because she knew exactly what her children were thinking, and her heart echoed it precisely. *A home!*

We're going to have a home!

Chapter 25

"We've figured out how to catch a herd of capys," Akira announced.

Sakura looked up from where she was working on trimming one of what seemed an unending series of wood planks which were going to be the stairs to their front door—well, actually, the *treads* of the stairs. Two big beams were the sides of the stairs, with notches cut in them where the planks would be inserted. The whole thing was designed to be able to be raised up by a pulley mechanism, so that if some of the larger predators came sniffing around, they couldn't get up without climbing, and climbing the columns wasn't easy.

But right now that was concept, and whittling wood was the practice. And they couldn't move in until this, and the stairway to the second floor, were done. "How, Dad?"

"It was partly Mel's idea, apparently from one of the adventure books she was reading. They have some clear paths that they follow, so if we get ahead of them in their grazing pattern and build most of a fence, once they enter the area we just have to drop down the last parts and they can't go anywhere."

"Won't they notice something's wrong?"

Her father considered, as he examined a support he was working on. "I don't think so, really. The fences will of course be made of natural materials, and look like sticks. Oddly positioned sticks, yes, and there will be some of our scent on them, but they haven't shown any aversion to us. The one herd actually seems quite comfortable around us."

"They way they reacted to us that one day...Dad, you don't think...well, they're not *intelligent*, are they?"

Her father chuckled, as did Whips, who was also working on something in the flickering firelight of this day-which-happened-to-be-at-night. "We've been trying to define 'intelligence' for hundreds of years, and I'm still not sure exactly what we mean by it. I'm not making fun of you, Saki. It's just that—especially for a biologist—that's not the easiest question to answer."

He was quiet for a few moments, but Sakura didn't disturb him. She knew that furrowed brow meant her father was thinking hard. Her Shapetool caught on a knot in the wood and then came loose suddenly, and she almost lost her grip on the thing. The speed with which it jabbed out made her very grateful that Whips had drilled into her over and over that all wood-carving motions were done *away* from you, with no other part of your body—or anyone else's!—in line with the motion. *If I'd been doing that towards me, I'd have stabbed myself. And I don't know if the omni monitoring it could get the Shapetool to reconfigure that fast.*

"In my best current opinion...no, not in the way you mean *intelligent*, Saki," her father said finally. "The behavior and interactions I have seen indicate that they are fairly high up on the scale, certainly, and I would consider them to probably be on the level of a smart dog. They recognize individuals, they have group and family loyalty, they have emotions of at least the general categories we recognize, all of these things, but—at least so far—I haven't seen any significant tool use, no sign of complex ideation or of long-term prediction or generalization of concepts." He grinned and shrugged. "Of course, even though I've spent a great deal of time studying them, it's not at all long by any reasonable standard, and I could easily be missing crucial aspects.

"But what I *have* learned is that they're reasonably gentle, vegetarian, and possibly tameable. I'd like to test the latter, although I would caution everyone not to get their hopes up. Domestication of most animals is actually a genetic process—a long-term breeding program to choose the best-compatible members and keep reinforcing those traits. Most wild animals, even ones that seem very similar to domesticated species, aren't able to be usefully tamed. I'm only willing to take the chance with these because they have shown multiple traits that are promising." He grinned. "Now, if we discover that they *are* on the sapient level with us, then we will of course release them and apologize, once we know their language."

"Great!" She held up the board. "Done! How many more, Dad?"

"I think . . . you're nearly done. Three more."

Three more! Her heart, which had been feeling rather depressed over the endless whittling, gave a little leap. "I can do three before bed!"

"I'll bet you can. Though a few months ago I don't know if you could have done three in a *day*."

It struck Sakura that her father was probably right. She wasn't in bad shape, but doing this kind of work was new to her. Whips, her mother and Caroline were the only ones who had any experience there. "Maybe. I don't think you could have, either, Dad!"

"*Touché*. I believe you are correct." He held out his hands, which—like Sakura's—had obvious, tough calluses and a multiplicity of healing scrapes and the roughness that comes from lots of handwork. "This adventure, at the least, has given me great respect for our forebears...and constant envy of those who still have electricity and power tools."

"*I*," Whips grumbled from the other side of the fire, "would give a great deal just for some old-fashioned iron and steel. It's much easier to shape than wood, in the long run, especially for some things. And there are so many tools that we could make with it. Perhaps we could find a meteorite?"

Caroline, who was relaxing off to the side with Hitomi, spoke up. "Well, there probably are some around somewhere. We've noticed two naked-eye comets since we've been here, and there's frequent meteors. But even relatively common meteorites will be really hard to find. On Earth in Antarctica, or Europa to some extent, you could find them lying around because they were about the *only* rocks you'd find on the surface." She gestured to the rocky debris around them in the landing scar. "Not so easy now."

Hitomi gave a little jump, then a laugh.

Sakura smiled over at her littlest sister. "Having fun?"

"This adventure's great! Who made the bubble cave?"

"That was me and Whips, though Mel wrote the story and all of us—even Mom and Dad—added stuff."

"Thanks, everyone!" Hitomi called, and various versions of "you're welcome" floated back through the night-day air.

"So, when do you think we'll catch us some capys and test your theory, Dad?" Sakura said, returning to the prior subject.

"Not for a while. We've got to finish getting the house ready, which is taking longer than we thought. Once we're settled in, then we can think about establishing things like farms and herds." He glanced over at Whips. "That for our water supply?"

"Yes," Whips said, holding up a section of pipestem, which was something like bamboo but with exterior ridges instead of internal sections; Caroline, in a rare burst of humor, had wanted to name it "pipeweed" after the tobacco-analogue in *The Lord of the Rings*, but she'd been overruled. "I'm carving sections to fit together."

"Making water pipes, of course. I saw the sketches of the system you were working on with Sakura—are you sure that will work?"

"It's an ideal use for the winch, I think. Only needs to be run a short time each day to bring water up to a tank on the top floor in some sort of tipping buckets. I'd like to figure a way to run it all the way to Blue Hole Lake, but for now I think we still have to have people bring water over by hand.

"Of course," Whips added, "that's if we don't get enough water from rain. We'll be trying to catch rain directly into the tank upstairs and if we keep getting rain at the same frequency we have, that probably will keep us pretty well filled up."

He looked at the pipe he was making. "The part

I'm worried about are the joins. They're probably not going to be tight enough, though maybe they'll tighten when they're wet. But we really need to find something like clay, or even a better gumlike adhesive, to seal them together. Plus if we had clay there's all sorts of other things we could make. Caroline, you said there are real soils here, do you think there might be clay or something like it?"

"Well . . ." Caroline tilted her head, visible as a slightly inclined shadow against the darker gloom, her eyes glinting in the firelight. ". . . maybe. There's silica in many of the foundation rocks, and there's plenty of weathering. Timescale is somewhat short, but if there's some places where water flowing down from an erosive area slows down and allows gentle deposition . . . could be."

She gestured to the distance. "We've seen a lot of streams that come down from the mountains, but don't know where they go to. Maybe we could take a hike inland to look." While the ridges that were visible farther inland didn't rise much more than three hundred meters or so, they were peaked and rugged enough that the family was willing to call them mountains.

"Worth a try, sometime soon. We certainly need to keep learning more about Lincoln, and exploring farther is necessary."

"I want to go on that one," Sakura said firmly. "Now that I'm allowed back out, that is."

Her father laughed. "You've learned your lesson, Saki. All right, we'll plan on a trek towards the mountains."

"Great!"

"But not if you don't get the ladder done," her father said wryly.

She realized she had stopped whittling a while ago. "Oops." She gripped the Shapetool in her aching hand, studied the phantom but clear lines projected on it by her omni, and started cutting. But she was still smiling.

Their house was almost done—and soon she'd be doing more exploring!

Chapter 26

"I can't believe we're really moving in, finally," Laura said, looking at the narrow but sturdy staircase in front of her, glowing a deep red-gold in the occasional slanting beams of the setting sun that penetrated through the jungle cover.

"Honestly, neither can I," Akira said. "I was so naïve to think that we could finish all that work in two or three weeks. It's been, what, more like eight weeks?"

"Nine and a half," Whips said. "A week or so of that was making the clear path to Blue Hole Lake and setting up my own safe niche in the lake, though."

"That counts," Laura said. "You're not so suited for treehouse life, unless we could put in some kind of wet room, and we're not there yet. So building that was your house, or your extension, anyway."

"Well, Whips, you did about eighty percent of the design and research work, you want to do the tour?"

The colors that rippled across the young Bemmie showed how pleased and proud he was. They'd all gotten very good at reading his signals. "I'd love to!"

Whips moved over to the staircase and quickly slid his way up. His rear anchor-feet and two front arms on the railings allowed him to go up surprisingly fast. Laura followed with Akira just behind, and the rest of the family came trailing along.

"Okay, this is the entryway. Right here's the crank to bring up the staircase. It's got enough mechanical advantage so that even Hitomi can probably crank it up." Whips gestured. "Why not give it a try, since we're all here?"

Hitomi bounced forward and grabbed the wooden handle. "Mmmmph . . ." she grunted. But then she threw her full weight on the handle and it moved, then started to turn faster as Hitomi got a feel for how to turn it best. "It's . . . going!"

"Oh, very good!" Akira was clearly pleased. "If Hitomi can do that, the rest of us will have no problems. How do we keep it there?"

"There's a carved ratchet on the side there, see? Once it's up where you want it, you just slide the catch over to the ratchet."

"Nice."

Hitomi was demonstrating her usual stubbornness; she continued cranking until the entire ladder was raised, and then managed to hold it steady until she'd locked the ratchet. "There!"

Laura laughed. "Very good, Hitomi. We'll have to let it down when we go to get the other stuff we're bringing up, though."

"I know, Mommy," she said, with just a hint of "I'm not stupid!" in the background. "But I wanted to see if I could bring it up all by myself."

"And you certainly did." Laura looked to the side. "I see we also have a door."

"Of course," Whips agreed. "We don't want wind

and rain coming in, and if anything *can* get up here we want to keep it out. Same for all the windows; they've got shutters to keep them secure.

"Now, you can see," he gestured around, "This is an entrance hall and a place we can leave things we carry in that we don't want trailing dirt everywhere, like tools we're using a lot. I've got a couple boxes over there for us to put things like that in. These stairs go to the second floor. But over *here*," he slid over to the door on the left, "is the kitchen, dining room, and pantry."

The revealed room was a full semicircle, more than half the useful space of the floor. "Now that we have lots of wood, we don't have to rely on the solar cooking method—which is good, since a good deal of our so-called 'days' are actually dark because Lincoln's rotation doesn't match up with human night-day schedules. The main firebox for the stove is right here."

"That's one of the metal pieces we used for building the fires to cut into the column, right?"

"The largest one, yes. For now, we've really just built a firepit with a big vent hood above it, and some attachments to put baking stones or pans or pots over the fire. Building a real stove's got me a little stumped, though."

"Don't worry about it, Whips," Caroline said with a laugh. "This is great. I love the way we have cabinets now! We can put things away *in order!*"

There was almost an excess of joy in Caroline's pronouncement—enough so that Laura found she couldn't quite stifle a giggle, and then the others started laughing.

For a moment Caroline looked mortified . . . and

then she started giggling too. "That did sound pretty dorky," she said after a moment.

"But it was definitely you," Sakura said, still smiling. "Where's the hood go to?"

"Hole on the outside—we widened one of the naturally occurring holes and put a grille over it to keep things from getting in that way."

"But . . ." Laura went and knocked on one of three rounded, columnlike structures on the wall. It gave a loud *tonk* sound; clearly hollow. "These are those vents you put in to let the column still 'breathe,' right? The ones that run all the way to the top? Why not just put the smoke vent into those?"

"Thought of that," Whips agreed, "But there were two reasons we didn't. First, the air can go into the column as well as out, so you could suddenly find smoke coming straight back into the kitchen. Still might, sometimes, with the wrong wind direction, but this might happen every time pressure changed, so that didn't seem like a good idea."

"The other reason," Akira said, "was that we've already been discussing the possible issue of a symbiotic defense for the islands. Now, we don't have much choice about doing some things that slightly disrupt the workings of the island, but it struck me that if any of the creatures here are sensitive to fire—the way that most animals are on Earth—having a constant source of smoke drifting in and out of the main airstream of the column might not be a wise idea. So we made a separate, isolated chimney. It's fairly well away from the windows on the next floor so there shouldn't be too much smoke coming in that way. If there is, we'll run an external stovepipe up past the top floor later."

"What about lighting?" Laura asked. "I see we've got one of our lights here, but there's no wires and solar cells are going to be not very reliable this far down in the canopy."

"That'll be one of the daily chores, like making sure the water's filled up," Whips said. "You're right, we couldn't put the solar cells down here and rely on them getting a lot of sunlight, and there wasn't a practical way to put them up on the top of the column. So we've put up a protected rack right near my sleeping pool. If someone comes down every morning, I can swap out charged cells for old ones and we can keep everything charged up."

"All right," she said, nodding. "And there are possible ways to make lamps if we can get enough burnable oil or something of that nature, I guess."

"And we might," Akira said with a nod. "Capys, and some of the other . . . mammal-analogues have a fair amount of fat in subcutaneous layers."

"The cupboards and cabinets have a lot of space!" Sakura said, half-inside one of the latter. "I guess so we have room for when we start getting more stuff, huh?"

"Right. No point in making things tiny now if we'd just have to make them bigger later."

"What's in here?" Melody asked, opening the large door on the other end of the room. "Oh! Hunting stuff!"

"Weapons for hunting and defense, yes. It makes the most sense to have them down here."

"I agree." Laura was most interested in what looked like . . . "Is this a sink?"

"The best we could manage, yes." Akira pointed to a covered section of log. "We burned and carved out this log to be a reserve tank for the kitchen; it has to be refilled by opening the valve on the top floor which comes from the main tank. We found that we didn't have anything yet that could keep it sealed with a vertical column of something like ten meters, so the main tank's kept shut off except when refilling the reserves or running the shower."

"Shower!" Sakura and Hitomi both shouted.

"Whoa, there, don't get too excited," Akira cautioned. "It's a cold shower for now, but since everything here's warm it's not *too* cold a shower. And we should be able to make soap soon, if the recipes Mel found work out. Heating shower water would be a big pain, so I'm glad it's warm enough here that we don't need to."

Sakura shrugged. "If it's a full-size shower, I don't care, much."

"It's good-sized, yes. Just remember that any water you use gets drained from the tank above, so someone taking long showers may be told to go get more water to refill it when they're done."

"What's the other room here, off the entrance hall?" Caroline asked. "I didn't work on . . . oh, it's a *bathroom*!"

"Well, a sort of inside-outhouse, but yes, no more digging trenches," Whips said, and was momentarily drowned out by the cheers. "There's a grid under it to keep nasty things larger than the bigger bug-type creatures from coming up, just in case, and the dump pipe for the main water comes down there so we rinse the whole thing clean when we do the weekly water purge."

"Water purge?"

Caroline nodded. "Of course. We don't have any

way yet to keep water clean and fresh everywhere, so we're going to have to clean out the water supply periodically. Maybe figure out some kind of disinfectant, just in case, but boiling water will probably be what we use at first."

Melody made a face. "Ugh. What a pain. That'll take time, won't it? Boiling enough water to rinse out all the pipes and make them hot enough?"

"I'm afraid so. But the advantage is having water available for things like showers, drinking, and cooking inside the house."

Mel sighed. "Well, okay. Worth it, I guess."

Whips now led the way up the set of stairs in the entrance hall, to a small squarish room a little more than two meters on a side with four doors. The first opened into a very large room—similar to the kitchen downstairs, most of a semicircle, though it did not continue around the center with pantry and storage space like the kitchen. "The master bedroom, for Akira and Laura. We'll just have the same sleeping pads for now, but pretty soon I'm confident we'll be able to figure out how to make driftseed-stuffed mattresses, at least."

"And this one?" Hitomi yanked open one door and then squealed loudly. "It's *my room!*"

Sure enough, the smaller bedroom next to theirs on one side had decorations that echoed Hitomi's favorite Jewelbug character, Waterfall Star, and sitting in the middle of the floor, as though waiting, was Skyfang. Hitomi ran in, grabbed up Skyfang, and started jumping around, her feet making satisfactory *thump* noises on the smooth wood. "My room, my room, my room!"

Melody's face was shining as she looked into the

room that was obviously hers—already supplied with a rocking chair and a little desk. "You...I didn't see you doing any of this!" she said, her voice trembling with surprised tears that brought a sympathetic, joyous sting to Laura's eyes.

"Sweetheart, we worked on your rooms when you were sleeping, so you'd have something to help make them home."

"Oh, Dad..." Caroline said, stunned, as she saw a whole set of sample shelves on the far side of her own room, which lay opposite the master bedroom. "You..."

Sakura was already charging up the other set of stairs. "So I'm at the top!"

"You are!" agreed Whips.

Akira looked over at Laura. "Sorry I don't have anything special for you in our room."

"We have a *room*, that's enough," she said, and hugged him fiercely, feeling happy tears going down her face as she heard the joyous exclamations of her daughters claiming their own rooms and really, truly having a home again. "I'm glad we spent time making sure theirs were already *theirs*, though."

"Oh, so am I," Akira said, and his eyes weren't dry either. "Now it is a home, and all these months of work are completely worth it."

"Come on up, Whips!" Sakura's voice came floating down the stairs. "Aren't you going to see this?"

"I thought I already..." Whips trailed off as he reached Sakura's room. "Mr.... Akira, Laura, you sneaked this past *me*?"

The two burst out laughing. "Yes, we certainly did. We moved the one wall over a couple of meters and put down a resting pad for you, so there's space for you to visit. Because the most special thing for Sakura is her very best friend."

Sakura's head, framed by her wavy ebony hair, appeared at the top of the stairs, also with happy tears. "You guys are the *best*."

Laura laughed again, and it was one of the most wonderful feelings, to be doing that inside a house, a big, roomy *house* and not a cramped little emergency shelter. "Well, thank you very much, Sakura!"

Then she clapped her hands. "All right, everyone, time to come back down. We've got to get everything here and *move in!*"

Chapter 27

Sakura approached the brilliantly glowing fire and the humped shadow near it, silhouetted in the darkness of Lincoln's long night—though by human time it was now about noon of another day. "How's it going?"

Whips didn't jump at the sudden voice—he wasn't really built for it, after all—but even in the firelight Sakura saw the jangling colors and the twitch of his multitudinous fingers. "Okay so far, but don't *do* that."

"Sorry. Is it that delicate?" She kept back from the fire, which was radiating a lot of heat.

"Well . . . yes and no," Whips said. "In concept this is dead-simple. About as simple as making lye—"

"—which Mom and Melody are starting now, and only Mom and Dad are going to be allowed near once the stuff starts, well . . . lye-ing."

"Ouch." She saw the ripple of humorous appreciation run down Whips' length. "So, with lye-making you basically take pure rainwater, and run it through the right kind of ashes until you get it concentrated enough for whatever job you have in mind. Instead of water, of course, I'm using fire, because what I want to make is quicklime."

238

"I kept forgetting to ask, but I know 'limestone' and limes that you eat, and lime like people put in gardens. Which is this?"

"None of them, exactly. The fruit's name, as far as I know, isn't related at all. The others are all calcium compounds, but limestone's going to be mostly calcium carbonate, and the lime you put on gardens is called agricultural lime."

Whips gestured to the roasting setup, which she'd seen partially assembled. The fire burned high below a metal bowl—one of the same pieces of metal wreckage that had been used to make the fireboxes for boring through the column. The bowl itself was held up by several carefully trimmed stones that fitted into hammered niches in the sides of the bowl.

"We crushed up shells and some limestone-type rocks that Caroline could identify—this is where we connect the different 'lime' things. The limestone and similar things get put in the bowl, and then roasted to high heat: over 825 degrees, or over about 1500 degrees in the old Fahrenheit scale." He shoved more charcoal from a large heap nearby into the fire. "That's why I've got to keep it really hot."

Sakura looked at him, as he inchwormed quickly back from the flames and went to splash water on his body. "Look, let me do that for a bit. You *really* don't want to get dried out. Shouldn't someone else be playing with fire?"

"This is *my* project."

She couldn't miss the pride in his voice. "So this stuff is for prepping leather, right?"

"Oh, much more than that!" Whips said. "Yeah, make sure the charcoal's distributed. Anyway, quicklime can be turned into what's called 'slaked lime' just by adding water. The two of them have a lot of uses ranging from taking hair off hides to making cement and plaster, food preparation, and even insecticide. We don't exactly have insects here, but it may well work on the analogues. A lot of uses for quicklime and slaked, even if we won't need all of them right away."

"Just from burned-up limestone and shells? I didn't know that." Sakura looked with more respect at the pile of smashed-up seashells and rock that was just visible inside the bowl from where she was squatting.

"Not exactly burned, more like roasted. Calcium carbonate gets heated, gives off carbon dioxide, and leaves behind calcium oxide, which is quicklime."

He raised himself up to get a good look. "Some of that stuff's already starting to turn; can you see the color change there? It's also losing coherence. It'll all be powder by the time I'm done." He reached over and picked up a thin metal strut. "Okay, step back a minute."

"You want me to—"

"No, I'm doing it. This is a bit dangerous."

She watched as he carefully, gently stirred the mass of rocks and shells that was, in fact, starting to crumble. "What's dangerous about it? The fire?"

"No, it's the quicklime itself. I picked a very windless night for a reason." He laid the piece of metal carefully down, far away from either of them. "Quicklime's very reactive, especially with water. You can actually use it as a heat source. Mel turned up references that said they used to have self-cooking meals in cans, which heated up due to reacting quicklime with water. Enough quicklime exposed to water could actually radiate enough heat to start fires. So you can imagine what that would do to us bags of salty water."

Sakura thought a moment, then shivered. *Everything inside us is wet.* "So if you breathed it or got it in your mouth..."

"A burning—quite literally—sensation is the least you'd get." He'd edged back again, and she joined him, leaning against his smooth, thick hide. "Your mom's a doctor, I'm sure you know enough to imagine what would happen."

"Yeah. Okay, I'll be careful. But you say you're going to add water to it?"

"Carefully, yes, after it's all cooled down. That makes slaked lime, which is what we need for making leather, and we need leather to make you guys shoes and stuff."

She looked down at her feet, currently encased in slightly padded barkcloth wrappings. "For real hiking! I'm looking forward to getting real shoes."

"I can't blame you."

She looked at the bright flames licking at the underside of the roasting bowl, and for a few moments they were quiet.

Something was nagging at her. She couldn't figure out what it was. It was somehow connected to this discussion, though. She tried going over everything in her head, but it wasn't quite gelling. "Time to add more charcoal?"

"Yes, you'd better. To keep the temperature up the fire has to be kept high."

She stepped up and carefully spread more charcoal around, avoiding the supports.

That's it!

"Hey, Whips," she said, looking at the supports, "I've got a question."

"Go ahead."

"Aren't most of the rocks here at least partly calcium carbonate?"

"Well, yes, though quite a few have—"

He broke off, staring, hide rippling in shocked colors.

At that moment, one of the supports *snapped*, and the bowl began to tip—straight at Sakura.

Everything went into dreamlike slow motion. Sakura could see the two pieces of the broken support, a puff of powdery dust surrounding the break and tinted red-gold by the fire, the two pieces drifting apart. The bowl tilted with a deliberate, almost dignified inevitability, the underside clearly glowing red-hot as it left the immediate area of the flames. Inside, the crumbling mass was starting to shift, slide towards her, parts of it clearly yellow, others white. She realized what was going to happen, knew she couldn't possibly get out of the way in time.

The image of her eyes burning themselves, of the powdery quicklime heating up within her lungs, suddenly rose in her mind. *Got to close my eyes! Hold my breath!*

She had no idea what she'd be able to do then, with only a minute or two before she'd have to breathe, but—

Cablelike arms whipped around her and *yanked*.

Everything sped back up. The bowl smashed down into the fire, spraying powder and burning coals everywhere. Whips gave a shivering, keening howl of pain as both struck his back.

But Sakura only felt a momentary sting across one

calf as Whips' panicked throw hurled her three meters and more from the fire, to land tumbling but unhurt in the brush.

She scrambled up, heart hammering. "Whips! *Whips!* Don't breathe it! Keep your eyes closed!"

The three eyes snapped shut and she heard his breathing cease momentarily. The young Bemmie slid away from the fire as fast as he could move, skin still rippling and shuddering with pain and shock.

"Mom! Come quick!" she shouted into her omni.

Whips let out his breath with a tremendous *whoosh*— but showed he was still thinking, because he breathed in with great, slow care. "Burning ... across back ..." he said, with an edge to his voice like a man gritting his teeth.

"Hold on! I'll sweep it off or something!"

She glanced around desperately. The scattered coals and partially decomposed quicklime were smoking, but she couldn't worry about the fire yet. *Leaves. Try the leaves!*

The area around the fire had been cleared of leaves, of course, but there were a lot scattered where she was. Grabbing two fistfuls, she held her own breath and squinted, making long, sweeping brushstrokes down the area of Whips' hide that was coated with white dust. Much of it came off, and she dumped the leaves, grabbed more, repeated it, feeling warmth on her own hands. Sweat was mostly water. It touched her and started reacting. But there was only a light coating of it.

There were three buckets of water near the fire. As she nerved herself to test something, her mother responded. "What is it? I'm coming!"

"Accident with Whips' quicklime experiment!" she answered, then grabbed the bucket and dumped water over her dusted hand.

For a moment it warmed, but as the water continued to pour it rinsed the quicklime away. *So it should work . . . I hope I'm right.*

She grabbed the buckets and dumped the water over Whips, successive surges of water picking up the quicklime and carrying it away.

Whips had tensed, but now started to relax. "Exactly right," he said, with a rippling sound that brought to mind her own shaking hands. "Rinse with large amounts of water to remove." He started shaking more. "*Sky,* Sakura, I'm so stupid! I'm sorry, oh, by the Sky and Vents I'm *sorry*! How could I—"

"Hey, it's okay, it's okay! I'm not hurt, much anyway, and it's an easy mistake."

Running footsteps became audible and both her mother and Caroline burst through the surrounding bushes. "Are you two all right?"

"I'm just a little banged up, Mom. Whips threw me clear. He's . . ."

"I see." Laura Kimei dropped to her knees to study Whips' broad back and tail area.

Caroline started towards the fires, but Sakura stopped her. "Some of that white stuff is quicklime. We don't want to step on it or get it on us. C'mon, let's get more water!"

Fortunately the jungle was basically wet. Even though it took a few minutes to reach Blue Hole and return, the fire hadn't spread far and they quickly got it under control. By then, her mother had stood up. "He'll be fine. Mostly superficial burns, and I've dressed the couple areas that were a bit more serious. His medical nanos are already responding."

"What about infection, Mom?"

Her mother gave her a reassuring smile and patted her shoulder. "Saki, I've been tweaking everyone's nanos to deal with the local microfauna. Remember Hitomi getting a runny nose a few weeks ago? That was actually one of the worst diseases we've run across here, and if we weren't protected it could easily have turned into something lethal. Usually, your nanos alert me when something strange starts happening and I can give instructions on how to counter it before you'll feel anything more than a little, oh, 'off,' so to speak. So don't you worry; a little infection won't bother Whips or any of us."

"I'm *sorry*, Dr. Kimei," Whips said. "It's my fault."

"What? Why?"

"I stupidly used rocks—*native* rocks—to prop up the roasting bowl. Which was roasting native rocks into a powder."

Her mother gave a loud guffaw. "Oh, I'm sorry, Whips, I shouldn't laugh, but...well, it's also relief. When Sakura screamed for help I was afraid it was worse."

Sakura restrained herself from arguing. *I didn't* scream.

"But," her mother went on, "I will agree that was stupid of you. Still, there's no great harm done, and you've obviously had a lesson in thinking ahead in more detail, haven't you?"

Whips spread his arms. "Oh yes, Dr. Kimei."

"Then I'll let the fact that you could have badly injured yourself or Sakura be the punishment."

"Yes, Dr. Kimei."

"All right then." She bent over and gave him a hugging grip to the base of his arms. "Then let's hear no more apologies, just remember the lesson."

She stood and then enveloped Sakura in a tight, tight embrace. Sakura hugged her mother back. She was still a little shaky from the whole thing, but the adrenalin was fading now. "I think we'll probably go back to camp, once we're sure the fire's out."

"All right. I've got to get back to Melody."

She went and stirred the ashes with the slender rod Whips had used earlier; a wisp of smoke came up, which she promptly doused. "Whips..."

"I'm—"

"Hey, no, Mom said we're done with that. I was going to say, let's just get this done. Tomorrow I'll help you put it back up ... with things that won't burn away under it."

Whips hesitated.

"Oh, come *off* it, Whips! We've all made mistakes. You were just telling me how important this stuff is—were you just making all that up?"

"No! No, not at all," Whips answered. "We need it, we really do."

"Then tomorrow we build it again."

He hesitated, then a ripple of calmer conviction showed across his body. "Yes. All right, tomorrow we build it again." He looked at the broken stones. "Build it *better*."

"That's the idea!"

Chapter 28

"This," asserted Sakura emphatically, "is dis-*gust*-ing."

Whips would have liked to disagree with her, given that what they were doing was so vital, but he was unable to even try. "We need leather, though. Those wrap-your-feet shoes you and Mel cobbled together—"

"I saw what you did there!" Sakura said, stirring the nauseating-looking soup with pieces of obvious brain still in them.

"What? Oh, yes, cobbled! Ha! I didn't notice!" He hadn't, actually, and suspected he'd never convince Sakura the pun was accidental. "Anyway, those things work okay on the mostly dry flat areas, and you can replace them pretty easily, but..."

"I know." Sakura glanced over at the four flat hides of capys—*not* from the herd they'd been following—that they'd managed to collect and salt. "But they don't protect us from a lot of things in rougher areas, and if we want to make a big expedition to the higher areas, with rivers and maybe swamps and who knows what else, we really need real shoes."

Whips glanced down at her feet, which were now heavily callused. "Of course, you're a lot tougher than you used to be. Still, walking unfamiliar rough territory isn't the same as the areas we're used to here near the shore."

He looked at the hides, remembering just how much work went into the process—skinning the animals, salting them immediately (and how very long it had taken to accumulate the kilos of salt needed!), soaking it in a dehairing solution made from slaked lime, scraping or, as Melody had said, "scudding" the hide, and now . . .

"I can't wait for this brain puree soup to be finished." Sakura said. "I'd *really* rather be working on soap."

"Your mother and father are not letting anyone else get involved where lye is concerned, at least not until they're sure how the whole process works out," Whips said, taking his turn stirring the solution. "And I can't blame them. None of us are chemists—your mom is the closest we've got—and while I think we've got all the information right, and she's pretty sure she's figured out the saponification values based on the chemical references we dug out of the omnis . . . but who knows? I don't need soap, much, and you guys have been doing okay with sand-scrubs and dips in the fresh water, but I know how much it would mean to you to get really clean."

Sakura nodded. "Boy, would it ever be great to have a shower or a bath with real soap." She looked down, wrinkling her nose. "I can't believe I am going to soak a capy hide in brewed capy brains."

"It's the simplest tanning method and doesn't use any other chemicals we need to make. Dehairing was—"

"Hairy?"

"Ouch. But yes, hairy enough." He rippled his

amusement at her. "Actually I'm glad we've done it for this. Now we know we can do it and have it work right, and that means, among other things, cement and concrete. Lime and lye are both really useful industrial chemicals."

He took over stirring the mess for a bit. "I guess we shouldn't complain. Some of the other tanning methods use other stuff that's even nastier. I saw one that used sulfuric acid as part of the process. And we haven't found a good source of tannin."

"Still disgusting, though. Will this work?"

Whips gave a rippling shrug. "The brain chemistry, especially the oils and fats, seems close enough. Your mother did a thorough analysis. The capys have more than enough brain mass for the job. And the only steps after that are smoking and stretching, and we already built two hollow-tree smokers for preserving food, along with salting."

Sakura stuck her tongue out with a nauseated expression. "Well, okay, but I sure hope the smoking and oiling afterward kills some of the smell." She looked enviously at Whips. "Boy, you're lucky you don't need clothes and stuff."

"I can't argue that." It was one of the things that made being a Bemmie clearly better than being a human, especially on an untamed planet like this one. His skin, as long as he kept it reasonably moist, was very tough, and his belly pad was thicker than a human boot sole, so it took something truly vicious to penetrate that.

"How long have we been here, anyway?" Sakura asked absently.

"Check your omni?"

"Duh!" She blinked absently for a moment. "Holy brain-soup. It's getting close to a *year*. Nine and a half...no, ten months since we crashlanded."

"Is it really only that long?"

"*Only?*" she repeated disbelievingly.

"Only, yes. Look at everything we've managed to do in that time, without a single qualified engineer, chemist, or even historian to help." He turned one of his eyes down into the boiling mix, and checked the bottom of the shell to make sure it was still holding up; sometimes they burned or cracked through without warning. "Some of what we've done surprises the *Sky* out of me. Oh, we've had our failures—"

"—like the jam that caught fire, or that first floor support that warped, or your first try at making the quicklime."

"Please, don't remind me of that, and I won't remind you of your naïve attempt to make spearheads by hammering metal pieces with a rock."

"Deal."

He looked around. "But really, Sakura, it's...kind of awesome. We weren't ready for this. We were colonists, yes, but...for a world with other people, with the right equipment, with everything understood, honestly."

She paused in her stirring, thinking, and he saw slow realization spread through her as she really thought about it. "You know...you're right. We could have died. So many times. We almost broke that one time. But...we're not dead. And we're not broken. We got up, we started rebuilding, and we've made a home again. And we're not stopping."

He gave a bright-patterned smile. "We certainly are not!" Whips glanced into the pot again. "Getting close to stopping on *this,* though. But then the real fun begins."

"Oh, ugh. Rubbing brain stew all over every one of those skins."

"Into every crevice, every fold, every edge, because if we miss even a small piece, we're going to end up with a part that isn't tanned."

She rolled her eyes, resignation clear on her features. "Yeah, yeah, I know." She gave the kettle another stir. "But *boy* do I hope they get the soap done soon."

Some of the solution spattered out, catching Whips. "Ouch! Watch it, Sakura."

"Sorry!"

"Just be careful." He couldn't restrain a flicker of mirth. "After all, this could turn me into one of your people's monsters."

"What are you talking about?"

"Well, if you get enough on me, you'd tan me, right?"

"I . . . guess . . ." she said, now looking at him with suspicious, narrowed eyes.

"Well, then I'd go from Little Bemmie to Mr. Hide."

"Do you want me to dump this whole thing on you?"

"An empty, empty threat," he pointed out, "since that would mean we'd have to start this over again. And we don't have more brains available."

"There aren't more *capy* brains available," she said, looking at his midsection meaningfully.

"A point," he conceded. He picked up the cloth broom and whisked off the flat rock surface they were going to work on one last time.

"I think that's it," Sakura said while he was still sweeping. "Looks smooth and it's heated to the right temperature, according to my omni."

"Then let's get to it."

"You'll have to hold the hides down and flat."

"I know." Despite other superiorities, Whips knew his manipulating tentacles were not really good at the spreading and kneading motions that would be required for this step; what he could do was to be an anchor and help in stretching the skins later. Sakura would do the majority of the rubbing and spreading of the brain tanning solution, which was sort of halfway between a soup and a paste.

I sure hope this works.

That was something close to a prayer, actually, even though he didn't really have a religion. The tradition of Those Beyond the Sky had dwindled a lot since the real people beyond the sky made contact with his. But if there were any unseen forces out there, he really hoped they would keep helping. What Lincoln had taught Whips most clearly was how hard it was to do the things that had seemed so simple in civilization; even the much more primitive civilization of his ancestor Blushspark's time, without the many reliable resources, processes, and skills taught and used throughout a large population.

Here, a single failure of an experiment could cost them weeks of effort, wiping out resources gained slowly over many days in a matter of seconds. The omnis helped—tracking their actions, highlighting key features, and so on—and taking their time to carefully work out the entire procedures they planned to use also helped a lot. That was, undoubtedly, why they'd had mostly successes.

But the failures . . . they really *hurt* when they happened, in a way that failure didn't hurt on board

Outward Initiative or back home in Europa or on Earth.

"Make sure your omni's tracking your work."

"Oh, yeah." Sakura grimaced. "Make sure I get brain-paste *everywhere*."

"Exactly," Whips said, with another flickering grin. "You always have to know how to use your brains."

Chapter 29

"Everyone ready?"

"I'm ready!" Sakura answered, trying to keep from bouncing. A day just exploring! It had been a long time!

"Ready, Laura," Whips answered. While Whips would slow them down to some extent in long walks, the fact that they were looking for watery areas made it important to bring their amphibious member.

"I wanna come!" Hitomi said, dangerously close to whining.

"Hitomi." Akira's voice was quiet, but the warning tone in it was enough to make Sakura wince even though she knew it wasn't directed at her.

"I wanna go *with* them!" Hitomi insisted stubbornly. "*Tired* of just staying here all the time!"

"We discussed this, Hitomi. We're going to a new area of this continent, and it could be dangerous."

"But—"

"*Hitomi.*"

This time the youngest Kimei stopped, though it looked like the effort to stop talking would make her explode.

Akira nodded. "Just in time. But good listening.

Your mother and I have made the decision, and you are not going to argue out of it. If you keep making a fuss, I'll give you more chores and no Jewelbug for three nights."

Hitomi bit her lip and looked down, angry but still quiet.

"Good. Now stay quiet for a few more minutes and I'll forget you were arguing with your mother."

Akira gave Laura a hug and a kiss. "You be careful." He looked to Caroline. "And you make sure you help watch over your sister and Whips."

"Don't worry, Dad, I will."

"You'll be all right with just Mel and Hitomi?"

"Fine. We'll work on some of the smaller things that we've been putting off."

Sakura found her self-control sorely tested as Mom and Dad continued talking. Finally she took matters into her own hands. "Okay, Whips, Caroline—time we got moving, right?"

Whips started moving forward in his deceptively jerky way. Caroline's sideways smile showed she knew perfectly well what Sakura was up to.

It worked, though. Her mother looked over, saw they were all starting to move, and sighed. "Well, Akira, I have to get going."

One more quick kiss and her mother jogged up to join them. "All right, I suppose I was taking a while, Sakura."

"'Sokay, Mom, we're going now!"

"How long do you think this will take, Laura?" asked Whips.

"Hard to say, exactly," Laura admitted. "You're able to maintain a bit more than three kilometers per hour walking, or crawling, speed, but like us you'll slow down when the underbrush gets too thick. The landing scar would give us some easier walking but we'd have to waste time getting there first. Caroline, how far is it?"

"According to our omnis, it looks like several streams come down the slopes—and disappear from anything we can see from a distance—about ten to fifteen kilometers from here. Have your omnis project the line for you." Caroline's phrasing reminded Sakura that Caroline still didn't have an omni, because hers was now mounted as a relay and alert sensor on the very top of Sherwood Column.

"So . . . five to eight hours each way, probably," Sakura said, adjusting time for the slowdowns they'd expect. "No wonder you and Dad had us pack for a couple of days."

"Yes," her mother agreed. "There's a good chance we're overnighting it."

"Oh, *that's* what the heavy package you added to my pack was," Whips said in understanding. "A section of the old shelter."

"Correct."

Ten kilometers. Sakura was still occasionally jolted by her changes in perceptions since they'd crashed. Back home, ten kilometers was, what, a few minutes in a car, or nothing in anything faster. Here . . . it was an epic trip.

And back home, pretty much everything along those ten kilometers from home would be familiar and safe. *These* ten kilometers might have something awesome to discover . . . or the most dangerous creatures they'd yet seen.

With Whips plowing his way steadily along beside her, Sakura followed Caroline and her mother past the Blue Hole, which happened to lie slightly "inland" of their column, and through Thin Column Meadow, and cautiously through what a vote of the family had christened "Stonetree Forest"—the jungle that covered much of this part of their floating continent. Hitomi had been very put out that her choice—Sherwood Forest, naturally—had been overruled, but she'd grudgingly agreed that since she'd already gotten to name the whole planet, other people should be able to choose some of the names.

Periodically, they passed a burned, broken stump and a trail of broken underbrush where a tree had been cut down. "Mom, do you think we're going to get, well, Lincoln mad at us?"

"Hm?" Her mother glanced back, saw where she was looking. "I hope not, honey. We are certainly doing *some* damage, but we've done what we could to spread it out a bit, and we're not concentrating on any one area." They moved on for a few moments in silence, her mother's face thoughtful. "Still, I know what you mean, and we should all watch for any signs of that sort."

"Hold up!" Whips said sharply. "Laura, I don't like the look of those growths ahead."

Sakura immediately saw what Whips meant. The slender, reedlike growths were covered with brilliant scarlet fuzz—fuzz that looked very painfully familiar.

Laura moved closer and pointed her omni at it, obtaining a better image. "Let me see . . . you may be right, Whips. Caroline?"

Caroline picked up a stick and gingerly poked at the

stand of red reeds. Immediately the "fuzz" snapped out and wrapped around the stick. Caroline pulled back. Most of the tendrils let go, but one of them had wrapped tightly enough around the branch that the tendril was broken off and came with the stick. "Here, Mom."

A few moments later, Laura nodded. "Very similar toxin, and the cnidocysts appear powerful enough to penetrate human skin but not Bemmie hide, just like the tree-anemone. Good catch, Whips."

They gave the stand of plantlike creatures, which Sakura dubbed fire-reeds, a wide berth as they continued on.

After that, they hiked for quite a distance without any particular incidents, until they noticed a shift in the light. "I think we're coming up on another clearing."

Caroline unlimbered her bow and nocked an arrow. The fire-hardened points had proven quite effective over the last few months, and Caroline was the best shot in the entire family—although Hitomi showed indications of being very good. Sakura carried a bow, but she really hoped she didn't have to use it. Hand weapons like her machete were her forte.

Unfortunately, the canopy krakens were not something you wanted to use hand weapons on. She'd been incredibly lucky in her one confrontation, and Whips, even though much larger than her, had needed his own share of luck facing three. And if they were coming to a clearing or something like it, the canopy krakens were likely to be there, waiting for things approaching or crossing that boundary.

"Whips, do you see anything?" Laura asked, holding the SurvivalShot at the ready.

"Nothing . . . no, wait. My omni's saying there's a pattern discontinuity up there. Two of them." He looked up with all three eyes, eyes which could make out the faintest gleam of light in the depths of Europa and were more sensitive to ultraviolet than human. "Yes, I see them now. Two krakens. Transmitting to your omnis."

With the enhanced vision from her omni projection, Sakura could clearly see the predators, crouched on the branches maybe five meters up. "Here, Caroline," she said quietly, and passed the omni to her big sister, who let the bow relax long enough to take the miniature wrist-computer unit and strap it on.

"Can we go around them?"

Whips looked in both directions. "It looks to me like the clearing, if that's what it is, must be pretty large, so yes. But no guarantee there aren't any others. Remember that we've seen . . . prides, packs, schools, whatever, of them, as many as seven."

"True." Sakura waited; this was her mother's decision.

"We'll go forward," Laura said finally. "Saki, you're the smallest and look the most vulnerable, you stay behind me and Caroline, and Whips, you bring up the rear."

The four of them moved slowly towards the forest edge. Knowing where they were, Sakura could make out the things with unassisted eyes now; anchored to the trees by their leg-tentacles, armor and skin shifted like Whips' body to match the surroundings, striking tentacles curled back, looking deceptively short.

She swallowed and gripped the hilt of her machete tightly; the memory of facing one on the ground, and nearly being killed by it, was all too clear.

Perhaps it was Whips' presence, much more massive

than any of the humans, or perhaps something about the way the group moved showed that they were well aware of the canopy krakens' presence and were still going straight through—an act which indicated minimal fear of the creatures. But for whatever reason, the two krakens never tried to grab any of them.

"Oh, *neat!*" Sakura said as they cut their way through the thicker brush at the edge of Stonetree Forest.

This was no clearing; the forest ended here, rather sharply, with only a few scattered trees and tree-animals spaced about. The land in front of them had a jumbled, wrinkled look that made it more rugged and clearly harder for trees and similar creatures to anchor well on.

"We've been making better time than I thought!" Caroline said, pleased. "I'd thought we were still half a kilometer from the edge, near as I could guess it with what we could see from the top of Sherwood Column."

The mountains, or tall hills, rose up perhaps five kilometers away, the ones farther behind tinted blue with distance. Three streams or small rivers were visible at this distance, coming down the flanks of the mountains and disappearing behind the jumbled terrain. What lay between them and the mountains wasn't easily visible, but even with the roughness of the land, Sakura thought they could move even faster.

"Let's go!" she said, starting forward.

"Slow down, Saki!" her mother said sharply. "Remember—this is a new kind of territory. We have no idea what kind of things live in this part of the continent."

"Sorry, Mom. You're right." *You'd think being stung*

by a pretty flower-thing would have taught me not to just charge ahead.

The thought of the sting reminded her of something else. "Hey, Mom . . . how are your medical supplies doing?"

"Getting a bit low," Laura admitted after a moment. She stepped over a moderate-sized rock and watched Whips go around it. "But on the positive side our personal nanos have been programmed with countermeasures for the toxins and allergens we've encountered so far, and they're holding up well. I've overridden their lifetime counters for now, but I think what I'm going to do is have them start concentrating out—probably in the urine."

"Oh, ugh. We'll have to save our pee."

"I'm afraid so, sweetie. But not for too long. Once I can replace them with some of our reserves, I can run a cycle where the reserves reprocess the old ones, make sure any long-term damage is purged and the units reset for use."

"We'll lose some nanos that way, though, won't we, Dr. Kimei?" Sakura noticed that whenever addressing Mom in her professional capacity, Whips suddenly became formal.

"Some. About ten percent. So we can't do this forever. But I also hope that by then our own bodies will be doing most of the work, since that's part of what the nanos are supposed to do—basically train and enhance our own immune systems. And with ten percent loss and needing a twenty percent reserve to do this process, well, I can do this a few more times. So we've got at least a few more years before it's an issue."

Whips dragged himself over another ridge, then waved one arm. "Hold up. I need a little rest."

"Gee, you seemed to be doing fine all the way here."

A rippling snort, combined with a red-black pattern of mild annoyance. "I know. But most of the forest and shore area is fairly flat. Sharp slopes, even short ones, and these blocks and boulders, those are harder for me." Another shimmer of light, this one less hostile. "Remember, in Europa we generally swim over every obstacle."

Sakura hadn't really thought of it that way, but it was obvious now that this kind of terrain—simple as it was for humans—would be a problem for Bemmies. They had to slide or hoist their ways over obstacles, and judging by the rise of the land they had another kilometer to go before they reached the top of this region and could maybe rely on gravity to help on the descent.

"A good place to stop," Laura said cheerfully. "Let's all have lunch, take a break. We've come a long ways and it's been several hours."

Sakura didn't object; her legs *were* getting tired. As they unpacked lunch, she looked to Caroline. "Hey, Caroline—can you tell me something?"

"Depends on whether I know whatever it is."

"Well, I hope so. We see three rivers over there, and I guess there's probably a lot more in other parts of this continent. But water wears through stuff, right? Why don't the rivers just cut through and then drop down out of sight into the hollow we know is there?"

Caroline smiled. "I can't know, but I can guess. First, I think the ... crust, for lack of a better term ... around here is pretty thick, and has a lot of the carbon-silica variant that's much tougher. Remember that the lifecycle for these floating landmasses probably has them regularly breaking and rolling over, so what we're looking at here is the former lower portion. So the mountains are like ballast, thicker parts of the continent that provide a counterweight to the stuff floating above."

Sakura nodded. "Makes sense."

"Second, I suspect that the island defenses actually include maintaining the crust. And it takes time for a river to wear through even soft rock, so the defenses can affect this river's course slowly. Look over there, the far left river. See above and to the right of that one loop, about in the middle from where we see? That's part of the river's prior course. It's shifted to the left. And I think I see similar shift indications all the way along its path, and that of the other two."

"So the island keeps the rivers flowing without falling through?" Whips summarized. "That's amazing."

"It is!" Caroline said emphatically. "Even more for Dad, really, since this is geology that's being built by living things. We're making major discoveries almost every week here." She looked wistful, and Sakura knew why, even before Caroline spoke again. "I just hope . . . someday . . ."

"I know, honey," said her mother. "So do we all."

The unspoken thought of *will we ever be rescued?* dropped a leaden blanket over the conversation, and Sakura decided she wasn't putting up with it. "So, everyone, I was thinking. If my omni's right, we're in the beginning of July back home."

"Well," Whips said reluctantly, "Probably. But I'm not sure of the relativistic—"

"Never mind about *that*. Not like anyone's here to argue whether the calendar's off by a couple days or whatever. What I was saying, is that we've been here for over ten months, and in just a month—July sixteenth—it'll be Hitomi's birthday."

"I never thought about that," her mother said, clearly startled. "I haven't . . . oh, dear. That means we've missed everyone else's birthday except Hitomi's and yours, in August."

Caroline looked thoughtful, then laughed. "Not quite. *I* got a brand-new room for *my* birthday."

"Really?" Sakura checked. "You're right. We moved into our house on your birthday!"

"But you're right to bring it up, Sakura. We're living here now, and that means it's time to start remembering things like birthdays, anniversaries, and so on." She looked at the others. "So what should we do for Hitomi?"

Talking about the birthday opportunities kept them busy until lunch was over. Sakura shouldered her pack again and looked up. "About a half a kilometer to go, Whips, and then we'll be at the top. Let's go!"

"Right behind you!"

Chapter 30

"What do you think, Caroline?" Laura asked.

Below and ahead, a brilliant green flatland was spread, with glinting pools and channels of water meandering through the wind-rippled green. There were scattered patches of bushes and a few stunted trees, but for the most part the growth was low and lush. Small hummocks of land, humps a few meters across, were dotted about the swamp.

Caroline was smiling. "Oh, that's *very* promising, Mom. Very. Look, over there, we see the streams coming in, and they slow down and go into this wetland. I want to get over to the far side there, where it looks like the stream's wandered around a bit."

She pointed ahead and to the right, where the ridge they were on curved around, gradually dropping in height until it became a low hill, merging into the base of the small mountain range. Not too far to the left of this, the wetland merged with the downslope. Laura could see the rippled shape of the land nearby that Caroline thought indicated a wandering of the stream itself.

"So you think we'll find clay there?"

"Don't get your hopes up too high," Caroline cautioned. "But if there is clay around here, that's a place I'd expect to find it."

"Cool!" Sakura said, but—Laura was glad to see—restrained herself from setting out.

"Whips? Are you all right to keep going?"

"Give me a few minutes and I will be," the young Bemmie answered, his breath a bit labored. "Downhill's easier, and a wetland looks *much* more my kind of place."

"Much less ours, though," Laura said, studying the deceptively beautiful flatland. "There's almost certainly deep mud there, and given everything else we've seen, there might be some very nasty creatures. I'll leave you to your own judgment on how far you want to go into that stuff, Whips, but I want the rest of my family staying on the solid ground as much as possible."

"No objection here," Caroline said. "Our new boots may seem to be waterproof but I don't see any reason to test that."

Sakura suddenly pointed. "Look there!"

Laura followed her daughter's gaze, and saw large ripples spreading across one of the many little ponds. "Did you see what made that?"

"Not really," Sakura admitted, "but I saw the movement. It was something pretty big."

"Keep an eye out then. Ready, Whips?"

"Ready. Let's go!"

The four made their way cautiously along the ridge. Whips dropped lower down and eventually was sliding along the edge of the swamp, ducking occasionally into small pools and then sliding up over the little hummocks, which were mostly covered with green, reedy growths. "Definitely fresh water," he called up to them. "Some minor jelly-stingers but nothing that bothers me. I've heard some movement that tells me there's a lot of life here. In fact . . ."

He hesitated, then lashed out with his arms; there was a sudden commotion in the water, and Whips turned and flung a fish measuring nearly a meter long up onto the bank near them. "Dinner, I think!"

Laura had the others stay back, studying the creature before risking getting close. Plenty of fish on Earth had spines and poison and really sharp teeth. Here they seemed to be at least as bad.

Like many other forms of life on Lincoln, the fish that Whips had caught was quadrilateral in its symmetry, with a four-part mouth that didn't seem to have many teeth. They were basically ridges with some very small back-pointing barbs. Sakura took careful aim and put an arrow through it. She might not be terribly good with a bow, but at this range she didn't have to be.

Once the writhing slowed, Laura moved forward and checked the fish-creature more carefully. "No defensive spines of note. Mostly non-toxic, too, though I'd avoid the internal organs. There are some concentrations of questionable materials in there, according to the nanos. Looks like you're right, Whips, you just got us dinner!"

"Great! I'll catch something else for me—that one wouldn't be enough."

They quickly filleted the fish and wrapped them in broadleaves—tough, non-toxic leaves from one of the trees in the forest that they'd brought for samples and for uses like this. "In these temperatures, wrapped like this, they'll keep for perhaps four hours," Laura said.

"That should get us up to the area we're heading for," Caroline said. "So Whips and Saki can get dinner ready then, while you and I do some trial digging."

Small creatures scuttled away through the under-brush as they walked; Laura caught a glimpse of the same feather-fur that covered the capys, but on something much smaller. This world's equivalent of mammals had multiple niches covered just as they did on Earth, she guessed.

The creatures were similar to mammals in several ways. Not only did they have a furlike covering, but they also seemed to give birth to live young and nourish them from their own bodies. This contrasted drastically with things like, say, the minimaws. Akira had recently determined that they were egg-layers whose larval forms turned out to be thin-legged small predators that Sakura had named "stilt-snakes." They must slowly lose their legs and become more and more burrowing creatures as they got older.

They made good time along the perimeter of the wetlands. Whips' speed was drastically increased with access to significant water and mud to go through, rather than dragging himself across dry land. In about three hours they came to the gently rippled land bordering one of the streams.

"This is good enough," Caroline said. The others, Laura included, promptly dropped their barkcloth bags with a sigh of relief. Whips slid up from the wetlands, accompanied by the familiar sulfurous smell of buried decay. "Eeew! Whips, go wash off, will you?" Sakura said as he approached.

"Sorry!"

This time he moved into the nearby clear stream

and rolled around until the black mud was gone. Only the faintest trace of the smell remained when he returned. "Better?"

"Much better," Laura agreed. "Did you get something to eat?"

"I grabbed smaller fish and things as we were walking. I'm set—don't worry about me."

"All right. I'll leave you and Sakura to get the fish cooked for the rest of us, then."

She got her pointed spade—wooden, of course, with an edge reinforced by a strip of metal—out of her pack while Caroline did the same. Caroline pointed out some areas of interest, and they started digging.

Digging with wooden shovels in ground that had never been tilled—even ground mostly without stones— wasn't easy. They also had to go quite a ways down, and Laura quickly found herself covered with more sweat than the hiking had managed to produce. "How are you doing, Caroline?"

Her daughter had just stopped and was kneeling on the ground. "Good! Hmm . . . well, we have deposition layers. Oh . . . oh, what's this?"

Caroline was squeezing something between her fingers. "That sure *feels* like it could be clay!" she said, excitement vibrating in her voice. She squinted down into the hole. "Layer's really thin, though. Not very good for digging it up. How far down are you, Mom?"

"About . . . fifty centimeters, according to my omni."

"I was down to seventy-nine, and my layer's at sixty-one through sixty-two and a half."

"Good Lord you're fast. I must be getting old."

Caroline laughed, still staring at the pale ball of maybe-clay she'd dug up. "I'm just used to digging.

Had to do a lot of it in my fieldwork a couple of years ago. How often do doctors have to dig holes in the ground?"

"Only when we make big mistakes," Laura said wryly.

"That's morbid of you, Mom!"

"Always glad to provide the more cynical humor," she answered with a grin. "Okay, I've gotten to about seventy centimeters now. Is that lighter layer what you're looking for?"

Caroline trotted over and took a look. "Yes, that's it . . . but it's even thinner here." She stood and gazed at the surrounding territory. Laura recognized the look as that of a the professional gauging their next move; something that looked the same on a doctor evaluating a patient for an operation, an engineer judging a design, or her daughter trying to figure out which way that layer of hopefully-clay would be thicker.

"Can I borrow your omni, Mom?" she asked after a moment.

"Of course."

While Caroline resumed her study of the surroundings, now with the omni to help, Whips gave a startlingly good imitation of a ringing bell. "Dinner's ready, come and get it!"

"Be there in a minute," Caroline said absently. Laura went over to the camp, where Whips and Sakura had gotten a fire going with the charcoal they'd brought and grilled the fish, as well as roasting some totatoes—tubers that had a distinctly tomato-ey taste—in the fire.

Sakura made a face as they started eating. "Awfully bland. And a kinda blah backtaste."

"Muddy," Laura agreed. "Catfish can taste that way. I seem to remember you can soak them in some things to reduce the taste, but we haven't got any of that." She took a couple more bites, as Caroline joined them. "If you eat it with a bite of totato, though, the backtaste disappears."

Sakura tried that and Laura had to smile at the surprised look. "That works, Mom!"

"My mother taught me that: it's not just what you eat, but in what order, and how you eat it, that determines what you taste."

"Gramma was real smart," agreed Caroline. "So, my best guess is that we need to head over there." She pointed across the stream. "The land flattens out between two rivers over there. It'll get wetter and mushier a bit, but I think we could end up with a much better layer of clay—and I'm pretty sure this is clay, now."

"That's wonderful!" Sakura said, beaming. "We'll be able to make pots and cups and—"

"Slow down, Saki!" Caroline said, though she was smiling too. "I said I'm *pretty* sure. But even if it is clay, it'll probably take a while to figure out how to make a kiln that can fire it, and how to make the right mix that doesn't shrink too much or break too easy, and glazes if we want to waterproof them. But . . . yes, I think so, eventually. And there are other uses for good ceramics, a lot of them."

"Then let's go!" Sakura said, standing. "I want to dig this time!"

"As soon as we finish eating," Laura agreed. "And you're welcome to my shovel, too."

After making sure the fire was well out, the four moved across the stream and headed for the area between the next two streams, a broad, lower plain area that blended almost imperceptibly into the wetlands. "We'll try to stay out of the actual swampy area," Caroline said. "But the wetter ground might be easier to dig."

A loud, booming cry, a deep-throated bellow, echoed from somewhere in the swamp; the whole party froze momentarily. "What was *that?*" Sakura demanded, gripping her spear.

"Don't know," Whips said. "It isn't any of the animals we've seen before."

"It was quite a ways off, though," Laura said calmly, though the unexpected roar had gotten her pulse racing too. "No need to panic. We're out in the open here and we'll have plenty of time to see anything approaching us."

"You're right, Laura," Whips said. "And I can sense things in the water pretty well."

It didn't take long to reach the area that Caroline had selected, and Sakura immediately attacked the ground with Laura's spade. The moister ground and Sakura's enthusiasm let the fifteen-year-old send dirt flying out of her hole at a startling rate. Caroline, though more experienced, was actually smaller than her younger sibling and dug in a more controlled, sedate fashion.

A few minutes later Sakura grunted. "Ow! That's not the same as the rest. It's hard to get through."

"Hard, or just . . . thick?" Caroline asked, putting her shovel down.

"Thick, I think. Kinda sticky . . ." With a grunt, Sakura yanked the shovel free. "Oh my God, is that—"

Caroline raised the end of Sakura's shovel, to which were stuck reddish-brown chunks of something. "I think it is," Caroline said, a broad grin spreading across her face.

She grabbed one of the chunks and pressed it

between her hands and then tried rolling it. In a few minutes, a long, slender rope of rust-colored earth lay in her hand. Caroline curled it around her arm; it only cracked slightly. "It *is!* Clay, Mom, Whips, Sakura—that's *clay!*"

The general cheer was louder than the distant bellow had been. "You're sure? No analysis?"

"Looking at the microcomposition in the omni's view, I'm sure. It's maybe not exactly like any Earth clay, but it's definitely clay."

"The stuff you found before was lighter, though," Sakura pointed out.

"Different compositions, probably from different weathering locations," Caroline said, answering the implied question. "The deposition area was where we predicted, but that didn't mean that composition couldn't be different. That might be useful, actually. Different types of clay have different uses. Let's dig up some of this clay, and then go back to the other holes and at least get some samples of the other clay so I can compare them back home."

Whips couldn't handle a shovel well, and he was best used as a watchman and guard anyway. With the three humans working together it took only a half hour to dig up and wrap about twenty kilograms of reddish clay. Divided up between them it wasn't very heavy.

"Great!" Caroline said. "Now we can go back to our first spot. She glanced at the sun, which was starting to get low; they were on the second bright cycle which meant that sunset would be coming later today. "I'd like to get home, but I guess we'll have to camp."

Laura nodded. "It will take too long to get back. We've been traveling for about ten hours total."

"That long?" Caroline's face showed her surprise, then she looked thoughtful. "I guess it has been that long."

"I think that we should make our camp at the first dig site," Laura said, as they started back, Whips sliding along the edge of the wetlands. "We can dig up the other samples in the morning-night, really—and then go straight home."

"Works for me."

They headed back towards the first site. As they walked, Laura was abruptly assailed by a nebulous feeling that something was wrong.

She turned towards Whips, but even before she could shout a warning, the Bemmie suddenly slewed towards shore, jetting furiously for dry ground. Even as he did so, one of the green-covered hummocks—a hummock that hadn't been there when they first passed—lunged towards Whips, rising up, revealing wide, dark eyes and the top of a savage, quadpartite mouth like a double crocodile. Twin *somethings* streaked through the water—and Whips' flight was halted as though he had run into a wall.

With a booming roar, the creature began to drag Whips back.

Chapter 31

The wetlands were full of the signals of life, and thick with confusing echoes and returns from the shallow water and masses of earth on all sides. It was only as he passed beyond one hummock and into a broad pool on the other side that Whips suddenly sensed that the mass at the farther side of the pool wasn't a hummock of dirt at all.

He spun and streaked for the land. Even if it, too, was amphibious, getting it on land would give the Kimeis a chance to help him.

Twin hammers slammed into his side, an agonizing double impact just above the base of his tail-anchors, and something *yanked* on him, trying to pull him towards the massive creature he could now clearly sense. It was huge—the size of an orekath, he thought!

That might have been a bit of an exaggeration, but the way it had ambushed him and was pulling him towards a multitoothed mouth was very much like that of the giant tentacled predators of Europa. He couldn't let himself be dragged backwards!

Lashing out with all three arms, Whips caught hold of an outcropping of stone—a projection of the corallike bedrock of the continent—with his right arm. His top arm could also get a good enough grip on that outcrop. The left arm couldn't, and he flailed frantically. He needed all three anchored or this thing would just drag him back anyway, maybe tearing his arms out at the base!

His sonar showed a faint, harder return below and to the left. He plunged his left arm deep into the mud and was rewarded with the feel of something solid. It might just be a boulder, but it felt big and heavy. Better than nothing.

Deeps and Sky, this hurts! The creatures' arms or claws or whatever were only partly penetrating his hide, but they had a grip on him that wouldn't be broken, and the immense mass of the thing was starting to stretch him.

Three sets of splashing footsteps suddenly detonated in the water near him. He heard Sakura shrieking something in both terror and fury, and the hillock-sized creature holding him twitched and gave vent to a howling growl. Instead of letting go, however, it tightened its grip and heaved.

Despite his desperate attempt to hold on, he felt his own grip slipping, several of his own capture-hooks starting to rip out. He couldn't keep from screaming, a loud, moaning shriek that could be heard both above and below the water. *I'm losing it!*

"Let . . . him . . . *GO!*" Caroline's frightened voice was no less determined, and he felt the impact of her spear echo through the thing's arms. Laura's struck in the same moment, and that caused the thing to bellow in agony.

One arm suddenly released him, but he still had lost most of his grip on the projection of rock. Desperately he fastened his other arms onto the boulder, but it, too, was being dragged backwards.

Then Laura gave a scream—a scream of shock and crushing pain.

Laura!

The thought was very, very much the same as *Mother!*

His pain was forgotten. All that mattered was that he had to act, had to act *now*. Using the strength of his own attacker, Whips pulled as hard as he could, and the boulder moved, water flowing now in around it, pulling out. The creature was dragging him swiftly towards it now, towards the huge jaws, but he was turning, arching his body like a sling, seeing Laura in the grip of the hulking thing and her two daughters reaching toward her—

And the boulder, still held in his arms, exploded from the muddy water, arching around, a morning star the size of Whips' entire body, almost tearing his arms out by itself, and he twisted around, pulling, let go *NOW!*

The dense, heavy stone struck like a bludgeon wielded by a giant, smashing against the monster's low-slung head, driving it down with a piledriver force that hammered it into the black, stinking mud below. The arms convulsed...and went limp.

Whips sagged down, sinking into the water, feeling the torn, strained, and bleeding agony of his arms. *Don't think...any of them are very good right now.*

His siphon and anchors still worked, though, so he ignored the stretching, grinding pain of some of his body plates and turned around, jetting to the thing's body...and Laura. "Laura! Dr. Kimei, are you..."

"Mother! *MOM!*"

"Don't pull on her!" Caroline snapped, just as Sakura was reaching for her mother, who was slowly sinking.

"But—"

"I *know!* But if you just pull on her and there's something wrong with her neck or back—Whips, can you support her?"

"Yes," he answered. His body was vibrating with the aftermath of terror and shock, and his arms and fingers did not want to move; pain and *wrongness*—of dislocation and torn muscle—echoed up all three of his arms. But he forced them to spread, to catch hold of Laura Kimei, and give her support as Sakura, sobbing but still moving, and Caroline carefully removed her from the slowly relaxing deathgrip of the thing's claw—which, he could now see, was a three-pincered affair.

I don't think I want to look at where it grabbed me, he thought. He could tell, just by feedback through his omni, that his medical nanos were in overdrive trying to negate blood loss, shock, and other effects of the combat.

He could see that Laura's eyes weren't completely closed, and she was still breathing, quickly, with tension showing her pain. That was good. She wasn't unconscious.

With great care, the three of them managed to get Laura well up the bank and lay her down very gingerly. By then, her eyes were open, and she managed a tiny smile. "Good...thinking, Caroline."

"Sorry, Mom," Sakura said shakily. "I..."

"Are you all right, Laura?" Whips asked tensely.

She raised an eyebrow—barely visible with the black mud, mixed with blood, smeared across her face. "I'll need...my omni back..."

Caroline practically tore it off her arm and put it around her mother's wrist. "You linked back in, Mom?"

"Working...fine, Caroline," Laura said faintly. "Now be quiet, I have to do some scans."

The next few minutes crawled by as though through the thickest mud he could imagine. But finally he heard a sigh from Laura.

"Well, Mom?" Caroline asked tensely. Sakura was wide-eyed and silent.

"I'm not going to die," she answered with a smile. "But I'm not going to be hiking right away, either."

Sakura and Caroline exchanged glances, and Whips' inward wince didn't have anything to do with his pain. If she couldn't walk...

"How bad is it, Laura?" he asked.

"Broken ribs—that claw crushed hard. Some minor internal injuries. It also managed to crack my hip. I can't move very far until that's patched up." Laura's voice was stronger. "The nanos are on that, of course, and fighting back the shock and other secondary effects, but they can't do magic." She looked at him. "You aren't much better off, Whips."

"Oh."

"'Oh,' indeed. You've got multiple dislocations in your arm plates, some in your main body, torn muscles, you've lost at least ten griphooks, and you took a hit that jarred your brain enough to produce a minor concussion. Your rear holdfast support was half crushed." She smiled wanly. "A lot of that damage you did to yourself, I think. I only saw what happened vaguely, but it looked like you threw a *hill* at that thing!"

He laughed, even though that really hurt. "I guess it would have looked like that coming down. It was awfully big and heavy."

"Good thing, too," Sakura said, looking at the

half-submerged, seven-meter-long carcass with a shudder. "Mom stabbed it in the eye but nothing else we did seemed to be even annoying it much."

"We have a problem, though," Caroline said slowly.

Laura nodded her head with care. "Yes. We don't have much with us, and two of us are basically crippled."

Sakura rose. "Then I'm going back."

"No, *I* am going back for help!" Caroline said flatly. "I'm older—"

"I can move faster than you!"

"You need to stay here and—"

"ENOUGH!"

Laura's agonized shout cut the near-hysterical argument short. She lay still for a moment, breathing shallowly. "Girls. Let's talk this out sensibly. Yes. One of you has to go for help. We don't have the supplies. Even if Whips or one of you could manage to get out there and cut steaks or something out of our now-dead adversary, we're still badly limited. At least one of you has to go back just to let them know what happened, since otherwise we won't show up when they expect us."

"So I should start out right away," Caroline said emphatically. "Sakura can help you both—"

"Sakura," Laura said emphatically, "will be the one going back."

"What? *Why*? Mom, she's only—"

"I know how young she is, Caroline. And how young *you* are. But Sakura's better at the fast, long-distance work. And you're better with the bow and arrow, and if we need to be protected, I want to use ranged weapons. We can't afford another close-up fight. Either way we'll have only one able-bodied person in camp with us. I want it to be my oldest daughter, who's the best at organizing and systematically taking care of things."

Caroline opened her mouth, then closed it slowly. "Yes, Mom," she said finally.

"Okay, I'm off."

"Saki!"

Whips had shouted at the same time as Laura, and Sakura stopped dead.

Whips continued, since Laura was once more in pain from shouting. "Jetting before thinking again? Even going as fast as you can, it'll take you hours. Refill your water bottles. Take some of the dried meat we brought. And whatever else, don't *run*. You'll just wear yourself out faster."

"But I . . . I . . ." Sakura took a deep breath, closed her eyes, and finally let it out. "Right. Sorry."

"That's my girl," Laura said quietly. "Go as fast as you can, but not faster. Right?"

"Right."

Sakura followed those directions. She even took Caroline's bottle (made, like the others, from the bamboolike pipestem) for extra water to support her trip. "Okay . . . *now* I'm off. You'll be okay, Mom, Whips, right?"

"We'll be fine, honey. Just make sure your father knows what happened."

"I will!"

Whips watched Sakura striding off—maybe a little faster than she should—until she disappeared over the ridge.

Now let's just hope nothing else comes after us while she's gone.

Chapter 32

I can't run. Can't run.

Sakura repeated that to herself, a mantra of restraint. She knew Whips was right. There was no way she could run the whole way back to Sherwood Tower, and even if she could, it was way too dangerous. This wasn't familiar territory that she knew like the back of her hand, like the forest around their home and the nearby beach and the Blue Hole. This was new, and she could run into something that would kill her, or just put a foot in a hole and break her ankle, and that would be it.

Don't run. Don't run.

But she *wanted* to run. The memory of her mother's face, pale, tight with pain, and of Whips, covered with the darker purplish blood of a Bemmie, screamed at her that she should run, push herself, to get back home as fast as she could.

She strode forward as fast as she could walk, and concentrated on her surroundings. They came down ... about *there*. She compared the view on her omni. *Little farther along ... yeah, there, I see Whips' skid-marks going down here.*

Following the flattened trail Whips left was, luckily, not too difficult. Sakura reached the top of the ridge and looked back.

Far, far away, across a wide expanse of the green, hummocked swamp, she could see two dots and a slightly larger brownish blob. She waved, and could just barely make out a return wave by the others; her omni enhanced the view and showed her both Caroline and Whips waving.

"Okay," she said into her omni. "Bye. Once I'm over the ridge I think I'll be cut off."

"Probably," her mother's pained voice answered. "Good luck, honey—and be careful."

"I will, Mom. I promise."

By the time she was halfway down the ridge on the other side, her omni showed signal had been lost. She was now alone on Lincoln—completely alone—for the first time since she had been on the alien planet, and that fact suddenly struck her, hard. There was no one nearby to help her. No one would hear her if she screamed or shouted; she could expect no answers if she transmitted.

Gooseflesh raised the fine hairs on her arms and for a moment the entirety of the wrinkled, jumbled plain was menacing, long black shadows in the slowly setting sun stretching towards her like claws. For a moment, Sakura shivered, and thought about just going back.

But she knew she couldn't do that. Her father needed to know what had happened, and there was no way for him to know until she got there. She swallowed and took a deep breath. "Okay, Saki, keep it together. Mom chose me, I've got to make it." She took a bite of the dried meat, then drank several swallows of water. The climate of Lincoln—at least where they were—was warm, but usually not stifling; but that did make it very easy to become dehydrated. She had to remember to drink regularly. It'd be really humiliating to keel over because she just forget to take a drink.

Setting her jaw, she started marching across the tumbled landscape, trying to follow the traces Whips' passage had left. Some of the land was pretty bare and tough, though, so it wasn't always easy to tell if she was following exactly. Fortunately, her omni had recorded the route so with that as an overlay she could tell if she was getting too far off.

Something warned her just in time. She jumped to the side as a minimaw lunged at her from its burrow. The creature gave a whistling hiss, but then backed down when Sakura jabbed at it with her spear.

"Come on! Come on, ugly, come on, I'll shove this thing through you and *eat* you!" she heard herself say, voice shaky and cracking.

Hungry or no, the minimaw apparently recognized a superior force when it saw the dull spear tip jabbing at it. With a more subdued hiss, it shrank back into its den. Sakura moved on, but her legs were shaky again, almost rubbery. She couldn't afford any mistakes out here.

It was definitely getting darker, and that was bad. Walking through Stonetree Forest by herself, at night? She shuddered, but realized there was no choice. She was traveling light, which meant that she hadn't brought any camping gear; that was all with Caroline, Whips, and her mom. So she couldn't just sit down and wait, even if Lincoln's day wasn't so darned long.

It wasn't going to be easy, though. She'd been up for, what, almost sixteen hours now? She was starting to really get tired.

And tired people made mistakes.

But she couldn't camp, either. Not in a place she didn't know, where she couldn't see anything without using her omni, and without anyone to be eyes for her while she slept. The omni could probably do a sort of sentry duty—Caroline's was programmed for that. She checked and was relieved to see that she had downloaded that app.

It still wasn't a good idea, though. Too many unknowns. If she was up and moving, anything roughly her size and smaller would probably not bother messing with her, and even bigger things might hesitate. Asleep...by the time the omni woke her up, it might be too late. She remembered her father the other day, pointing to a carcass crawling with large crants—short for "crab-ants."

"Be careful around those things," he'd told her. "They nest like ants, and I'm a little suspicious they might be predatory as well as scavenging. Army ant-type behavior in these things would be very nasty."

She shivered again. That would be an even worse death than the giant four-jawed gator-hill-thing. No, she'd keep awake and keep going.

There was movement ahead of her, some squeaky grunts and burbles. She tensed, then relaxed. *Those* noises she knew. Capys, a herd of them. They weren't dangerous if she didn't do anything they thought was a threat.

Capys and *threat* made her think of canopy krakens, though, and her gut tightened again. The edge of Stonetree Forest was coming up, and the krakens had been there before...

Her omni, familiar with the target patterns, soon projected the augmented-reality overlay she feared. There were indeed still krakens in the trees, waiting. They were pretty high up the food chain, though. If they weren't the top land predators, they couldn't be far off. Which meant there couldn't be too many of them. They certainly couldn't be in every tree at the edge of the forest.

Of course, if she moved too far, she'd have a ways to go to get back on track. She had to trust the omni's record to help her get back, at least until she was back in areas she knew.

She could head for the coast and follow the sea down. Eventually she'd get to the scar and from then it would be an easy route to follow.

But that would add a lot of distance, and time. She sighed. It occurred to her, belatedly, that her current mission was maybe not so well considered. They all been worried and half-panicked. It might have been better to wait until she was rested.

But... Then she'd have started in the night cycle of Lincoln. Picking her way along the swamp edge... No, that would have been worse.

The capys murmured to each other sleepily, and that sparked an idea in her head. If she got some of them moving towards the forest edge, that'd distract the krakens, and then she could get through.

She was sure she could pull it off. She knew how the capys reacted to startlement and other stimuli, so she could get them stampeding towards the forest pretty easily. And the canopy krakens would then drop down and grab up a feast, keeping them busy for a couple of days.

She looked at the peaceful feather-furry creatures and shook her head. No. She couldn't do that. It was one thing to kill them for meat, fur, hide...but completely different to just send them to be killed as a distraction.

She slowly moved down the edge of the forest, staying at least fifty meters away from the treeline. After about a quarter of a kilometer, she found a stretch of trees without a single kraken in it...that she could see, anyway. She knew better than to assume that her omni was perfect. Still, it was the best chance she'd seen.

Her heart began to thump so hard that she could feel her chest vibrate as she approached the forest. She kept the omni focused above her, picking her way along carefully more by feel than anything else. The spear was held vertically; if one of the things tried to drop directly on her, it would have a very painful surprise.

To the tree edge. Nothing yet, and the omni still didn't show telltale shapes or movement.

No. Wait.

There *was* a canopy kraken—a lone creature, but a large one, resting in the branches of a tree about twenty meters to her left.

It wasn't directly above her, but she was uncomfortably close. Twenty meters was within striking distance, though long. Still, she was committed now. Backing up would send exactly the wrong signals. She continued moving slowly forward.

The creature stirred, shifting. She brought the spear

around, pointed directly at the canopy kraken, and kept it that way as she moved.

The hard-shelled, tentacled predator slowly settled back. She didn't know if it had given up on her, or just been shifting for other reasons, or if the fact she'd been moving and keeping her weapon pointed at it had made it wary. She just kept moving, and only turned away from it when she was a good sixty meters past it.

Now she was alone in Stonetree Forest.

The darkness was almost absolute. If her omni hadn't been able to use multispectral imaging and considerable light intensification, she would have been as blind as though she were in a cave. The enhanced-reality view painted the darkness with fairy-light structure, showing her trees and stones and all the details she needed to pick her way through the forest. Slowly, a green path became visible as she closed in on locations that the omni thought corresponded with the path they'd followed on their way out.

She breathed a sigh of relief as she reached that phantom landmark. She couldn't actually *see* any difference, but though this world lacked navigation signals and stable landmasses, the omni had been recording her movements all day with dead-reckoning from accelerometers, optical flow, and key features of the natural world. If it thought this was the right area, it was probably right.

"Not home yet, Saki. Keep moving," she told herself.

She paused for some more water and another bite of jerky. Around her, the forest whispered and shuffled, wind moving the branches above, and other things— small and not so small—moving below. The enhanced vision showed infrared signatures of small creatures scuttling away as she moved, and larger ones—fortunately not on her projected path—that turned slightly, showing they were aware of her presence.

She glanced back, and up, frequently. *No one's going to ambush me, no way.* She tried to move silently, attract as little attention as possible, and suddenly she was reminded—forcibly—of the last day, the same day the accident had happened, and how she had been playing the stalking game with Whips just before.

Well, I won that one. This one... I can't afford to lose.

It seemed to be hours that she spent, moving slowly but steadily through the forest; she almost ran into the fire-reed patch before realizing what she was seeing. Once she'd skirted that, though, her heart began to lighten. Not that far away. Maybe she was in calling range?

There was no obvious signal, but they knew that altitude made a huge difference. She took the omni off and held it up, as high as she could reach.

A faint light pulsed, showing the barest beginnings of a signal. Not quite enough to transmit... but she was getting close!

Then as she lowered her arm, something snarled, not close, but not all that far away, either. She jumped—

And her foot caught on a projecting branch. Sakura went suddenly sprawling, the wind knocked out of her.

But that was nothing. At the same time, the *darkness* hit her, almost as much a physical force as the ground. Her omni! It was...

The omni's coupling was resonant and short-range, unless tuned in advance to track on one signature at greater range. It had fallen somewhere farther away than it could resonate with her iris displays!

Now she truly understood what *dark* meant. On Lincoln, there were no cities. There were no villages. There were no artificial light sources anywhere on the planet other than their little camps. When the sun was set and the moons not high, darkness held absolute sway over the land and sea. Beneath the forest canopy, she couldn't even see the stars, make out even the faintest movement or shape.

And the thing that had snarled was still out there. Maybe too far away...maybe getting closer.

She reached out and found the shaft of her spear. *Okay, I'm still armed. Breathe! Don't panic!*

That was one of the hardest instructions she'd ever given herself, but she made herself concentrate on those two words. If she panicked, she'd probably never get out of here alive. There were still a lot of hours—a *lot* of hours—until Lincoln permitted its sluggish dawn to start.

Got to remember. What direction did it go?

She felt the root that tripped her, remembered the way her foot had hooked it. *I fell...that way. So my arm was out like that...which means it had to fall somewhere over...there.*

Sakura prayed she'd gotten the general direction right. If she hadn't, her chances of coming back to the right area to search were near zero.

But she didn't have to actually find it. She just had to get near it. Two meters was the transmission range for the omni. Short indeed, but the great advantage was that she didn't have to identify the thing by touch, search through the debris on the jungle floor trying to find the little curved bracelet. She just had to get close *enough*.

Using her spear as a blind man's cane to explore the area in front of her, Sakura slowly moved forward. One step. Two. Three. *How far did it go?*

It could have gone quite a distance, she admitted to herself. And over a fairly broad arc. If she didn't find it soon, she could spend hours looking—and she'd have to. Searching for the omni here would waste time, but trying to make her way home through the darkness without it? Utterly hopeless.

A low, rumbling growl floated through the air behind her. Sakura whirled, holding the spear stiffly before her. No. It wasn't that close yet. But it was closer than it had been.

I have to find that omni!

She knew what her hesitancy would look like to a predator; something wounded, or lost, separated from its herd, vulnerable. If it chose to attack—whatever it was, because she didn't recognize the rattling growl or the snarl—she'd have one stab in the dark to stop it, and then she'd almost certainly be dead.

Ignoring the crawling between her shoulder blades, the certainty that something was going to spring on her, she turned back and continued the methodical movement forward. *Swing the spear left, step, right, step, left, step . . .*

The sound was on her left, now, a little closer. It *was* stalking her. That was classic predator's behavior, surveying the prey, closing in, cautious but confident at the same time.

Flicker.

It was the faintest spark of light, but her heart gave a tremendous leap. It was here! Nearby!

Another step forward, and her iris displays lit up.

The omni recognized that it was separated, and generated a homing image. She lunged forward and caught the little bracelet up, sliding it on, even as she heard stealthy footsteps, faint on the fallen, rotting leaves around her.

The forest burst to visibility in fairy light and she spun swiftly towards the soft, padding sounds.

Scarcely ten meters away it crouched, preparing to spring: a lithe, armored form that combined the worst features of panther and centipede, with the remnant dual back ridges of spines that some creatures of Lincoln sported. It snarled, revealing a mouth that also crossed the worst characteristics of arthropods and mammals. It was nearly three meters long from nose to end of tail.

But Sakura wasn't going to give it the initiative. *Scare it! Show it who's boss, or it'll keep doing this!* Despite the terror that told her legs to start running, Sakura tightened her grip on the spear and gave a short, vicious lunge, jabbing the spear tip at the thing and shrieking her own challenge, a shrill cry that hearkened back to her primate ancestors.

The creature growled and crouched down, easing backwards, but still not convinced, not intimidated. It paced deliberately, patiently around Sakura, looking for an opening.

Keep the offensive. Make *it back off.* She knew that was what her father would tell her. She gritted her teeth, then yelled and stabbed outward again, this time charging far enough that her spear would connect, if the thing didn't react.

It gave a frustrated squall, dodging her thrust but not countering. It moved slightly off, as though puzzled. She pursued, knowing that she had to establish that she was *not* prey, *not* an easy kill, not *anything* this creature wanted to deal with.

This time it hunkered down and then slashed out with a clawed leg—one of several. The impact against the spear shaft sent pain shivering through Sakura's fingers, but she wouldn't let go. Instead, she shoved forward, right down the leg and ramming the fire-hardened point into the juncture between leg and armored body.

The beast shrieked and lunged back, slashing at her again with its claws—but not to attack. It was now trying to make *her* back off so it could scuttle away, its gait slightly uneven with its one injured leg.

Sakura stood still for moments, panting, shaking with relieved terror. So close. It could have killed her if it had really tried. She convinced it not to, but it could have.

She drained the rest of her one water container. She had to be close now. She just needed to keep going.

She moved forward as fast as she dared, the fairy-outlined forest even more sinister and dangerous. She stumbled more often. She was exhausted. That wasn't just because of the time and effort she'd expended. The two big scares had taken a lot out of her as well.

But she kept moving.

There! A flicker of light... And it's getting more steady!

As soon as the light of reception glowed steadily, Sakura began shouting. "Dad! *DADDY! Wake up!*" She didn't care that she was sounding like a kid again. The panic she'd kept at bay was still there and she *felt* like a little girl again.

"Mommy's been hurt!"

Chapter 33

"Caroline," Laura said, trying to speak slowly and ignore the stiff, dull pain in her chest.

Her eldest daughter was instantly up, an enhanced-glowing shadow in the night. "Yes, Mom?"

"Any sign of scavengers?"

"Not yet. Maybe the thing screaming in pain scared things off."

"Or they're coming underwater, where we can't see them. I want to move farther up the slope."

She could see Caroline's frown. "*Can* you move, Mom?"

"Slowly, I think. No damage to my spine. The medical nanos have the pain under control for the most part, though most of mine are concentrated on my hip."

"Still," Whips' deep, rippling voice broke in, "maybe we should just stay put."

"I'd really feel more comfortable with more distance between us and the water. I can't be sure, Caroline, but it looks to me like up *there*," she pointed and had her omni transmit a highlight for the same region she was pointing at, "is a fairly large section of bare stone. Am I seeing right?"

Caroline looked. "Hard to be certain in the dark . . . but it does look that way. Hold on." A pause. "Okay, checking the imagery we got during the day, yes, I'm pretty sure you're right. Is that where you want to go?"

"Yes. We've got the little bit of camping gear so we can make the rock more comfortable, and bare rock keeps fire under control and pests have a harder time crossing it."

Despite the nanos, this much talking was making her chest burn. She didn't look forward to moving at all, but she knew it was the right choice. Another of those monsters could be the scavenger that showed up. Predators usually had no problem with adding fresh carrion to their menu.

Caroline was looking at Whips. "Do you think you can make it up there?"

Whips hesitated. Laura couldn't blame him; his arms were badly damaged, and she wasn't in any shape to reposition the shoehorn plates or try to guide the ligaments and tendons to realign. He contracted into himself but answered, "I think so. Won't be fun, but I think I can."

Caroline sighed. "Okay. I don't know if this is a good idea, but you're the boss, Mom. Lean on me, right?"

"Believe me, honey, I'll take all the help I can get." She looked apologetically at Whips. "Whips, I'm sorry, but I don't think either of us can do much to help you."

He gave a shimmering laugh that was phosphorescently visible even without the omni helping. "I outweigh any two of you put together, maybe any three of you. I know you can't do much without a winch. I'll get there somehow. Just . . . keep an eye on my telltales, okay?"

"Wait until I'm up there, then. I want Caroline to at least be able to follow along with you."

Whips slumped down comfortably, or as comfortably as his injuries would allow. "Waiting I can do."

Laura couldn't help but suck in her breath loudly as Caroline helped her up. "Mom!"

"It's...okay." *That's a lie, and she knows it.* "I have to get up there, so it doesn't matter that it hurts." *That's the truth.*

Caroline walked beside her, helping her with each painful step. The nanos could dull all the pain, but she didn't like that. Pain was the body's warning mechanism, and she wanted to hear the warning bells clearly. *When I'm going to sleep, that's different, but not when I'm up.*

"Do you think we're really in danger, Mom?"

"I'm...afraid so, yes. That's a huge kill out there, and the scavengers and other predators won't leave it alone for long. If your father's right about the possible behavior of the insectoid creatures like the crants and the shieldlice, we don't want to be in their path if they start heading for the smell of a kill, either."

Caroline nodded.

Progress up the slope was slow, torturous in the literal sense. The site wasn't more than two hundred fifty meters up the slope, but it took Laura and Caroline an hour, with frequent stops, to finally get Laura deposited, on top of one of the precious sleeping pads, on the smooth, weathered coral-rock surface. "Whew," she said as she sank back in relief. "Oh, God, it feels so good to be just lying down."

"I'm going back down to Whips," Caroline said. "Will you be okay?"

She forced herself to a sitting position. "Prop me up on the tent roll, all right?"

Caroline positioned the rolled-up shelter and Laura leaned back. It supported her well enough. She took out the SurvivalShot and laid it across her lap. "Now I'll be okay."

Caroline nodded and jogged back down the hill.

It took even longer for Whips to get up the hill. Without Caroline to act as a guide and anchor, Laura suspected he'd never have made it, and once or twice she nearly called the whole attempt off. The last thing they needed was the poor Bemmie hurting himself just because she was being cautious.

But finally he slid onto the smoother rock surface and sagged down in relief, so exhausted that his whole body flattened out. "Made . . . it."

"You did great, Whips!" Caroline said.

"Just relax, Harratrer," Laura said, using Whips' real name to emphasize her words. "I'm going to turn up your nanos—and mine too, so don't either of you start—so you can really try to get some sleep." She shook her head. "I hate to do this to you, Caroline—"

"Don't even say it, Mom! I can stay up a while longer if I have to, and you guys need rest about a hundred times more than I do."

"All right."

There was silence for a few moments. Then Whips spoke up, asking the real question that she'd been shoving to the back of her mind for hours now. "How do you think Sakura's doing?"

Her mind invented about a hundred scenarios of horrifying disaster in the instant before she responded.

"It's been, what, six hours? I'd guess she's near the Stonetree Forest by now. Maybe in it."

"Did we do the right thing, Mom?" Caroline asked slowly. "I mean...it...we were all still panicked."

"I hope to heaven we did do the right thing, honey," she said, in as comforting a voice as she could. "Someone had to let your father know what had happened. If we'd waited...well, to make sure she wouldn't be in night at all, we'd be waiting for a long time before she could even leave."

She looked down at the SurvivalShot in her lap. "If she doesn't make it..."

"She will." Whips' voice was certain. "Sakura's not going to give up, and she'll find a way to get there. We just have to stay alive until then."

Laura knew part of that was bravado, but part of it was Whips' genuine faith in her daughter, and that warmed her as though the sun were still shining. "You're right." Laura felt the weariness stealing over her as the nanos finally drove pain into the background. "Okay, Caroline...keep a watch."

"I will."

When Laura woke up, she could tell it was several hours later. The stars had shifted quite a bit. Her omni helpfully informed her it had been almost seven hours. "Caroline?"

"Yipe!" The startled yelp was accompanied by a jump. Caroline turned, embarrassment written clear across her face. "Sorry, Mom. It'd just been so quiet for so long..."

"Nothing near the carcass?"

"Actually, there have been noises from there. Infrared

shows various shapes moving around it. Not sure how many or how big. A couple shapes have moved up near the shore, maybe onto it, but none going farther. I haven't seen any specially nasty things anywhere near us, though."

"Give me a hand up," Laura said reluctantly. "I need to..."

"Oh." Caroline looked around. "Over there. Wait, let me dig a pit first."

"You don't—"

"We should, even here. It'll just take me a few minutes."

Sure enough, Caroline finished her preparatory work quickly and took Laura to the improvised latrine. Once Laura was done, she got up, with difficulty, and let Caroline fill it in.

"All right. Just give me a little food and water, and you can get some rest, Caroline."

"I...could use that. I was starting to nod off a bit even when I was walking." Her eldest daughter looked at the stars for a few moments. "Mom...do you think Sakura..."

"I think she must have gotten there by now and your father's probably going to be on his way immediately," she said firmly. "Now get your rest."

Guard duty was eerie. Her omni painted the darkness with clear outlines and enhanced data—probably better than Caroline's. Sitting on this exposed ridge above a swamp, in territory they didn't know was enough to make anyone tense. But looking down, Laura saw a lot more to worry her.

There *were* shapes down there. They flickered in and out of view as they rose and submerged, since infrared didn't penetrate any depth of water, but it looked very much like a school of sharks around a whale carcass. The animals looked to be two to three meters long, if she took a guess at how much remained underwater. There were other smaller things, too.

Some did pause at the water's edge, even seem to pull themselves a short distance up; she got an impression of a flattened, rippling body that didn't look like anything they'd seen on Lincoln before. That wasn't surprising. They'd only seen one tiny part of one floating continent so far. Most things were going to look different.

In the quiet of the night, with an undertone of susurrations and night-calls that sounded almost like those you might hear on Earth at night, she could now hear something else; ripples and breaths, sounds of tearing, snorts. *They're feeding. Well, if the carcass keeps them satisfied, they won't bother us.*

But the question was whether it *would* keep them satisfied. After all, if new, hungry creatures kept coming in to replace those sated, or if something disturbed them...

She caught her eyelids drooping. *No. Can't allow that. It hasn't been long enough. Caroline needs her rest, and so does Whips. He's worse off than I am. He almost tore himself in* half *with that crazy, heroic stunt.*

She glanced over and smiled fondly at Whips' sleeping form. Objectively, he probably looked as scary-monstrous as any of the things out there. But he was family, and that made him look as helpless as her kids when he was asleep. Even if he was the size of a small horse.

She turned her attention back to the swamp below, after casting a wary glance around the rest of the terrain. It would be ironic to be watching so carefully for danger down there, and not notice some stalking predator coming from the hills.

There *had* been a couple of forms creeping down towards the water, but they were small—about half the size of Hitomi, no more—and probably wouldn't cause any trouble.

She felt something on her barkcloth pantleg, flicked it off. *Crant. Large one.* The crants didn't put out significant heat, being cold-blooded, but if you looked carefully you could still see them on IR due to varying emissivities. There were quite a few now, mostly heading down towards the water.

Laura was strongly tempted to build a fire. They only had a fairly limited store of fuel—they'd had to pack it with them, and they'd used some to cook the fish earlier—but fire was one of the few sovereign weapons. The discovery of plains-like areas and of real wood trees—and the fact that with sufficient heat a lot of the non-wood "trees" would, in fact, burn—had encouraged them to believe that the land animals of Lincoln would know and avoid fire, and a few tests had confirmed it. They knew what it was, and that it was something to be avoided.

She decided to wait. The crants weren't a real problem yet, and nothing else was approaching them. Better to save it for when and if things got worse.

Her thoughts turned to Sakura. With no one else awake, no one else depending on her to be stable, she could not fight off her fears: Sakura with a broken leg, fallen somewhere on the way back; bitten by a venomous minimaw, her nanos desperately fighting off the poison; seized and devoured by a canopy kraken; lost and wandering, somewhere, with no one to help her or guide her . . .

"Stop that," she muttered to herself. She had to believe that Sakura would make it. She wouldn't give up, and she wouldn't stop, and she wasn't stupid. She'd stay out of the reach of the minimaws and the krakens, and she'd follow the route. Which meant that by now Sakura would have reached home, let her father know.

She knew Akira. He'd get ready as fast as he could and be on his way—probably bringing everyone with him, because he couldn't leave Mel and Hitomi alone, even with Sakura. He was probably on his way now, and *he* was the biologist, with more field experience than anyone else. He would make it here as fast as anyone possibly could.

There came a faint splashing and a dragging sound. She saw that another of the unknown things was moving around on the shore. It moved hesitantly upward, an undulating, slithering motion that made her skin crawl just to watch it. But it stopped and turned slowly back towards the water. *Thank goodness. Well, that certainly woke me up.*

Laura activated the medical imaging package and checked Whips' progress. His nanos were keeping inflammation down and she could see that healing had started. The internal bleeding had stopped and there was no systemic damage, thankfully. She'd have to realign those plates, though.

She kept the pain damping on her own body very high—just enough left to let her know if she was doing something that would be really damaging—and cut off all sensation to Whips' arms. It was a good thing that modern medical nanos for colonization types could be used for anesthesia since they didn't have any chemicals for that.

The worst off were the basal shoehorns. Whips had nearly pulled his own arms off with that impossible stunt. One of the basals was cracked, and all three were pulled from their ball sockets. It was incredible that he'd managed to continue to function as well as he had.

With the inflammation kept down, however, it was possible to reseat them. She aligned the ball with its socket, and then pushed as hard as her ribs would allow. As her force peaked, she triggered a spasm of Whips' own muscles surrounding the basal, and it popped back into place with an audible *thump*.

Despite the dull pain, she smiled. *Good! I can get this done!*

It didn't take long to seat the other two. The cracked one she did last, making sure she pushed as straight along the main shoehorn axis as possible. Whips should find his arms already feeling better when he woke up.

Another quick survey of the area reassured her that—as of yet—nothing significant was approaching them. She swept a bunch of crants from the stone and off of Whips' body. She'd have to keep an eye on that. If they decided he was tasty, that could get very bad.

Tending to Whips' injuries, though far from restful, was at least helping keep her awake and alert, so she spent another half-hour realigning as many of his arm-plates as she could. At least one of his arms should end up being functional soon.

With a start, she realized that she could now make

out Caroline's sleeping form, a few meters away, without enhancement. Dawn was finally approaching.

That meant it had been sixteen or seventeen hours since Sakura left. Akira must be well on his way. With Sakura's data on the trip there and back, he could make good time even at night. Hitomi would slow him down a bit, but she was a good little trooper and wouldn't complain or drag her feet. Neither would Mel, not knowing what was at stake. So they should be here soon.

She refused to think of the alternative.

Caroline stirred. "Mmmmm... Oh, ow. This sleeping pad needs to be thicker. I'm stiff all over. How're you doing, Mom?"

"All right. I did some work on Whips while I was up."

"He's still asleep?"

"Bemmies don't sleep like us nearly as often, but when they're badly hurt or exhausted they will for quite a long time, until their body thinks they've recovered enough. Still, I think we should wake him soon. I want to see how he feels, get some food and water in him."

"How are things down there?" Caroline nodded towards the vaguely discernible bulk in the black-ink water below.

"Plenty of somethings eating away. Seen them come up on shore a couple of times, but—"

The two of them caught sight of it at the same time: a huge shape, glowing with infrared in the enhanced vision, emerging from the water only a few scant meters from the carcass. It let loose with a rumbling bellow that vibrated Laura's chest even at a range of over two hundred meters. They could see other creatures fleeing, retreating in all directions from the new arrival. It was of the same species as the dead one, though slightly smaller. Having announced its claim, the creature bit into the carcass and tore free a large chunk with a splintering, ripping sound.

Whips gave a whooping noise that Laura knew was a mild curse and exclamation of startlement. "What . . . oh. The big one's arrived."

"Yes, and it's trying to scare all the competition away."

Laura looked down, and a new chill went down her spine. "That could be very bad for us."

Several of the rippling things—that the slowly growing dawnlight now showed to be glistening, gray creatures about a meter across, shaped something like a double-winged stingray—were now on the shore, and starting to move upward. One, in the lead, was zig-zagging from side to side. It halted abruptly, then turned and began heading straight up the hill towards Laura, giving vent to a hissing, bubbling cry. Immediately, the other creatures turned and started upward as well.

"Oh, no," Caroline said softly, even as she unlimbered her bow. "They've found your blood trails."

Laura nodded grimly. "Yes, they have."

Chapter 34

Whips turned himself slowly to face the approaching creatures. He still hurt, but he could feel his arms responding better, much less sense of *wrongness* in the way they moved and turned. He realized that Laura must have done work on him while he was out.

Even so, he could tell that only one arm—the left one—was even close to really working, and even that one was badly hurt in areas. But it didn't matter how much it hurt; if he had to, he'd fight. Nothing was getting Caroline or Laura while he could move!

"How's the SurvivalShot, Laura?" he asked.

She glanced at the telltales. "About fifteen shots stored. I've got plenty of little pieces of metal wreckage in my pouch for ammo, so I can shoot it that many times. Now that the sun's coming up..." She spread the solar panel on the stone nearby and connected it to the pistol. "Takes a while, but every little bit helps. I might get another shot or two, depending."

She surveyed him. "How about you?"

"I'm better than I was. You fixed me up a bit, I can tell." He reached out and grasped one of the curve-shafted spears he'd had in his equipment. "I can use the spear in this arm. Won't be perfect, but it's better than nothing. Shame I couldn't get it out when I was swimming before."

"I should have told you to stop swimming entirely." Laura's voice held sharp self-recrimination. "With all the—"

"Laura ... Mom," he said, deliberately, which got her attention and a startled smile, "if I hadn't, maybe one of those things would've ambushed us as we came by. Who knows? Don't beat yourself up over it, as Sakura would say."

She gave him a quick hug to the base of his arms. "Thank you, Harratrer. And calling me 'Mom' almost made me cry."

"I don't think my mother would complain."

"No, she wouldn't. Any more than I would." Her voice was affectionate, and that just strengthened Whips' resolve.

"Oh, crap," Caroline said. "Mom, Whips, there's a *lot* of these things."

More were emerging from the water, following the liquid-bubbling calls of their kindred. Whips counted nine already. "Do you think we could throw them off?"

"Off the trail, you mean?" Laura shrugged. "I don't know how."

Caroline looked down apprehensively. "They're not that fast, but they're going to be here pretty soon. I don't know if it would make any difference; but I think those glints at the front are eyes, so if we don't move out of their way quick, they'll know we're what they're trailing anyway."

"Then we're going to have to try to hold them off. Caroline, how many arrows do you have?"

"Twenty-two, Mom. Sakura was carrying some for me and she left those here." She glanced down. "The crants are starting to gather, too."

"Whips, take the barkcloth wrapping stuff we have and sweep the crants off. Can you do that?"

"On it." The little armored creatures were large enough for that to be effective. Fortunately; it wasn't like brushing away the smaller Earth ants he'd seen pictures of, or trying to shoo away *tinnak*, very small plankton pests native to Europa, which were about the same size. A few of the crants tried to bite or pinch him but couldn't get a grip on his tough skin, and his actual cuts were covered by barkcloth-toughened dressings. So he thought he was safe from them, at least for the present.

"Caroline, maybe if we kill one of them they'll back off."

"Or eat their own fallen comrade, if they're like sharks. It might slow them down, anyway."

Caroline stood, nocked an arrow, and drew back, sighting carefully. The bow made a clear, sharp *twang!* as she loosed the arrow, and the shaft streaked true.

The lead creature gave a choked howl and writhed in a circle, tendrils extending out from beneath and yanking futilely at the arrow's shaft. It was unable to move forward or backward, the arrow having gone all the way through and into the ground beneath.

The other animals had scattered away with surprising speed and nimbleness, flowing with eerie and smooth precision to a considerable distance from their comrade. When nothing more happened, they slowly closed in, and circled, poking at it, flowing over it, bumping cautiously into the arrow shaft.

Then the first creature gave another howl, as the others grasped it with their tendrils and pulled. Slowly, with a sucking hiss, the creature's flesh parted around the arrow, and it popped free.

The things turned slowly and resumed their rippling approach up the hill. The injured one moved more slowly, but it continued up the hill, trailing darker fluid.

Whips shuddered. "What in the Sky was that?"

"They helped their . . . pack-mate, or whatever . . . move. And he's still alive." Caroline looked nauseated. "Ripped a quarter across him, but he's alive and moving."

"We don't know how they're built," Laura said tensely. "So wherever you hit didn't do it lethal damage. Or at least not right away. We need to hit them somewhere vital."

"Maybe they don't *have* vital spots," Caroline said, looking at the glistening, oozing approach.

"Anything moving like that has to have some kind of vital spots—lungs or gills, brain, whatever," said Whips. "Try between those points that look like eyes."

Caroline drew, aimed, and let fly again.

This arrow drilled almost precisely between the eyes of the new lead creature, and the result was spectacular. It gave a single, high-pitched shriek, and flipped over in convulsions. This arrow had gone more parallel to the ground and hadn't stuck in. In flipping over, the thing also exposed an underbody with multiple gray tendrils and a sucking mouth with hints of ripping structures inside. That was a scavenger's design, primarily, but the creatures were obviously willing to act as predators also.

The others once more scattered—though, Whips

noted with concern, not nearly so far—and then returned.

They poked at the victim, which was now subsiding into quivers, and flowed over it. The tearing, ripping sounds that followed showed that this time, they were not trying to help. Laura's eyes were narrowed, and Whips could see her shiver. *If they get to us . . .*

"Mom!"

Whips realized that Caroline was looking *behind* them.

Something—more than one something—was stalking into view from behind a ridge. These were sleek, six-legged things, moving in a way that reminded Whips strongly of a film he'd seen of a mountain lion or, perhaps, a wolf. They didn't look to be as heavy as a mountain lion, though, or maybe even a wolf. The body was partially armored, with a dual spine ridge, and the head was clearly that of a predator.

"Fantastic," muttered Laura. "The smells and sounds finally got the land animals in on the action." She raised the SurvivalShot. "Time to see if a gun can scare them."

Taking time to aim, Laura drew a careful bead on the approaching predator and fired.

The loud, flat blast of the pistol echoed across the land far and wide. At the same time, Laura's target gave a rasping yelp and stumbled, falling, its face smashing into the ground.

That seemed to be more than convincing for the other three of the land creatures. They dashed off, disappearing behind the ridge. The first one managed to get up, but its flight was much slower and uneven. Whips didn't think it was going to live long.

The echoing sound had not, however, deterred the

oozing, glistening horde of amphibious . . . things. They were closer now, and more were now emerging from the water. The one that Caroline had shot first had slowed down, and when the second group caught up with it, they were not so helpful as the first had been.

"How many are there?" Laura asked in an unnaturally casual voice.

"I think . . . about a dozen and a half right now." Caroline's voice was shaky.

"Well, you still have twenty arrows. Not so bad."

"If I'm Robin Hood, maybe," Caroline said, taking a deep breath.

The nearest creatures were now about thirty-five meters away. The bodies of the two eaten ones were now visible; the remains seemed to include a radial structure of supports for the flattened bodies. "You definitely won't do much shooting at most of the body. The area behind the eyes and just in the center of the body look like the only ones with vital structures."

"He's right," Laura said.

"Great. Smaller targets are always easier to hit," Caroline said sarcastically. She drew, sighted, and let loose again.

This arrow nicked the side of one, but struck nowhere vital. "I suppose if I could pin all of them down, that would be good enough."

"You don't have enough arrows for that," Whips said dismally. "Look."

Still more of the creatures were emerging, farther down each side of the shore, and converging on their location. Whips gave a whistling sigh. "This isn't good."

"No," agreed Laura darkly. "And we're starting to run out of tricks."

Whips reached out and grabbed their packs. "Time to start a fire, I think."

Laura nodded. "We'll keep them back as long as we can. After that..."

"I know."

The charcoal was easy to ignite with tinder and a metal-ceramic striker Whips had devised. He focused on building the fire, trying to ignore the twanging of the bow, the sharp reports of the SurvivalShot, and the shrieks and burbling cries of the creatures as they slowly closed in.

If this area was drier, like plains, they could set it all on fire and be safe on this flat area of rock. But none of this vegetation would burn well.

But they still did have fire. "It's burning, Laura!" he said.

"Good! See how they react to something hot, then!"

He was shocked to see that the nearest ones were now only fifteen meters off. From what he'd seen, the things had enough speed that soon they'd be close enough to try a lunge. "All right!"

He took the cooking pan, scooped up some burning coals, and scattered them across the oozing horde.

The ones struck shrank back, with high keening noises, and the others stopped, flowed slowly backwards. "Oh, they don't like *that* at all!"

He looked at the fire. "I can't do that too many more times, though, Laura. And we don't have much more that's flammable."

"Maybe we won't have to. A few more times might discourage them."

Laura's voice didn't carry conviction, and Whips said nothing. These things didn't seem to care much about injuries. Even the ones hit had stopped moving away. They needed something that really could hurt them, a lot of them, to convince them to run.

He looked over. Caroline's quiver was almost empty, and from the way Laura was looking at the SurvivalShot, she didn't have many shots left. He gripped his spear tightly. It was going to come down to close-quarters combat, and they were heavily outnumbered. He glanced one eye towards the east.

The sun was coming up, shedding its brilliant light over the land, showing the brilliant greens and browns of the land.

It was ironic, Whips thought, turning back to face the oncoming creatures. Dawn would arrive in time to let them really see what was probably going to take them down into the deepest night.

Chapter 35

"How much farther, Sakura?"

"Just over that ridge," Sakura pointed, "and then head towards the mountains around the edge of the wetlands you'll see when we get to the top. If things haven't changed much, we'll be able to see Mom, Whips, and Caroline from the ridge."

The whole run back through the night-dark forest had an air of unreality to it. Her father had known he couldn't leave her behind, so he'd reluctantly put one of the stim codes into her nanos, overriding the need for sleep and keeping her alert, but a part of her knew she really should have been in bed and dreaming a long, long time ago.

But no way am I sleeping until I know Mom's all right!

She glanced back. Hitomi was still doggedly following, stumbling, but amazingly tenacious, not complaining as she carried a bulky slung sack that looked nearly as big as she was. Melody, longer-legged than Hitomi, was staying next to her little sister, ready to help. Her face was starkly white against her night-dark hair, and her expression was grim. Of them all, Melody was the best at visualizing things, and in this case, that wasn't helping. "You guys okay?"

"Okay . . . Saki," Hitomi said breathlessly. Mel just gave a nod and a quick thumbs-up from the hand that held her own carryall.

"Let me know if you need help," she reminded them, then turned her attention to clambering up the tumbled ridge. They'd gotten so much tougher since they arrived on Lincoln. Sakura couldn't even imagine Hitomi getting this far before they crashed. For that matter, she couldn't imagine *herself* getting this far before we crashed.

She looked up at her father, climbing just ahead of her. His slender frame moved with a calm unvarying rhythm like an unstoppable machine, and she saw the absolute focus in his gaze. It made her feel better. *Daddy won't let anything hurt Mom.*

Lincoln's sun came up as they crested the ridge, or maybe the ridge being a tiny bit higher up let them see the sun that much earlier. She looked down, seeing the same dappled green landscape, eyes following it across . . .

What was that?

She triggered a zoom and enhance from her omni. "Oh, no. *Mommy!*"

Akira stared, frozen for a moment. He saw what she did—a mass of writhing, rippling movement like a mob of landborne jellyfish, oozing steadily towards three figures higher up on the slopes.

Akira set his jaw, and looked at the three of them. "Hitomi, Mel—we have to run, now. I know we're all exhausted, but they're almost out of time. Can we run that far?"

"I promise I will!" Hitomi said.

"Try my best," Melody said, daunted by the distance.

"I can," Sakura said, and started down the hill at the fastest jog she dared. "Dad, don't get too far down. It looks smoother near the edge of the swamp, but it gets softer, and we don't want one of those monsters ambushing you."

"Neither...do I..." he said, breathing deeply as he matched her pace.

"You could run faster—"

"No. We can't get too separated." He spoke the words with tense reluctance, but certainty. Sakura understood that her father wasn't going to risk them while trying to get to her mother in time.

A part of her understood that; the other part just wanted him to run flat-out.

Now she saw a streaking glow from where her mother and the others were, multiple streaks that caused the approaching things to withdraw. *What was that?* she wondered, then saw the infrared glow nearby. *Oh, that's smart. A fire. They're throwing fire at the things. They're from the water, maybe...*

But the creatures were regrouping; she heard her father say "*Kuso...*" and from the curse knew how frightened he was.

The gray, repellent, undulating things closed in, starting to give surprisingly quick lunges. Whips was jabbing at them. Then he lifted his spear with one writhing on the end, impaled, and threw it off. Some of the others diverted to swarm the dying one. Her mother was backing up, jabbing with her own spear, but even from this distance Sakura could see that she couldn't put much force into her blows.

Caroline was the only one in good shape, and she was *incredible*. She stabbed one completely through, hurled it aside, pirouetted—no, *jumped* completely over one that darted at her, landing with both boots *hard* on its central bulge, then over to Whips' side, stabbing hard, another dead, and a dancing leap back to Mom.

Sakura would have cheered her on, but she had no breath to spare; a dull ache was starting at the base of her chest, and she glanced backwards.

Hitomi was staggering grimly onward, her face a mask of iron determination, with Melody helping balance her. Sakura saw her father look back, make a face, and abruptly he darted over and hoisted Hitomi onto his back.

"Daddy! Can you—?"

"Only a little farther. Yes, I can."

There were a hundred yards more to go, but her legs felt like they had steel clamps on them. The ache in her chest spread up and in, each breath requiring another effort, but now they were closer, and she had to *think*. Where? Which direction . . .

"Dad, it's from the north right now! The wind, I mean."

He nodded, stumbling, almost falling, somehow recovering, setting Hitomi down. "Good. We come in from this side and just a little lower. It will be dangerous."

"We know, Dad."

She reached into her bag, grasped the pipestem container, and saw Melody do the same. Hitomi slowed, knowing she had to stay back and keep the bag that was in her care safe.

They were close now, very close, and they could hear the wet-sucking movement of the creatures and their bubbling hungry cries, and a curse from her mother, a hiss of pain from Whips as one of the things fastened onto one of his arms—

"NOW!" Akira shouted.

Sakura wrenched the sealed top from the container and lunged forward, jabbing the open end like a spear towards the creatures.

A fountain of white, dusty gravel erupted from Sakura's, Melody's, and Akira's tubes and scattered across the mass, dust spreading farther with the north-blowing wind.

There was a pause, a shout of *"Akira!"* from her mother—and then the creatures shrieked, a cry of shocked and unbelieving agony. An undertone of hissing became audible, and she could see steam rising from the things, which now writhed and struggled and rolled over, desperate to escape the hideous pain that was all over them. Creatures which had not yet been touched moved in and tried to flow over those who were struggling. But her father already had another tube out and doused the next group.

With the second outbreak of terrified pain from multiple creatures, the approaching swarm finally broke. Turning, they fled for the water, away from the terrible burning things in the air. Many of them never made it; some that reached the water hissed and steamed more spectacularly.

"Laura!" Akira said, dropping his pack and running to her. Sakura and her sisters followed only slightly more slowly.

"I knew you'd come, I knew you would, but oh *God* that was close!" Her mother was almost babbling in her relief, hugging Dad as hard as she could with her ribs. Sakura let them do that, went to Whips instead.

"Great...timing, Saki," he said, slowly.

"What in the world did you *do* to them?" Caroline asked wonderingly, seeing still-hissing pellets in the wet ground—and crants writhing in death in the white dust that had scattered with the pellets.

She held up her second tube and shook it. "Quicklime."

"Of course," Whips said, in a tone of voice that said *Why didn't I see that right away?* "They were all wet, amphibious; hitting them with that..." He shuddered. "Well, we heard. Who came up with *that* idea?"

"Me." Hitomi held her hand up.

"Really?" Laura asked, startled.

"Really," Sakura confirmed. "We were packing, trying to figure out what we could take that might give us a chance against a large group of somethings, and Dad said that he wished he had something that could burn when he threw it."

"I was thinking of oil or alcohol," Akira admitted with a smile, sitting down on the flat rock, "but then little Hitomi just said, 'Daddy, didn't you and Whips say that lime stuff would burn if it got on us?'"

"And it certainly did," Laura said.

Sakura finally let herself drop to the ground and started shaking. She tried to control herself, but the shakes became sobs, and even when her mother gently touched her hair and tried to hug her, the sobbing grew worse. Caroline didn't collapse, but she stood shaking, the horror of the siege finally getting to her.

"I...can't...Mom, I thought...Mommy, I thought you and Whips and Caroline were..." Sakura said, disjointedly.

Both her mother and father knelt next to her and

hugged her. "It's all right. You were fantastic, Sakura. You made it there and back—"

Her mother paused and shot a concerned glance at her father. "Did you . . . ?"

"I had no choice, Laura. I couldn't leave her there, even if she would have stayed—which I knew she wouldn't—and so I had to make sure she could keep going."

Her mother bit her lip, then shrugged. "I suppose that was exactly the sort of situation I gave you those codes for. So all right. But now we're setting your nanos back, young lady."

She finally got herself under control. "I'll probably go straight to sleep then."

"Exactly what you should do. We don't have any more blankets, though."

"We brought more food and more camping supplies," Akira said, "as well as weapons. Don't worry."

"All right." Her mother turned back to Sakura. "Then you lie down on this pad, and I'm shutting off the stimulants."

Almost instantly, Sakura felt a tsunami of exhaustion wash over her; her eyes started to droop as though weights were hung on them. "We're . . . okay now?" she managed to say.

"Everything is okay now, Saki," her mother said, and kissed her on the forehead, just as though she were tucking Sakura into bed. "Go to sleep."

She tried to ask another question, but somewhere between taking the breath and opening her mouth, she slid straight into slumber.

Chapter 36

Laura sat up suddenly with a pained gasp, but found that the lancing agony wasn't from an oozing tendriled beast but just one of her ribs—which complained at the sudden movement.

"It's okay, Laura," her husband said. "Nothing's been bothering us. Even the crants are mostly gone; a lot of them ran into the quicklime dust and died. And we hauled the carcasses away to keep them from drawing more predators." He nodded toward the distant pool. "More of them came out of the water to drag them in. There must be an underwater connection between that pool and a much larger subterranean lake of some kind. There's no way a body of water that small could support so many predators and scavengers—and such large ones."

She calmed her breathing, which made the pain subside. Not quite as bad as it had been, either. Looking around, she saw Caroline stretched out on another pad nearby, covered with one of the survival blankets, with Sakura next to her and Whips ending the little row of sleepers. Hitomi was sitting a bit farther up-slope, playing with her omni, and Melody was putting together some sandwiches.

"You're going to need some sleep too, hon," she said finally.

"I know, but I was waiting for you to get back up." He hugged her gently. "Your telltales say the hip is getting better. I think we're here for at least another three, four days, though."

"I really would like to get out of here before then," she sighed, and looked with a shudder towards the water where a few things still moved sluggishly around the carcass, "but you're probably right. Whips' injuries need to get better and that fight didn't help either of us."

He saw her look at Melody and Hitomi. "Oh, I made them sleep too. Once they saw you were all okay, it didn't take much convincing. They were practically dead on their feet."

She shook her head, feeling so much pride in her heart that her eyes stung with tears for her children. "And they made it all the way here, through the night and the morning."

"For you and Whips and Caroline? Of course we did." He touched Caroline's hair gently.

"She's stayed sleeping?" Laura remembered that she'd had to trigger a sedative setting in Caroline's nanos; once the emergency had ended, panic had taken over. Caroline had stood, rigidly, hyperventilating and unable to get control over herself, until the sedative effect took over.

"Yes. That was exactly what she needed, really. She was fighting for the two of you out of terror, I think, and her body didn't know how to stop. She's been completely out ever since."

Laura grimaced and moved towards Melody and

the sandwiches. "I'm afraid all three of us will have a few nightmares about this."

"*I'll* have nightmares about it, Laura!" Akira said emphatically. "Seeing those . . . things about to wash over you, that was a horror show. I can't imagine what it must have been like to be in the middle of it."

"Well, it's over now," she said. "Thank you, Mel."

"You're welcome, Mom," Melody said, and suddenly hugged her tight enough to make Laura's ribs complain.

Still, she hugged back, and felt Melody sniffling against her chest. "Ease off, Melody. It's all right, but Mommy's still hurt. Gently."

A few minutes later Melody let go and sat back down to finish making the sandwiches for the others. "There's a big chunk of smoked blockcrab in Hitomi's bag for Whips," she volunteered. "And the SurvivalShot's got ten shots recharged now. We can probably fish or hunt for something else—oh, we also recovered most of Caroline's arrows."

She made a face. "That was ucky, pulling them out of the carcasses. But between the ones recovered and the ones we brought, we now have twenty-four arrows."

"My God, you thought of everything," Laura said, impressed.

Her husband shrugged. "We packed as much as we could carry, knowing that we could take our time coming back but that we might need to stay a while."

Laura looked down at the pool. "What *were* those things, anyway? It was terrifying, the way they just kept coming. Predators usually avoid fierce opponents."

"Very interesting creatures. I dissected one of them. They're related to the tree anemones, actually."

"Really?"

"Really. Their behavior mainly results from the fact that they just aren't that intelligent. Adjusting for body mass, their brains are no bigger than a crant's. Admittedly, that's an order of magnitude or more better than the anemones, but still not very impressive. That's why they kept attacking even after suffering casualties that would make brainier predators run away. Like those six-legged puma analogs you told me about."

He paused for a moment, considering. "But they're not invertebrates, like real anemones on Earth are. Instead, they have this interior support structure that looks like an old-fashioned barrel. These things," he gestured at the remains downhill, "evolved from that same structure. The 'barrel staves' stretch outward along with the body, and have interconnects and muscles that allow it to swim or move on land with that rippling motion—and can contract a bunch of them simultaneously to do those lunges we saw. The mouth is now on the underside and evolved a contracting, cutting assembly for active predation and scavenging."

"So the tendrils sting, too?"

"Not much. They have some cnidoblasts over their surface but they seem mostly for discouraging minor pests. The tendrils have evolved into much better grasping tools. An impressive set of adaptations, but the price they paid for it was a simplified neurological system."

"Well, I for one hope I never run into them again."

"I can't blame you," he said with a chuckle, "but they *are* fascinating, in a biological sense. I think I'll call them raylamps—cross between lamprey and stingray, if you see what I mean. I could call them lamp*rays*, but that would be confusing."

"As long as you don't study them near me, you can call them anything you want." She took up the SurvivalShot. "Now, you should get some sleep yourself."

He nodded, and she could see him already sagging down with exhaustion as he let himself recognize how tired he was. "On the condition that after I wake up you tell us everything that happened *before* Sakura had to come get us."

"Deal."

By the time Akira woke up, all the others—even the exhausted Sakura—had also awakened and eaten. So as her husband ate his own breakfast, she—with help from Sakura, Caroline, and Whips—told the others everything, from their journey through Stonetree Forest through the rough, folded country in between, to their discovery of clay near the wetlands just before Whips was attacked, finally ending with the battle and Whips' heroic finish of the giant predator.

"And once we realized how badly Whips and I were hurt," she finished, "I sent Sakura after you and, well, that's pretty much it."

Akira's sideways smile showed he recognized how much she was downplaying their vigil and siege, but he wasn't going to ask her to go back over anything that traumatic. "So, you turned yourself into a trebuchet, eh?" he asked Whips.

"More like a sling, really," Whips said. "Just a big one."

"*Very* big," Akira agreed. "That's the stone there, right?"

The body of the large predator had settled slightly after death, and the stone's weight, plus the scavengers coming after, had caused it to sink ever lower. Even so, a fair-sized, dark, irregular dome of rock still protruded from the inky water. "Yes, that's it."

The size of the boulder really was impressive. She seemed to remember it was roughly spherical, which would mean it was somewhere between sixty and seventy centimeters across. "I wouldn't have thought you could lift anything that big," Laura said.

Caroline shook her head. "Remember that most of the rocks around here are fairly light corallike stuff. That thing probably weighs less than Whips does, although maybe not by much. Still a big rock, and it sure did the job."

"And I didn't really *lift* it. We're not great on lifting, us Bemmies, not the way you humans do it," Whips added honestly. "That four-jawed gator-thing was doing a lot of the pulling." His arms—clearly better than they had been a day or two ago—made a small rippling motion that harmonized with the pensive colors running over his hide. "Still, it felt really heavy, I'll say that." He paused, colors still rippling. "I mean, I know how strong I am and how tough my arms are. I don't think a stone that light would have hurt me that bad. Am I wrong, Laura?"

Laura frowned. "Well . . . it's really hard to tell that, sometimes. We humans can throw out our backs by doing something that seems trivial. But still, you should have a good sense of what your own body can do."

She turned to her second-youngest. "Melody? Can I borrow your omni's number-crunching for a minute?"

"Why?" Mel asked, then answered her own question. "Oh, for a biomech sim. Sure, hold on . . . There, I'm out."

Laura used her omni to provide the data on Whips' healthy biological parameters, then combined that with one of Akira's biomechanics applications and a sim that used a considerable chunk of processing resources from all three omnis.

The results were startling. "You know, Whips, I think you're right. No matter what assumptions the model starts with, that rock *has* to be heavier than you are. Akira?"

"Hmm . . . yes, everything looks correct. I would say that, based on your models, it's actually well over Whips' mass."

Caroline blinked. "But that would put it somewhere close to a specific density of *four*. More than three, for sure." She suddenly stood up. "Whips, are you feeling good enough to help me get close to that thing?

"Now wait a minute, Caroline!" Laura could see her oldest girl's face pale as paper. "You know some of those—"

"I know!" Caroline stopped herself, took a deep breath. "Sorry. Sorry for shouting, Mom. I know. Those things terrify me. But . . . if I don't force myself past that, I might be scared of going *anywhere* I can't see things, and here . . . we can't afford that."

Laura opened her mouth to argue, but she couldn't. Caroline was right. "Whips? You're not nearly fully recovered."

"No," he agreed equably. "But I get less pressure on me in the water, and now that I know what to look for, those big things aren't going to sneak up on me again. The raylamps . . . I'm a *lot* bigger than they are, and without me acting injured, I don't think they'll want to mess with me in the water. I think I could escort her out and back; it's not that far, only about fifteen, twenty meters."

The thought of her little girl—because adult or not, they would always be her little girls—going wading into that black water where some of those oozing *things* might be waiting sent chills down her spine. But telling her she couldn't go might be a worse choice.

"All right," she said after a moment. "Just be careful."

"Oh, believe me, Mom, I will."

The rest of the family watched tensely as Caroline and Whips made their way to the edge of the water. Akira and Sakura followed, ready to back them up if something happened.

Whips entered the water first, with a deliberate splashing lunge that announced to anything nearby, "Here I am, I'm not afraid of you." A few moments later his one arm reached out of the water and gestured. "Okay, Caroline. There were a couple but they've run off," he said, voice burbling slightly in the water. "Follow me and I think we'll be okay."

Caroline stood at the water's edge, shivering slightly, paler than a ghost, and Laura almost called her back. But then Caroline's hand tightened on her spear, and she stepped resolutely into the water, wading in with a determined stride that shouted out her need to finish this before she ran screaming back to shore.

The distance was only twenty meters—sixty feet in old-fashioned measurements, the length of a small house, barely farther than the distance across Sherwood Tower, nothing, really, something to be crossed in a few quick strides on land. But it seemed to take forever, the thick mud on the bottom impeding Caroline's walk, Whips cruising ahead of her slowly, sometimes circling her to ensure nothing could approach her without him knowing.

Finally the two reached the half-sunken boulder and Caroline took out her kit. It took her some considerable effort to hammer one of the chisels made from wreckage of the *LS-5* into what was apparently a crack in the rock's surface, but after several minutes a chunk broke away. Clenching it in her fist, Caroline immediately turned and began heading for shore. Laura watched tensely. She was moving towards shallower water. If anything wanted to catch her, now was the time . . .

Whips made a sudden backwards lunge. Caroline gave a *yip!* of startlement and floundered up to the water's edge, but nothing attacked her. Whips glided slowly up onto the shore. "One of them started to try to sneak up on us, but I smacked it down. If it's not dead, it's hurting."

"I'm just glad you're both out of there safe," Laura said. "Well, Caroline?"

Caroline's hands were shaking slightly, but color was returning to her face and her voice was steadying. "You guys were right. Just carrying this I can tell it's a lot denser than the other rocks around here." She held up the wedge-shaped chunk, black on two sides but with a brighter, yellowish-brown color showing where it had just been broken free of its parent stone. "Let's see if I can figure out what we're dealing with here. It's really intriguing. I can't figure out what kind of a rock we'd find here that would . . ."

She trailed off as she examined the stone, first turning it in her hand, then scraping it firmly against a flat piece of hardened composite scrap. The rock left a brownish streak on the hardened composite, but scratched softer composites and some of the standard corallike rocks of Lincoln. "Mel, help me boot up that spectral analysis program," she said, and there was something in her tone of voice that made them all look up again.

"Okay...yeah, it's running. You're using ambient, so make sure the filters account for the sun's spectrum as filtered through atmosphere."

"Mmm-hmmm," Caroline agreed absently. A few moments went by, and then, without warning, Caroline leapt into the air with a shout of triumph that startled them all, especially coming from the usually reserved and controlled Caroline.

"What?" demanded Sakura. "What is it?"

"It's *limonite!*" Caroline shouted, her face in a broad grin. When the others, including Laura, blinked at her blankly, Caroline laughed. "It's *bog iron*, everyone."

"Bog..." Whips went rigid, even as Laura felt a rising joy in her own heart. "You mean it's *iron ore?*"

"Twenty-seven percent iron!" Caroline confirmed, and laughed again, seeing answering smiles dawning all around her. "Forget wreckage and fire-hardened tips and the Paleolithic—welcome to the Iron Age!"

Chapter 37

"Listen to that wind howl," Whips muttered.

"Nasty," Sakura agreed, and winced as a particularly savage gust rattled the shutters of Sherwood Column. "Is this a hurricane, Mom?"

Her mother, across the kitchen from her and Whips, nodded. "That's what we think. We're drifting around the right latitudes for hurricanes, and the wind out there is easily over a hundred and forty kilometers an hour." Rain hammered the shutters and something more substantial rapped loudly as it smacked the column's side. "There will be more than a few trees down from this."

"Is . . . is our house going to be okay?" Hitomi asked nervously, peeking in from the stairway.

"Don't worry," Whips said with a luminescent chuckle. "This thing was meant to take a *lot* worse. Even with the holes we've put in it, it's going to be just fine."

"He's right," Sakura reassured her sister. "This is like reinforced concrete, like a tower back home. Wind's not going to hurt it."

"Okay!" Reassured, Hitomi scampered back upstairs.

She turned her attention back to the gently boiling concoction on the fire, stirring it. "It's getting thicker."

"I don't doubt it will thicken. The question is what we get out of it when it's boiled down enough—which should be pretty soon."

She looked over at the assortment of plants and fruits on the table. "I think this one will work. We've got other candidates, of course."

The current project was an attempt to make a concentrated sweet syrup, or possibly even sugar, by boiling down the juice of the sweetest plants they'd found. Knowing that Earth plants from sugarcane to maple trees to beets could be used to make sugar, Sakura was pretty confident that they could get sugar out of at least one, and maybe several, of the plants available on Lincoln.

This particular batch was using pearberry, which of course looked like pears but were small berries about the size of blueberries, and tasted to Sakura rather like kiwi fruit with a hint of cherry. They were quite sweet and so she thought there should be enough sugar in them for this purpose.

With the storm going on, almost everyone was doing something in the kitchen. It was lower down, warmer, and large, and there were plenty of projects to work on in the area of improving cuisine. The big outdoors projects, like iron and ceramic works, obviously couldn't move forward in this weather.

Sakura caught a whiff of sharp odor from across the kitchen, smiled. "Is that working?" she asked her mother.

"I think so." In the container—made from a small blockcrab shell—was a mass of slightly off-white material.

What made it impressive was that it was now near the top of the container, and what had been put into it—an hour or two ago—had been much smaller.

"Yeasts are very common, not just on Earth but other compatible planets," Akira sad with a nod. "Which is another of the points the panspermians like to use to push their hypothesis. But it took a while to find one that worked for bread." Dad gave Mom a quick kiss and then went towards another niche. "I think that our first batch of vinegar is almost ready, and that means pickling and other things—not to mention a very good cleaner for various uses."

She hadn't realized that vinegar took a two-step process to make; somehow she'd always thought it was what naturally happened if you left things like apple juice to go bad, but her father and mother—and the references in their omnis—had shown that the key ingredient, the acid, came from a breakdown of alcohol-containing material, which meant that you *first* had to ferment your fruit juice, and *then* have it turn into vinegar.

Now that they could do both, that meant maybe wines and things like that (more an interest for Mom and Dad) but more importantly if they could figure out a still, concentrated alcohol which would have a lot of uses. Plus, as Dad said, the vinegar meant pickles, and the thought made her mouth water. She hadn't had a pickle since the dinner before the disaster, and she loved pickles. Sakura hadn't let herself think about pickles since the crash, because they were just about the worst thing to miss: completely nonessential, and impossible to make without a lot of work.

"Dad . ... can I try?"

"What? Oh, the vinegar?" He looked into the covered container. "Well...doesn't seem to be anything dangerous in it. Your mother and I have watched that closely. So, I suppose so."

She left Whips to stir the thickening pearberry juice and went over to her dad. "You made it from the opals, right?"

"Right." Opals, or more correctly, Hitomi's Opals, were an iridescent fruit Hitomi had found and brought to them because it was so pretty; they had also proven to be very sweet and common in certain parts of the forest. If the pearberries didn't work out for syrup, Sakura planned on trying a batch with the opals.

The sharp smell from inside the container set her mouth to salivating. Some people hated the smell of vinegar, but Sakura loved it, and this smelled...

She firmly squashed her rising enthusiasm. Sure, it might have the acetic acid content, but the other components could make it terrible. With trepidation, she took one of the small spoons, dipped it in, and dropped some on her tongue.

An instant burst of puckery sourness spread joyously throughout her mouth, with a faint burn and fruity notes that echoed the opals from which it had been made. She paused, savoring it, and resisted the urge to get another spoonful; instead she just licked what was left off the spoon. "That's perfect, Dad!"

He laughed. "And you can't wait for us to start pickling things, can you?"

"Nope. Let's start today!"

"Hold those horses. This batch will be for flavoring. Dressings, maybe cooking, too. Now that we know it works, we'll start making more."

"Sakura, this is really getting thick. You want to test it?"

"Coming!" She ran back to Whips, seeing the liquid now boiled down significantly and not swirling as water but trailing slowly. "That sure looks like syrup to me."

She dipped her spoon in the boiling liquid and pulled it out, blowing on it. For a few moments it seemed to just sit there, but then she saw a faint but unmistakable clouding in the yellow-orange stuff. "I think this might just be working!"

Popping it into her mouth, she was rewarded with a concentrated fruity sweetness, and—for a moment—an unmistakable almost-sandy texture that dissolved away. "Gentlemen, we have achieved *sugar!*" she shouted.

"Now it's my turn to try!" Akira said, crossing to their place in two strides. Sakura felt her own grin widen almost painfully as she saw her father's near-ecstatic expression upon tasting it. Dad had the sweet tooth of the family.

"You could not have timed that more perfectly," her mother said.

"How so?" Whips asked.

"Well, I hadn't said anything because I didn't want to get any hopes up—or get us anticipating something that didn't work out. But now that it looks like this loaf of bread will actually *be* a loaf—a risen loaf—I want to give a slightly delayed birthday party for Hitomi. We can make something like a cake, or maybe pancakes and syrup, for a special treat—"

"Oh, that's a great idea, Mom!" Hitomi and Melody were the only ones not in the kitchen at the moment. They were cleaning the upstairs rooms (and probably playing, which was likely to make the cleaning a bit haphazard). "We're almost finished with the next Jewelbug adventure, too. If Whips, me, and Mel take the time tonight, I think we could finish it and have that be her big present."

"And I think I could probably finish up her new driftseed carder by then," her father said. "Not much of a present, maybe . . ."

"She'll love it," her mother asserted firmly. "Hitomi, fortunately, hasn't ever quite reached the point where she thinks work and fun have to be separated, and she really likes things like that kind of singleminded work that, honestly, drives me insane."

"Okay, so it's settled!" Sakura and Whips lifted the syrup off the fire and scraped it into a large, solid pipestem container at the side. She painted it around the edge with the thicker remains of the syrup—the skin that had formed around the edges of the boiling part—and wrapped a barkcloth top over it. "Okay! That'll keep for a while, I think."

She and Whips moved over to join her parents, and Caroline, who was cutting capy meat into thin strips for smoking. "So let's plan the best Lincoln celebration ever!"

Chapter 38

"Can't I look yet, Mommy?" Hitomi asked.

"Almost, honey," Laura said, unable to restrain her smile. "Just another couple of steps . . . there we go . . . ready . . . okay, open your eyes!"

Hitomi's eyes opened just as everyone shouted *"Surprise! Happy birthday, Hitomi!"*

The youngest Kimei's hazel eyes widened in incredulity as she stared at the table, with what looked like . . .

"A . . . a birthday cake? With *candles*?"

"As close as we could come to a cake, yes, honey." The family burst into a rendition of "Happy Birthday," and the still-astonished little girl was guided to a seat at the table, staring in wonder at the seven glowing flames. Laura gave her a hug. "Now make your wish and blow out the candles."

Hitomi closed her eyes tight, then opened them and with impressive force blew out every candle with a single breath.

Everyone laughed and clapped, and Hitomi grabbed one of the candles off the red-and-blue-streaked cake. "Ow! It's a real candle! Where'd it come from?"

"We've been rendering tallow from the capys and

a couple other animals for soap, and once we got enough of that I remembered that books often talked about tallow candles," Akira said, and kissed Hitomi's forehead. "And what better time to try it than for a birthday?"

"Wow." Hitomi said. "So now we can have light when we want it, even better than the fat lamps you made."

Laura smiled, feeling proud and happy that even Hitomi appreciated what that meant. A tiny part of her noted with bemusement how awestruck everyone—including her—felt at achieving something that would have been so laughably trivial to her a year or so ago. "Now, let's cut your cake."

Hitomi nodded, somewhat shaggy golden hair bobbing with the motion. They still had a ways to go with their barbering skills. "It's...like a stack of pancakes?" Hitomi said as she took a closer look at the cake.

"Making a good real cake takes something like eggs, and real frosting...well, we haven't figured out all the things involved yet. But this is good enough, isn't it?"

"It's great, Mommy! I don't care how it's built!" Hitomi sliced through the cake with Laura's guidance, then pulled the knife away and did the second cut—very neatly—by herself. "Can I..."

"Of course you can, honey. It's *your* birthday."

Reassured that she wasn't being greedy, Hitomi moved her piece of stacked-cakes birthday cake to her nearby plate; as the others cut their pieces, she grabbed a spoon and took a bite.

Her eyes widened again, and she said—somewhat muffled by cake—"It's good!"

Laura agreed. The driftseed pancakes had come out well—after she'd wasted half a bowl of laboriously manufactured flour experimenting on the exact thickness and method of whipping air into the batter. But it was Sakura's pearberry and opal syrups that really made the cake into a treat. She could see Akira restraining himself with heroic resolve from eating two slices right away.

"One piece for now, everyone," she said. "As soon as we're done with those, it's time for the birthday girl's dinner!"

Sakura jumped up. "Got to check the roast!" She ran over, glanced inside the firebox, then grabbed triple-thickness barkcloth potholders and pulled out the largest of their pans, with a dark-red and black something on it. As it came into the light, Laura could see that it looked like a rib roast from a very large capy, but the color was very different from the others, and the *smell* that came wafting out . . .

Akira laughed at her expression, and did a little dance with Sakura at everyone else's surprise. "Snuck it past you, did we?" Akira said, grinning.

"What *is* that?" Laura asked.

"Capy, of course, but with a glaze of pearberry syrup, salt, Lincoln pepper, and our very own opal vinegar," he said proudly.

"It smells *totally bestest*, Daddy!" Hitomi said.

"Um . . . Akira," Whips said hesitantly.

"Don't worry, Whips," he said with a smile. "We've got another one just for you, without the pepper or syrup."

Laura smiled. Akira wouldn't forget important things like that. The "Lincoln pepper" was a seed from a smooth-barked, slender tree that had a high concentration of something very like Earth's piperine, which was responsible for the spiciness of black and white pepper. This made it a tasty spice for humans, but unfortunately piperine and its close relatives were toxic to Bemmies. Whips himself also wasn't terribly fond of sweet things, but did like acidic flavors.

The capy roast was incredible. Laura tried to remember when she'd tasted anything so good, but couldn't. "Honey, this is just . . ."

"*Bestest* bestest!" Hitomi said firmly.

"It really is, Dad, Sakura," Caroline said, wonder in her voice. "I'd almost forgotten what food can taste like when it's prepared with different flavorings."

"We're just getting started!" Melody said emphatically. "There's got to be *dozens* of spices and flavorings we can find here, if we keep looking."

And she would keep looking, Laura thought with pride. One good thing about Lincoln was that their constant struggle had brought Melody a long way from her habitual laziness. Oh, it was still her natural state, but now she had come to enjoy showing off what she could *do* as much as what she *knew*, and that made a huge difference.

Hitomi's birthday dinner was a deliberately huge feast. There were fresh opals and smoked platefish, minimaw, and blockcrab; a salad with emerald seaweed, brushweed, and green filegrass, sprinkled with sweetened vinegar; steamed older filegrass stems, which were sort of like asparagus crossed with water chestnuts; and of course more of the birthday cake. Laura ate until she simply couldn't eat any more, and saw even the ravenous Sakura slowing down.

"And now," she said with a smile at the birthday girl, "presents!"

As she had expected, Hitomi was actually ecstatic at the new carder when she unwrapped it from its barkcloth coverings, and she appreciated the extra clothes that Caroline and Melody had finished in time for the birthday party.

"Hitomi," Sakura said with a grin, "have your omni do its update."

Hitomi did, and suddenly squealed in glee. "A new adventure! A new Jewelbug adventure!"

"Happy Birthday!"

Hitomi bounced up and hugged Sakura, then Whips, then Melody, and around to everyone else, ending with Laura. Laura hugged her back, tightly.

"Mommy, can I play?"

Laura laughed, as did everyone else. "Of course you can. All you want, today."

Hitomi looked around, and straightened, and for a moment she looked a lot older than the seven she now was. "Thank you. Thank you, everybody, so much. I know how hard all this was to make . . . and this is the best birthday *ever*."

She was getting older, Laura thought, another sting of maternal pride causing her eyes to water. *And still herself.*

Hitomi sat down to play Jewelbug, and the others started to clean up.

She leaned over to Akira as they started washing dishes. "Somehow, it really feels like a home now."

"Because we've gotten enough ahead to have a real celebration? Yes. Oh, we have so much more to do, and so many more things could go wrong," he looked momentarily distant, "like that other island that's getting a bit close, but . . . yes. We can live here.

We've survived many dangers, but in spite of them we've started to build a little civilization here. If we're never found . . ." He shrugged and smiled. "We'll still make a very good run of it. We will have pottery and iron and steel soon—pottery in a week or three, iron and steel in a few months, perhaps. We lost almost everything . . ."

She hugged him, knowing exactly what he was going to say; she finished with him, ". . . but not the most important things."

Chapter 39

Whips tilted the big log container slowly, letting water pour from the top.

He was almost completely recovered, he thought with satisfaction. Even tipping this heavy tank of clay slurry—which was settling into clay—was only causing slight ghosts of pain instead of the agony that had been his almost constant companion for many days after the battle against the raylamps. The capture hooks he'd lost . . . well, a couple had actually been torn out to the root and he'd never get those back, but most were regrowing by now.

"A little more . . . a little more . . . Okay, that's good!" Caroline said, and he let the tank tip back with some relief. Caroline looked in, poked and stirred with a stick. "This batch looks a lot better than the last one."

Whips flickered in a cynical pattern. "That's what you said about the last one and the one before."

"And it's been true every time," she said serenely. Caroline glanced over at the pile of broken clay shards. "We're learning. I really think this one will work. We'll test it with small items again, and if those all hold, then we can make a furnace."

"Have you decided on whether you're going to build it in layers from the ground up, or use a form?"

Caroline scrunched up her face in a thinking expression. "I keep going back and forth on that. The layer approach is really the most solid design, but it's going to take a lot more clay. But making the mold or form for the smelting furnace is also going to take time . . ." She shrugged. "I think we'll probably use the mold approach, though. If we design it right—and we turned up a couple good sets of pictures and diagrams in Mel's omni—we can reuse the forms, and something like that will also make for a good start at a kiln. With the regular rocks around here tending to decompose whenever you heat them up, we really can't make a kiln from them that will survive more than a firing or two."

Smoke drifted by them, and Caroline gave a small cough.

"Sorry!" Sakura said contritely. "Wind shifted again."

"It's okay, we know you're not in charge of the weather yet," Whips said. Sakura, Melody, and Hitomi were burning wood for charcoal—something they were going to need a lot of—while on the other side of this cleared section of the landing scar, Akira and Laura were working on a large bellows.

Making things to make things to make things to make other things, he thought—not for the first time. When you were in a ship traveling between the stars, or in a comfortable home in Europa or Earth, you kept forgetting how ridiculously long the chain of operations was between the raw materials in the ground, water, and sky and the food you were eating and the gadgetry you used to prepare it.

But Lincoln reminded you of it every day. Now they were working on making clay out of the raw material dug out, so that they could prove that they had the right quality of clay, by firing it in an improvised kiln that would probably be used up just by the test, and then make a wooden mold so they could build a furnace with the clay which they would fire with wood and then heat with charcoal they were making from wood, which they would then use to smelt ore, using the bellows that they had made to keep the fire hot, into crude iron that they would refine more by working it, which they would then use to make tools that were better than the ones they had now. So they could make more stuff.

Just *thinking* that almost made him run out of breath.

"How're our provisions, Mom?" he called over to the two adults.

Laura flashed a smile. "Pretty good. I think we could spend another couple of days before we need to go hunting and gathering again. I'd really like you to go fishing again, too; we're still finding new treats in the ocean, and you're the best at that. Now that you're better—"

"You don't have to argue me into it," he interrupted, flashing his enthusiasm. "I haven't gone on a good water-hunt since we almost got killed. I'd love to go out and spend a day—"

A moaning, shuddering vibration ran through air and ground; flying things took off from the distant forest in grayish clouds.

"What—"

Caroline had straightened. "It's hit. That island we were watching."

"I thought it had been drifting farther away!" Akira said, his tones conveying his concern.

Caroline nodded. "It was. But we've had a strong wind from the south for the past two days, and I think that overcame whatever drift it had."

The juddering, rumbling vibration grew stronger, and Hitomi looked scared. "Mommy!"

"I know, honey. But there's nothing we can do."

Whips couldn't keep from tensing, even though, as Laura said, there wasn't anything he could do. Uncountable tons of floating island were colliding with their own floating continent, and the real fear was that, somewhere, a seam existed, a crack—perhaps caused by their own crash-landing—that would suddenly give way, causing their section of Lincoln to break apart, spear into the sky, hurling the castaways and everything they'd built into the sky or plunging them into the depths of a nearly bottomless sea.

Sand and earth cascaded from the edge of the landing scar, miniature landslides echoing Whips' fears, as the grinding collision continued. Sakura glanced up, and then screamed *"Down! Everybody down!"*

Whips, of course, was pretty much as far down as he could get, but he still flattened himself as much as possible while the humans all dropped to the ground.

Black and gray masses fell all around them, embedding themselves deeply into the ground. Hitomi and Melody both screamed as one smashed down not two meters away, showering them with filthy water and pulverized sandy rock. One suddenly materialized in a puff of dust and muck-smelling water almost directly in front of Whips, a six-meter shard of what he knew was the outer shelf of one of the floating landmasses. *Just a few meters over and...*

But the vibrations were fading, finally, the grinding sounds diminishing, turning to a faint murmur...gone.

For several minutes, the entire family lay frozen, waiting, to see if the impact had done enough damage to destroy everything they'd built. As they lay there, slowly the sounds of life returned around them. The crants began to scuttle towards the now-beached lifeforms on the displaced chunks of continental skirt, and the smaller flying creatures began their usual hum.

Finally Laura rose to her feet. "Okay, everyone. I think we're okay."

"I wish I could have watched it," Caroline said wistfully. "But we couldn't spare days just to watch the drifting island."

"I almost wish you had, though," Akira said wryly. "It would have been nice to have a little warning before that happened. Are we sure that this part of the continent won't just break up in a few days?"

"Sure? No," Caroline's answer was candid, if not entirely comforting. "but we do know that these islands have to maintain themselves somehow, so I'd guess that if we're still intact in a couple of days, we'll be okay. Once the repair crews get to work, so to speak, it'll be more stable. And I don't feel any extra movement or hear anything suggesting a big crack's open."

"There really isn't anything we could do about it, is there?" Melody finally said.

Whips saw the others hesitating and decided to plunge forward. "No, not as we are. We saw what a—pretty small—piece of this floating continent-sized reef breaking off looks like. We can't hold it together, or stop it, and if it started tipping like that piece we'd be lucky to get thrown clear instead of getting crushed or dragged down."

"What if we still had the *LS-5*?" she asked.

"If it were *intact*?" He considered. "Well...if we were living inside it, and we reacted quickly, we might be able to take off and get out of the way. But if we were outside at the time, I think by the time we could get back inside and take off, it'd be too late." He waved and flickered an ironic grin. "Of course, if we had the *LS-5* we'd be doing a lot of things differently."

He waved towards the forest. "I suppose we could build a few rafts and keep them stocked with key supplies, put them somewhere that they might somehow end up floating after such a disaster. But the chances of anyone living through that to get to the rafts doesn't look too good to me."

"Except maybe for you," Sakura pointed out.

"Well...yes." He couldn't argue that point. If he wasn't crushed, or thrown so far up that coming down would kill him, he had a good chance of survival; he could live in the water as well as he could on land, and even if he got dragged far down, he could survive—even here, with higher gravity and thus pressure with depth.

But none of the humans would be likely to survive. "But if I was the only survivor, I'm not sure I'd want to live," he said, very quietly.

Everyone else was silent for a moment; then Hitomi came up and hugged him. "Well, we would want you to, anyway."

He hugged her back. "Okay. I'd feel the same way. But I'm glad it doesn't look like I'll have to."

"So are we all," Laura agreed. "We're all okay, right? Anything major get wrecked in that stone-shower we just had?"

Fortunately, it appeared nothing had—here, at least.

"All right. Akira, I'm going to just hike over and make sure nothing hurt Sherwood Tower."

"Be careful, love," Akira said, a faint warning tone in his voice. "This may be like a forest fire; animals may be a bit panicky."

"I will." She picked up her spear and checked the SurvivalShot before heading out.

"All right," Caroline said after a moment, "let's get back to this clay. Time to pour a little more water off."

Whips reached out and twined his arms around the tub of clay again. "Here we go!"

Back to making things to make things to make things...

Chapter 40

Akira Kimei always felt a bit guilty whenever he made another entry in his special journal. The guilt came partly from the simple fact that the journal was secret—even from his wife. It was the only thing he had ever kept secret from Laura, but his contractual obligations had been clear and non-negotiable. The journal was maintained in a portion of his omni that was hidden as well as encrypted.

Mostly, though, the guilt came from the subject matter of the journal itself. As he had done more times than he could remember, the first thing he did when he opened the journal was glance at the heading.

ETHOLOGICAL REPORT ON
BEMMIUS NOVUS SAPIENS

There followed page after page after page of dry prose; the sort of prose that a biologist is careful to maintain when compiling data on a subject he knows to be potentially explosive.

Ethological. That term was another source of guilt. "Ethology" was a branch of biology, specifically the study of animal behavior. Using the term for a study such as this one had always seemed rather demeaning to Akira. But when he'd suggested substituting the term "ethnographical," the Board had slapped him down.

"Akira, we're not interested in the *culture* of *Bemmius novus*," said Boris Yermolov, the chairman of the Board. "We already know all we need to know about that."

He shrugged. "Basically, it's just Europan Bemmie culture with a heavy admixture of human elements. The real issue here is whether or not—as *animals*, just as we ourselves are animals—the new Bemmies are a viable species. Can they handle adverse and unpredictable situations? Can they adapt when necessary?"

"Not that we'd take any undue measures against them if the reports are negative," interjected Hasumati Chopra.

Yermolov gave her a sour look. "Yes, yes, of course. We are not contemplating anything punitive. Still, leaving *Bemmius novus* in peace—just as we would do with anyone suffering from mental or psychological defects—is a far cry from actively encouraging their growth as a species. *Especially* in such an intrinsically perilous enterprise as interstellar colonization."

His tone had been every bit as sour as the look he'd given Chopra. There had been a wide range of opinion concerning the wisdom of modifying the Bemmie genome to produce what amounted to a brand new species. That range was narrower on the Colonization Board than in the public at large—there were certainly no members calling for outright euthanasia—but it was still pretty wide. And the chairman of the Board occupied a position near to one of the edges.

To be precise, the edge of opinion that argued the new species was completely untested, of dubious provenance—a species modified from a species that had *already* been modified—and far more likely to be a hindrance than a help in the great project of spreading human civilization through the galaxy.

There are been other members of the Board, however, who argued just as vehemently that there was no reason to assume that *Bemmius novus* would pose any problems at all. No one questioned the viability of *Bemmius pelagica,* after all. It would be awfully hard to do so, given that the species had thrived and even evolved into intelligence in the very difficult environment of Europa's ocean.

The modifications that had been made to the *Pelagica* genome had been fairly restricted and limited entirely to physical changes. Basically, a species that was adapted to a marine environment had been modified to a more amphibian *Bauplan.* The new species was actually closer to the original Bemmie stock than their direct *pelagica* progenitors—and no one could possibly question the viability of that original species, given that they had managed the supreme feat of crossing the vastness of interstellar space.

In the end, the Board had decided to put the issue to a test. They would run an experiment, essentially, by including a small number of *Bemmius novus* in the next colonization expedition. Akira had been one of the four members of the expedition assigned the task of assessing the outcome of the test. In fact, he'd been appointed the coordinator of the project.

"Project Triton," they'd decided to call it. That seemed more...diplomatic than "Project Can The New Bemmies

Cut The Mustard?" And given the very delicate nature of the experiment, it had been kept secret from anyone except Board members and the four assessors themselves.

Akira had no idea what had happened to the other three people assigned to the experiment. They might all be dead; they might all have reached their original destination; some might be alive and some might be dead—there was simply no way to know.

For all intents and purposes, therefore, Akira had to act as if he were the only assessor left. And he had to assume that his report would be the only one the Board would consider.

That assumed, of course, that the Colonization Board would ever discover the journal. But that was a different problem and one that Akira was now confident he would have years in which to figure out a solution.

Years—which he would have in no small part because of the youngest member of *Bemmius novus* who had come on the expedition.

Slightly more than a year had now passed, according to Akira's omni, and he had decided to discontinue the experiment. The result of the test was in—had been for quite a while, really—and it was time to record the result.

For that, he decided he could finally abandon the academic prose in which he'd recorded the data. Whatever purpose it had once served, it was no longer needed. Indeed, it would now be inappropriate.

The issue is settled. It would be hard to devise a more difficult test than the one Harratrer has passed—and passed with flying colors. Marooned on a water planet with almost no resources beyond personal omnis; with no companions of his own species and only a small number of human ones; on a drifting continent full of dangers...

Compared to this test, the one the Board designed would have been laughably easy. A year has gone by, and our impromptu little colony is doing quite well. Thriving, in some ways, although our lack of numbers will obviously continue to pose a great challenge—an insoluble one, in the end, if we do not make contact with other humans.

But I now have great hope that we will do so. Not soon, no. But given enough years I believe we will be rescued. And I am confident that we will have those years. Even decades, should we need them.

A large part of my confidence comes from the fact that Harratrer is part of our colony. He has been invaluable in a multitude of ways. His skills are superb, especially for such a young being. His courage and steadiness are by now unquestionable. It is no exaggeration to say that he has saved all of our lives more than once.

The reverse is also true, to be sure. We humans have saved his life more than once too. But that simply highlights what I believe may be the single most important outcome of this experiment—and the one that was the least predictable.

Harratrer's ability to form close emotional bonds with his human companions—all of us, and especially with one of my daughters—is something I don't think any of us could have foreseen. Not to this extent, certainly. Human relations with members of Bemmius pelagica *have always been friendly, but the difficulties each species faces when operating in the other's environment has served as a barrier to close personal relations. With members of* Bemmius novus, *that barrier is almost completely removed.*

I am aware of the dangers of generalizing from a single example, but I have observed many members of Bemmius novus, *and it is my considered professional opinion that while Harratrer is an exceptional individual, I do not believe he is any more exceptional than any human being chosen to be part of an interstellar colonization expedition—certainly no more extraordinary than my wife or my daughters, or the other human colonists on board* Outward Initiative.

A year, under these extreme conditions, is more than time enough. The experiment has been concluded. The test is over. With no reservations of any kind, I recommend strongly to the Colonization Board that members of Bemmius novus—*and in considerable number—be included in any and all future colonization expeditions being sent to planets whose environment is sufficiently marine or aquatic.*

In practice, that meant *all* colonization expeditions in the foreseeable future. Humans were not amphibious, but they still much preferred environments with plenty of water. There were so many inhabitable planets that there was no need to contemplate settling desert planets. Not now, not for centuries—quite possibly not for many millennia.

Akira wasn't concerned with millennia. Years and decades were his business.

He looked forward to those years and decades.

All that remained was . . .

> *Signed, Akira Kimei*
> *Coordinator, Project Triton*

He paused for a moment. Then, smiling, decided to add a curlicue that not even a curmudgeon like Boris Yermolov would miss.

The Bemmies—both *pelagica* and *novus*—had a custom very similar to that of some human cultures. Like Arabs, they used teknonyms, adding the title of "father of" or "mother of" to their name when they had offspring. Arabs used "abu" for the former and "umm" for the latter.

There were some differences, but the customs were still quite close.

Certainly close enough for his purpose. He deleted the signature and replaced it with:

> *Signed, Akira Kimei allu-Harratrer*
> *cnet-Caroline cnet-Sakura cnet-Melody*
> *cnet-Hitomi*
> *Coordinator, Project Triton*

Chapter 41

Sakura pulled gingerly on the wooden frame. *Please, please let the oil have worked...*

"Careful!" Melody said nervously. "If it's stuck, you'll pull the clay apart!"

"I *know*, Mel," Sakura snapped back. Then she paused, took a breath. "I know. Sorry."

"Both of you relax," their father said sternly. "Melody, you can watch, but don't critique people while they're working. I've told you about that before."

"But—" Sakura saw her father's eyebrow rise, a warning sign that Melody obviously caught because she immediately stopped whatever protest she'd started. "Yes, Dad."

"Good. And Sakura, I'm glad you caught yourself and apologized. But if you're that tense, maybe I should do it."

Sakura looked at the furnace—or the furnace-to-be, anyway, a semi-conical structure of clay formed around a greased wooden mold, and thought to herself just how much work had gone into it. Dragging the clay here, purifying it, working the right proportions of the different clays together to make the right kind for this furnace, then making the mold... "Let you do it? Dad, I'm kinda tempted, you know?"

"I know exactly what you mean; if *I* do it and something goes wrong, I get to take the blame, not you."

"Yeah. All that clay, plus all the work on the forms, and the days waiting for it to dry..." She looked again, then shook her head. "Nope. I'm going to do it. This will work."

That was a little more confidence than she really felt. She carefully avoided looking to the left, where the ruins of the first attempt lay collapsed. Instead, she glanced to the right, seeing Hitomi sitting on a rock a ways away, playing with her omni. Caroline, Mom, and Whips were away—hopefully almost back—getting as much of the bog iron as they could drag home. There was already a huge stack of charcoal under one of the shelter tarps. If they could finish the smelting furnace...

Okay, Try again. Stop being so hesitant! She remembered advice like that in some of the books. On things like this, hesitating or going too slow could be about as bad as going too fast. She had to assume the mold pieces would come off, and pull as if they would.

Sakura lay back down on the ground, looking into the lower opening of the furnace. The key pieces were at the bottom; if she could remove those, the higher ones would be able to drop and separate, and they could be removed by reaching in—carefully—from the top. Once that was done, they'd build a small fire in it, keep it burning for a while, and slowly increase it until the whole furnace was completely dry. It wouldn't *quite* be like firing the whole thing, but it would make it hard and strong enough for this purpose, especially at the base.

She reached in suddenly, decisively, and grasped the small handle that had been designed into the mold. Offering a small prayer to anything that might be listening, she gave a quick, authoritative pull.

The mold section resisted for a moment, then popped loose, so suddenly she almost banged her arm into the side of the furnace—which could have been disastrous; any impact with the not-yet-dry clay could easily break it. "Got it!"

"Excellent, honey! Can you get the one on the other side?"

"I hope so." The second one was actually easier. She found that with the handle's leverage she could do just a tiny bit of a twisting motion that broke the seal between the wooden mold and the clay packed around it. Now, if she could just dislodge the bottoms of the chimney mold pieces...

One dropped so suddenly it landed on her pinky. "*OW!*" she said, and rolled away, cradling the injured digit. "Ow, ow, ow, *OW!*"

"Are you okay?" Her father and Mel were instantly there, and Hitomi was watching from her rock with worried eyes.

"Think so..." she said, forcing herself to ignore the pain.

She could see her father studying his omni display, staring into apparently empty air. *That's right, Mom gave him the codes so he could check our medical nanos.* After a moment, Akira relaxed. "Says it's just a bruise. Nothing to worry about, Saki."

"Okay." She gritted her teeth and got up. "Well, they came loose easy enough. If I can get them out..."

It turned out to be pretty easy. The trickiest part

was the bottom section of each mold piece, since that was the widest, but the design that Whips had finalized had taken that into account and there was enough room to remove them safely, if you were careful. Sakura was *very* careful.

"All out, Dad!"

"Fantastic!" They stood and admired the now-all-clay (with some of the grasslike, carbon-silicon hydroid-grasses woven in for support) furnace for a few moments.

Then Melody clapped her hands briskly, a gesture she had gotten from some book she'd read. "Right! Let's get a fire started, then!"

Within a few minutes, a thread of smoke started to come from the chimney of the little furnace. "If this works—if it really works . . . we'll have to make something bigger, something where we can get a lot of iron out," Melody said. "This little thing won't make much."

"Several kilos, if what Caroline and Whips say is correct," Akira said. "And that's enough for a number of knives or other relatively small things. But you're right, we'll want to figure out a way to do more. There are other processes to make iron and steel, but a lot of them take more advanced technology." He glanced down at his omni. "We're lucky we have these, but unfortunately they don't help much with the heavy work."

"You can say that again!"

The familiar voice from above startled Sakura. Looking up, she saw her mother looking down, breathing heavily, with Caroline looking equally winded next to her. Whips hove into view slowly. "We have to . . . do all the heavy work," Laura said with a smile.

"Mommy!" Hitomi bounced up, then realized that she couldn't run straight to her mother because she was still up on the edge of the landing scar. That only delayed her a second, and then she started jogging towards the path that led to the top. Sakura followed her closely.

"Hello, honey. Akira, we've got as much of this as we could bring."

"Any problems?"

"I'm dragging part of a problem," Whips said, "but it's a tasty part, I hope."

By then, Sakura and Hitomi had reached the top. The draggable sleds were bent under the weight of the bog iron, and on Whips' was a large piece of . . .

"A hillmouth?" Sakura said in surprise. That was the name they'd eventually given to the giant four-jawed creature that had nearly killed Whips. "One attacked you?"

"Tried to," Whips said. "But I had plenty of warning this time, and tough as it is, your mom's a crack shot with that pistol, and Caroline's mean with that bow. It got about fifteen meters out of the water and dropped dead. Turns out it's perfectly edible meat for humans or Bemmies, so we figured we could bring some back."

Closer up, she could see it was actually several pieces, already partly seared from fire. "Started cooking it, I see."

"Well, we killed it yesterday. It takes a while for things to go bad around here for some reason," her mother said, "but no point in taking chances. We cut it up and did some cooking last night."

"So how is it?" Akira asked, looking at the large meaty chunks with interest.

"Not bad at all. A bit tough, but I figure we could do roasts or something of that nature. Maybe a pot roast."

"Mmm. Sounds great. And you managed to bring back a lot of ore."

"Well, at roughly one-quarter iron, and with that furnace's efficiency—or, to be accurate, lack thereof," Caroline said, "we'll want quite a lot of it to be sure we get a good deal of usable iron out of this operation."

"True. Well, let's get this down to the smelting area. You can see that we've started to harden the furnace."

"So it stayed together this time?" Whips' color pattern was relieved. "Wonderful. Just remember to keep the fire going."

"Oh, I will," Sakura said firmly.

"All right, you keep tending the fire while we get the cargo down," her father said.

Hitomi, having given and received the much-needed hugs from her mother, skipped back down and sat on her chosen rock, her omni back on.

Sakura tended the fire carefully, making sure that it burned steadily, and slowly expanded it as time went on. That didn't take all her attention, of course. She could take frequent breaks to check that Hitomi was still in sight and see if she was needed for anything else.

Lunch was rolled sandwiches Dad and Melody had put together before they'd left that morning; Hitomi was clearly engrossed in her game and concentrated on the empty-air display in between bites. *Wonder what's got her so focused? I thought she'd finished the last adventure.* On the other hand, she might have missed some of the side adventures, or be playing something other than Jewelbug. Obsessive focusing was, of course, Hitomi's main characteristic.

Another smell wafted through the landing scar valley: the smell of something cooking. She saw the others working on breaking the ore into smaller pieces, with either Mom or Dad occasionally breaking away to check on one of their pots, sitting over another fire. That must be the pot roast they mentioned. It smelled good.

Just watching the fire was kind of boring, but she could play some games of her own in the intervals. But she did still keep an eye on Hitomi, and finally she noticed that there were frown lines on the little girl's forehead.

"Got a problem, Hitomi?" she asked, coming up to her smallest sister.

"Puzzle," Hitomi answered shortly. "Gotta solve it."

"Have you been working on one puzzle all this time?" She was surprised. Hitomi was good at solving the logical puzzles common in Jewelbug—figuring out sequences of switches to activate to open doors, color patterns for solving riddles, that sort of thing.

"Yes! I *have* to solve it! Rubine's gonna *die* if I don't!"

"Die?" That made no sense. She hadn't designed any adventures that would kill any of the major characters, and she was astonished that Whips or Melody had. *Maybe one of the side adventures we discussed, for when she's older?*

"Can I see? Maybe I can help."

Hitomi relinquished control of her omni reluctantly; she didn't like being interrupted or failing to finish something on her own. The fact she was letting it go at all told Sakura how hard this challenge must be.

As soon as she saw the Jewelbug world come up, she was even more perplexed. *Where the heck did* this *cavern come from? That doesn't look like any design that we...*

She froze.

Then she paused the game, checked status.

Last update: 22 hours 57 minutes.

But they hadn't done an update since Hitomi's birthday, two months ago!

And then she understood, and was up, sprinting towards her parents, screaming as loudly as she could.

"Mom! Dad! We're not alone!" She waved the omni as she came, and seeing their confusion, finished, "Hitomi got a satellite update from a Jewelbug server! A day ago!

"Someone else is here!"

ACKNOWLEDGEMENTS

No book is written in isolation,
and I would like to thank some of the
people who made *Castaway Planet* possible:

Our publisher, Toni Weisskopf,
who let Eric and me start a brand-new adventure
in the Boundaryverse that we built together

My beta-reading group,
who always catch me when I stumble

And my wife Kathleen,
who gives up a lot of time to allow me to write!

—R.S.

1636: The Devil's Opera   HC: 978-1-4516-3928-5 ◆ $25.00
(with David Carrico)   PB: 978-1-4767-3700-3 ◆ $7.99

1636: Commander Cantrell in the West Indies
(with Charles E. Gannon)   978-1-4767-8060-3 ◆ $7.99

1636: The Viennese Waltz
(with Gorg Huff & Paula Goodlett) HC: 978-1-4767-3687-7 ◆ $25.00

RING OF FIRE ANTHOLOGIES
Edited by Eric Flint

Ring of Fire   978-1-4165-0908-0 ◆ $7.99
Ring of Fire II   HC: 978-1-4165-7387-6 ◆ $25.00
                          PB: 978-1-4165-9144-3 ◆ $7.99
Ring of Fire III   HC: 978-1-4391-3448-1 ◆ $25.00
                          PB: 978-1-4516-3827-1 ◆ $7.99

Grantville Gazette   978-0-7434-8860-0 ◆ $7.99
Grantville Gazette II   978-1-4165-5510-0◆ $7.99
Grantville Gazette III   HC: 978-1-4165-0941-7 ◆ $25.00
                          PB: 978-1-41655565-0 ◆ $7.99
Grantville Gazette IV   HC:978-1-41655554-4 ◆ $25.00
                          PB: 978-1-4391-3311-8 ◆ $7.99
Grantville Gazette V   HC: 978-1-4391-3279-1 ◆ $25.00
                          PB: 978-1-4391-3422-1 ◆ $7.99
Grantville Gazette VI   HC: 978-1-4516-3768-7 ◆ $25.00
                          PB: 978-1-4516-3853-0 ◆ $7.99
Grantville Gazette VII   HC: 978-1-4767-8029-0 ◆ $25.00

MORE . . .
ERIC FLINT

THE CROWN OF SLAVES SERIES *with David Weber*

Crown of Slaves	978-0-7434-9899-9 ◆ $7.99
Torch of Freedom	HC: 978-1-4391-3305-7 ◆ $26.00
	PB: 978-1-4391-3408-5 ◆ $8.99
Cauldron of Ghosts	HC: 978-1-4767-3633-4 ◆ $25.00
	TPB: 978-1476780382 ◆ $15.00

THE JOE'S WORLD SERIES

The Philosophical Strangler	978-0-7434-3541-3 ◆ $7.99
Forward the Mage (with Richard Roach)	978-0-7434-7146-6 ◆ $7.99

THE HEIRS OF ALEXANDRIA SERIES

The Shadow of the Lion (with Mercedes Lackey & Dave Freer)	978-0-7434-7147-3 ◆ $7.99
This Rough Magic (with Mercedes Lackey & Dave Freer)	978-0-7434-9909-5 ◆ $7.99
Much Fall of Blood (with Mercedes Lackey & Dave Freer)	HC: 978-1-4391-3351-4 ◆ $27.00 PB: 978-1-4391-3416-0 ◆ $7.99
Burdens of the Dead (with Mercedes Lackey & Dave Freer)	HC: 978-1-4516-3874-5 ◆ $25.00 PB: 978-1-4767-3668-6 ◆ $7.99

The Wizard of Karres (with Mercedes Lackey & Dave Freer)	978-1-4165-0926-4 ◆ $7.99
The Sorceress of Karres (with Dave Freer)	HC: 978-1-4391-3307-1 ◆ $24.00 PB: 978-1-4391-3446-7 ◆ $7.99

The Best of Jim Baen's Universe	1-4165-5558-7 ◆ $7.99